Julia Hamilton

Steve Hamilton attended the University of Michigan and won the prestigious Hopwood Award for writing. His first novel, *A Cold Day in Paradise*, won the PWA/SMP Best First Private Eye Novel Competition and the Edgar and Shamus Awards for Best First Novel. In 2006, Steve won the Michigan Author Award for his outstanding body of work. He lives in Cottekill, New York, with his wife and their two children.

THE LOCK ARTIST

Praise for *The Lock Artist* . . .

"*The Lock Artist* is far more than a suspenseful heist caper. It's the story of a boy emerging into his own life. . . . The talent Steve Hamilton has developed over the course of the Alex McKnight series is in full bloom here in this daring and deeply satisfying novel." —*ReviewingTheEvidence.com*

"Propelled by an aching desire to recover his voice, Mike has brushes with the law, flirts with romance, and makes alliances with criminals, from rank amateurs to consummate professionals. Along the way, Hamilton drops tantalizing clues about Mike's troubled past and his uncertain future. Readers will hope to hear more from Mike." —*Publishers Weekly*

"Sharp prose and a strong cast." —*Kirkus Reviews*

"Intense and involving." —*Booklist*

"Hamilton has a knack for weaving a complicated web of intrigue and irony and a knack for hoisting the system on its own petard." —*Chronogram* magazine

"Hamilton maintains a seamless narrative of escalating suspense as he juggles alternating adolescent and late-teen story lines that merge in the revelation of Mike's brutal secret. With this absorbing coming-of-age tale scarred by horror and adversity, the New York author breathes new life into the oldest chestnut of all, the redemptive power of love." —*Winnipeg Free Press*

"Hypnotic . . . a proven master of suspense moves in a brand-new direction—and the result is can't-put-it-down spectacular." —Lee Child

"I haven't read a book this captivating in a long time. *The Lock Artist* is gutsy, genuine, and, flat out, a great read. You won't be disappointed." —Michael Connelly

Also by Steve Hamilton

Night Work

A Stolen Season

Ice Run

Blood Is the Sky

North of Nowhere

The Hunting Wind

Winter of the Wolf Moon

A Cold Day in Paradise

THE LOCK ARTIST

Steve Hamilton

Minotaur Books

A Thomas Dunne Book

New York

THE LOCK ARTIST. Copyright © 2009 by Steve Hamilton. All rights reserved. Printed in the United States of America. For information, address St. Martin's Press, 175 Fifth Avenue, New York, N.Y. 10010.

Book Design by Rich Arnold

www.thomasdunnebooks.com
www.minotaurbooks.com

The Library of Congress has cataloged the hardcover edition as follows:

Hamilton, Steve, 1961–
    The lock artist / Steve Hamilton.—1st ed.
      p. cm.
    ISBN 978-0-312-38042-7
    1. Lock picking—Fiction. 2. Criminals—Fiction. I. Title.
    PS3558.A44363L63 2010
    813'.54—dc22

                              2009034523

ISBN 978-0-312-69695-5 (trade paperback)

10 9 8 7 6 5

To the Allens

Acknowledgments

I am indebted to Dave McOmie, real-life safecracker extraordinaire, for all the assistance with the safecracking material—we got it right enough to be convincing, but wrong enough to make sure this book isn't a training manual. Thanks also to the aptly named Jim Locke for getting me started with locks in the first place, to Debbie Noll for the help with the American Sign Language, and to George Griffin for the help with the motorcycles.

Thanks to Bill Massey and Peter Joseph for working extra hard with me on this one. I can't tell you how much I appreciate it.

Thanks as always to Bill Keller and Frank Hayes, to Jane Chelius, to everyone at St. Martin's Press and Orion UK, Maggie Griffin, Nick Childs, Elizabeth Cosin, Bob Randisi and the Private Eye Writers of America, Bob Kozak and everyone else at IBM, Jeff Allen, and Rob Brenner.

To the good people of both Milford and River Rouge, Michigan, I'd like to say that the portrayal of both places in this book is based on memories so imperfect they might as well be from a fever dream. I know this is worlds away from real life.

For some great insight into how traumatic events affect the human mind, I recommend *The Inner World of Trauma: Archetypal Defenses of the Personal Spirit*, by Donald Kalsched (Brunner-Routledge, 1996).

Finally, more than ever, I owe everything to Julia, who really had to help me get through this one, to Nicholas, who will be driving away in a car soon, and to Antonia, who is very glad I took out the octopus.

THE LOCK ARTIST

One
Locked Up Tight for Another Day

You may remember me. Think back. The summer of 1990. I know that's a while ago, but the wire services picked up the story and I was in every newspaper in the country. Even if you didn't read the story, you probably heard about me. From one of your neighbors, somebody you worked with, or if you're younger, from somebody at school. They called me "the Miracle Boy." A few other names, too, names thought up by copy editors or newscasters trying to outdo one another. I saw "Boy Wonder" in one of the old clippings. "Terror Tyke," that was another one, even though I was eight years old at the time. But it was the Miracle Boy that stuck.

I stayed in the news for two or three days, but even when the cameras and the reporters moved on to something else, mine was the kind of story that stuck with you. You felt bad for me. How could you not? If you had young kids of your own back then, you held them a little tighter. If you were a kid yourself, you didn't sleep right for a week.

In the end, all you could do was wish me well. You hoped that I had found a new life somewhere. You hoped that because I was so young, somehow this would have protected me, made it not so horrible. That I'd be able to get over it, maybe even put the whole thing behind me. Children being so adaptable and flexible and durable, in ways that adults could never be. That whole business. It's what you hoped, anyway, if you even took the time to think about me the real person and not just the young face in the news story.

People sent me cards and letters back then. A few of them had drawings made by children. Wishing me well. Wishing me a happy future. Some people even tried to visit me at my new home. Apparently, they'd come looking for me in Milford, Michigan, thinking they could just stop anybody on the street and ask where to find me. For what reason, exactly? I guess they thought I must have some kind of special powers to have lived through that day in June. What those powers might be, or what these people thought I could do for them, I couldn't even imagine.

In the years since then, what happened? I grew up. I came to believe in love at first sight. I tried my hand at a few things, and if I was any good at it, that meant it had to be either totally useless or else totally against the law. That goes a long way toward explaining why I'm wearing this stylish orange jumpsuit right now, and why I've been wearing it every single day for the past nine years.

I don't think it's doing me any good to be here. Me or anybody else. It's kind of ironic, though, that the worst thing I ever did, on paper at least, was the one thing I don't regret. Not at all.

In the meantime, as long as I'm here, I figure what the hell, I'll take a look back at everything. I'll write it all down. Which, if I'm going to do it, is really the only way I can tell the story. I have no other choice, because as you may or may not know, in all the things I've done in the past years, there's one particular thing I *haven't* done. I haven't spoken one single word out loud.

That's a whole story in itself, of course. This *thing* that has kept me silent for all of these years. Locked up here inside me, ever since that day. I cannot let go of it. So I cannot speak. I cannot make a sound.

Here, though, on the page . . . it can be like we're sitting together at a bar somewhere, just you and me, having a long talk. Yeah, I like that. You and me sitting at a bar, just talking. Or rather me talking and you listening. What a switch that would be. I mean, you'd really be *listening*. Because I've noticed how most people don't know how to listen. Believe me. Most of the time they're just waiting for the other person to shut up so they can start talking again. But you . . . hell, you're just as good a listener as I am. You're sitting there, hanging on every word I say. When I get to the bad parts, you hang in there with me and you let me get it out. You don't judge me right off the bat. I'm not saying you're going to forgive everything. I sure as hell don't forgive it all myself. But at least you'll be willing to hear me out, and in the end to try to understand me. That's all I can ask, right?

Problem is, where do I begin? If I go right to the sob story, it'll feel like I'm already trying to excuse everything I did. If I go to the hardcore stuff first, you'll think I'm some sort of born criminal. You'll write me off before I get the chance to make my case.

So maybe I'll kind of skip around, if you don't mind. How the first real jobs I was involved with went down. How it felt to be growing up as the Miracle

Boy. How it all came together that one summer. How I met Amelia. How I found my unforgivable talent. How I got myself heading down the wrong road. Maybe you'll look at that and decide that I didn't have much choice. Maybe you'll decide that you would have done exactly the same thing.

The one thing I *can't* do is start off on that day in June of 1990. I can't go there yet. No matter how hard other people have tried to convince me, and believe me, there were a lot of them and they tried pretty damned hard . . . I can't start there because I already feel claustrophobic enough in here. Some days it's all I can do to keep breathing. But maybe one of these days as I'm writing, I'll get to it and I'll think to myself, okay, today's the day. Today you can face it. No warm-up needed. Just go back to that day and let it fly. You're eight years old. You hear the sound outside the door. And—

Damn, this is even harder than I thought.

I had to take a little break, get up and walk around a little bit, which around here isn't very far. I left the cell and walked down through the common area, used the main bathroom and brushed my teeth. There was a new guy in there, someone who doesn't know anything about me yet. When he said hey to me, I knew I had to be careful. Not answering people might be considered rude on the outside. In here, it could be taken as disrespect. If I were in a *really* bad place, I'd probably be dead by now. Even in here, in this place, it's a constant challenge for me.

I did what I usually do. Two fingers of my right hand pointing to my throat, then a slashing motion. No words coming out of here, pal. No disrespect intended. I obviously made it back alive because I'm still writing.

So hang on, because this is my story if you're ready for it. I was the Miracle Boy, once upon a time. Later on, the Milford Mute. The Golden Boy. The Young Ghost. The Kid. The Boxman. The Lock Artist. That was all me.

But you can call me Mike.

Two

Outside Philadelphia
September 1999

So there I was, on my way to my first real job. I'd been on the road for two days straight, ever since leaving home. That old motorcycle had broken down just as I crossed the Pennsylvania state line. I hated to leave it there on the side of the road, after all it had given me. The freedom. The feeling that I could jump on the thing and outrun anything at a moment's notice. But what the hell else choice did I have?

I took the bags off the back and stuck my thumb out. You try hitchhiking when you can't speak. Go ahead, try it sometime. The first three people who stopped for me just couldn't deal with it. It didn't matter how nice my face was or how used up I might have looked after all those lonely miles. You'd think I'd stop being surprised by how freaked out people get when they meet a man who is always silent.

So it took a while to get there. Two days since the call and a lot of trouble and hardship. Then I finally show up, tired and hungry and filthy. Talk about making a good first impression.

This was the Blue Crew. These were the guys the Ghost called steady and reliable. Not quite as top of the heap, but professional. Even if they were a little rough around the edges sometimes. Like most New York guys. That's all I'd been told about them. I was about to find out the rest for myself.

They were holed up in a little one-story motor court just outside of Malvern, Pennsylvania. It wasn't the worst place I'd ever seen, but I guess if you were stuck there for an extra day or two, it would start to get to you. Especially if you were trying to keep a low profile, ordering pizzas instead of going out, passing a bottle back and forth instead of seeing what the local bars had to offer. Whatever the reason, they weren't all that happy when I finally showed up.

There were only two of them. I didn't think I'd find such a small crew, but there they were, both staying in the same room. Which I'm sure didn't help their mood any. The man who answered the door was the man who seemed to be the leader. He was bald and maybe twenty pounds overweight, but he looked strong enough to put me right through the window. He spoke with a pronounced New Yorker accent.

"Who are you?" He stared me down for five seconds, then it hit him. "Wait a minute, are *you* the guy we've been waiting for? Get in here!"

He pulled me inside and shut the door.

"You're kidding me, right? This is a joke?"

The other man was sitting at the table, in the middle of a hand of gin rummy. "What's with the kid?"

"This is the boxman we've been waiting for. Can't you tell?"

"What is he, like twelve years old?"

"How old are you, kid?"

I put up ten fingers, then eight more. I wouldn't turn eighteen for another four months, but I figured what the hell. Close enough.

"They said you don't talk much. I guess they were telling the truth."

"The fuck took you so long," the man at the table said. His accent was a lot thicker than the first guy's. So thick it sounded like he was standing on a Brooklyn street corner. I nicknamed him Brooklyn in my mind. I knew I'd never get real names.

I put my right thumb up, moving it slowly from side to side.

"You had to hitchhike? Are you kidding me?"

I put my hands up. No choice, guys.

"You look like shit," the first man said. "Do you need to take a shower or something?"

That sounded like a great idea to me. So I took a shower and rummaged through my bag for some clean clothes. I felt almost human again when I was done. When I stepped back into the room, I could tell that they had been talking about me.

"Tonight's our last chance," Manhattan said. That was the nickname I'd already settled on for the leader. If they had brought three more guys with them, we could have covered all five boroughs. "Are you sure you're up for this?"

"Our man comes back home tomorrow morning," Brooklyn said. "If we don't hit him now, this whole trip's a fucking waste."

I nodded. I understand, guys. What else do you want from me?

"You really don't talk," Manhattan said. "I mean, they weren't pulling my chain. You really don't say one freaking word."

I shook my head.

"Can you open the man's safe?"

I nodded.

"That's all we need to know."

Brooklyn didn't look quite as convinced, but for now he didn't have much choice. They had been waiting for their boxman. And their boxman was me.

About three hours later, after the sun had gone, I was sitting in the back of a panel van marked ELITE RENOVATIONS. Manhattan was driving. Brooklyn was riding shotgun, turning every few minutes or so to look at me. It was something I knew I'd have to get accustomed to. It was like the Ghost had said, these guys had already done all of the legwork, had scouted out their target, had watched their man's every move, had planned the whole operation from beginning to end. Me, I was just the specialist, brought in at the last minute to do my part. It didn't help that I looked like I hadn't even started shaving yet, and that beyond that I was some kind of mutant freak who couldn't even say one word out loud.

So yeah. I didn't blame them for being a little skeptical.

From what I could see out the front windows, it looked like we were heading into some prime real estate. This must have been the Main Line I'd heard about. The old-money suburbs west of Philadelphia. We passed private schools with great stone archways guarding the entrances. We passed Villanova University, sitting high on a hill. I found myself wondering if they had a good art school. We passed a long sloping lawn with strings of lights and white furniture set out for some sort of party. All of it in a world I'd never get to see in any legal, legitimate way.

We kept going until we hit Bryn Mawr, past another college I didn't catch the name of, until we finally took a right off of the main road. The houses started to get bigger and bigger, yet still there was nobody to stop us. No uniformed men with tin badges and clipboards to check our credentials. That was the thing about these old-money houses. They were built years before anyone ever dreamed of "gated communities."

Manhattan pulled the van into the long driveway, drove it all the way back, past the loop that would have taken us to the front door, instead going around to the back of the house, where there was a large paved area and what looked to be a five-car garage. The two men put on their surgical gloves. I took the pair they gave me and put them in my pocket. I had never tried doing any of this with gloves on, and I wasn't about to experiment now. Manhattan seemed to make a mental note of my bare hands but didn't say anything about it.

We got out of the van and made our way across a large veranda to the back door. There was a thick line of pine trees surrounding the backyard. A motion sensor light snapped on as soon as we got close to the house, but nobody flinched. The light did nothing but welcome us, anyway. Right this way, sirs. Let me show you fine gentlemen exactly where you're going.

The two men paused at the door, obviously waiting for me to perform the first of my specialties. I took the leather case out of my back pocket and got to work. I chose a tension bar and slipped that into the bottom of the keyhole. Then I took out a thin diamond pick and started in on the pins. Feeling my way through those pins, back to front, pushing each pin up just enough for it to catch against the shear line. I knew that on a house like this, the lock would have to have mushroom pins at the very least. Maybe even serrated pins. When I had all the false sets done, I worked my way through them again, bumping each pin up another tiny fraction of an inch, keeping the tension exactly right. Shutting out every other thing in my mind. The men standing around me. The simple fact of what I was doing here. The night itself. It was just me and those five little pieces of metal.

One pin set. Two pins set. Three. Four. Five.

I felt the whole cylinder give now. I pressed harder on the tension bar and the whole thing turned. Whatever doubts these men may have had about me, I had just passed the first test.

Manhattan pushed in past me, going right for the alarm station. This was the part they needed to have worked out already on their own. There were so many elements that could be compromised in an electronic alarm system. Bypassing the magnetic sensors on a door or window. Disabling the entire system itself or just disconnecting it from its dedicated phone line. Hell, even getting to the person who was sitting in the alarm company's control room. As soon as you have a real live human in the loop, things get easier, especially if that real live human being is earning $6.50 an hour.

Somehow these guys knew the pass code already, which is the simplest way of all. They might have had a connection inside the house. Either a housekeeper or a service man. Or else they had just watched the owner closely enough, with enough magnification to see the buttons as he pressed them. However they did it, they had the number, and it took Manhattan all of five seconds to turn the whole system off.

He gave us the thumbs-up, and Brooklyn split off to keep watch or whatever else he was supposed to be doing. This was obviously routine for them. Something they felt totally comfortable with. Me? I was in my own little zone now. That warm little buzz, the way my heart rate would speed up until it was finally in sync with that constant bass drum inside my head. The fear I lived with every second of every day finally draining away from me. Everything peaceful and normal and in perfect tune, for just those few precious minutes.

Manhattan gave me a little wave to follow him. We walked through the house, as perfect a house as I had ever seen. It was decorated more for comfort than for show. A huge television with chairs you could disappear into. A fully stocked bar with glasses hanging from a rack, a mirror, bar stools, the works. We went up the stairs, down the hallway, and into the master bedroom. Manhattan seemed to know exactly where to go. We ended up in one of the two big walk-in closets, rows of expensive dark suits on one side, expensive casual clothes on the other side. Shoes arranged neatly on their slanted platform. Belts and ties hanging on some kind of electric contraption. Press the button and they would all start rotating into view.

Of course, we weren't here for the belts and ties. Manhattan carefully slid some of the suits aside. I could see the faint rectangular outline in the back wall. Manhattan pushed on it and it popped open. Inside that door was the safe.

He stood aside for me. Once again, my turn.

This is where they really needed me. They could have gotten through that back door if they had really wanted to. It might have taken them a little longer, but these were smart, resourceful men, and they would have found a way. The safe? This was a different matter. It was one thing to find out the security code for the whole house, but the combination to the safe hidden in the master bedroom closet? No, that would live only inside the owner's head. Maybe in the wife's head. *Maybe* in one other person's head, a trusted confidant or the family lawyer, in case of emergency. Beyond that . . . well, you could go ahead and find the owner, tape him to a chair and stick a gun in his mouth, but then you'd have a whole different kind of operation. If you wanted to do this clean, then you needed a boxman to get you into that safe. A bad boxman would probably end up cutting through the wall and dragging the safe right out. A better boxman would leave it in the wall and use a drill. A great boxman . . . well, that's exactly what I was hoping to demonstrate.

The problem was—and I was glad Manhattan didn't know this—up until that point in my young life, I had never once opened a wall safe. I mean, I knew it was the same idea. It's just a regular safe built into a wall, right? But I had learned on freestanding safes, where I could really get my body up next to them and feel what I was doing. As the Ghost had said so many times, when he was teaching me how to do this . . . It's like seducing a woman. Touching her in just the right way. Knowing what was going on inside of her. How do you do that if every part of the woman except her face is hidden behind a wall?

I shook out my hands and stepped up to the dial. I tried the handle first, made sure the damned thing was actually locked. It was.

I could see the Chicago brand plate, so I dialed the two "tryout" combinations, the preset combinations that the safes are shipped with. You'd be amazed how many people never change them.

No luck on either of those. This was a conscientious safe owner who set his own combination. So now it was time to go to work.

I pressed myself against the wall, putting my cheek against the safe's front door. I was already assuming three wheels, but it was my first time, after all, so I wanted to make sure. I found the contact area, that area on the dial where the "nose" of the lever was coming into contact with the notch on the drive cam. Once I had that, I parked all the wheels on the opposite side of the dial, then spun back the opposite way, counting all of the pickups.

One. Two. Three. Then I was clear. Three wheels.

I spun back, parked all the wheels at 0. Then I went back to the contact area.

This was the hard part. This was the almost impossible, should-be-impossible part. Because of the fact that no wheel can be exactly, exactly round and no two wheels can be exactly, exactly the same size as each other, you're going to have some imperfect contact when you pass over the open notches on each wheel. It's just unavoidable, no matter how well the safe is built. So when you're sitting over a notch and you go back to the contact area, it's going to feel a little different. A little *shorter* as that nose dips down a little farther on the drive cam.

On a cheap safe? You can feel it like a pothole on a smooth road. On a good safe? A good, expensive safe like the man who owned this house would have built into his closet?

The difference would be so small. So tinier than tiny.

I parked at 3. Then at 6. Then at 9. Going by threes to start out with, testing each time. Waiting for that different feel to come to me. That slightest shortening in the contact area. Such a fine difference that no normal human being could ever perceive it. Absolutely never ever in a thousand years.

12. Yes. I was close.

Okay, keep going. 15, 18, 21.

I worked my way around the dial, spinning quickly when I could, slowing down when I needed to feel every millionth of an inch. I heard Manhattan shifting his weight around behind me. I put up one hand, and he was still again.

24. 27. Yes. There.

How do I know?

I just know. When it's shorter, it's shorter. I just feel it.

Or something beyond feeling it, really. That little piece of hard metal touches the notch a hair width's sooner than the last time around, and I can feel it, hear it, see it in my mind.

When I had finished the dial, I had three rough numbers in my head. I went back and narrowed those down until they were exact, moving by ones this time instead of threes. When I was done with that, I had the three numbers in the combination, 13, 26, 72.

The last step is a little bit of grunt work. There's no other way to do it but to grind right through them. So start with 13-26-72, then switch the first two, then the second and last, and so on, until you've worked your way through all six possibilities. Six being a lot better than a million, which is how many combinations you'd have to go through if you couldn't find out those numbers.

Today's combination ended up being 26-72-13. Total time to open the safe? About twenty-five minutes.

I turned the handle and pulled the door open. I made sure I was watching Manhattan's face as I did that.

"Fuck me," he said. "You can just fuck me with a stick right now."

I stepped aside and let him do what he needed to do. I had no idea what he was hoping to find in there. Jewels? Hard cash? I saw him pull out about a dozen envelopes, those brown paper envelopes that are just a little bit bigger than business size.

"We got 'em. We're ready to roll."

I closed up the safe and spun the dial. Manhattan was right behind me with a white rag, wiping everything down. Then he swung the outer door shut and slid the suits back in place.

He turned the light off. We retraced our steps down the stairs. Brooklyn was in the living room, looking out the front window.

"Don't tell me," he said.

"Right here," Manhattan said, holding up the envelopes.

"Are you shitting me?" He looked over at me with an odd little smile. "Is our boy here like a genius or something?"

"Or something. Let's roll."

Manhattan keyed in the security code to rearm the alarm system. Then he closed the back door behind us and wiped off the knob.

This is why they called me. This is why they waited around for a kid they'd never met before to ride halfway across the country. Because with me on the job, they leave absolutely no trace behind them. The owner of this house would come back the next day, open the door, and find everything exactly as he had left it. He would go upstairs, take some clothes out of his closet, turn the light back off. Only when it was time to go into that safe would he dial his combination and open that door and see . . .

Nothing.

Even then, he wouldn't comprehend what had happened. Not right away. He'd fumble around for a while, thinking that he must be mistaken. That he must be losing his mind. He'd accuse his wife next. You're the only person in the world who knows the combination! Or else he'd call the family lawyer, put him on the spot. We were gone for a week, eh? You decided to make a little visit to our house?

Finally, it would dawn on him. Somebody else had been here. By that time, Manhattan and Brooklyn would be safely back home, and I'd be . . .

I'd be wherever it was that I went next.

I never did find out what was in those envelopes. I didn't care, not in the least. I knew going in that it was a flat fee job. When we were back at the motor court, Manhattan gave me the cash and told me it had been a real pleasure seeing me work.

I had some more money now, at least. Enough to eat for a while, to think about finding a place to stay. But how long would that money last?

He peeled off the magnetic ELITE RENOVATIONS sign from each side of the van and put those in the back. He took a screwdriver and undid the Pennsylvania license plates and replaced them with New York plates. He was about to get behind the wheel when I stopped him.

"What is it, kid?"

I took out an imaginary wallet from my back pocket, made like I was opening it.

"What, you lost your wallet? Go buy a new one. You're flush now."

I shook my head, pretended to take a card out of that same imaginary wallet.

"You lost your ID? Just go back to where you came from. They'll give you a new one."

I shook my head again. I pointed to that invisible card in my hand.

"You need . . ."

Finally, the lightbulb went off.

"You need a *new* ID. As in, a whole new fucking identity."

I nodded my head.

"Oh, shit. That's a whole different deal right there."

I leaned in close, put one hand on his shoulder. Come on, friend. You gotta help me out here.

"Look," he said. "We know who you work for. I mean, we're gonna send him his cut, right? That's how this deal works. We're not gonna stiff him, believe me. So if you got a problem like that, why don't you go back home and get it straightened out there?"

How could I explain this to him? Even if I *could* speak? This strange sort of limbo I was in now. I was a dog who couldn't go home, who didn't have a place on his master's floor. Or even in his backyard. I had to stay on the run, scrounging for scraps in the garbage cans.

Until he finally called me. When the master stuck his head out the door and called my name, you better believe I had to go running back to him.

"Look, I know a guy," he said. "I mean, if you're really in a jam."

He took out his own wallet, pulled out a business card and then a pen. He turned the card over and started writing on it.

"You call this guy and he'll—"

He stopped writing and looked up at me.

"Oh yeah. That might be tough. I guess you should probably just go see him in person, eh?"

I took out the money he had just given me and started peeling off bills.

"Wait, wait. Stop."

He turned around and looked at Brooklyn. They exchanged a couple of shrugs.

"I'd ask you to promise not to tell my boss," he said, "but somehow I don't think that's gonna be a problem."

I got in the back of their van. That's how I ended up in New York.

Three
Michigan
1991

Back up a little bit. Not all the way back. Just to when I was nine years old. Right after it happened. By that time, I was pronounced more or less physically recovered, except for that one little oddity they couldn't quite figure out. The not talking business. After being shuffled around to a few different beds, I was finally allowed to go live with my uncle Lito. The man who had such a studly Italian lover's name, even though he was anything but. He did have black hair, but it always looked like he was one month overdue for a trim. He had long sideburns, too. They were turning gray, and from the amount of time he spent fussing with them in the mirror, he must have thought they were his best asset. Looking back, those sideburns, the clothes he wore . . . hell, the whole combination would have been impossible if he had ever gotten married. Any woman in the world would have blown him right up and started from scratch.

Uncle Lito was my father's older brother. He didn't look anything at all like my father. Not even close. I never asked him if either or both of them had been adopted. I think the question would have made him uncomfortable. Especially now that he was the only brother left. He lived in a little town called Milford, up in Oakland County, northwest of Detroit. I'd never spent much time with him when I was little, and even when I did see him, I don't remember him ever taking much interest in me. But after everything happened, hell, it had obviously changed him somewhat, even though he wasn't directly involved. It was his brother, for God's sake. His brother and his sister-in-law. And here I was, his nephew . . . eight years old then and officially homeless. The State of Michigan would have taken me away otherwise, put me God knows where with God knows whom. It's hard to even imagine how my life would have worked out if that had happened. Maybe

I'd be a model citizen right now. Or maybe I'd be dead. Who knows? The way it worked out, it was Uncle Lito who took me to his house in Milford, about fifty miles away from that little brick house on Victoria Street. Fifty miles away from that place where my young life should have ended. After a few months giving it a try, they let him sign the papers and he became my legal guardian.

I know he didn't have to do it. He didn't have to do *anything* for me. If you ever hear me complain about the man, don't lose sight of that bottom line, okay? Here's the first problem, though. If you want to start your life over, you need to move more than fifty miles away. Fifty miles is not far enough to get away from your old life, or to avoid having everyone you meet still know you as the person you were.

It's not nearly far enough if you've already become famous for something you want to forget forever.

And the town of Milford itself . . . well, I know it's a yuppie little "exurb" now, but back then it was still just a working-class little hick town with a Main Street that ran cockeyed under a railroad bridge. No matter how many flashing lights and big yellow signs they put up, they probably averaged two or three accidents every month. Just from the drunken idiots who couldn't negotiate that sudden little jog in the road that took you within inches of the concrete embankments. Hell, just my uncle's customers alone . . . because his liquor store was right next to the bridge. Lito's Liquors. On the other side was a restaurant called the Flame. If you've ever eaten at a Denny's, just imagine that same dining experience except with food that's about half as good. You'd think I wouldn't have ever eaten there more than once, like most people, but because the Flame was so close to the liquor store, and because there was this one waitress my uncle had a thing for. Anyway, it sounds like an old joke, but if there was anything that would have ever gotten me to finally speak up, it would have been the food at the Flame.

Beyond that, there was a park down Main Street with rusty old swing sets and monkey bars you'd be a fool to touch without a tetanus shot. The park sloped down to the Huron River, which was littered with old tires and shopping carts and stacks of newspapers still in their bindings. There was a bank against the river where the railroad ran over it, and that's where the kids from the high school hung out at night, blasting their car radios, drinking beer, smoking pot, whatever.

I know, you think I'm probably exaggerating. If you saw Milford now, you'd think I was crazy, with all the upscale housing developments they've got there now, and Main Street with all its antiques and healthy sandwich wraps and salons. There's a big white gazebo in the park now. They do concerts there in the summer. If you tried to smoke a joint under the railroad bridge now, the cops would be there in three seconds.

It was a different place back then, is what I'm trying to say. A lonely place, especially for a kid just turning nine years old. With no parents. Living in a strange house with a man he barely knew. Uncle Lito had this little one-story thing behind the store, this sad little house with mint green aluminum siding. He took the poker table out of the back room, and that became my bedroom. "Guess we won't be playing poker here anymore," he said as he showed me the room for the first time. "But you know what? I was losing money most of the time, so maybe I should thank you."

He reached out his hand to me. It was a gesture I'd come to know well. It was like a playful slap or maybe the way you'd knock your best buddy on the shoulder. You know, a little horseplay between two guys, but more tentative, like he didn't want to touch me too hard. Or like he was leaving open the possibility that I'd step closer and he could turn it into an awkward sideways hug.

I could tell Uncle Lito was trying hard to figure out what to do with me. "We're just a couple of bachelors," he said to me on more than one occasion. "Living off the fat of the land, eh? What do you say we go to the Flame and get a bite to eat." As if the Flame's food qualified as the fat of the land. We'd sit in the booth and Uncle Lito would run down his day to me in great detail, how many bottles of this or that he sold and what he needed to reorder. I'd sit there completely silent. Of course. Whether I was really listening to him, it didn't seem to matter much. He just kept up his end of a one-sided conversation, pretty much every waking moment.

"Whaddya say, Mike? You think we need to do some laundry today?"

"Time to go to work, Mike. Another day, another dollar. You feel like hanging around in the back while I clean things up a bit?"

"Getting low on supplies here, Mike. I think we need a trip to the store. Whaddya say we pick up a couple of honeys while we're out, eh? Bring 'em back here? Have a party?"

This habit of his, this jabbering on and on all the time . . . it's the kind of thing I'd run into a lot, wherever I went. People who naturally like to talk, it takes them a minute to get used to me, but once they do they just turn it on and never turn it off. God forbid there be one moment of silence.

The quiet people, on the other hand . . . I usually make them uncomfortable as hell, because they know they can't compete with me. I'll out-quiet anybody, in any venue for any stakes. I'm the undisputed champion of keeping my mouth shut and just sitting there like a piece of furniture.

Okay, so I had to feel sorry for myself for a little while there. Put the pen down and lie on my bunk. Stare at the ceiling. That always helps. Try it sometime if you don't believe me. Next time you find yourself in a cage for a few years. Anyway, back to the story. I won't drag you through all the doctor visits I sat through. All the speech therapists, the counselors, the psychologists . . . Looking back on it, I must have been the ultimate wet dream for these people. To every one of them, I was the sad, silent, totally lost kid with the messy hair and the big brown eyes. The Miracle Boy who hadn't said one word since that fateful day he cheated death. With the right treatment, the right coaching, the right amount of understanding and encouragement . . . that doctor or speech therapist or counselor or psychologist would find the magic key to unlock my wounded psyche, and I'd end up bawling in their arms while they stroked my hair and told me that everything was finally going to be all right.

That's what they all wanted from me. Each and every one. Believe me, they weren't going to get it.

Whenever we'd leave a new doctor's office, Uncle Lito would have a new diagnosis to recite to himself on the way home. "Selective mutism." "Psychogenic aphonia." "Traumatically induced laryngeal paralysis." Really, in the end, they all amounted to exactly the same thing. For whatever reason, I had simply decided to stop talking.

When people find out I grew up behind a liquor store, the first thing they ask me is how many times the place got robbed. Every time, guaranteed. The first question I get. The answer? Exactly once.

It was that first year after I moved in with him. One of the first warm nights of that summer. The parking lot was empty, aside from Uncle Lito's ancient two-tone Grand Marquis with the big dent in the back bumper. This man, he came in and took one quick lap around the store, making sure the place was really as empty as it looked. He stopped dead when he saw me standing in the doorway to the back room.

Now technically, I wasn't supposed to be on the premises at all. I was nine years old then, and this was a liquor store. But Uncle Lito didn't have a lot of options, at least not in the evenings. Most of the time I'd sit in my little spot in the back room. My "office," as Uncle Lito called it, with walls made from empty boxes stacked five feet high, and a reading lamp. I'd sit back there and read every night, mostly comic books that I'd get from a store down the street, until it was time to go home to bed.

So even though I wasn't supposed to be there at all, let alone every night, who was going to bust us? Everybody in town knew my story. Everybody knew Uncle Lito was doing the best job he could with me, with no real help from anyone else. So people left us alone.

The man stood there for a long time, looking down at me. He had freckles and light red hair.

"You need any help back there, friend?" Uncle Lito's voice from the front of the store.

The man didn't say anything. He gave me a little nod of his head and walked away from me. That's the exact moment I knew he had a gun.

You're going to have to go with me on this one. Nine years old, and somehow I knew this. You're thinking I'm just looking back at it a certain way, and because I was about to find out what happened next, somehow in my mind I'm filling in this detail. That in my memory I'm adding this part. But I swear to God. You can freeze time right there and I already knew exactly what was about to happen. He was going to go back up and he was going to take the gun out with his right hand and he was going to point the gun at Uncle Lito's head and tell him to empty out the cash register. Just like in one of my comic books.

As soon as the man turned away from me, I closed the door. There was a phone in the back room. I picked up the receiver and dialed 911. It rang twice, and a woman's voice answered. "Hello. Do you have an emergency?"

An emergency. Maybe that's what it would take. When it was time for me to speak, when I really *needed* to . . . the words would come.

"Hello. Can you hear me? Do you need help?"

I held the phone tight in my hand. There were no words coming out. It wasn't going to happen. I knew that. I knew that without any doubt at all, and in that same moment I knew something else. The sick feeling I had been living with . . . the living, breathing *fear* I had been feeling, every second of every day . . . it was all gone. Every bit of it. At least temporarily. For those next few minutes, when I did what I did next. It was the first time I didn't feel scared about anything since that day in June.

The operator was still talking, her voice fading to a faraway squeak as I dropped the receiver and it hung swinging by its cord. Turns out that was enough to get the police there, by the way. You call 911 like that and leave the line open, they have to come check it out. But on this night, it wouldn't be soon enough to stop the robbery.

I opened the door and walked out into the store. Down the long aisle of bottles. I could hear the man talking in a quick, high voice.

"That's right, man. All the money. Right now, man."

Then Uncle Lito's voice, an octave lower. "Just take it easy, friend. Okay? Nobody has to do anything stupid here."

"What's that kid doing back there? Where'd he go?"

"Don't you worry about him. He's got nothing to do with this."

"Why don't you call him up here? I'm getting nervous. You don't want that."

"He can't even hear me if I tried. He's deaf and dumb, okay? Just leave him out of this."

That's when I turned the corner and saw them. I can still remember every detail in that scene. Uncle Lito, paper bag in one hand, bills from the open register in the other. The wall of sample bottles behind him. The coffee can on the counter, my picture taped to the rim, above it the sign asking for money to help out the Miracle Boy.

Then the man. The robber. The criminal. The way he stood there with the gun gripped tight in his right hand. A revolver shining in the fluorescent light.

He was scared. I could see that as clearly as I could see his face. This gun in his hand, it was supposed to take the fear away, to make him the master of this whole situation. But it was doing exactly the opposite. It was making him so scared he could barely think straight. This was an instant lesson for me, even at nine years old. It was something I'd remember forever.

The robber looked at me for the first two seconds, swung the gun my way in the third.

"Michael!" he said. "Get the hell out of here!"

"I thought you said he was deaf," the robber said. He came over to me and grabbed my shirt. Then I felt the barrel of the gun pressing against the top of my head.

"What are you doing?" my uncle said. "I told you I'll do anything you say."

I could feel the robber's hands shaking. Uncle Lito's face had gone white, his own hands outstretched like he was trying to reach me. To pull me away. I didn't know which one of them was more terrified at that point. But, like I said, I wasn't scared myself. Not one little bit. It's the one advantage you have maybe, being scared all the time. When it's time to *really* be scared, when all of a sudden you're finally *supposed* to be scared . . . it just doesn't happen.

My uncle fumbled with the money, trying to stuff it all into the paper bag. "Take the money," he said. "For God's sake, just take it and get out of here."

The robber pushed me away, grabbing the bag with his left hand while he kept the gun aimed with his right, swinging it back and forth between us. Me, my uncle, me again. Then he backed away, toward the door, passing right by me. I didn't move. When he was two feet away, he took one quick look down at me.

I didn't try to stop him. I didn't try to take the money away from him, or try to take the gun. I didn't stick my finger in the muzzle and smile at him. I just stood there and looked at him like he was a fish in an aquarium.

"Fucking weirdo kid." He pushed the door open with his left elbow, nearly dropping the bag of money. He recovered and ran to his car and drove away, spinning his wheels as he hit Main Street.

Uncle Lito scrambled out from behind the register and went to the door. By the time he got there, the car was out of sight.

He turned back to me. There was so much adrenaline pumping through his body by now, he was practically vibrating.

"What the hell is wrong with you?" he said. "What in goddamned hell . . ."

He sat down, right there on the floor, breathing hard. He stayed there until the police showed up. He kept looking at me, but he didn't say anything else. So many questions in his mind, I'm sure, but why bother asking them when he knew he'd get no answers?

I sat down next to him, to keep him company. I felt a tentative hand on my back. We sat there and waited, sharing the silence.

Four
New York City
Late 1999

It seemed like the last place on earth to me, this little Chinese restaurant on the ground floor of an eight-story building on 128th Street. The family who ran the place had a lease for the first floor only, and the top floors were supposedly locked up tight and scheduled for renovation by the owner at some undetermined point in the future. So naturally, those boards that were blocking the stairwell got taken down and a number of people ended up living upstairs. Extended members of the family first, the cousins and second cousins who came over to America to work ninety hours a week in the restaurant. Then the occasional outsider who could be trusted to keep his mouth shut, and who could pay the family a certain amount of money every month. In cash, of course.

I was passed along to the family, after the man who sold me my new identity passed me along to this other guy he knew, who in turn passed me along to somebody else. My room ended up being on the third floor. That was about as high as you wanted to go. Any higher and the heat from the first-floor kitchen wouldn't quite get to you. Plus nobody had an extension cord that was long enough to reach to the fourth floor. So it was dark and freezing cold, and on top of that the rats had already claimed those floors as their own.

I hadn't thought to change my appearance yet. That would come later. But I figured being officially on the run from the State of Michigan, a violator of my terms of probation, and having done my first real money job . . . No turning back now, right? Hence the New York driver's license with the made-up name of William Michael Smith and the made-up age of twenty-one. I didn't use it to get into bars, though. Believe me. I stayed inside as much as I could, because I was convinced that every police officer I saw was

actively looking for me. Even in the middle of the night, when I'd hear a siren down on the street . . . I'd be convinced that they had finally found me.

It was getting colder every week. I stayed inside and I drew and I practiced on my portable safe lock. I ate the food from the restaurant that the
Chinese family gave me. I paid them two hundred dollars a month cash to
stay in the upstairs room they didn't own, and to use the bathroom and
shower in the back of the kitchen. I had one lamp that I had plugged into the
extension cord. I had paper and art supplies. I still had my motorcycle bags
with all of my clothes in them. I had my safe lock and my lock picks.

I had the pagers.

There were five of them, all in a beat-up shoebox. One pager with white
tape on it, one with yellow, one with green, one with blue. Then the last with
red tape. The Ghost had told me, if any of the first four pagers go off, you
call the number on the little screen, you listen to what they say. They'll
know that you can't speak in return. If they don't seem to understand that,
it's a good sign that the wrong person is on the phone and that you should
hang up. Assuming they're on the level, you listen to what they say, and then
you go to meet them at the location they indicate. If everything still feels
right, you go do the job with them. You handle your business the right way
and everybody wins. They'll take care of you because they know if they don't,
you won't be picking up that pager the next time they call.

They'll also take care of sending the ten percent "usage fee" to the man
in Detroit. Because they want to keep living.

That's for the first four pagers. The last pager, the one with the red
tape . . . that's the man himself. The man in Detroit. You call the number
right away. You do what the man says. You show up exactly where and when
the man says to show up.

"This is the one man you do not fuck with." The Ghost's exact words.
"You fuck with this man, you might as well go ahead and kill yourself. Save
everybody the trouble."

I knew the Ghost had been telling the truth. I had seen enough myself to
know that this was the one piece of advice I should never forget. But what
was I supposed to do while I was waiting for the next job? How long would
I have to stay here, hiding out in this abandoned room above the Chinese
restaurant on 128th Street, before somebody paged me and I got to make
some money again?

Would I starve first? Would I freeze to death?

The Ghost never covered that part.

By the time Christmas rolled around, I was finally leaving the building once in a while. I'd go to a park a few blocks to the south and sit on one of the benches. I finally had to buy some new clothes. I wasn't broke yet, mind you. I had been well paid for the job in Pennsylvania. Still, I could do the math and see where it was all headed.

To make matters a little worse, one of the men who worked in the restaurant told me I needed to help him if I wanted him to keep giving me food. He gave me a big stack of menus and told me to go to all of the buildings in the neighborhood, to get inside somehow, and to put one menu under each door. I knew that some of the buildings had a doorman at the entrance, and that at the other buildings you had to have somebody who lived there buzz you in. So I wasn't sure how I'd be able to deliver the menus. I mean, I could have found the back doors on most of these buildings and picked the lock, but was that really worth it?

"You have nice fine face," the man said. His English wasn't quite up to speed yet. "People let you in."

So I took my nice fine face and my stack of menus and I went to the buildings, one by one. I figured instead of hiding it, I'd come right out and let everybody know exactly what I was doing. Show them the menus, make like I was slipping one under a door. I'd throw in a little sign language once in a while, too. That seemed to help. I got into more buildings than not.

One day, when I was working my way down a long hallway, a door opened just as I was about to slide a menu under it. Before I could even stand up, I felt two hands on my shoulders. I was pushed backward against the far wall, so hard I lost my breath.

I looked up and saw the man's face. It took me all the way back to that man who held up my uncle's liquor store when I was nine years old. It was that same animal fear in his eyes. A horrible smell of unwashed clothes, urine, maybe that fear itself, it all washed over me. I kicked at his knees and he fell back away from me. Then he ran down the hallway. He slammed open the door and disappeared down the stairs.

I got up, rubbing my shoulders. When I looked through the open doorway, I saw the wreckage inside. The man had trashed the place, looking for anything of value. So he could buy more drugs. Or whatever it was he needed in his life so bad. I could see the refrigerator still open, even the food inside ransacked and ruined now. I closed the door to the apartment and left.

When I got back down to the street, I wrote the apartment number on the back of a menu and gave it to the doorman. Then I went back to the restaurant.

I went up to my room. I counted what was left of my money. I'm living on borrowed time here, I thought. How long until you turn into that man breaking into apartments?

It got colder and colder. The snow came down that night. White at first, but dirty by morning.

I woke up to hear one of the pagers beeping.

I met the men in a diner in the Bronx. A simple cab ride over the Hudson River. It was the yellow pager they had called me on. Now, I knew what the Ghost had said about the yellow pager. This was the general number that just about any knucklehead could use to reach me. Therefore proceed with extreme caution. But I was feeling especially motivated, shall we say. So on that cold afternoon I went into the diner and stood there for a few minutes until I got waved over to a booth in the back, right next to the kitchen doors. There were three men sitting there. One of them stood up, grabbed my right hand, and pulled me close to him for a halfway hug.

"You must be the kid," he said to me. He was wearing a bright green New York Jets jacket and a gold chain. He had a close-cropped Caesar haircut that he probably spent too much time on. He had one of those razor-thin lines of stubble that ran perfectly along each side of his jaw, meeting in a little soul patch on his chin. You know, a white boy trying to look anything but white.

"These are my boys," he said, gesturing to the other two. "Heckle and Jeckle."

So at least he was saving me the trouble of thinking up nicknames. He slid back into the booth and made room for me.

"You want something to eat? We just ordered." The thin little beard thing seemed to make his mouth look bigger somehow, and I'd come to find out he could never let a minute pass without saying something. Or many somethings. So right off the bat I nicknamed him Bigmouth. He called over the waitress, and she got a menu for me. I pointed to a hamburger.

"What, you don't talk?" she said.

"That's right," Bigmouth said. "He don't talk. You got a problem with that?" She took my menu from me and walked away without another word.

"I heard about you," he said when she was safely out of earshot. "You just did a little something with a friend of a friend of mine."

That answered my first question, about how on the phone he had seemed to know I was in the city somewhere. I couldn't help imagining a thousand more shady characters out there, all of them knowing my general location at all times.

"I mean, damn," he said. "I heard you were young-looking, but God damn."

Heckle and Jeckle weren't saying anything. They had milkshakes in front of them, one chocolate and one vanilla it looked like, and they were content to suck on their straws and nod their heads at everything Bigmouth said.

"So here's the basic situation," he said, lowering his voice. "We've got this buddy of ours . . ."

He's actually doing this right here, I thought. He's laying out the whole plan in a diner.

"He works at this bar uptown. They've got this fancy room upstairs for parties and big events and stuff. So couple weeks ago, they got this Christmas party going on. Bunch of Jewish guys from the diamond district. Wait a minute, did I just say a bunch of Jewish guys were having a Christmas party?"

Heckle and Jeckle spit up their milkshakes over that one. That's exactly when I should have got up and walked out.

"A holiday party, I mean! A Hanukkah party, whatever. Anyway, they're having this party, and this one guy, he gets totally lit up, right? I mean, he's just falling down drunk. And my buddy, he's helping the other guys carry him down to the street, so they can call a cab for this guy. They get him down to the coat check room, and they sit him down there, you know, so they can find his coat and everything. My buddy goes off to find it, and when he's gone, this drunk guy gets talking to his friends. Nobody else is around, right? They're just having this private conversation. And this drunk guy, he's saying about how he's got all of these diamonds stashed away at his house in Connecticut. Like a million dollars' worth, all in a safe. And this guy's friends are like, watch what you're saying, man. You can't go around talking like that or the wrong person will hear you. You know? And the drunk guy's going, oh, you guys have been in business with me for years, I'd trust you with my life. That whole thing. Only the whole time they're having this conversation, my buddy's right around the corner there in the coat check room, and he can hear every single fucking word they're saying!"

The waitress came back with the food just then, so Bigmouth hushed up until she walked away. Then he finished his story while we were eating. Bottom line, his friend looked up the man's name on the invitation list, then found out where his house was in Connecticut. It was just over the state border, in Greenwich. When the friend called the man's place of business, they told him that the man was down in Florida until after the new year.

So lo and behold, these guys were going to break into the house and steal that million-dollar stash of diamonds. With my help, of course. Then Heckle and Jeckle would finally get to do their part in this whole deal, by turning those diamonds into cold hard cash. They both had connections in the jewelry business, I was assured, and they'd be able to move them even if they had laser-inscribed identification numbers.

Now, I had already gotten my bad feeling about these guys the first second I saw them, and everything that happened next just made me feel even more uneasy. I remembered what the Ghost had said about this kind of situation, how I should just get up and walk away if my gut told me to.

But hell. I needed to make some more money eventually, right? They were talking about a big score, and they seemed to have everything covered.

So I got in the car with them. Okay? I got in the car.

Bigmouth was driving. Heckle and Jeckle were in the back. I had shotgun for once in my life. "The seat of honor," Bigmouth said as he opened the door for me, making a big deal out of it. "For the man of the hour."

It was New Year's Eve. Did I mention that yet? We were riding up to this man's house on New Year's Eve.

"My buddy lives in New Rochelle," Bigmouth said. "We'll pick him up on the way. It'll be just the five of us. That sounds about right, eh?"

He looked over at me. He was driving fast on I-95, heading straight to Connecticut. Like a lot of New Yorkers, I figured, he didn't drive more than once a month, and it showed.

"So this is what you do, eh? You're a safecracker? I mean, that is so fantastic. How'd you ever get started doing that?"

I shrugged. I didn't figure he'd know any sign language.

"Hot damn, you really don't say one fucking word. Ever! That is so fucking cool, isn't it, guys?"

Heckle and Jeckle both agreed that it was fucking cool.

"You're like a silent assassin. Except you assassinate safes instead of people, right?"

The Ghost was right, I thought. You walk away. No matter how big the score seems to be, if it doesn't feel right, you turn around right then and there and you walk away.

"Besides, what's this guy doing with all those diamonds in his house, anyway? Am I crazy here? Isn't he just *asking* somebody to come take them?"

But how do I do that now? I can't tell him to stop the car, tell him to leave me here by the side of the road.

"I mean, just the sheer stupidity of this guy, right? Actually talking about it in public? Are you kidding me? We need to do this just on general principle, wouldn't you say?"

More nodding in the backseat. I looked out my window as we whizzed by every car in the right lane.

It didn't take us more than a half hour to hit New Rochelle. We rolled up to a little house not far from the Long Island Sound. Bigmouth's buddy came out and squeezed into the back with Heckle and Jeckle. He reminded me of half the football players back at Milford High School. Big in a white middle-class kind of way, strong as an ox, but probably just as slow on his feet.

"This is the kid," Bigmouth said to him. "Shake his hand."

The Ox put his right hand over the back of the seat and squeezed mine. "Fucking kid is right. Are you sure you can do this?"

"He don't talk," Bigmouth said. "He just opens safes. That's all he does."

We got back on the expressway. Through Mamaroneck and Harrison, past a dozen golf courses all closed up for the winter. To the Connecticut state line.

"So here's the deal," the Ox said. "The safe is right in the guy's office. On the first floor. There's a window there that's already open and waiting for us."

"Vinnie did a little advance work on this," Bigmouth said, actually dropping his friend's name. "What he did was, he went to the guy's house and tried a couple of the windows, until he found one that was open, right? He opens it and then he runs away. And he waits. Does the alarm go off? Do the cops come? He waits and he waits. Nobody comes. So he goes back, throws like what, a big rock through the open window?"

"A branch," the Ox said.

"A branch, okay. He throws a big branch in there, in case they've got one of those motion sensor things, right? He runs away again, he hides. He watches for somebody to come. Nobody comes. So he goes back *again*! He climbs right in the window, right? Walks around, I don't know, does jumping jacks. Climbs back out, runs away, and hides. Nobody comes."

"So then I finally know the alarm system isn't on," the Ox said. "So I go in and look around the place. First painting I see on the wall, right there in the office . . . Bam! I lift it up and there's the safe."

"It's right there waiting for us," Bigmouth said. "We go and we get it. Happy New Year."

"I think I get a little bigger share, too," the Ox said. "I mean, all the advance work I did? Putting my neck on the line, crawling into the house? Not to mention the fact that this guy was my lead to begin with."

I tuned them out at that point. They wrangled over the shares while I ran down all the things that could go wrong. It actually sounded pretty simple. As long as everything the Ox was saying was true, we should be able to get in there, take the diamonds from the safe, and be back on the road in half an hour. Forty-five minutes tops. The only problem might be getting my share of the haul, but I figured what the hell. If I'm out, I know I get nothing. I was already getting nothing today. If I'm in, at least I've got a chance at seeing some big money.

Another half-baked idea, I know. The wrong way to think about it. I know!

We rolled over the border, into Connecticut. The house was only a few minutes farther. The more money you've got, I guess, the closer you can live to New York City, even if you're in a different state.

The Ox directed Bigmouth to the house. It was a big brick Tudor-style mansion, on top of a long sloping lawn. We drove past it and turned about a half mile down, looping back to a playground that was just on the other side of the house's backyard. I didn't like the sight lines on the back of the house, but it was thirty degrees outside, the sun was going down, and the playground was totally deserted.

Bigmouth pulled off the street and turned the car off. We all sat there for a few minutes, waiting for somebody to say something.

"We're actually gonna do this shit," Bigmouth finally said. "Can you believe this?"

"Piece of cake," the Ox said. "What are we waiting for?"

"You're the expert," Bigmouth said to me. "What do you think? Do we go now or do we wait a while?"

As if I hadn't already known this was Amateur Hour. I shook my head and opened my door. Everyone else followed me. When we were outside, I put my hands up to stop them.

"What? What is it?"

I put one finger up. Then I pointed to my eyes, pretended I was looking around in every direction. Then I pointed to the steering wheel of the car and pounded on an imaginary horn.

"Somebody should stay here and be the lookout? Is that what you're saying?"

I gave him the thumbs-up. Either Heckle or Jeckle got elected for that job. Then the rest of us were on our way to the house. We walked down the edge of the backyard. I kept looking around us, trying to find a potential problem. Everything looked clear.

When we got to the back of the house, I stopped everyone again and pointed to my eyes again. Whichever of Heckle or Jeckle was still with us got positioned on the corner of the house, where he could see up to the car in one direction and down to the street in the other. That left Bigmouth, the Ox, and me to go inside.

The Ox carefully raised the window he had left ajar. I was thinking maybe I should make us all wait again, but then I thought, hell, let's just go for it here. Assume the dumb bastard did everything he said he did and the alarm system is really off. Why would a rich man go to Florida for the holidays and not turn his alarm on? Because like Bigmouth said, some people are just plain stupid and deserve everything that happens to them. That's the one thing Bigmouth got right that day.

The Ox climbed into the window first, with about as much grace and delicacy as I would have expected. I went in next. Bigmouth came in behind us. We were already standing in the office. The Ox went right to the nearest painting on the opposite wall. A sailboat battling the waves, the usual high-class crap. He made a big show of putting one finger on the picture's frame and lifting it from the wall. There was a safe there, all right, recessed a few inches into the wall's surface.

"Do your thing," Bigmouth said to me. "How long's it gonna take, anyway?"

I went over to the safe. The Ox stepped aside. I could feel them both staring at my back now as I put my fingers on the dial. It was a brand I'd never seen before. Some European-sounding name. A tiny ray of doubt started to flicker in the back of my mind. What if this one was different from every other safe I'd ever opened before? I certainly didn't know the tryout combinations, so I wouldn't be able to try those first. Which was a shame, because a man who leaves his alarm system off is the same kind of man who'll buy a safe and never change the combination.

But first things first. Try the handle, see if the damned thing is even locked. I put my hand on it, gave it a little twist. I didn't really expect it to move. It's just the thing you do first, to eliminate the possibility.

The handle moved.

I froze on the spot. In two seconds, I saw the whole thing unfolding in my head. When the Ox got in here the first time and found the safe, he didn't even bother trying the handle. If I open the door right now and show them that it's unlocked, they'll know that they didn't need me here at all. Hell, I didn't even open the back door for them. We came in through the damned window.

So what'll happen next? They'll jump right in here, take the diamonds. They'll take me back to New York, at least. I hope. Then they'll dump me on the street corner and say, Thanks for nothing. Unless they're honorable thieves, of course. Fat chance. Or unless they ever want to work with me again. Fat chance again. Like this isn't a once in a lifetime thing for all of these guys.

I could feel that the bolts were already retracting into the door. One little pull and the door would be open. I slowly let the handle slide back. Then I turned and sneaked a look back at Bigmouth and the Ox.

"Is it a hard safe?" Bigmouth said. "Can you do it?"

I shook out my hands, worked my neck around like I was about to attempt the impossible. I pointed at my eyes, then out the room in one direction. At my eyes again, then in the other direction. You two guys get the hell out of here and keep watch.

They both seemed a little reluctant to leave, but I stood my ground. I didn't move a muscle until both of them were gone. Then I let my breath out.

I went back to the safe and opened it. There was a black velvet bag inside. Like something out of a movie, exactly what you'd expect to see holding a million dollars' worth of diamonds, right? With a little drawstring on top? It was perfect.

I opened the drawstring and looked inside. Twenty, maybe thirty glittering stones. Not quite as much as I would have expected, but what did I know about diamonds? I took a few of them out, thought about maybe keeping some for myself. Then I realized that was probably stupid. I'd never be able to do anything with them, and I'd just be reducing the overall take. So I closed up the drawstring and put the bag on the floor. Then I went back to the safe. I knew I needed to kill a few minutes, so I thought I might as well check out the locking mechanism. I spun the dial a few times, pretended that it was locked and tried to open it. I parked the dial, picked up three wheels. Pretty standard so far. I cleared the dial and started going through the numbers, feeling for the contact area. It seemed very well defined to me. When I got to the first short contact, it stood out immediately. This was *not* a hard safe. I was almost sorry that I didn't get to crack it.

What the hell, I thought. At least I'll know this now, if I ever see another one. In the meantime, no sense taking any longer than you have to. Let them think you're really, really fast at doing this.

I wiped off the dial and closed the door. Then I replaced the picture on the wall. I left the room and found Bigmouth standing by the front door, looking out the little window. He almost jumped through the ceiling when I tapped him on the shoulder. He got over that when I handed him the bag.

"What? Are you kidding me? Did you open it already?"

He looked inside the bag. He seemed at a loss for words, maybe for the first time ever.

"Happy New Year," he finally said. "Happy Fucking New Year."

We collected everybody and got back in the car. I rode shotgun again. This time, when we got back on the expressway, I put my hand on Bigmouth's arm and got him to ease up on the gas. Everybody was just a little bit too excited, and I didn't want us all to get killed on the way back.

"He did it!" Bigmouth screamed, for the third or fourth time. "How long did that take, like four minutes? Five minutes? The kid is a fucking genius!"

"He's ice," the Ox said. "I gotta admit it now. I had my doubts at first, but this kid is a fucking ice cube."

"Hey, I just thought of something." Bigmouth took his eyes off the road to look at me. "When you were in there alone, you didn't put any of those diamonds in your pocket, did you?"

"I could pat him down," the Ox said. "You think?"

"No, no. I'm just saying. All he has to do is look me in the eye and tell me he didn't put any of those diamonds in his pocket. Then we're cool."

The car went quiet. Everybody was staring at me. I put my hands up. Like what the hell, guys? What am I supposed to do here?

Then everybody started laughing. The moment passed. The radio came on. A bottle of schnapps got passed around. I declined. Bigmouth kept driving too fast, until I reminded him with my hand on his arm, again and again, to take it easy. We didn't stop at New Rochelle to take the Ox home. He needed to be with his boys that night, to celebrate until the sun came up.

When we were back in the city, I pointed to the sign for the Hamilton Bridge. They seemed eager to do just about anything for me, so they went ahead and took me over the river and down to 128th Street, let me off across the street from the Chinese restaurant.

"You gotta move to a better neighborhood," Bigmouth said as I got out of the car.

I had one last card to play that night. I figured what the hell, it might be the only thing I get out of this. I stood there on the sidewalk and pulled out both side pockets.

"Fucking A, why didn't you say something?" Bigmouth got out his wallet, made everybody else in the car do the same. He collected together about three hundred dollars and gave it to me. That didn't seem like quite enough to him, so he parked the car and he made everyone march right down to the bank on the corner.

"Whatever your fucking limit is," he said. "You hear me? Your absolute max. It's the least we can do for the kid."

Between the four of them, they were able to withdraw another thousand dollars.

"That's just an advance, kid. Wait till we unload those diamonds! I'll be beeping you to pick up your share! I promise! As soon as we have the money, I'll beep you!"

A few more hugs and handshakes and carrying on. Then they piled back into the car and took off down the street.

When they were out of sight, I crossed the street and went into the restaurant. I paid the family the two hundred dollars I owed them for the month. Then I went upstairs and celebrated New Year's Eve in my empty room. I couldn't help but think about my uncle. I wondered what he was doing, back in Michigan. Probably having a busy night, selling champagne.

I thought about Amelia. Of course.

Then I got out my paper and my pencils and I started drawing. I put my whole day on the page, panel by panel, playing the whole thing back for her. Showing her what I had been through. It was the thing I did almost every day, just for my own sanity, and for the small amount of hope it gave me. That maybe someday these pages would find their way to her. That she'd read them and that she'd understand why I had to leave her.

As I finished the last panel, I looked back over the whole thing and it seemed totally comical. The more I thought of it, the more I realized that I'd probably never hear from them again. I mean, they had no reason to contact me with my share of the money, right?

No more amateurs, I told myself. Never, ever again. Even though you did make thirteen hundred bucks today.

I went back to Amelia as I turned off my light, got in my sleeping bag on that cold dusty floor, and closed my eyes. I would have given anything to have her right there with me. For just one hour. I would have given my life for it.

Happy New Year to me.

The yellow pager woke me up the next morning. I went downstairs and used the pay phone. I dialed the number. It was the same number I had used the day before.

"Hey, kid," Bigmouth said. "Hope I didn't wake you. Is everything okay?"

I waited for him to realize he wouldn't get an answer.

"Sorry, I'm kinda hungover. Not thinking straight. Anyway, can you come back to the diner? Soon as you can? We've got a little problem."

Five
Michigan
1991 to 1996

After the robbery, Uncle Lito went out and bought himself a gun. It was a handgun, but it was a lot different from the gun the robber had used. The robber's revolver, with the shiny bright metal . . . It looked like a classic six-shooter, the kind you'd see in a Western movie. Uncle Lito's gun was a semi-automatic. No spinning cylinder. No bright metal. It was dull and black, and somehow it looked twice as deadly.

He hid it behind the register, thinking I'd never see it. That lasted about five minutes. He didn't talk about the gun. He didn't talk about anything having to do with the robbery at all. But I could tell he was thinking about it. For the next few weeks, whenever he was quiet, I could tell he was replaying the whole thing in his head. Not just the robbery itself, but the strange way I had reacted to it.

I have to feel a little bad for him now, looking back on it. It's not like he had anybody else to talk to about me. There was a woman from the state who'd come by and see how I was doing, but she only did that once a month or so, and after the first year, she stopped coming altogether. Even if she had kept up her visits, what the hell was she going to do with me? By all appearances, I was doing okay. Not great, but okay. I was eating, even if half the time it was at the Flame. I was sleeping. And yes, I was finally back at school.

It was this place called the Higgins Institute. It was mostly deaf kids who went to this place. Deaf kids with money, I mean. Besides them, there were a few kids with what they called "communicative disorders," some kind of defect that prevented them from hearing or talking or both. I was put in that category. I had a "disorder."

I was nine years old, remember. I hadn't been to school in a year and a half. Let me tell you, being the new kid in school is bad enough. Try doing it in a school where hardly anybody can talk to you, even if they want to. And you can't talk back.

That turned out to be the first problem they tried to fix. I needed to learn some way to communicate, some way that would be better than carrying around a pad of paper and a pen for the rest of my life. Which is why I started learning American Sign Language.

It didn't come easy for me. I didn't *have* to use it, for one thing. I never went home and kept on using it. I never practiced it at all unless I was at school. Meanwhile, all of the deaf kids were totally immersed in it. It was their whole culture. It was their own special, private code. So I wasn't just the "different" kid. I was the foreign invader who barely knew the language.

On top of everything else, there were still plenty of psychologists and counselors poking at me. That never let up. Every day for at least forty-five minutes or so, I'd be sitting in somebody's office. Some adult with jeans and a sweater. Let's just kick back, Michael. Let's just hang out here and get to know each other, eh? If you feel like talking to me . . . and by talking I mean you can write something for me, or draw me a picture. Whatever you want, Mike.

What I wanted was for them to leave me the hell alone. Because they were all making one big mistake. This business about me being too young to "process" the trauma, that I'd have to bury it in my little mind's backyard until somebody came along to help me dig it up—I mean, I still get upset to this day just thinking about it. The condescension there. The stunning, absolute ignorance.

I was eight years old when it happened. Not two years old. Not three years old. I was eight, and like any other kid my age, I knew exactly what was happening to me. Every single second, every single moment. I knew what was happening, and when it was all over, I could go back and replay it in my mind. Every single second, every single moment. The next day, I could still do that. A week later, I could do that. A year later. Five years later. Ten years later. I could still go back to that day in June for the simple reason that *I had never left it.*

It wasn't repressed. I didn't have to go digging to find it. It was always there. My constant companion. My right-hand man. Every waking hour, and more than a few of the sleeping hours . . . I was and am and always will be right back there in that day in June.

Nobody ever got that. Not one person.

Looking back, I'm probably being too hard on everybody. They were trying to help me, I know, and it's not like I was giving them anything to go on. Problem was, I don't think they *could* have helped me. At all. And hell, I think I just made everybody uncomfortable, you know? Like they couldn't forgive me for what had happened to me, and how that made them feel when they thought about it. So they tried to help me so that *they* could feel better.

Yes, that's it right there. All those years. That's what I was thinking. They were all so freaked out about what had happened to me, they were just trying to make themselves feel better about it. I think that's why they gave up on me in the end. After five years at the Higgins Institute, because I wasn't "responding" well enough. Maybe it was a mistake to have you come here in the first place, they said. Maybe you should have been around speaking kids all along. So that maybe . . . someday . . .

That's what they said. Just before they kicked me out and made me go to Milford High School.

Imagine that summer for me. Just counting down the days to September. I mean, I had already been the odd man out at the institute. How much more of a freak would I be walking down the halls of a public high school?

There was only one thing that could distract me that summer. You see, there was this metal door in the back room. It opened out to the parking lot. When the delivery trucks came, that's the door they'd use to wheel in the boxes. The door was usually locked, but when the trucks came, Uncle Lito would have to start fiddling with the dead bolt to get it to open. There was a real trick to it. You'd have to give the bolt a quarter turn in the wrong direction, then pull hard on the knob while you eased the bolt back the way it was supposed to go. Only then would the damned thing decide to cooperate. And forget about opening it with a key from the outside. One day, he got sick of it and bought a whole new lock. I watched him take out the old lock and throw the two separate pieces in the garbage can. When he put the new lock in, it turned beautifully on the first try.

"Just feel that," he said. "It's like butter."

But it was the old lock I was interested in. I took it out of the garbage can and joined the two pieces together again. I could see immediately how it was designed to work. Such a simple idea. When the cylinder turns, the cam goes with it and the bolt is retracted. Turn the cylinder the other way and the bolt is extended again. Eventually, I'd take the cylinder apart and see the five little pins inside. All you had to do was line up those pins just right so the thing could turn freely. At least that's the way I got it to move after cleaning out the dirt and gunk and spraying a little oil in there. Uncle Lito could have put that lock right back in the door and it would have worked just fine again. But he'd already bought the new lock, so there was nothing else to do with the old one except to keep playing around with it, to watch how the key went inside and how it pushed up each pin exactly the right amount and no farther. Then, finally, the really interesting part. The absolutely most fascinating and satisfying part of all, how I could put a little bit of tension on that cylinder with something as simple as a paper clip, and then with a thin piece of metal I had taken from the edge of a ruler, say, how I could push up each pin, one by one, letting the tension keep them in place as I moved on to the next, until finally all five pins were lined up perfectly. How the lock, without the use of a key, would then slide smoothly and magically open.

I sometimes wonder how my life would have gone if not for that one old lock on that one back door. If it hadn't gotten stuck so much, or if Uncle Lito had been too lazy to replace it . . . Would I have ever found that *moment*? Those metal pieces, which are so hard and unforgiving, so carefully designed *not* to move . . . Yet somehow with just the right touch it all lines up and God, that one second when it opens. That smooth, sudden, metallic release. The sound of it turning, and the way it feels in your hands. The way it feels when something is locked up so tight in a metal box, with no way to get out.

When you finally open it . . .

When you finally learn how to unlock that lock . . .

Can you even imagine how that feels?

Six

Connecticut
New Year's Day 2000

I didn't have to go back to that diner that day. I know that. But I did. I honestly don't think it was the ignorance of youth or anything like that. Hell, maybe it was nothing more than simple curiosity. I mean, they got the diamonds from the guy's house, right? What could the big problem be? Were they having trouble converting them into cash? Maybe, but if that was the problem, why call me? Just to let me know that I wouldn't get my share for a while? Or that my share would be a lot smaller? Either way, that would mean that I *was* getting a share at least, and they weren't planning on stiffing me.

Damn, I thought, could it be that these guys think that they *have* to pay me? Or else? I mean, if they found me in the first place, that meant they probably had to know about the man in Detroit, right? I wasn't just one kid on one pager. Maybe they figured there must be plenty of other people on other pagers, some of whom could set their feet in concrete and drop them into the Hudson River on a moment's notice. That's right, I thought. You don't mess with the Kid. Let 'em all think that.

Either way, there I was, in another cab, riding over the river on a clear, cold New Year's morning. I had given the driver the same address in the Bronx, written down on a piece of paper. He talked about the "Y2K" thing the whole way there, how nothing was supposed to be working that day, the first day of the year 2000, and yet how everything seemed to be humming along just fine. I sat in the backseat and nodded. When we finally got to the diner, I paid the man and got out. I went inside. My four new friends were sitting together, at a bigger table this time because now we were a party of five. I went over and slid in next to Heckle and Jeckle. Bigmouth and the Ox were on the other side. All four of them looked like hell.

The same waitress came over. She seemed to recognize me. I pointed at the Western omelet. The boys seemed to be done eating, but I didn't care. If they were gonna drag me out here again, I was going to get breakfast out of it.

"So here's the problem," Bigmouth finally said. He was wearing the same green New York Jets jacket.

"Not here," the Ox said.

"I'm just giving him the general idea."

"What, you want everybody in the restaurant to know what we did yesterday? Just save it, all right?"

They had no problem talking about it yesterday, I thought. Then again, the Ox wasn't here yesterday. He was obviously the one man in this outfit with any sense at all.

When my breakfast came, there was a tense silence hanging over the table. I have lifetime immunity to tense silences, but this one seemed to be taking years off of Bigmouth's life. He sat there rocking back and forth on his hands, looking out the front window. The Ox just sat there looking at him sideways. Heckle and Jeckle both looked like they were about to throw up.

When I was done, Bigmouth slapped some money down and hustled us all out of there. He got behind the wheel of his car. The Ox rode shotgun this time. Heckle and Jeckle waited to see if I was going to get in the backseat.

"Come on, we'll go somewhere safe and talk about it," Bigmouth said to me. "It's a solvable problem. Really. You want your share, right?"

I slid into the backseat. Heckle and Jeckle got in on opposite sides so I'd be stuck in the middle. It was a little thing, but it was already making me feel sorry I had come.

Bigmouth put the car in gear and took off down the street. A few minutes later, we were on I-95. Heading east, toward Connecticut. I tapped on the back of his seat and raised both hands. What the hell, guys?

"Okay, here's the deal," he said. "Those rocks we stole are totally fake. They're not even good cubic zirconium. They're just junk. It took my experts here about three seconds to find that out, once they sobered up."

Neither of them said anything. The one on my right shook his head slowly.

"It didn't make any sense," the Ox said. "This guy buys and sells real diamonds all the time. Why would he put a bunch of fake rocks in his safe?"

"So what we're wondering is—" Bigmouth said.

"What *I'm* wondering," the Ox cut him off, "like I told these numb-nuts today, is whether there's another safe in the house. One that's a lot harder to find, with the real diamonds in it. You see what I'm getting at?"

I had to think about that one for a few seconds. Then it all came together. The Ox was right. That safe was in such an obvious spot. The first place you'd look, *way* too easy to find. Then the fact that the safe was *open*, which of course these guys didn't even know. Turn the handle and there it is . . . a perfect, beautiful little black velvet bag with—

God damn, how could I have not seen right through that? It was the perfect last line of defense. So perfect you could almost be forgiven for being so sloppy with everything else. Here they are, boys! A million dollars in diamonds! All yours! Don't bump your heads on the way out!

"So we were figuring," Bigmouth said, "if you don't mind another little trip . . ."

"Our man can't be back home yet," the Ox said. "I mean, he's away for the holidays, right? Who comes back home on New Year's Day?"

I could hear the Ghost's voice in my head. Walk away, hot shot. Just turn around and walk away.

Not that I could really do that at the moment, hurtling down the expressway.

But you can't hit the same place twice, can you? Isn't that just asking for trouble?

Or maybe this doesn't even count. We really didn't hit it at all yet, right?

That's the line of bullshit I had running back and forth in my head, all the way back to that house in Connecticut. Some things you've got to learn the hard way.

We parked around by the back of the property, on the same playground. The house looked just as deserted today. I mean, the Ox was probably right about that. If the owner was gone yesterday, he'd probably be gone today, too.

Nobody stayed with the car this time. "We gotta find that second safe," Bigmouth said. "We need all the eyes we've got."

Another mistake, of course. This was no time to get sloppy. But I wasn't going to start a fight over it. So all five of us went down along the tree line to the house. The same window was unlocked. The Ox pushed it open, and Bigmouth climbed inside. I went in next. I was assuming that *somebody* would stay outside to keep watch, at least. I mean, you can't be *that* dumb, right? I guess I should have known better by then, but at that point I just wanted to find that second safe so we could get the real payoff and then get the hell out of there.

I knew I wouldn't find it in the office. I went to the front of the house, then up the stairs. It was one of those houses with the sweeping staircase and the twelve-foot chandelier hanging over the foyer, but I didn't have time to admire it. I went straight down the long hallway, looking into each room. Bedroom, bedroom, bedroom, bathroom. Everything museum quality and looking like nobody had ever lived there. Finally, I got to what had to be the master suite. I went right to the walk-in closet, pushed the clothes aside, and looked carefully at each wall. I didn't find anything.

When I came back out, I saw Bigmouth looking under the artwork, pulling each frame away from the wall and then letting it back in place. Something told me he wouldn't find what he was looking for. Not that way. If your decoy is behind a painting, the real thing won't be.

Bigmouth looked more and more frantic as he went through the room, eventually getting to the point where he was pulling the furniture away from the walls. When he got to the lady's dressing table, he knocked over at least fifty bottles, nearly every one exploding when it hit the hardwood floor. A few seconds later, my nose was overwhelmed by several thousand dollars' worth of high-class perfume.

"The fuck is this thing supposed to be?" he said. "If you were some kind of rich Jew bastard, where the fuck would you hide your safe?"

The more agitated he got, the more I felt totally calm. I shuffled through a few of the letters sitting on the desk. I picked up five or six of them and handed them to Bigmouth.

"What? What are these?"

I pointed to the name that appeared on every envelope. Robert A. Ward.

"His name is Ward. So what?"

The coin finally dropped in his head.

"Oh, what? So he's not Jewish? Is that what you're saying? Okay, excuse me, he's not a rich Jewish bastard. He's a fucking rich gentile bastard? Are you happy now? Are you gonna stop clowning around and help me find the fucking safe?"

I pointed to the bed. It was a king size, with a Persian rug underneath it. The only rug in the room.

"What? You think he hid the diamonds in his mattress? Are you trying to be funny again?"

I took one corner of the rug and waited for him to take the other. As we pulled, the rug and the bed on top of it both slid across the smooth hardwood floor. When we had pulled it as far as we could, I went around and looked at the floor we'd uncovered.

There it was. If it's the most precious thing in the world to you, whether you think about it consciously or not, you want it right underneath you when you sleep.

There was a recessed handle in the floor, with an iron ring that fit inside like an old-fashioned trapdoor. I pulled up on the ring and opened it. The door to the safe was round and only about six inches in diameter. The way it was embedded so far under the floorboards . . . This is going to sound a little strange, but it actually made me feel claustrophobic. To this day, I still feel that a safe should stand free, so you can see the whole thing, run your hands along every inch of its skin.

I had to get down on the floor with my face as close to the safe as possible. Then I had to get my fingers on the dial. Instead of a turning handle, it had a simple knob that you'd pull up once you had the right combination dialed. I gave it a quick pull, but I knew this time around it wouldn't be open.

"Do your magic," Bigmouth said to me. "See if you can get this one open even faster, eh?"

Fat chance of that, friend. I started spinning the dial, parked all of the wheels, and then reversed. I picked up a wheel, then another, then another, then another.

Then one more.

Five wheels! I'd never even *seen* a safe with five wheels before. Meaning this wasn't gonna be easy.

I felt for the contact area, parked the wheels on 0, and started doing my thing. Go back to contact, park at 3, back to contact.

Was that one already?

I went to 6. Damn, this was so hard. I felt like I was reaching down a well.

"How long you think this is gonna take?" Bigmouth said. Living up to his nickname yet again. "You about half done, ya think? A quarter done?"

I sat up for a moment, shaking out my hands.

"Is it open?" All excited now.

I shook my head, put both hands up, and shooed him away.

"Okay, okay," he said. "I'll be right over here. Quiet as a mouse."

I wouldn't bet on that, I thought, but I'll do my best to pretend you're not here.

I went back to the dial and kept working my way through. I could feel the contact area well enough, but it was so damned hard to tell when it was getting short on me. I had to keep my neck at an uncomfortable angle to get close enough, with most of my weight on my right arm. It kept falling asleep on me, so I had to keep stopping to shake it again.

"We're getting deep into the game here." Bigmouth was sitting over on the bed now. "I bet the other guys are starting to get anxious down there."

When I looked up this time, I saw that he had taken off his jacket. There was a gun tucked into his waistband. It's official, I thought. On that checklist the Ghost had drilled into my head . . . sure signs that the crew you're working with is nothing but a bunch of fucking amateurs who will surely get all of you sent to prison or even killed. Yeah, these guys had just checked off every single box.

I took a deep breath and went in again. Time to really focus here, I thought. Get in, get out, get away. And never look back.

When I was finally through with my first pass, I thought I had four numbers. I knew I needed one more. If you set the combination yourself, you can use the same number twice, but most people don't do that.

I went back through and narrowed down the numbers I had. When I got to the 27, I felt it narrow down to 26, and then also to 28. Aha, I thought. Now I've got them. Come to think of it, I've got a 1, 11, 26, 28, 59 here. That's 120 different possible combinations, but I'll bet anything you used your birthday here, plus your wife's birthday. Then maybe the year you got married? If the birthdays are first, then we're talking what, only four possibilities instead of 120. For which I would thank you very much.

I started on the first possibility, 1-11-26-28-59. It takes a long time to spin out a five-number combination, because you've got to pass the first number four times, then the second number three times, then the third number twice, then the fourth number once, then go to the fifth number and then finally go back the opposite way to trip the lever. I worked it all the way through and pulled up on the knob. Nothing.

I heard Bigmouth standing up. He was walking across the floor now. I shut him out and kept going. Second possibility, 1-11-26-59-28. Four passes, three, two, one, back, turn. Nothing.

Bigmouth was saying something. The words not even registering now. I am far, far away, at the bottom of the sea. I am so close to opening the treasure chest.

Third possibility, 1-11-59-28-26. Four passes, three, two, one, back, turn. Nothing.

Pop pop pop. Just like that. Noises from somewhere on the surface.

"Oh shit." Bigmouth's words breaking through. "Holy fucking shit."

His feet pounding on the boards now. I am yanked back to the surface, blinking and gasping for air. The last of the four combinations left down there behind me, unspun. I slide over to the window where Bigmouth had been standing. I see the black van out front, parked haphazardly, both front doors wide open.

Then the noises again. Louder this time, coming to me even through the closed window. Pop pop pop.

As I struggle to my feet, I see the man running down the driveway. It is Heckle or Jeckle, whichever one of them will carry which imaginary name because it's about to be carved on his tombstone as another man comes into view behind him. He moves quickly for his size. He's wearing a gray jacket with white letters across the back. Before I can read what the letters say, he crouches and extends the gun in his hand, both hands on the grip in a way that tells me he has done this many times before. He has practiced this exact thing over and over again. Shooting at a paper target perhaps, but the geometry is exactly the same. He squeezes off two more rounds. His target is fifty feet away from him, but I see the dark little circle appear on Heckle or Jeckle's back. He goes down with his arms spread wide, like he's doing a swan dive onto the hard ground.

Another man, wearing another gray jacket, comes into view. As he looks at the dead man on the ground, the shooter turns and runs toward the front door of the house. A second later, I can hear the door opening, directly below me. Meaning it would be a good time for me to move.

I leave the master bedroom, move down the hallway as quickly and quietly as I can. When I get to the end, I can see down into the foyer. The front door is open now. I don't see anyone, but I can hear footsteps not far away. I don't want to make a break for it yet. The stairway is too long, and whoever is down there will have such a clear shot at me, he'll have time to pull up a chair before shooting.

I know this feeling. Sitting here and waiting. Trying to stay silent. This is familiar country for me.

Another sound from downstairs. Smoothly mechanical. Metal on metal. Then footsteps. Moving slowly.

A crash. A yell. Feet scrambling on the floor. Then the blast, obliterating every other sound in the world. Until the ringing in my ears fades and I hear the inhuman, not-even-animal screaming of something way beyond pain.

That goes on forever as I back up down the hallway. Footsteps coming up the stairs now. I need to make a choice. Jump out a window? Risk breaking both my legs? There must be some other way out, another door through another room, another set of stairs, because you wouldn't build a house this way, not with one long deathtrap of a hallway, but I don't have time to find that other door.

Unless I just take my shot and hope for the best. I open a doorway to a bathroom, then another to a bedroom. I go inside and close the door softly behind me. Another high window, this one overlooking the side of the house. Another thirty-foot drop.

Okay, think. He doesn't know how many of us are in this house. That's one thing that works for me. Although wait . . . did Bigmouth even get downstairs yet? Is that him screaming down there right now?

I go to the door and listen hard. A minute passes. Two minutes. If he opens this door, I thought, I'll hide behind it and try to surprise him. It's my only shot.

Another minute. Then finally a voice.

"I give up!" Bigmouth, from somewhere down the hall. "Don't shoot, okay? I'm unarmed!"

No response.

"I'm coming out now! I'll have my hands up, okay? There's no reason to shoot me!"

A door opening. Footsteps in the hallway.

"You see? No gun, man! I totally give up. You got me."

Then heavier footsteps, from the other end, coming closer.

"Hey, wait a minute. Hey. Hold on now. Let's not do anything crazy, huh? Hey, come on."

The footsteps louder, closer. Bigmouth's voice on the edge of hysteria.

"No! Hold on! Wait!"

One second I'm standing behind my door, the next second the door is exploding and knocking me backward. Bigmouth is falling on top of me. He clutches at me like he means to use me as a shield. I knock his hands away, and he's on his feet now. He's going back toward the door and then he stops, as the man with the shotgun is right in front of him now. A silver badge on his gray jacket. But he's not a cop. No, sir. He's private security, which means he could do just about anything at this point. The double-barreled monstrosity in his hands is aimed right at Bigmouth's chest.

I have just enough time to see the man's face. Ugly and red. The sick little smile of a man who finally has the license to use his gun on real flesh and blood.

The next second . . . Bigmouth reaches for his belt. Then the blast, more than just sound, a hard metal *thing* punching in through my ears. The side of Bigmouth's head disappearing. Not so much exploding or falling but just . . . not there anymore. A sudden spray of blood and bone and gore on the wall and the window and the curtains and in my eyes. Bigmouth's body still standing, not even aware of what has happened yet. Until it finally starts to tilt sideways against a chest of drawers like a man leaning against a lamppost, then finally collapsing, his legs folding and the top half of his body falling backward in a way that no living thing would ever fall.

The man with the shotgun stood there watching this. Then when it was done he finally seemed to notice me. I was crouching against the far wall. He looked at me for a while, not moving.

"You're just a goddamned boy," he said.

I didn't know if that meant I was off the hook. Then, as if to answer that very question, he breached the shotgun and rummaged around in his pocket with his left hand. I pushed off the wall and came right at him, with as much force as I could gather.

He tried to swing the butt of the shotgun, but because it was breached he didn't have any leverage or any reach with it. At the last moment I ducked down and hit him low, taking out both knees. I tried to keep rolling through him, even as he grabbed at me with his free hand and tried to pin me with his legs.

I kicked at him until eventually I struggled free. Then I was on my feet and running down the hallway, imagining him grabbing for the shells and reloading. Down the stairs, on the edge of falling with every step. A great pool of blood at the bottom, the Ox's torn-apart body in the middle of it. Then another mind-shattering blast, ripping through the chandelier and raining down glass all around me.

I was through the open door. Into the cold air. That's when something came swinging at me from out of view. The arm of the other gray-jacketed man, hitting me across the neck like a branch from one of those trees I could see in the distance.

I was on the ground now. Looking up at the sky, which seemed to be spinning counterclockwise. It made me think back to the only other time in my life I had been captured like this. Only I had no reason to fear for my life then. I had no reason to wonder if they'd stand me up against a wall and rip me apart with a shotgun.

I felt myself being turned over, the handcuffs being slapped tight on my wrists.

"We've got you now," a voice said. "You ain't going nowhere."

Seven
Michigan
1996 to 1999

There was an antique store a few blocks down from the liquor store. They had a few old locks there, and the old man who owned the place seemed to already know about me, so I didn't have to break him in with the whole pantomime routine. I found the locks, some with keys, some without, took them all to the counter, and the owner looked them over and charged me five dollars total.

I took the locks apart and put them back together again. I practiced using my makeshift tools to open them. I had four picks now, and two tension bars, all of them just thin strips of metal I had filed down into different sizes, all of them stuck into rubber erasers that I could use as handles. I was learning by trial and error, and it didn't take me long to figure out it was all a matter of touch. How much tension you put on the lock, and how you lift each tumbler, one by one, until the whole thing turns free.

I got damned good at it. I really did. That was my summer. Me and a pile of rusty old scrap metal.

Then the day came. The Wednesday after Labor Day. They were just about to start fixing up the high school around then, so you're going to have to trust me to paint the right picture here. Start with a main building that hadn't been touched in forty or fifty years. Tired gray bricks, windows that were too few and too small. Surround the whole thing with concrete and fencing and tall light poles. Then spread a dozen trailers all over the place, as if dropped at random. Those were the temporary classrooms to handle the overflow of students.

Or let me put it another way. The day I came to this prison I'm sitting in right now, the day I stepped out of the Corrections Department van and took my place in line at the processing center—I was ready for it. I was ready because I had been through something pretty similar once before. The way it looked that day, the soul-crushing *grayness* of the place. Above everything else, the way my stomach turned inside out at the thought of spending so much time there, unable to leave.

Yeah, I'd been there. All on that Wednesday after Labor Day, when I stepped off the bus and took my place as a member of the incoming freshman class at Milford High School.

The first thing I noticed was the noise. After those five years at the institute, to suddenly find myself surrounded by over two thousand kids with healthy, normal voices. That main hallway was as loud as a jet engine, everyone talking and shouting on that first day of school, some of the boys chasing each other, pushing each other into the lockers, aiming sharp-knuckled punches at each other's shoulders. I felt like I was walking into an insane asylum.

There were a lot of other new freshmen, of course. Most of them probably looked as overwhelmed as I was, and probably didn't say much more than I did, either. Even so, it didn't take long for me to stand out. Every class I was in, the teacher would make a big deal about introducing me and telling everyone else about my "unique circumstances." The "challenge" I was bravely facing. Everybody welcome Mike, eh? Just don't expect him to say thank you in return. Ha ha.

I'm not sure how I got through that first day. It's all a blur now, looking back on it. I didn't eat lunch, I remember that much. I kept walking through the hallways, eventually finding myself back at my locker. I felt utterly lost and alone as I stood there, just spinning the dial on my locker, over and over.

The next morning, as I was getting ready to go back to that school again, I admit it . . . I started thinking about suicide. I rode on the bus in my own little cocoon of silence among the roar of the other kids.

The next day, when I got home I actually started looking around to see if I could find any pills. Uncle Lito had his own bathroom. I usually didn't have any reason to go in there, but that evening, while he was minding the store, I took inventory of his medicine cabinet. There was aspirin and cough syrup and hangover medicine and jock-itch cream and a thousand other things, but nothing strong enough to do what I had in mind.

I wasn't driving yet, but still, I thought maybe I could take his car, get up some speed, and then aim right for a tree. Or hell, for those concrete embankments under the railroad bridge. Talk about a proven death trap. My biggest worry about that was that I wouldn't get the car going fast enough, or that I'd hit something else first and end up just wounded and fucked up and in huge trouble but still very much alive.

What a cheerful turn my little story has taken here, I know, but this was pretty much a running theme for that whole first semester at the high school. Nobody talked to me. I mean nobody. As that first semester went on, it got colder, and darker. I was getting up at six in the morning, in total darkness, to catch the bus at six forty to get to school by seven fifteen, not just going to this place I hated so much, but doing it before the sun even started thinking about coming up.

It makes my heart ache, just thinking back on that time in my life. How lonely I was. How out of place I felt every single minute of every day.

When I went back to school for the second semester, there were new classrooms to find, a new set of kids to get used to me sitting in the back of the room, never making a sound. And right off the bat, a new class for me. Freshman art, or, excuse me, Art Foundations. The teacher was a man named Mr. Martie. He was younger than most of the other teachers in the school. He had a beard and permanently red eyes, and he spent most of that first class mumbling to himself about the size, shape, and color of his headache.

"Let's not get too excited on the first day, eh?" He walked among the art tables, ripping off sheets of drawing paper from a large pad. When he came to me, he ripped off a sheet and I got maybe eighty percent of it, most of one corner still on the pad. "Just draw something today. I don't care what."

He passed by me, not giving me a second look. Not pausing to single me out like most of the other teachers did. So he had that going for him already. With any luck, this would be one class where I could really disappear into the wallpaper.

He went back to his desk and tilted his head back. "I would murder for a cigarette right now," he said, his eyes closed.

There was a small basket of art supplies on each table. Mine had a few broken pieces of charcoal-looking crayon things and a couple of pencils. I took out one of the pencils and stared at the blank piece of paper. Three square corners of nothing, and one jagged edge.

"You've got to give us a subject," a girl in the front row said, apparently with the authority to speak for all of us. "We don't know what to draw."

"It doesn't matter," Mr. Martie said. "Draw a landscape."

"A landscape?"

Mr. Martie looked up at the girl. There was a lifetime of regret in his face, that the years spent studying art would lead him to be here in this classroom on this January morning, the windows still dark, sunrise a half hour away. "Yes," he said. "A landscape. A place, you know? Draw a place. Draw your favorite place in the world."

"In my last school, the art teacher always gave us something specific to draw. Something that we could see, right in front of us. We never just drew from memory."

He let out a sigh, got to his feet and went to a cupboard, and pulled out the first two things he put his hands on. A gray cylinder, about one foot high, and a gray wedge about the same height. He went to the empty table at the front of the room and put the cylinder down, then the wedge down right next to it.

"For those of you who wish to do a still life . . ." He sat back down and closed his eyes again. "The rest of you are on your own."

The girl in the front row raised her hand again, but he wasn't about to make the same mistake and notice her this time. Finally, she just gave up and started drawing, presumably tackling the challenge of the cylinder next to the wedge.

Meanwhile, the kid sitting next to me had already started on drawing a house. It was a rectangle with smaller rectangles inside, windows and doors. Then he drew a chimney on top with a curl of smoke coming out.

I picked up a pencil and thought about what to draw. I had this fascinating still life up there I could try. But no, instead I started sketching in the railroad bridge in the center of town. I imagined myself standing on the other side of it, away from the liquor store. From there I'd see the restaurant, the big sign, THE FLAME in block letters, 24 HOURS just below that in smaller letters. More details coming to me as I pictured it in my mind. The flashing lights on the bridge embankments, the door to the liquor store barely visible through the archway. The iron bars on the front window.

This certainly didn't qualify as my favorite place in the world, as my fine teacher had suggested, but it felt so familiar to me. It felt more like home than anywhere else, this one particular bend in the road with a beaten-down liquor store waiting on the other side of a beaten-down railroad bridge. I started to shade in some of the darker areas, the way the bridge would cast a shadow on the door to the restaurant. The newspaper boxes lined up outside. It needed some trash now, some random cans and bottles rattling around in the parking lot. It needed dirt and dust and stains and misery. I didn't think I could ever capture the whole thing, if I spent the rest of my day here, using up every pencil in the basket.

Then, in my reverie, lost in the picture and not aware of what was going on around me . . . Mr. Martie had stood up. He had asked everyone in the class not to commit any actual felonies while he stepped out of the room for a moment. It didn't register until later, until after he had passed behind me on his way out the door. Then he reappeared behind me. He was looking over my shoulder now as I struggled to make my drawing look just like the picture in my head. It took me a moment to realize that he was standing there.

He didn't say anything. He put one hand on my shoulder and gently moved me away so he could get a better look at the drawing.

So began the only good and decent chapter in my life.

Two and a half years, that's how long it lasted. It's funny how your life can turn on one thing like that. One talent that you don't even know you've been given.

By the end of the week my schedule had been rearranged. Instead of going to that first period freshman class, I was doing a double period of Advanced Independent Study in Art in the afternoon, right after lunch. It became an oasis in the day for me. The one chance all day I had to stop holding my breath.

I even made a friend. Yes, an actual, living human friend. His name was Griffin King. He was one of the other twelve students in the advanced art class. I was the only freshman, and he was the only sophomore. He had long hair, and he acted like he didn't care much about anything in this world except being an artist one day. It was a tough way to think in Milford, Michigan, believe me. On my second day in the class, he came over and sat next to me. He looked at the drawing I was working on. It was one of my first attempts at a portrait. My Uncle Lito. Griffin kept watching me struggle with it until I finally stopped.

"Not bad," he said. "Have you done a lot of this?"

I shook my head.

"Who's the model? Did he sit for this?"

I shook my head.

"What, you're doing it from memory?"

I nodded.

"That is freaky, man."

He bent down to look more closely.

"Still, it's kind of flat," he said. "You need more shading to bring out the features."

I looked up at him.

"I'm just saying. I mean, I know it's not easy."

I put my pencil down.

"How's this school treating you, anyway?"

I looked at him again, lifting both hands as if to say, do you not know anything about me?

"I know you can't talk," he said. "I think that's totally cool, by the way."

What?

"I'm serious. I talk way too much. I wish I could just . . . stop. Like you."

I shook my head. I looked up at the clock to see how much time we had left until the class was over.

"I'm Griffin, by the way." He extended his right hand. I shook it.

"How do you say hello, anyway?"

I looked at him.

"I mean, you must know sign language, right? How do you say hello?"

I slowly raised my right hand and waved at him.

"Ah, okay. Yeah, that makes sense."

I put my hand down.

"How do you say, 'I hate this town and everything in it. And I wish everyone would just die'?"

I had never been that good with the sign language, remember, but it all started to come back to me as I taught him a few signs every day. Eventually, a few of the signs became his favorites. He'd flash them at me when we were in the hallway, like they were our secret code. Grabbing the thumb and waving for "incompetent." The double twist to the nose for "boring." If a particular girl was walking by, the hand pulled away from the mouth for "hot." Or his own invention, both hands pulled away, meaning "double hot," I guess.

We ate lunch together every day, then we went to our art class. Me and my friend. You have to understand what this meant to me. It was something I'd never had before. Between hanging out with Griffin and the art I was trying to do—hell, it was almost like I had a real life now. Everyone in the school started treating me a little differently, too. I mean, it wasn't like I was suddenly a sports star or anything. Kids who were good at art or music were way down on the totem pole, but at least I was *on* the totem pole now. I wasn't just the Miracle Boy anymore, the mute kid with the mysterious trauma in his past. Now I was just the quiet kid who could draw.

Like I said, this was such a rare time in my life. In a way, I don't even want to keep going with my story. Just stop it right there, let you think, yeah, this kid turned out all right. He had a rough start, he found something to do with his life. Everything worked out okay.

Of course, that wouldn't be the truth. Not by a long shot.

Fast-forward to my junior year. Griffin's senior year. I was sixteen and a half then. My hair was such an unruly mess I had to finally prune it back just enough to see where I was going. I could tell that the girls in school were looking at me differently now. I was allegedly a decent-looking guy, although at the time it would have been news to me. But hell, if you add in the mysteriousness factor, I guess I could see how I'd be worth a look, at least. I even thought about the possibility of going out on a date. There was this new girl in our art class. Nadine. She was blond and pretty and was apparently on the tennis team. Not like the other girls in art class at all. She'd give me a shy smile whenever I saw her in the hallway.

"She wants you, dude." Griffin's voice in my ear one day. "Go ask her out. I mean, hell, I'll do it for you. I'll be your messenger."

I had a car now. Uncle Lito's old two-toned Grand Marquis. We could have gone and seen a movie or something. It was just . . . I don't know, the thought of sitting there in a restaurant before the movie. Or driving her home afterward. I'd listen to her, of course. I'd listen to whatever she'd have to say. Then what? She couldn't talk forever. Nobody can, not even an American high school girl. When the silence finally came, what would I do? Start writing her notes?

So maybe I wasn't ready for that scene yet. Still, I hadn't ruled it out. Nadine wasn't going anywhere. In the meantime, a few people were actually saying hello to me when I walked past them in the hallway. They were showing my artwork in the big display case at the front of the school now. I was still doing a lot of pencil and charcoal then. Griffin had a big painting out there, too, with his outrageous splashes of color. I wasn't sure what I'd do the next year, when I was a senior and Griffin was long gone to art school, but I wasn't worried about that yet.

We ended up in gym class that semester. Of all the places in the world for my whole life to start turning . . . it was that very first day, when we were opening the padlocks on our little gym lockers. I couldn't help noticing that if I pulled down while I was spinning, the dial seemed to catch in twelve different spots, and one of those spots just so happened to be the last number in the combination. Was it my imagination or did that spot feel a little different from the other eleven?

When I went home that night, I was still spinning the dial on that padlock in my mind and thinking about what was going on inside. By then I had already gone about as far as I could go with key locks. I mean, I was pretty sure I could open just about anything. But this was a new challenge that made me remember why I had been so drawn to locks in the first place. As I worked the dial one direction, then the other, I could feel how it made the separate cams turn underneath it. It made me wonder how hard it would be to open the damned thing if I didn't know the combination.

So I went back to that same old antique store, I bought a few combination locks, and I took them apart. That's how I learned.

It was that same semester. In November, the week of the big game against Lakeland. You see, Lakeland was the newer high school in the district, a few miles to the east. Milford was usually pretty good at football, and they'd been dominating the big game ever since Lakeland got built. I suppose because we still had our shabby old dump of a school, it must have felt pretty good to kick Lakeland's ass in anything. That had changed the year before, when Lakeland finally won for the first time ever. Because the varsity players usually only played for two years, that meant that the Milford seniors had just one more chance.

Our best player was a senior man named Brian Hauser, a.k.a. "the House." We didn't exactly move in the same social circles, Brian and I, but even I could see that he was bouncing off the walls in school that week, getting himself psyched up for the last game of his high school career. Griffin and I were still getting through our semester of gym, and our class happened to be last period, so by the time we were getting dressed, the football players were usually getting ready for practice. That always got Griffin going, hearing the whole team making a racket on the other side of the locker room. He'd always have a running commentary for me on what the football players were saying, how sophisticated their conversation was, how much sensitivity they showed to the opposite sex, and so on. He kept his voice down, because he didn't actually want to end up stuffed in a locker. But today, we could really hear the football team going at it. Brian Hauser, in particular, was making a hell of a racket and banging on his locker like a madman.

"Motherfucking son of a bitch! Stupid whorebag fagbiscuit!"

Then more voices from his teammates.

"Fagbiscuit! What the hell is a fagbiscuit?"

"That's a new one, House."

"I know what a fagbiscuit is—"

"No, man. Don't even go there. I don't want to know what a fagbiscuit is."

"When I think they can't get any wittier," Griffin said to me, "they surpass even their own high standards."

There was more banging, followed by laughter. I don't know what possessed Griffin to go check it out at that point, but he went around to the end of the row of lockers, still buttoning his shirt. I followed him.

As soon as we both peeked around the corner, we saw Brian slamming his fist on the locker. There was already a fair dent in it. The rest of the team was almost dressed, but Brian was still in his street clothes.

"What's the problem?" one of his teammates asked him. "Did you forget the combination?"

"It's three whole numbers," someone else said. "I can see how that would be a challenge."

"Yeah, fuck all of you," Brian said. "I didn't forget the combination. It's a new lock, all right?"

"Did you check the little sticker on the back? That's how you learn it the first time."

Someone else reached for the lock to verify exactly that, but Brian knocked his hand away.

"It's not there, genius. I left it at home, all right? I bought a new lock because the old one was a piece of shit. I had the combination in my head this morning, but now I'm just . . . Fuck."

"What are you gonna do, get a hacksaw?"

"Why don't you call your mother? Maybe she can find the piece of paper with the combination."

"There was a seventeen in it," Brian said. "God damn it. Then it was . . . Wait."

"Think, man. Think."

"Will you guys shut the fuck up? I can't concentrate."

Now, I knew that Griffin would do some crazy things now and then, but I had no idea he'd actually step around the corner and walk right into the middle of the football team. What was going through his head, I couldn't possibly imagine . . . until he opened his mouth and dragged me right into it.

"Hey, Brian," he said. "You need some help?"

Brian Hauser was about six-four, and he had to weigh at least 250 pounds. They didn't call him "the House" for nothing. He was a little soft around the edges, one of those fat kids who manage to sprout up and become athletic for a few years, before losing the battle for good by the time they're thirty.

"What do *you* want?"

"My associate here can open your lock, if you'd like," Griffin said.

"Your *associate*?"

As you can probably guess . . . yes, once I had opened up those padlocks from the antique store and saw how they worked, I had to show off to *some-body*. So I had grabbed Griffin's lock one day and opened it for him. It had taken me about two minutes.

That was obviously a mistake. Which, as I stood there and watched him offer my lock-opening skills to Brian Hauser, I was about to pay for.

"Come on over," Griffin said to me. "Show him how it's done."

The whole football team was looking at me now. I didn't think I had much choice. I looked at Griffin and put an imaginary gun to my head, then pulled the trigger.

"Don't be shy," he said. "We're all buddies here."

He was showing them up, I thought. He was making fun of them and they didn't even know it.

"What the fuck are you gonna do?" Brian said. "Try all thousand combinations?"

Actually sixty-four thousand, I thought, but who's counting? I went to his locker and grabbed his lock. I pulled down and spun the dial past the fakes and felt for the real sticking point.

I won't drag you through the whole thing, but here's the basic idea. The combination to my gym lock happened to be 30-12-26, and the combinations to those two locks I bought at the antique store were 16-28-20 and 23-33-15. Notice how all of the numbers are either even or odd, first of all. Then notice how the first and last numbers are in the same "family," and that the middle number is in the opposing family. By that I mean that 0, 4, 8, 12, 16, 20, et cetera are one family, while 2, 6, 10, 14, 18, et cetera are the other family. Once you get the touch for finding the real last number out of the twelve "sticking points," you can work backward from there, trying all of the combinations that start with a number in the same family, then a number in the other family, and then the final number. You can even learn to "super set" all of the second numbers once you know how that second cam can be bumped four numbers at a time without having to start the whole thing over. With a little practice, you can go grab most any combination lock from the junk drawer and have it open in a matter of minutes.

Got that?

So on Brian's lock, I could tell that the last number of the combination was 23. So far so good. Clear the cams, spin to 3, and start on the super sets.

"Somebody get a hacksaw," Brian said. "He's gonna be here all day."

"Give him a chance," one of his teammates said. "Maybe he has ESP or something."

"What the hell are you talking about? That wouldn't be ESP."

Everybody shut up, I thought. Go away and leave me alone for a few minutes. I worked it back to 9, then to 23, then to 13-23, then 17-23, working my way up the dial, bumping that second cam, feeling it move just the right amount and then staying smooth on the reverse to make sure I didn't jar it out of position.

Wham! Brian slammed his fist on the locker next to me. "Are you seriously going to open this lock? Is that what you're telling me?"

"He's not telling you anything," Griffin said. "In case you hadn't noticed . . ."

"Yeah, okay. I get it. He's a fucking mute."

I looked up at him for one second, then went back to the lock. I started the second set, hoping to God that the second number wasn't all the way up the dial. Hoping to God that I could do it at all. What the hell was Griffin thinking, anyway? Why the hell did I have to do this in front of everybody?

7 next. I went 7-13-23, then turned back to keep the set going.

I heard a door open.

"Shit, it's Coach!"

Mr. Bailey, the football coach, came into the room. "What's going on in here?" he said. "Brian, why aren't you dressed?"

I dialed 7-17-23.

The lock opened.

"What are you doing, young man?" Coach Bailey said to me. "Are you his personal servant now? He can't even open up his own locker?"

He was holding a playbook in one hand. I made a writing motion to him. He took a blank page from the book and handed it to me. Then he fished a pen out of his pocket. I wrote *7-17-23* on the paper and gave it to Brian. Then I gave the coach his pen back. Nobody else had said a word yet.

"Everybody outside while Mr. Hauser gets himself dressed," Coach Bailey said. "Have you forgotten what week this is?"

That's how it began. I remember it so well because I can trace so much of what would happen next right back to those few minutes. If I had had any idea . . .

But no, I hadn't learned that lesson yet. I hadn't learned that some talents cannot be forgiven.

Ever.

Eight
Connecticut
January 2000

It was the second time in my life I had been in handcuffs. The man lifted me to my feet and pushed me back inside the house. We stepped through the broken shards from the chandelier. Past the spreading pool of blood and what was left of the Ox's body.

"Holy fuck," the man said. "I can't believe this."

His partner was standing there in the foyer. He had come down the stairs, the shotgun still poised in the shooting position. The barrel was pointed at my chest.

"Put the gun down," the first man said.

His partner didn't move. He was looking at me now like he was in some kind of trance. That sick little smile still on his face.

"Ron, put the gun down!"

That seemed to snap Ron out of it. His eyes came back into focus, and he lowered his weapon.

"Ron, I don't even know what to say right now. Did you call the police yet?"

Ron shook his head.

"Come on," the man said to me. He led me into the kitchen and put me on one of the tall stools, next to the center island. He picked up the phone and started dialing. From where I was sitting, I could still see Ron standing out there in the foyer. He was looking down at the floor. At the carnage he had created.

The man got through to the police, gave them the address, told them to expect a horrible scene when they got here. But the last remaining suspect was in custody, he said. As I listened to him, I could feel the cold steel of the handcuffs biting into my wrists.

The man hung up the phone. "Ron, they're on their way!"

He came over to me. He wiped his face with both hands and then leaned over the little sink that was set into the island. For a moment, I thought he was going to throw up, but he pushed himself back up and looked at me.

"What the hell just happened?" he said. "How many men did he kill? Four?"

The man went to the refrigerator and opened it. He pulled out a can of Coke and pulled the tab. Then he drained half of it in one gulp.

"Ron, what are you doing in there? Are you okay?"

He listened for an answer. After a few seconds, we could hear Ron saying something, but it sounded like he had moved farther away from us.

"Why don't you come in here with us? Where are you?"

We started to make out the words. Something like, "The suspects were armed I saw the guns the suspects were armed I saw the guns the suspects were armed I saw the guns." Over and over again.

"Holy shit," the man said. Then he came over to me and put his can of Coke down on the island, right in front of me. He went behind me and undid one of the handcuffs. I had no idea what the hell he was going to do, until he brought the free cuff around and fastened it on the faucet, below the handle.

"You stay right here, son. I'll be right back."

Then he left the room to go see what his partner was up to. Leaving me alone there. Just me and the handcuffs.

I looked at them closely. I remembered what I had been thinking, the one other time I had worn them. How simple they were. The way the teeth on the loop fit into the ratchet. How the ratchet seemed to be the only thing holding on . . .

I heard the man calling for his partner. I didn't know how long I'd have.

I saw a pair of scissors on the far side of the island. If I stretched out my arms, could I reach them? I stood up and tried.

Stretch for it, damn it. A few more inches.

I felt the handcuff biting into my left wrist, but with one more lunge I was able to put one finger into one handle of the scissors. I pulled them over and put them down in front of me. Then I grabbed the can of Coke and transferred it to my cuffed hand. I picked up the scissors again and jabbed the sharp point into the soft aluminum.

I started cutting. I was spilling Coke all over, but I didn't care. When I had a thin strip cut out, about two inches long and maybe a quarter inch wide, I put the can down and started working the end of the strip into the handcuff's ratchet.

If I can just slip this in over the teeth, I thought, the ratchet will have nothing to grip anymore. The whole loop should slide right out.

The metal was so thin and brittle. It was taking me too long to work it in. Damn it! I could hear sirens in the distance now. They'd be here soon.

Relax. Concentrate. Don't force it. Let that thing slide right in. Right over those teeth. That's it. A little more. A little more. One more notch—

Boom! It was open.

Just as I saw the face of the man coming back into the kitchen. His eyes grew wide as I pushed the stool over and went for the back door. I pushed it open and I was outside in the cold air, running toward the trees, the man yelling behind me.

I saw the last dead man to complete the foursome, Heckle or Jeckle, this one lying on his back at the edge of the garden, his lifeless eyes staring right up at me as I jumped over him. The voice still yelling at me to stop. I ran into the woods, the branches whipping at my face. Running as hard as I could, past the point of suffering, until I could not breathe anymore. Not looking back until I was sure I was alone.

I kept going through the woods until the sun went down. Moving as fast as I could, looking over my shoulder every few seconds. I found a stream and washed the blood from my face and hands, the water so cold it made my skin ache. My jacket was still splattered with the inside of Bigmouth's skull, and I couldn't get it anywhere near clean. So I had to take it off, even though it was already not warm enough. Not for being outside in the woods for this long.

I stumbled around and hid behind trees as I heard sirens in the distance. I imagined a team of men coming after me, beating their way through the underbrush, led by a pack of baying bloodhounds.

In the end I came upon a train station. There were several taxicabs waiting out front, the drivers standing together in a pack and smoking. I circled around and came up on the station from the track side. There were no trains in sight, but I was hoping that I'd have one more shot to catch one back to New York City.

I tried the door to the waiting room, but it was locked. The sign told me that the lobby hours were over at nine, and that if I didn't have a ticket already, I could buy one on the train. I looked in at the clock, saw that it was almost ten. I didn't know when the next train would be coming. A cold wind hit me and I started to shake.

I looked over at the cabdrivers. There was no way I could approach them. A seventeen-year-old kid with no coat, his hair still wet. The police no doubt looking for me, with a decent description from my brief custody. Even the train would be a risk, but what choice did I have?

I sat down with my back against the cold brick wall, waiting to hear the rumble of the train. I sat there and shivered, feeling hungry now on top of everything else. I must have dozed off somehow, because the next thing I remember was being jarred awake by the train releasing its air brakes. The train was right there in front of me, huge and humming. I got up slowly, feeling as stiff as a ninety-year-old man. The doors opened and people started getting off. Well-dressed men mostly, a few women, all of them making the late trip back home from the city. Now they were ready for a good meal with their families. I stayed on the edge of the scene like a stray dog.

Then I realized that this train had come east from the city and would keep going east, deeper into Connecticut. Maybe I should get on anyway, I thought. Get the hell out of here.

No, I thought. I don't want to do that. I want to go back home, even if home is nothing more than a single room above a Chinese restaurant. It was all I had in the world just then, and I would have given everything I had to be back there.

Most of the passengers were getting into their cars now. Starting them, turning on the lights, driving away. A few passengers were taking taxis. I had two choices now. Either wait for a westbound train, or pretend I just got off this one. Try to blend in with the crowd here, get into a cab, and pay him to take me all the way to back the city.

I knew it was less than forty miles. Not that outrageous, especially if I showed the driver some money up front. I had a couple hundred dollars with me, some of the money Bigmouth had given me the night before. I took out five twenties and walked up behind the last man waiting for his taxi. When it was my turn, there was only one cab left. A good omen, I thought. He'd be glad to have me as a customer now.

"Where you heading to, sir?" The driver was black, and he had a soft Caribbean accent. Jamaican, maybe.

I made a writing motion. He looked at me with confusion until he finally got the message. He took out a pen and tore a sheet out of a notebook he had lying on his front seat. He watched me as I wrote on the paper. That slightly entertained look, what an interesting twist this is, a man who must write me a message, what will happen next? The whole scene I usually hated so much, but on this night I just wanted the man to understand me as quickly as possible.

I need to go to the city, I wrote. *I know it will be expensive.*

I handed him back the pen and paper, and then I showed him the twenties in my hand.

"You want me to take you all that way?" That singsong lilt in his voice. "I'd have to charge you for the round-trip."

I nodded my head. Good enough, kind sir. Let's get rolling.

He didn't move yet. He looked me up and down.

"Are you okay, young man? You don't seem good to me."

I put my hands up. I'm perfectly good, no problem here. Thanks for your concern.

"You're wet and cold. Please, get in the cab."

Glad to, I thought. I got in and counted the seconds until he finally put the cab in gear and left the station. My ears were still ringing from the blast of the shotgun. I could still smell the blood. I wasn't sure if the driver could smell it, or if it was just me. Something I'd be smelling for the rest of my life.

The driver picked up the radio. This is it, I told myself. The dispatcher will know about the search for the fifth man, the one who got away. The driver will turn and look at me, and he'll know in an instant. If I'm lucky he won't run the cab right off the road, will simply tell me to sit back and not to try anything funny, because he has to turn around and take me to the police station.

Somehow, though, the dispatcher hadn't gotten the word. Thank God for bad communication between law enforcement agencies and public transportation. The driver kept driving. I didn't relax even then, because every time a voice would break through the static on the radio, I'd figure it would be the bulletin finally coming through. Maybe a special code that I wouldn't recognize but the driver would know. Code 99 or whatever the hell it would be, meaning watch out for a fugitive on the run. Respond with the appropriate code if the fugitive is in your cab. The police will set up the roadblock for you.

The code never came. The driver took me all the way into the city, softly humming a tune the whole way. I took the paper back from him and wrote down an address a few blocks away from the restaurant. Don't let him know exactly where you're going. One more precaution, just in case.

The fare ended up being $150, including tip. The man thanked me and told me to get inside because it was too cold to be running around like a fool with no coat. He seemed to want to tell me a few other things, but I tipped an imaginary hat to him and walked away.

When he was gone, I went down the street, turned the corner, and saw the restaurant. The lights were glowing in the dark. Customers were lined up at the counter, even this late at night. I went through the side door, up the stairs, and into my little room.

There, in the shoebox, the white pager was beeping.

Nine
Michigan
June 1999

Last day of school. I had one more year left, of course, but it still felt like a big day to me. Griffin would be going to art school in Wisconsin. Not far enough away from home to suit him, but he apparently didn't have many other options. I wasn't sure how well I'd do without him, but Mr. Martie took me aside that day and told me that a couple of the art schools were asking about me. They had seen some of my stuff at a district-wide portfolio day, and they were already liking my "special circumstances." It made a good angle for them, I guess. The Miracle Boy healed by art.

"This could be your big ticket," he said. "You know what happens to you at art school?"

I shook my head.

"All that good natural technique you have? All that detail? They'll beat it right out of you. They'll be so threatened by it, they'll make you start throwing paint at the canvas like a monkey. By the time you graduate, the only thing you'll be able to do is teach art to high school kids."

Okay, I thought. I'm glad he's excited for me.

"On the plus side, you'll probably get laid a lot."

I gave him a nod and a quick thumbs-up. He patted me on the shoulder and then left me alone.

I kept thinking about it for the rest of the day. Maybe I'd end up at Wisconsin with Griffin. Or hell, any art school that would take me away from this place. I had this feeling in my chest, this helium lightness that I'd never experienced before. When school let out and we all had this long summer stretching out in front of us, I wondered what the evening would hold for me. There were parties, of course. I wasn't exactly a party animal, as you can imagine, but I knew Griffin and all of the other art students would be doing *something* that night.

He had arranged to pick me up at the liquor store right after dinner. I was waiting outside when he arrived in his red Chevy Nova with the plaid seats. When he got out of his car, I pointed at myself and made a driving motion.

"No, I'll drive." He looked over at Uncle Lito's old Grand Marquis. "Come on, get in."

I pointed at him, made a drinking motion, spun my hands around both ears, then made like a man driving like a maniac. He got the general idea then. So that's how we ended up in the Grand Marquis. It was total style, of course, with the two-tone finish, light brown and dark brown. Big dent in the back fender. Just over a hundred thousand miles on it, and smelling like a cigar factory. It was the only way to hit a summer night in Milford, Michigan, on the last day of school.

We drove to the house of one of the girls in our art class. There were a dozen people sitting around in folding chairs, looking bored. We hung around a few minutes, then moved on to the next. The sun went down. The air was turning cool.

We kept making the rounds and ended up at another art student's house. It hadn't been a winning formula yet, but here, finally, things were looking up. There were a lot of people there, for one thing, and the growing darkness seemed to be a signal to everyone that the real party was just beginning. There was loud music coming from the backyard, smoke rising in the sky from a barbecue. I found my classmate and shook her hand, didn't flinch when she wrapped her arms around me. She whispered in my ear that I could have anything I wanted in my life if I kept working hard enough. The kind of thing you say only after a few beers on an empty stomach.

She dragged me into the backyard, where the music was so loud it hurt. She was into obscure techno music, as I remember, so all the kids were dancing away or voguing or whatever the hell they were doing. Another six or seven kids were jumping up and down on a trampoline, bumping into each other and almost falling off the damned thing. The one oblivious adult stood flipping burgers at the grill, a thick pair of acoustic headphones on his ears.

My classmate tried to yell something to me. I couldn't make out what she was saying. She gave up and pointed to a group of girls who were standing in the far corner of the yard. Nadine spotted me and waved me over.

I caught an elbow in the ribs as I made my way through the crowd, from somebody doing some kind of robot dance. When I finally got to the other side, I saw that the girls were all standing around a huge silver tub filled with ice and beer bottles. Nadine separated herself from the other girls and came to me, one bottle in each hand. She was wearing shorts and a sleeveless blouse, looking more like a tennis player today than an art student. She handed me a bottle.

I opened it and took a sip. It was cold enough to taste good, even if alcohol was still not high on my list. You see enough drunken wreckage walking into a liquor store every day, it sort of puts you off the stuff. But tonight . . . What the hell, right?

She tried to say something to me. I couldn't hear her over the music. I leaned in close, and she spoke right into my ear. "It's good to see you here." I could smell her soft scent as our heads came together. I could feel her breath on my neck.

We stood there for a while, watching everyone jumping around and having a great time, or just standing on the fringes trying to look cool. I didn't see Griffin anywhere, but I figured he could take care of himself for a few minutes. The stars were coming out. I had only drunk half the bottle of beer, but it went down fast and it was enough to make me feel a little dizzy. It wasn't a bad feeling.

Maybe best of all, it was okay to be standing next to Nadine and not saying anything. Everyone in the party was effectively just as mute as I was, because nobody could hear a damn word you were saying anyway.

Nadine went to get another beer for herself. I couldn't help wondering how many she had already had before I got there. When she came back to me, she put her hand on my arm. She left it there. I wasn't sure what I was supposed to do in response.

The music stopped for a moment. The sudden silence roared in my ears.

"Mike," she said.

I looked down at her.

"Come here."

I know I must have looked a little confused. She wasn't more than eighteen inches away from me. How much more here could I get?

She grabbed me by the shirt and pulled me closer. Then she kissed me.

"I've been wanting to do that," she said. "I hope you don't mind."

I didn't respond in any way. I just kept looking at her. The music started again, just as loud as before.

The other girls she was with pulled her away from me. She waved at me to follow them. So I did. I found Griffin on the way out, gave him a little head bob. Follow us. When we were back in front of the house, away from the assault of the music, she told me that they were all going to another party and that I should follow them. I stood there feeling a little bit embarrassed by the Marquis.

Nadine got into her car. One of her friends rode shotgun, and the four other girls piled into the backseat. A couple of them looked like they were on their last legs already, and it wasn't even eleven o'clock yet.

Griffin and I got into my car and followed them across town.

"What do you think?" he said. "Is tonight the night?"

I looked over at him.

"You and Nadine? Hot summer night?"

I shook him off, but I couldn't help noticing how her kiss was still right there on my lips.

We were headed west, out toward the proving grounds. Nadine turned down a dirt road, and as I drove behind her, her car kicked up a cloud of dust in my headlights. Finally, she pulled off, parking on the side of the road behind a line of other cars. As I got out, I could see the cars stretching all the way down to a long driveway. This was obviously the A-list party of the night.

"Where the hell are we?" Griffin said. "Whose house is this?"

I put my hands up. No idea.

"You really want to go in?"

I looked at him. Like, what do you think?

"I suppose we could check it out."

We caught up to Nadine and her friends. I walked beside her. She kept brushing her hair back and tucking it behind her ears. I was terrified of the idea of trying to hold her hand. She kept smiling at me.

The house was made of logs, not a rustic-looking Abe Lincoln log cabin but one of those nicer log homes with lots of windows and high beamed ceilings. It overlooked a good acre of lawn that ran all the way down to the tree line. Next to the house sat an empty Michigan State Police car.

There were citronella candles burning every few feet to keep away the mosquitoes. There was music playing, of course. I could feel the thump of the bass notes as we went through the front door, but thankfully the volume was only turned up to nine this time. Instead of weird techno, it was good old-fashioned white boy rock music. Van Halen, Guns N' Roses, AC/DC. There were so many people in the house, there was barely room to stand.

Nadine's friends formed a wedge and started leading us through the house. I saw a photograph on the wall of a state trooper in full dress uniform, standing proudly next to his German shepherd. There was an open sliding door ahead, past the dining room table. That seemed to be our target.

It was just as crowded outside. There was a huge banner mounted on a clothesline, at least ten feet long and four feet wide. MILFORD KICKS ASS, in big block letters. With a drawing of a foot kicking an actual set of buttocks, in case you didn't get the point. Right below the banner, there was a keg on ice. Nadine and her friends all grabbed red plastic cups and got in line. She handed me a cup, and I stood next to her. Then I felt a strong hand on my shoulder.

"Hot damn! It's my man, Mike!"

It was Brian Hauser. The House himself, the senior hotshot whose lock I had opened back in the fall. Right before he and the rest of the team got trounced in the big game against Lakeland High School. He was wearing a Hawaiian shirt with every shade of blue and green ever invented. It seemed like he was taking a little bit of extra effort just to put his words together tonight.

"How's it hanging, man? I'm glad you made it! Who you got here?"

He took a quick scan. Nadine and her friends. Griffin.

"Okay, then," he said. "The party's complete now. Hey, can I talk to you for a minute? There's something I've been wanting to ask you."

I looked at Nadine and Griffin.

"Will you ladies excuse us for a second?" he said to her. "And you, sorry, what's your name again?"

"Griffin."

"Yeah, it'll just be one moment. We're gonna step into the VIP Room here. You go ahead and hit that keg. We've got a few more lined up, so don't worry if it's running out."

Brian led me away to his "VIP Room," which apparently was the upper level of his back deck. There was an actual red velvet rope strung from the posts. Brian untied the rope from one post and let me through, then retied it as we headed up the steps. There was a patio table up there, with a big green umbrella and padded chairs. There was a hot tub. Two other seniors were sitting on the edge, their feet in the water. Trey Tollman, the quarterback, and another guy from the team named Danny Farrely.

"Hey, look who I found," Brian said to them.

Danny nearly fell over himself as he came barefoot from the edge of the hot tub.

"Michael, my man!" Like I was his long lost friend.

"You know Danny and Trey," Brian said. "From the team."

"I want to tell you something," Danny said. He pulled me away from Brian and wrapped his arm around my neck, the sickly sweet smell of hard alcohol on his breath. "You're okay. You know that? You really are. You're like an inspiration to me."

"Okay, leave him alone," Trey said. "You're slobbering all over him."

"Come over here," Brian said, pulling me back. "You want something to drink? Trey, you got any of that punch left?"

"Hell, yeah," Trey said. He grabbed a cup from the table and poured a tall drink from the pitcher sitting next to it. "Give this a try. It'll fix you right up."

I took the cup from him and tried it. It tasted like regular old fruit punch to me.

"That's the Sucker Punch," Brian said. "Don't drink it too fast, eh?"

"God damn," Danny said. "The artist himself." He went back to the edge of the hot tub and put one foot back in. "The fucking Rembrandt of Milford. Fuck, this water is hot."

"Don't be a pussy," Trey said. "You're not going to melt."

"I don't see *you* getting in."

"Yeah, well, if anybody's getting naked back here, it sure as hell ain't gonna be just us guys, I can tell you that."

"The VIP Room! When are we gonna get some girls up here, anyway?"

"So let me ask you," Brian said, brushing his friends aside. "You remember that day you opened up my lock?"

I nodded.

"How did you do that?"

They all looked at me intently, like they were actually expecting me to answer. I put my hands up.

"It's complicated," Brian said. "Is that what you're saying? You just have to know how?"

"He's an artist," Danny said. "With a paintbrush or a padlock."

I took another sip of the drink. It was sweet and it went down easy. The deck started to move under my feet. Just a little bit at that point. Not the full-blown Tilt-A-Whirl.

"So then, let me ask you this," Brian said. "Can you open up other kinds of locks?"

I gave him half a shrug, half a nod.

"Like key locks? Can you open those? You probably need tools, though, right?"

"I bet you he can," Danny said. "He's an artist, I tell you."

"What kind of tools would you need?" Brian said. "I mean, I'm just wondering."

I didn't have my homemade tools with me. I should have just waved him off and tried to go find Griffin and Nadine. Funny how it's hard to change the subject when you can't speak, though. You can't help but be a captive listener.

"If I get my old man's toolbox, will you show me? I think it's just amazing that you can do that."

"He's amazing," Danny said. "He's the amazing artist of art and . . . something. Wait."

"Will you shut up with that, already?" Trey said.

"You're just jealous because you're not amazing."

"Here, come on down," Brian said. "I'll get the tools."

He led me back down the stairs, practically towing me behind him. Danny and Trey followed us. I tried to find Griffin and Nadine, but I couldn't see them anywhere. I was about to go inside, but Brian blocked my path as he came back out with a big metal toolbox. I started to feel a little bit nervous about this. I took another couple of sips from the Sucker Punch. Probably not the best idea in the world.

"So what do you need here?" Brian said. "I've got no clue."

I closed my eyes for a moment, took a deep breath, and felt myself starting to float away. I opened my eyes and knelt down next to the toolbox. I pulled out a long thin screwdriver to use as a tension bar. I rummaged through the rest of the tools, but there was nothing even close to a usable pick in there.

"What are you looking for? What do you need?"

I put my fingers together and then pulled them apart, like I was holding something long and straight. Then with one hand I made a jabbing motion.

"A pin? Is that what you need?"

I gave him the thumbs-up.

"Be right back."

People were starting to gather around me now. The music was still pounding. Beyond the burning candles in the yard it was pitch black all around us. I took another long sip from my cup.

"I found a big safety pin," Brian said as he came back outside. "Will this work?"

I gave him the thumbs-up again. Then I took the safety pin from him, opened it, and used a pair of needle-nose pliers to bend the tip up about forty-five degrees.

"Fuckin'-A," Brian said. "Can you really open a lock with that? What can you open, like this door over here?"

He went to the big glass sliding door, pushed a couple of people away, and then closed it. He reached into his pocket, took out his key ring, fumbled for the right key, and then put it in the lock.

"How about this one?" he said, rattling the handle to make sure it was locked tight. "Can you open this now?"

I went to the door and felt my legs creak as I knelt down by the handle. I put the cup down and looked at the lock. It was a basic, inexpensive lock. Probably just five regular straight pins. Under normal circumstances, I probably could have cracked it in under a minute, but now, using makeshift tools, with everyone watching, especially with the Sucker Punch tumbling through my bloodstream . . . I wasn't so sure I could do it at all.

"Hey, turn off that music," Brian said.

The music didn't stop.

"Hey, I said turn off the fucking music! There's an artist at work here."

If everyone hadn't been focused on what I was doing, they sure as hell were now. I could see them piling against the glass from the inside. I could feel them standing right behind me on the deck.

"Give him some room," Danny said. "Let the man do his magic."

I put the screwdriver into the lock, keeping it toward the bottom so I'd be able to reach all of the pins. I turned it just enough to feel the tension. Then I slipped the bent safety pin into the lock and went to work. I felt for the back pin, pushed it up with the pin, felt it stick in place. One down.

"Go," Danny said. "Go . . . Go . . . Go . . . Go . . ."

Everybody joined in with him. Everybody was chanting as I worked the next pin.

"Go go go go go go go."

I could feel the sweat dripping down the back of my neck.

"Go go go go go go go go."

I had the third pin up now. Then I felt the pin slip in my fingers. I pulled everything out and shook the tension out of my hands.

That's when I finally saw Griffin standing in the crowd. Nadine was next to him. Griffin had a smug smile on his face, but Nadine obviously had no idea what to make of this whole scene. I could have given up then. I could have stood up and shrugged my shoulders and given Brian his tools back. But I kept going. I gave her a little nod, and then I went back to the lock.

"Everybody be quiet," Brian said. "You're distracting him."

I reset the tension and went in for the back pin, lifted it just enough, and then went on to the next. Keeping just enough tension on that screwdriver, because that's the whole game right there. Having that touch. I blocked everything else out, the people standing all around me, the dizzy sick feeling that was building in my gut. Everything. It all faded away as I worked each pin one by one, feeling them with my fingers. Each one sliding up to just the right position until I finally came to the next one. Here's where I'd find out if they were regular pins or something more complicated. If they were mushroom pins, they'd have that extra little notch in them and I'd have to keep the tension just right and go back and lift each pin a second time. But no. The last pin was up and the lock seemed to spring free on its own now, like it wanted to be open all along. I turned the handle and opened the door as everybody went wild all around me, screaming and carrying on like I had just defused a deadly time bomb.

It felt good. Okay? I admit it. It felt good.

"That's awesome, man." Brian pulled me to my feet and gave me a big slap on the back. "That's fucking awesome."

"That was the coolest thing I've ever seen," Danny said. "I'm not lying to you. That was the single coolest thing ever."

"I gotta admit," Trey said, hitting me in the shoulder. "That was impressive. You're like a superspy, right? You can go anywhere you want."

Griffin was still standing at the back of the crowd, shaking his head. That same smile on his face. Nadine was gone. When I pointed to the spot next to him, he looked around the deck and shrugged.

I didn't think she'd just leave, but hell, maybe she was mad at me for leaving her there in the beer line while I went up to the VIP Room. Or maybe I had no idea *what* she was thinking. Her or any other female in the world.

I went inside and made my way through the dining room to the front door, looking everywhere for her. I felt more people slapping me on my back. The words seemed to swirl all around me, coming too fast for me to comprehend. Then one voice broke through all the rest.

"It's true," the voice said. "He was clinically dead for, like, twenty minutes. That's why he can't talk. He's like brain-damaged."

I stopped. I tried to find the source of the voice, but there were too many people crushed all around me. It could have been one of a hundred people.

"Come on," Griffin said, pushing his way through the crowd. "I think you need some air." He grabbed me by the elbow and took me out the front door.

I almost fell off the front steps, regained my balance, and stood there blinking in the harsh glow of the porch light.

"You okay?"

I nodded.

"That was quite a show you put on. All of a sudden, you're the prince of Milford High School."

I looked at him like, yeah, you've been drinking too much beer.

"I think they're hatching up a crazy idea. Are you up for it?"

Before he could explain, Brian, Trey, and Danny came out through the front door. Brian had taken down the huge MILFORD KICKS ASS banner and was rolling it up.

"We've got the most awesome idea, dude. You gotta help us out here. Whaddya say?"

I looked at all of them, one by one.

"Come on," Brian said. "I'll explain on the way."

He led us to his Camaro, parked next to his father's state trooper car. I couldn't help but wonder where his father was that night, but there was no time to think about that or anything else because a few seconds later Brian was holding the back door open and waiting for us to pile in.

"Wait a minute," he said, looking at Griffin. "We only got room for four guys here."

"Fine," Griffin said. "We'll just be on our way, then."

"Hold the phone," Brian said. "You know what? Maybe we shouldn't be taking this car anyway. It's kind of conspicuous. You know what I mean?"

"You got a point there," Trey said. "Everybody in town knows the House's Camaro."

"You guys got a car?"

So yeah. That's how I ended up driving. Brian sat up front with me. Danny, Trey, and Griffin squeezed into the back.

"We're just gonna play a little joke on somebody," Brian said to me. He smoothed his hands over the rolled-up banner. "Don't worry, it's nothing hardcore."

I looked in the rearview mirror, caught Griffin's eye. He put his hands up. Like, why the hell not?

Brian told me to head to the center of town. We rolled down Main Street, past the liquor store. I was still feeling the effects of the Sucker Punch, so I ended up having to brake hard as we passed under the railroad bridge. For one moment I thought with absolute certainty that we'd hit the embankment and we'd all be killed. Then I pulled out of it just in time.

"I hate that fucking bridge," Brian said. When we hit the edge of town, Brian told me to keep going. We were on a lonely stretch of road now, nothing but trees whizzing by us on both sides. We were heading east.

"You figured out where we're going now?" Brian said.

I shook my head.

"There's somebody we really need to give this banner to."

I shook my head again.

"It's right up here," he said. "You're gonna take a left."

We came to a sign that said WELCOME TO LAKE SHERWOOD. This was one of the original big subdivisions, built before all the other McMansions started popping up all over the place. More importantly, being in Lake Sherwood meant that we had crossed the line that divided the school district into its two separate parts. Milford High School and Lakeland High School.

"There's a party up there," Trey said. "Better be cool."

"I see it, I see it." Brian had me stop as we came up on a line of cars parked on the street. We could see the big house with every light on and a swimming pool in the backyard. There were twenty or thirty people having a hell of a party.

"It's right there," Brian said, nodding to another house, directly across the street. This house was mostly dark, save for one light in the front window.

"You're sure they're gone?" Trey said.

"They're up at Mackinac Island. A little graduation present for our friend Adam."

It all made sense now. This was the house of Adam Marsh, Brian's archrival. The one man he could never beat on the football field or on the wrestling mat.

"I don't see any of those alarm signs on the front lawn," Trey said. "You know what I mean? Those signs to let you know the place is wired?"

Brian didn't answer him. He was too busy unbuttoning his Hawaiian shirt. Underneath, he had on a dark blue T-shirt.

"So Mike," he said. "Here's what I want to ask you now. Do you think you can get us inside Adam's house so we can give him this present?"

I noticed he had the screwdriver in his hand now, the one I had used to open his door. I looked closer and saw the bent safety pin in the other hand.

"We're just going to string it up in his bedroom. So when he comes home . . . Bam! There it'll be. A special little good-bye from his friends at Milford."

Who couldn't actually beat him on the football field, I thought. So this is the best they can do.

"Can you imagine?" Trey said. "He is going to shit his pants."

"Fucking scholarship to Michigan State," Brian said. "I *know* he does steroids. Did you see how much he grew since last year?"

"Oh, like no doubt, man. He's juicing."

"I'm not so sure about this," Danny said. It sounded like he had gotten about half sobered up on the way over here. "It's breaking and entering, isn't it?"

"We're not gonna rob the guy. We're not gonna do *anything*. Just leave the banner in his bedroom."

"I think it's a bad idea," Danny said. "I'm just saying."

Nobody said anything for a minute. I tried to catch Griffin's eye in the rearview mirror again, but he was staring out his window at the Marshes' house. In the distance, we could hear the faint sound of the partiers splashing in the pool.

"What about you?" Brian said. "Griffin, right? You'd think I'd remember a fucking name like that. Are you gonna pussy out like Danny? Or are you with us?"

"I'm there," Griffin said.

Brian turned around and shook Griffin's hand. "You, sir, are officially no longer an art fag."

"Thank you, Mr. Wizard. Do I get a diploma like the Tin Man?"

"What?"

"Never mind."

"Whaddya say?" Brian said, turning back to me. "Are you our man tonight? We can't do it without you."

"Do it for the whole school," Trey said. "It's our last chance to get this asshole."

I looked out at the Marshes' house. The high windows, the perfect lawn. It looked like a castle to me. I couldn't even imagine living in a house like this.

I opened my door and got out of the car.

"Fuckin'-A," Brian said.

"I'm staying here," Danny said. "I'm not going."

"Yeah, whatever," Brian said as he closed his door. "We don't need you."

So it was the four of us. Brian, Trey, Griffin, and me. Two jocks, two art geeks. The Sucker Punch had almost worn off by now. I was feeling every step with an absolute clarity. We were about to illegally enter somebody else's house. Somebody I had never even met.

We walked a short way down the street and then slipped behind the fence when we got to it. There were plenty of lights all over the place. Streetlights every hundred feet or so, plus all of the lights that were shining on us from the house across the street. I didn't know enough yet not to feel exposed. I didn't know yet that these so-called security lights meant to thwart us were actually our best friends that night. You light up the front of a house, you turn everything else that isn't directly lighted into a perfect cloak of invisibility. You light up the back of the house, where nobody else can see you anyway, you just make it all that much more convenient for someone trying to break in.

There was a good lock on the back door, but I had it open in two minutes. My three partners all stood there rocking back and forth, looking over their shoulders every few seconds. They didn't know enough not to be nervous. Nobody had any kind of sight line on us here. We could have set up a net and played volleyball.

When the door was open, we all piled inside. We stood there in the kitchen for a full minute, taking it all in. There was just enough light to see the huge metal stove with the restaurant vent over it. The double refrigerator. The marble countertops that seemed to glow with their own light.

"Fuck," Brian said. "We're actually doing this."

"Let's go," Trey said. "Let's go find his room."

"I can't believe this," Brian said. "This is some heavy duty shit right now."

"Don't wuss out, man. Are you coming or not?"

I knew Trey would never dare talk to him that way under any other circumstances. It was my first lesson in how different people react when they find themselves in a situation like this. The guy who did all the talking could suddenly become the one having cold feet. One of the guys along for the ride, he suddenly finds himself getting into it. For whatever reason, he rises to the occasion. Maybe too much. While the other guy along for the ride can't even get out of the car.

Griffin? I couldn't tell what he was thinking. He just stood there, not making a sound.

And me? I felt nothing. I swear to you, as soon as we stepped foot into that house, everything drained out of me. That ever present buzz, the constant humming from that one moment in my life, playing out in my head, over and over, becoming like a constant static on my internal radio . . . As soon as I opened the door to a stranger's house and stepped inside, the static was gone.

I'd get to know that feeling. Or rather that *lack* of feeling. I'd get to know it very well. On this night, though, I was just standing there in a rich man's kitchen while Trey gave Brian a little bump to get him moving forward. Griffin still hadn't moved.

"I think we should just stay right here," he finally said to me. "Be the lookouts. Whaddya think?"

It was too dark to see his face.

"Okay, maybe this was a mistake," he said. "I'm sorry. We shouldn't have gone along with this. I was just thinking it would be . . . I don't know, like something *real* for once. You know what I'm saying? Didn't it feel that way?"

I didn't want to stand there listening to him. I wanted to see more of the house.

"Where are you going?" he said.

I didn't answer him. I left the kitchen, walked into the living room. There was a fireplace with a big art print hanging over it. A woman in a tight sleeveless dress, hat shading her eyes. Next to her, a sleek black panther on a leash. Real classy.

There was cream-colored leather furniture. There was a television bigger than any I had ever seen. On the opposite side of the room, there was an even bigger aquarium. The air pump was humming away. There was a treasure chest on the bottom, with a lid that would open every few seconds, releasing a stream of bubbles. I counted the fish. There were four of them. I stood there, watching the fish swim back and forth in that bright rectangle.

Until it exploded.

The tidal wave was soaking my pants before I could even process what was happening. A few seconds later, I was looking across at Trey's face, on the other side of what had just been glass and water. He was holding a long iron poker from the fireplace.

The way he looked down at the ruin he had caused, the cruel smile on his face. How happy this made him, the sheer mindless destruction in that one moment. I hated it. I hated it like a sickness and I knew I'd never forget it.

A voice came hissing down at us, from upstairs. "Trey! What the fuck are you doing?"

"Just saying hello to the fish," Trey said.

"What the hell's the matter with you? They're supposed to come inside and be surprised when they see the fucking banner! You just ruined everything!"

"Well, then let's do something even worse in the bedroom," Trey said. He winked at me and dropped the poker. Then he went upstairs. I stood there for a while, watching the fish flopping around at my feet. I picked up two and took them to the kitchen.

"What the hell was that?" Griffin said. He hadn't moved from the door.

I went to the sink, ran some lukewarm water, and then dropped in the fish. I went back into the living room and picked up two more. I put those in the sink and turned the faucet off. All four fish were swimming around now like it was just another day at the office.

"I think we need to get out of here," Griffin said. "Let's just leave those idiots here, eh?"

I held up one index finger, left the kitchen again, and went upstairs. I poked my head into the first room. It looked like a sewing room or something. It was untouched.

I kept going down the hall, poked my head into the master bedroom suite. There was a king-sized four-poster bed and two walk-in closets. I took a look in the master bathroom, saw a big whirlpool tub, a separate shower, a marble sink with gold fittings. That's the kind of house this was.

I stepped into the last bedroom. This was a Lakeland house, remember, so I didn't know anything about the family. I didn't know that Adam had a brother. Or at least that was my first thought. I was assuming it was a boy's room. There were posters all over the walls, for rock bands I had never heard of. Then I noticed that the bedding was bright red, and that there was a big black heart-shaped pillow on it, along with about a dozen stuffed animals.

"Mike! Where are you?" Griffin's voice coming to me from downstairs. I ignored it. My attention was fixed instead on a large portfolio lying on the dresser. I knew exactly what it was. I had one myself, for carrying my drawings. I untied the string and opened it. Then I reached back to the wall switch and turned on the light.

"Mike! Come on!" The voice louder now. It could have been a megaphone in my ear, I wouldn't have moved an inch. I was lost in these drawings.

The first was of a young girl, sitting at a table and looking up at something or someone out of the frame, her face showing both fear and hope simultaneously. The next drawing was of two men, standing in an alley, one man lighting a cigarette for the other. The next a simple still life, one single apple sitting alone on a table, with a knife stabbed into the top of it.

The drawings were good. There was talent here. There was something else, too. I remembered something that Mr. Martie had said to me, about how I needed to find a way to put more of myself into my work. Something I tried so hard *not* to do.

This is it, I thought. This is how you do it. Even if it's just a drawing of a young girl, or two men smoking, or even just an apple with a knife in it. Whoever had done this work . . . she was on these pages, too.

I was about to close the portfolio when I noticed the second portfolio that had been lying underneath it. Whereas the one on top had been one of the cheap cardboard portfolios they give you at school, this portfolio on the bottom was made of black leather and had a zipper along three sides. I hesitated for a moment, then unzipped it.

"Mike, we gotta get out of here right now!" The voice was frantic now, but it didn't register with me. I wouldn't even hear it until I played the whole scene back in my mind an hour later.

There were several drawings of a woman. Thirty years old, maybe. Very pretty in a sad, used-up kind of way. Long hair tied back. A tight, self-conscious smile. In the first drawing, she was sitting in a chair with her hands folded in her lap. Indoors. In the next, she was sitting on a bench outside, the same look on her face. Like she wasn't totally comfortable. There were a few more drawings of the same woman. Judging from the different types of paper and the different shades of pencil, I was guessing they had been done over a fairly long period of time. You could even see an improvement in the ability of the artist.

Then the very last drawing . . . a new subject. Younger. I could tell from the way the paper was worn thin and creased around the edges, by the eraser marks around the eyes and mouth . . . this was something the artist had worked very hard on, had come back to again and again. I could practically feel the sheer effort, trying to capture something in this simple drawing of one person's face.

This was her, I realized. This was a self-portrait. I was looking at Amelia's face for the first time.

From somewhere outside, the sound of tires screeching on asphalt. Then a sweep of headlights across the wall, finally breaking my trance. I dropped the drawing. I went into the hallway and then down the stairs. I could see the car stopped diagonally in the driveway through the front window. I ran out the back door. A mistake. You should find a window on the far side of the house, away from any doors, if you're going to make a run for it.

There were two of them. They tackled me in the backyard. They knocked the wind out of me. I couldn't breathe for a full minute. That old familiar feeling coming back to me, from nine years before. You cannot breathe, Mike. You cannot breathe and you are surely going to die.

"Where are the others?" A voice hot in my ear. My breath slowly coming back to me.

"Tell us where they went! Who was with you?"

I didn't say a word to them. So they just picked me up and hauled me off to the police station.

Ten
Los Angeles
January 2000

Before I went to the bus station that next morning, I cut off most of my hair. No more shaggy curls for me. I cut as close to my scalp as I could, going for as drastic a change in my appearance as I could manage. When I was done I looked like someone who had just finished his last round of chemo.

I also bought a pair of sunglasses with the lightest lenses I could find, so I could wear them all of the time. Combined with the short hair, I truly looked like a different person. I didn't feel any different, but some things you just can't change that easily.

I bought a new pair of jeans, a new shirt, a new coat. I threw the clothes I had been wearing into the Dumpster. I knew I had to watch my money, but a man needs to wear something, right? And it's not like I was shopping at Saks.

I packed up everything I owned. A few more pairs of underwear and socks. An extra pair of shoes. A toothbrush. A half tube of toothpaste. A bar of soap and a mostly empty bottle of shampoo. My practice safe lock. My leather wallet filled with tension bars and picks. A thick folder of every drawing I had done while sitting alone in that room above the restaurant. That was it. That was everything.

Oh, and my pagers. I packed the white pager, the red pager, the blue pager, the green pager. I was tempted to leave the yellow pager right there on the windowsill. Let it beep away all it wanted, until the batteries finally ran out. Or hell, maybe some new member of the Chinese family would find it, would call the number on the little screen, speaking in Mandarin or broken English. Maybe the rank amateur on the other end of that call would cancel his operation, and end up not getting his head blown off his body.

But no. In the end, I took that pager with me, too. I packed everything up and caught a cab downtown to the Port Authority. I paid for my ticket in cash, waited for the bus, got something to eat. I got on the bus, and as it pulled out I said good-bye to the city. You'd think I would have been glad to be rid of it. That I would have sworn I'd never step foot in the city again. But I actually felt a pang of regret to leave the place. As miserable as it had been, I had survived it. I had proven that much to myself. That I could make it on my own if I had to.

The bus kept going, all through the night. I slept on and off. In the morning I saw cornfields and trucks and billboards. In the evening I saw cows and red dirt. The miles rolled by.

By the end of the second day, I was in Los Angeles.

It was a hell of a long trip, but this was the white pager we're talking about. These were the guys that the Ghost called money in the bank. True professionals. The best of the best. I figured it was the ultimate lucky break for me, that they'd be the guys beeping me next, after the yellow pager disaster. I was ready for something to go right for a change.

The man on the phone who had given me the address in L.A. told me it was a nice, clean motel up in the Glendale area. He told me the man at the desk would be expecting me. That I should indicate to him that my name was Stone and he'd show me to a room on the back side of the building. He and his associates would come for me at the motel and knock on my door. At which time the details of the operation would be shared with me.

It all worked out exactly as he said. I got off the bus, wrote down the address, and gave it to a cabdriver. He rolled out onto the expressway, which was already jammed with midday traffic. We bumped along for almost an hour until we got up to the motel. I paid the man and got out. It was a dry, sunny day in Los Angeles. An even seventy degrees, everything looking brown and dried out. There was a slight sting of smog in the air.

The motel was a double-decker, not too cheap-looking but not exactly the Ritz, either. The pool looked clean, but nobody was swimming. The parking lot was half full. I went in and wrote down one word on a piece of paper, *Stone*, the name the man had given to me. I gave it to the man behind the desk, and that got him right off his chair.

He insisted on personally showing me the way around the parking lot to my room. It was up on the second floor. He opened the door, showed me where the phone was, the towels in the bathroom, everything else that I could have found myself quite easily. He gave me the key and told me not to hesitate to call him if I needed anything. I'm not sure that he even noticed I hadn't said a word to him the whole time.

When he was gone, I sat on the bed for a while, wondering how I'd gotten there. On the other side of the country, with nothing to do but wait for a stranger to knock on the door.

On the other hand, this was a step up from the room above the restaurant on 128th Street. There was a television, a clock radio, clean towels. Hell, a bathtub! I couldn't remember the last time I had had a hot bath. Even at Uncle Lito's place, I only had the shower stall.

I went into the bathroom and started running the hot water. I looked out the window at the parking lot and the scrubby-looking palm trees. When the tub was full I took my clothes off and got in. It felt good after all those miles on the bus.

When I was done, I dried off and sat on the bed wearing just the towel around my waist. I counted what was left of my money. I turned on the television. Then I got out some paper and started to draw.

I caught up with my ongoing story. The second trip to Connecticut. How it all fell apart and how I was the only one to make it out alive.

If Amelia ever reads these pages, I thought, what the hell is she going to think of this?

I waited for two days. Watching television, drawing, spinning my lock. Walking down the street to buy some food and bringing it back to the room. The third morning, I heard a knock on my door.

I had been wondering all along what these guys would look like. This small band of professional thieves, supposedly the best of them all.

It was time to find out.

The first face I saw when I opened that motel room door was a woman's. A very attractive face, actually. Young, Hispanic. Full lips and big dark eyes. She was smiling, like someone else had just said something funny. As soon as she saw me, the smile faded.

Then I saw another face. A man, just as young as the woman. Maybe even younger, but still a few years older than me. Stubble around his chin. Sunglasses. Curly hair that looked sort of like mine, at least back when I *had* hair.

"Are you the Young Ghost?" he said.

"He's a little kid," the woman said. "He's, like, still wearing diapers."

They stepped past me into the room. They were both wearing black leather jackets. I was about to close the door, but the receiving line wasn't over yet. Another man came in, also in black leather. Rail thin. He was just as young, but from the scars on his face you could tell he'd seen a lot more hard miles. He had a tattoo of a spiderweb on one side of his neck.

Then the fourth. Another young woman, in even more black leather, with even *more* hard miles on her if that was possible. She looked tired and strung out, with one eyelid slightly closed. A chipped tooth. Yet she wasn't ugly. I mean, there was just something about her. Like a raw animal beauty that couldn't be erased, no matter what she did to herself.

These were four bizarrely attractive human beings, all right, and not one of them looked older than a college undergrad. This could *not* be the White Crew that the Ghost had been raving about, could it?

"You said this place was nice," the first man said to the second. He looked out the window at the tired palm trees.

"It's just fine," the second man said. He walked in a tight circle around me, looking me up and down.

"My name's Julian," the first man said. He was obviously the leader of this outfit, whoever the hell they were. "That's Gunnar."

"Charmed." He slid off his jacket to reveal a black T-shirt with the sleeves cut off. He had absolutely no body fat on him whatsoever. You could see every muscle, every tendon.

"That's Ramona," Julian said, indicating the young Hispanic woman. She nodded once to me and then sat down on the bed.

"And that's Lucy."

She came up to me and stood a few inches too close. I could smell cigarettes and open road, and some kind of perfume that jogged a distant memory. She looked at me with her uneven eyes, put one finger under my chin, and pushed upward. Then she let me go.

"So, Young Ghost," Julian said, "what's your name?"

I took out my wallet and extracted the driver's license. I handed it to Julian.

"William Michael Smith?" He held the license up to the window. "You're kidding me, right? Could this thing be any more fake?"

Here I was, thinking it was a perfect forgery, but then what did I know? I went and took the license from him and pointed to the middle name.

"Michael. That's your real name?"

I nodded. It was the first time anyone had called me Michael since leaving Michigan.

"So it's true," Julian said. "You really don't talk."

I nodded again.

"That is so fucking cool. Talk about meta. It's just transcendent."

Whatever you say, I thought. Then I figured it was time to get everything straight. Because I couldn't quite believe what seemed to be happening here. I pointed to him, to Gunnar, to Ramona, to Lucy. Then I put both hands up. Like, who the hell are you guys?

Julian smiled at that one, looked at his friends, one by one, then turned back to me. "The first time the Ghost saw us, he was a little skeptical, too. Then when he worked with us . . . I mean, we ended up making him a lot of money. And that guy he works for . . . the guy *you* work for. Have you actually met him?"

I nodded. Oh yeah. I've met him.

Julian shook his body like some kind of cartoon character. Like a man seeing a vampire. "Is he not the scariest fucking human being you've ever seen? I mean, seriously. We made damned sure he got his cut out of anything the Ghost helped us with. I assume you come with the same tax? Or did he raise the rates this year?"

"How's he gonna know?" Gunnar said. "We're three thousand fucking miles away."

"Please disregard my boy over there," Julian said to me. "He hasn't actually met your boss yet, so he doesn't know any better."

"I don't care *who* this guy is," Gunnar said. "And I'm not your boy."

"So tell me," Julian said, waving Gunnar away like a mosquito. "What exactly did the Ghost say about us? Did he tell you we were the best of the best?"

I nodded.

"What else? I'm dying to know."

I shrugged. He said something about if I ever met them someday, I shouldn't let their looks deceive me. Which I guess made sense now.

"Okay, but you were expecting some real straight-looking, serious fuckers, right? Clean and white and like, what was that guy's name? Who played on that show?"

"Robert Wagner," Ramona said.

"Yeah. *It Takes a Thief,* right? Real smooth guy? Dressed up in a tux all the time? Playing baccarat and then sneaking away to steal the jewels?"

"You should wear a tux sometime," she said.

"I might. You never know."

"Can we get to the point?" Gunnar said. "Can this teenager here really open a safe?"

"It says right here he's twenty-one," Julian said, handing me back my license. "Seriously, dude, we gotta get you a better ID."

"Cut the bullshit," Gunnar said. "I mean, come on, look at him."

"I told you what the man said. The Ghost should know, right?"

"I want to see him do it first. Then I'll believe it."

"Well, of course he's going to do it first," Julian said. "What do you think we are, a bunch of amateurs here? Come on, this dump is giving me the creeps."

"He's not riding with me," Gunnar said. "You take him."

"You know how to ride a motorcycle?" Julian asked me.

I nodded.

"I mean, a real bike?"

I nodded again.

"What do you think, Ramona? Can he take yours?"

"Are you fucking kidding me?"

"Come on, he's our guest here. He came all this way. Are you gonna make him ride bitch?"

"Are you gonna make *me* ride bitch?"

"You used to love riding behind me, remember? Wrap your arms around me? Whaddya say?"

I knew this was way beyond reasonable. You don't ask somebody to give up their bike. Was he testing her? Testing me?

Ramona looked at him for a long moment. I wondered which part of his body she'd take off first.

She stepped up to me and grabbed me by the shirt. "If you wreck my bike," she said, "I swear I will kill you."

Four Harleys were parked in the lot. There was one extra helmet, just for me. We mounted up and rolled out onto the street. If nothing else, it felt damned good to be on a bike again.

They took off fast. I had to really gun it to keep up with them. They pulled onto the busy street and started weaving their way through traffic. Lucy kept looking back, but the two men seemed to be racing each other now, like they had forgotten all about me. We went through West Holly-wood, then Beverly Hills. Tall palm trees, big houses, brown grass. The whole city looked like you could light one match and burn it to the ground.

Just as we started to get close to the ocean, they pulled off onto a quiet side street. Another couple of turns and they were all stopping their bikes in front of a modest little house on Grant Street. The house took up most of the lot. The tiny front yard was all gravel, with a fence around the whole thing. Julian took off his helmet and opened the gate for us.

"How was the ride?" he said.

I gave him a quick nod and handed him my helmet. When we were in-side the place, I could see that the outside was deceiving. There was a state-of-the-art kitchen, a big wine rack filled to the ceiling with bottles, lots of ultramodern spot lighting hanging from the ceiling. If these people were really thieves, they were making a good living at it.

"What can I get for you?" Julian said. "Wine? Cocktail?"

I passed on those, eventually accepted a cold beer. The first sip took me right back to that summer night in Michigan. The night I first got arrested. As I sat there and drank my beer, Julian kept watching me.

"You're like a work of art," he finally said to me. "I mean, look at you. You're just perfect."

Okay . . . thanks. I guess.

"And you're just so . . . silent. You're like a living Buddha or something. I can't stand it."

I took another hit off the beer.

"Ramona," he said to her. "Come over here. Look into Michael's eyes. What do you see?"

She came over to me. She bent down and put a finger under my chin, just like Lucy had done to me at the hotel. She looked into my eyes, and then she shook her head.

"*La fatiga*," she said.

"Like he's seen way too much already," Julian said. "Even though he's what, seventeen, I bet? Eighteen?"

"How old are you?" she said to me.

I put up ten fingers. Then seven.

"How did you get here?"

I kept looking up at her.

"Okay, us first," she said. "Julian, tell him your life story."

"Just like that," he said, smiling.

"Yes. I think this is one man who can keep a secret."

So he spent the next few minutes giving me the rundown. He had been born into money, had gone to private schools, was tops in his senior class and on his way to either Pepperdine or Gonzaga. He hadn't made up his mind. Then he got busted for his second DUI, ended up spending a month in a youth program. Where he met Ramona, Gunnar, and Lucy, all of whom came from abject poverty, abusive parents, broken homes. He and Ramona had been together ever since. They stayed off the rap sheet while Gunnar and Lucy kept drifting in and out of trouble. Then finally those two got clean and reconnected with Julian. The four of them had lived here in his house ever since.

He didn't tell me how they ended up working together on high-end robberies. Or how they had met the man in Detroit. Or the Ghost. That part of the story would come later.

"We should talk a little business at some point, eh? But first things first."

He took me to a bookshelf on the back wall of the house.

"Okay, I swear to God," he said. "This was here when I bought the place."

He pushed on the shelf, and the whole thing turned like a revolving door. There was another room behind it. When I stepped through, I saw maps and photographs pinned to the wall. File cabinets. A computer and printer. And in the corner, solid, metallic . . . downright heartwarming . . . a safe, about four feet high.

"Welcome to the Bat Cave," Julian said.

"You're not being very careful," Gunnar said. "I mean, with somebody we just met."

"Ramona says he can keep a secret. So I trust him. Besides, you want him to prove he can open the safe, don't you?"

"Just drag it out and have him open it in the living room."

"I'd like to see *you* drag it out."

"Boys," Ramona said. "Behave."

They didn't have to tell me what to do next. I was already on my knees in front of the safe. As I did this, Lucy, who hadn't said one word since we rode back to the house, got down on her knees right beside me. When I reached out my hand to touch the safe, she looked like she wanted to stop me.

"It's all right, Lucy." Julian came over behind her and started to rub her shoulders. "It's okay. Just watch."

Gunnar pushed Julian away from her. I realized that the whole dynamic between these four people was wound tighter than piano wire, and something I'd probably never quite understand.

"Did you really work with the Ghost?" Lucy said to me.

I nodded.

"At that place in Detroit? With the eight safes?"

Yes.

"I was there, you know. He tried to show me how to do it. I worked so hard at it . . ."

Yes. I know how hard it is.

"This is the safe we'll be breaking into," she said, touching the handle. "The exact model. We don't leave anything to chance."

It made perfect sense. My first indication that these seemingly insane people really knew what the hell they were doing.

"So can you do it? Can you really open this safe without breaking her?"

Her, she said. She really did study under the Ghost. Or at least she tried.

"Show me."

I took a deep breath and started. I turned the dial, clearing the wheels so I could count them. She watched me carefully. I knew she knew everything I was doing. It was a strange feeling for me, and yet comforting. She knew.

Four wheels. Park at 0. Go to the contact area. My familiar rhythm now. She watched intently, but as I closed my eyes and felt for the slightest tiny difference, I knew I was leaving her behind. There was no way she could see this part.

I kept working my way up the dial, finding the short contacts. All the way to 100, then back again to verify them and to narrow them down to the exact numbers.

I made a writing motion. She gave me a piece of paper and pen.

There were tears in her eyes as I wrote down each number. I was sure she knew the combination. She had probably set it herself. She also knew that, at this point, finding the numbers was all that really mattered. Getting the right order was the easy part.

She grabbed the paper from me and crumpled it into a ball.

"Does he have it right?" Gunnar said.

"Yes."

He nodded, didn't say anything else.

"You can't show me how you did that," she said to me. "It's just something you can do. Or can't do."

I just kept looking at her. At that moment, I honestly wished that I *could* show her.

"Okay," Julian said, his voice quiet now. "That's why Michael is here. Lucy, you know you're here for a reason, too. You know that, right?"

She didn't respond. She got up and left the room.

He shook his head slowly. Then he looked at his watch.

"If we're going to do it this week," he said, "then now's the time. We all need to get into character."

He reached out a hand to me and pulled me up from the floor.

"I'm glad we called you," he said to me, taking me over to one of the maps on the wall. The whole city of Los Angeles, laid out before us.

"Welcome to the City of Angels," he said. "Let me show you which piece of it we're going to own tonight."

Eleven

Michigan
June and July 1999

So there I was. Sitting in the back of a police car. I had a shiny pair of hand-cuffs on. For the first time ever. They didn't lock them behind my back, so I could sit there and study them, wondering how hard it would be to get them open.

Once the two cops had given up on me telling them anything, they had put me in the back of the car and had tried to recite me my Miranda rights. You have the right to remain silent, et cetera. When they got to the part where I had to acknowledge that I understood them, things got interesting. I nodded my head, but one of the cops told me that wasn't good enough. I had to give them a verbal acknowledgment. Instead, I just gave them a long string of sign language, even with the cuffs already on my wrists, hoping they'd get the idea.

"He's deaf," one of the cops said to the other. "What do we do now?"

"He has to read his rights and then sign a statement that he understands them. I think."

"So give him your Miranda card. Let him read that."

"I don't have it. Give him yours."

"What? I don't have one. How could you not have one if you just read it to him?"

"I didn't read it. I have it memorized."

"Oh shit, *now* what are we going to do?"

"Just take him down to the station. They'll know what to do with him."

I was going to try to convince them I wasn't deaf, but then I thought, what the hell. Maybe they'll stop talking to me. By then, another two police cars had already pulled up. Everyone from the party across the street was gathered around now, watching us.

They took me to the Milford station on Atlantic Street, just around the corner from the liquor store, in fact. It was after midnight now. They stuck me in an interview room for what seemed like another hour, until finally the two cops who had arrested me came into the room, along with two other men. One was a detective, and as soon as he saw me, he looked very confused. The other man was a professional sign language interpreter, who looked like he had just gotten dragged out of bed. One of the arresting officers started talking while the interpreter did his thing, signing to me that I was in the Milford police station, which I had obviously already figured out myself, and that they had to make sure I understood my rights before we went any further.

When it was my turn, I dusted off just enough sign language to convey the one important message they all had to finally understand. Point to self, put hands in front and draw them apart like an umpire signaling safe, one finger to right ear, then both hands, palm out, coming together.

"I am not deaf," said the interpreter. He was speaking for me, automatically, before he even realized what I was saying.

"You're Mike," the detective said. "Lito's nephew, right? Over at the liquor store?"

I nodded yes.

"He can hear just fine, you clowns," the detective said to the cops. "He just can't talk."

That led to some general embarrassment and a dismissal of the now pissed-off interpreter. The detective read me my rights and had me sign a statement that I understood them, while the two cops kept looking at me like I had made a special point of tricking them and making them look bad. Then the detective gave me a blank legal pad and asked me if I wanted to say anything. I wrote a big *NO* and slid the pad back to him.

They fingerprinted me. They gave me a breathalyzer test, even though I was pretty sure I was stone cold sober at that point. Then they had me hold up a little sign with my name and case number as they took two pictures of me, one facing front, one sideways. Then they put me in a holding cell by myself while they called Uncle Lito.

I sat there in the cell for another hour or so, until I heard some footsteps at the end of the hallway. There was a door there with a little observation window in it. I saw Uncle Lito's face appear behind the glass, his eyes wide and his hair sticking up like something out of a cartoon. Another half hour passed. Then a cop came to my cell and took me to another interview room.

There was a woman waiting for me. It had to be two o'clock in the morning by now, but this woman was wide-awake and very well dressed.

"I've been hired by your uncle to represent you," she said to me as I sat down across from her. "We need to discuss a few things before you're released. First of all, do you understand everything that's happened to you so far?"

She had a legal pad ready for me. I picked up the pen and wrote *Yes.*

"I understand you have not given the police any written statements yet? Is that true?"

Yes.

She took a deep breath. "They want to know who else was involved in this," she finally said. "Are you willing to tell them?"

I hesitated, then I started writing. *What happens if I don't say anything?*

"Michael, you have to understand something here. I can't help you if you don't tell me everything that happened. I need to know who was with you."

I looked away from her.

"Are you going to tell me?"

I want to go home and sleep, I thought. Figure this all out tomorrow.

"I understand that there was a party going on across the street from the residence you broke into. I'm sure the police are talking to everyone who was there. *Somebody* will have seen your . . . friends running away."

One friend, I thought. One friend and two other people I couldn't care less about. But I couldn't see how to give up just the two of them without Griffin getting pulled into it. Even if he was already in Wisconsin by now. They'd find him and bring him back.

"Your car," she said. "It's parked down the street from the Marshes' house?"

I nodded.

"Do you even know the Marshes? I'm sure there's a reason you drove all the way over there, *all by yourself,* if you expect anyone to believe that, and broke into their house."

I closed my eyes.

"All right," she said. "We'll talk about this tomorrow. I'm going to go get you released now so you can go home and get some rest."

Another half hour of waiting, and then I was out of the holding cell. The lawyer drove us home. Uncle Lito sat in the front seat, not saying a word. I was in the backseat. When we got to the house, he thanked the lawyer and got out. I slid out and followed him. I kept waiting for the big blow-up. What the hell got into you, what the hell were you thinking. Something like that. Maybe even some physical confrontation. For the first time ever. But he just opened up the front door and let me in.

"Go to bed," he said. "We'll deal with this in the morning."

I went to my room in the back of the house and got undressed. As I lay down and turned off the light, I saw his silhouette in the doorway.

"Do you have any idea how much this lawyer is going to cost?"

I stared at the dark ceiling.

"I didn't realize it was this bad, Michael. I mean, I know what you had to go through . . ."

No. You don't know.

"I thought you were getting over that now. I thought you were doing okay."

He closed the door and left. As I went to sleep, I saw the aquarium shatter again. The water running onto the floor. The fish lying on the floor, mouths gaping in surprise.

The next day I woke up late, expecting the worst. I figured by the end of the day, I'd be hauled off to prison, or to some special place where they send juvenile delinquents. What I didn't know was that the county prosecutor was already working on his second headache of the morning.

"Okay, here's where we are," the lawyer told us, as soon as we were both sitting in her office. "The police believe that the Marsh residence was entered around ten thirty last night," she said, reading from her yellow pad. "By Michael and some unknown number of accomplices."

"I want the names," Uncle Lito said to me. "Do you hear me? You're going to write them down and you're going to do it now."

"Hold that thought for a moment," she said. Then she went back to her pad. "According to the police, various witnesses at the party across the street reported as few as two and as many as five young men fleeing the scene when the squad cars arrived. It's not uncommon to get differing accounts from different people. In any case, several witnesses state that one of the young men was very large."

She looked at me, measuring my reaction.

"That leads them to believe that a Milford student named Brian Hauser may have been on the scene. Apparently, he and Adam Marsh have some history. Is any of this ringing a bell yet, Michael?"

I didn't move.

"As far as the charges themselves go," she said, "there were no apparent signs of forced entry. Which leads the police to believe that the back door was unlocked. A lucky break for whoever wanted to get in."

Nothing about the safety pin, I thought. Or the screwdriver. The police had taken them from me when I was arrested, but I guess it didn't even occur to them that I could use those things to open the lock.

"A large aquarium in the living room was shattered, apparently by a fireplace poker. That resulted in a fair amount of water damage to the carpeting and furniture. Although the fish themselves were found unharmed in the kitchen sink. I suppose, what, you broke the aquarium and then felt bad about the fish? Or was the whole thing just an accident?"

I could really feel Uncle Lito staring a hole through me now.

"A large banner was left in Adam Marsh's bedroom. Something to the effect that Milford High School kicks ass. Aside from that, there were no further damages, and nothing was reported as stolen from the house."

"So it's not burglary," Uncle Lito said. "I mean, if nothing was stolen . . ."

"If you unlawfully enter someone's house to commit a crime, it's still technically a burglary charge."

"But it's not as serious?"

"It's still a felony. If they choose to play it that way."

I felt Uncle Lito's hand on my arm. "Michael, who else was with you? We need those names now. We'll tell the judge they made you do it. That's what happened, right? That big guy the police are talking about, was it that kid? Brian . . . what was it?"

"Brian Hauser," she said.

"Brian Hauser. Was it him? Did he put you up to this?"

"Actually," she said, "I'm not so sure we need a definite answer to that question right now."

"What do you mean?" Uncle Lito said. "How could we not need an answer?"

"Because whether he was part of this or not . . . well, let's just say that if it's an open question, it might work in our favor."

"I don't understand."

"Here's what's happening." She put her pad down. "I've already talked to the prosecutor this morning. First of all, we talked about my concerns with the way the police handled Michael's arrest, and how long it took for you to be contacted. Even with their little 'misunderstanding,' it doesn't look good. Not with a juvenile involved."

"So what does that mean?" Uncle Lito said. "Is that enough to get him off?"

"He's not 'getting off,' no, but along with their other problem, it gives us a good chance at some broad leniency."

"What's their other problem?"

"Brian Hauser. You see, without even getting a statement from Michael yet, the police have already been over to his house. Like I said, just based on the witnesses and the personal history. Maybe even talking to the Marsh family already, getting their input. I mean, they really jumped the gun here."

"How's that a problem?"

"Did you know that Brian Hauser's father is a Michigan State Trooper?"

"No. Does that matter?"

"Mr. Hauser claims that Brian was home at his party for the entire evening. That he never left the house."

"He's covering for his son. You don't think a father would do that?"

"Maybe he would. It wouldn't be the first time, I'm sure. But look at it from their side. They've got a state trooper saying his son couldn't possibly have been involved."

"So what does this all mean?"

"What this means is that nobody is particularly anxious to see this case go any further. The prosecutor doesn't even want to touch this."

"So give him a piece of paper. We'll have him write the names down right now."

She hesitated. "Let me try to put this the right way," she said. "Michael is going to go down for *something*, whether he takes these other kids down with him or not. If he goes it alone, he makes life a lot easier for everyone else."

"So he's going to take this rap by himself. Is that what you're telling me?"

"I'm saying . . . given the motivations of the parties involved . . . not to mention the special circumstances surrounding Michael's personal history . . ."

Nobody said anything for a while. I could hear the traffic on the street outside her window.

"So what's the bottom line?" Uncle Lito finally said. "What are we looking at here?"

"One year probation. Then disposition of the charges. Meaning the charges are completely stricken from the record."

"That's it?"

"He'll have to do some community service," she said. "You know, cleaning up trash on the side of the highway, something like that. Unless the judge has something more creative in mind."

"Like what?"

"Like a little restorative justice. It's the big thing right now. Have the guilty party make things right for the victim."

"You mean, like fixing the damages?"

"It could mean that. It could mean almost anything. That'll be up to the judge and the probation officer. And Mr. Marsh. The victim."

So there it was. My big lesson of the day, something I'd take with me and never forget. The whole legal system—If you think it's just a big set of rules, you're dead wrong. It's really a bunch of people sitting around and talking to each other, deciding what they want to do with you. When they make their decision, then they pull out whatever rule they need to make it happen. Get on the wrong side of these people and you have no hope. They'll turn a parking ticket into a bus ride to the penitentiary. On the other hand, if they decide that it's in their own best interests for you to be spared, then you will be.

That's how it went. A few more days ground by while everyone talked it over some more. Finally, I stood up in circuit court while my lawyer entered a guilty plea and I listened to the judge tell me how lucky I was to get this chance to wipe my slate clean.

The next day I was sitting in a conference room with a probation officer and the man whose house I had broken into. Mr. Norman Marsh. He was big, overtanned, loud, totally gung ho. It was no surprise that his son was a high school football star. Mr. Marsh could have killed me on the spot if he wanted to. One look in his eyes dispelled any doubt about that fact. But the whole point of the meeting was just to make sure we all understood the program, that I had admitted my guilt and that I would be working for Mr. Marsh that summer to make restitution. Mr. Marsh sat up straight in his chair, looking smart in his perfect suit and tie. He shook my hand with a strong but not bone-crushing grip when it was finally time to do that.

"I think this is going to be a positive experience for both of us," he said. "Maybe it'll teach me a few things about forgiveness. And I hope I'll be able to share some of my own life experiences with young Michael here."

In other words, he was saying all the right things, and I'm sure the probation officer was impressed as all hell. He was already putting this one in the win column. Maybe even imagining all the good press he'd get for setting the Miracle Boy onto the right path. Yet another headshrinker with a dream.

___

It was almost two weeks now since the big crime, me taking the rap alone and getting ready to report to the Marshes' house the very next day at noon sharp. I was outside the liquor store that night, sitting on the back of Uncle Lito's car. It was a hot night, the beginning of a real heat wave. The two yellow lights on the bridge embankment blinked on and off. Yellow on top. Yellow on bottom. Yellow on top. Yellow on bottom.

I watched the cars rolling down Main Street, some of them with their windows open, music pumping out into the night air, the ashes from glowing cigarettes trailing behind them. I wondered how many of these people were on their way back home to a television and a late dinner. Surely one person in one car was on his way to somewhere far, far away from Milford, Michigan. If he happened to see me sitting there in the cheap light of the liquor store, maybe he'd assume I was just another local kid who'd never go anywhere my whole life. He wouldn't know about my history, about the day in June or the fact that I'd been silent for nine years. Or that I *couldn't* go anywhere, now that I was officially an offender on probation.

Another hour passed, the night refusing to cool off any. Not one single degree. A bad sign for the next day. Finally, a car came by and instead of sweeping its headlights past me it locked them right on my face, blinding me. The car turned into the lot and stopped. When the engine was turned off, it kept ticking in the heat. The driver didn't get out. He just sat there.

I knew the car. A red Chevy Nova with plaid seats. I sat there for a while, figuring he'd have to open that door eventually. A full minute passed. Then another. Then I slid off the back of Uncle Lito's car and went to him.

Griffin was sitting behind the wheel. His face was lit up enough for me to see that he was crying. I went to the passenger's side, opened the door, and sat down beside him.

"Is it okay for me to be here?" he said.

I put my hands up. Why wouldn't it be?

"I mean, is it safe?"

I crossed both fists against my chest, then opened them. With a look on my face that said, of course it's safe.

"I wanted to turn myself in," he said. "I really did."

I put my hands down.

"I'm serious. I was going to do it."

I made a *Y* with my right hand and shook it in front of my forehead. Ridiculous.

"I still can, Mike. Do you want me to? Would that help you any?"

I shook my head.

"Are you sure? I can tell them everything."

I hit him in the shoulder, a little harder than I meant to.

"Those other guys," he said. "I bet they don't feel bad at all. I bet they haven't been dying inside like I've been."

I nodded at that, thinking, yeah, thanks a lot. I looked out the window.

"I still feel bad. I'm going out to Wisconsin. You know, that summer program thing, before school starts in the fall. I feel like I'm just abandoning you here."

He thought about it for a minute.

"Still," he said. "I mean, one more year until you graduate. Then you can go to art school, right? Maybe even come out to Wisconsin and join me? That would be cool, right?"

I shrugged. He stopped talking again for a while.

"I owe you one," he finally said. "Okay? I'm totally serious. Anything you ever want. I totally owe you."

I nodded again before I got out of the car and watched him drive away. I couldn't help wondering if the visit had made him feel any better.

No, he'll still feel just as guilty, I thought. Maybe more than ever. He'll never be comfortable around me again. The only real friend I ever had. He's going to leave town now, and I'll never see him again.

I was right.

The next day, I drove over to the Marshes' house. I knew being late would be Strike One, so I got there at eleven fifty-seven. It felt strange to be there at that same house again. It looked even bigger in daylight, the white paint so clean you needed sunglasses to look at it. I parked the car on the street, only a matter of yards from where I had parked just a few nights before. I walked to the front door, feeling the sun burning down on my head. I knocked on the door and waited.

Mr. Marsh opened the door. Instead of the perfect suit and tie, now he was wearing a white sleeveless workout shirt and a pair of tight blue compression shorts. He had a headband on to complete the effect.

"It's you," he said. "You're here."

Like I had a choice?

"Come this way." He left the door open and turned away from me. I closed the door and followed him.

"We'll have a little chat in my office," he said. "After you see this." He led me through the living room, where the aquarium had been replaced, and where the exact same fish were now swimming around as if nothing had happened. All of the other damage had apparently been fixed as well. There was no trace of the invasion.

"Twelve hundred dollars," he said. "Between the new tank, the water damage on the rug and the furniture . . ."

He stood there and waited for me to react in some way. To acknowledge what he was saying.

"I should have waited to let you do it, but hell, that wouldn't have made any sense. What were you going to do, glue the glass back together?"

Now you're arguing with yourself, I thought. I'd better do something here. So I lifted both hands a few inches, then let them fall back to my sides.

"Yeah, sure. You're damned right. What else is there to say?"

He turned and went to a door just past the stairs. He opened it and gestured for me to enter. It was a room I hadn't seen the first time around. There was a bookcase of dark wood on one wall, a huge projection television screen on another wall. A large picture window looking out over the backyard on the third wall, and on the fourth, the biggest goddamned stuffed fish I'd ever seen. It was one of those huge blue marlins, at least eight feet long with another three feet of spear nose. It was stuffed and mounted and lacquered, looking so real you'd think it was still dripping wet.

"Have a seat." He indicated the leather guest chairs in front of his desk. He sat behind the desk, the great fish just behind his head. He produced one of those little rubber exercise balls and started squeezing it. For a long time, he didn't say anything. He just looked at me and squeezed.

"I caught that damned thing off Key West," he finally said, without actually looking up at the thing. "I fought it for three hours."

He squeezed some more. He didn't take his eyes off of me.

"Okay, I admit, I'm a little torn here. Part of me still wants to kill you right now."

He paused and watched me, no doubt measuring the effect of his words.

"The other part of me just wants to hurt you really badly."

This isn't the way this was supposed to be going, I thought. Not according to my probation officer.

"Let me ask you this. Have you ever had your home broken into?"

I shook my head.

"Do you have any idea what it feels like?"

I shook my head again.

"It feels like you've been violated. Like someone has reached right into your guts . . ."

He held up his ball and squeezed it as hard as he could.

"Like someone has taken something away from you that you'll never, ever get back. Your whole sense of security. Of being safe in your own goddamned home. Do you understand what I'm trying to say to you?"

I sat there and looked at him.

"What's with the not speaking, anyway? What's that all about?"

With his free hand, he reached over and picked up a framed photograph that had been facing away from me.

"I have a daughter who's the same age as you," he said. "Ever since the break-in . . . ever since the violation of this house . . ."

He turned the frame toward me. I saw her face.

"Things have been hard enough for her, is what I'm trying to say. Since her mother's been gone."

He stopped for a moment.

"Since her mother took her own life. A few years ago. I'm telling you that just so you know what she's already been through, okay? Amelia's been living in her own world ever since. Getting better, maybe. I don't know. But now . . . fuck, with you breaking in here . . . I can't even imagine how scared she must be. You have no idea, do you? You have no fucking idea."

In the picture, she was wrapping herself up in a hooded sweatshirt, her hair whipped around by the wind off a lake in the background. She wasn't smiling.

But she was beautiful.

"I hope to God you have kids someday. I hope you have a daughter like my Amelia. Then I hope you have a few cheap lowlife punks break into your house and terrorize her. So you get to feel what I'm feeling right now."

Amelia. It was the first time I heard her name out loud. Amelia.

He turned the frame back away from me. I had a bad feeling in my stomach now, hollow and raw. I hated the idea of her being afraid in her own house. Someone who had been through at least some of the same things I had been. Someone who could draw those drawings I had seen in her bedroom.

"Now, my son . . . Adam . . ." He picked up the other picture on the desk. This picture was twice as big, which should have told me something right there.

"He's on a full scholarship to Michigan State. My alma mater. He's already up there for summer conditioning."

He turned the frame so I could behold the full glory of his son. Adam was in his Lakeland uniform, kneeling on the ground with one hand on his helmet.

"I know what happened here," he said. "I know why you guys broke into this place. Why you felt you had to put that banner in Adam's bedroom. I mean, after four years of him beating your team up and down the field. Hell, it must have been pretty frustrating. I guess I can understand that part."

He actually smiled at that point, for the first time. He put Adam's picture back on the desk, carefully aligning it until it was in just the right place. Then he opened up a drawer in his desk and took out a small pad of paper and a golf pencil. He slid them over the desk until they were directly in front of me.

"So let me ask you something, Michael. You feel like writing some names down for me?"

He leaned back in his chair and began passing the exercise ball from one hand to the other.

"I know this didn't come out in court. This is just between you and me, is what I'm saying. It doesn't leave this room. I know that Brian Hauser was one of the gang who were with you that night. I mean, let's not even *pretend* that he wasn't here. Are we good so far?"

I sat there.

"That buddy of his, the quarterback . . . Trey Tollman? Who can't even throw a ball forty yards? Are we talking about him, too?"

Another moment of silence.

"They used to be friends, you know that? Adam and Brian, I mean, back when they were in junior high school."

He paused for a while, thinking about it.

"Then Brian goes to a different high school and starts taking cheap shots at Adam. You know he almost destroyed Adam's knee once? Could have ended his whole career. Funny how a kid can turn into an asshole so quickly. Guess it runs in the family. You ever meet his dad? The state trooper? Couple of useless fat fucks, both of them. Anyway, I know you took the rap for him, Mike. I know it and you know it. So like I said . . . just between you and me . . . Nod your head if I'm right so far."

This wasn't my battle. God knows none of those other guys ever thanked me for taking the blame for him. And yet . . .

"I'm waiting."

And yet fuck this guy. I wasn't moving a muscle.

"Come on, Mike. Don't be a chump. It's not worth it."

I can do this all day, I thought. I'll sit frozen in this chair while you keep talking.

"Okay," he finally said. "If that's the way you want to play this."

He stood up and came over to me. I still hadn't moved yet. I waited for him to put his hands around my neck.

"You know what? One phone call from me and they'll find something else to do with you. If I tell them you're not being a good little probationer here. You follow me? They'll send you to one of those camps with all the other juvies. I'm sure your little silent act will go over real big with those guys. Is that what you want?"

I finally looked up at him.

"You're putting me in a real difficult position here. I get you from what, noon to four, six days a week? So get your ass out of my chair and come outside."

I stood up and followed him. He led me through the kitchen, through the very same door I had opened with a screwdriver and a safety pin. He opened it and was about to head into the backyard. Then he stopped suddenly and looked at the doorknob.

"By the way . . . this was the door you came in through, right?"

I nodded.

"Was it unlocked?"

I shook my head.

"Then how the hell did you open it?"

I made like I was holding something in each hand.

"What, did you get a key somehow?"

I shook my head and made the motion again. Two hands. A tool in each.

"Are you telling me you picked the lock?"

I nodded.

He bent down and examined the knob. "You're lying. There's not a scratch on this thing."

Whatever you say, I thought. I'm lying.

"We're not getting off to a great start here," he said, almost laughing. "That's all I can say."

He stood there looking at me for a moment.

"Last chance. Are you going to tell me who else broke into my fucking house, or not?"

I didn't tell the police, I thought. Why the hell would I tell you?

"Okay, fine," he said. "I guess we've got to do this the hard way."

Twelve

Los Angeles
January 2000

The motorcycles went into the garage on the back end of Julian's lot. A gunmetal gray Saab came out. It seemed a little understated for this crew, but then maybe understated is exactly what you need sometimes.

We all got in the car. Julian driving, Ramona shotgun, me in the back with Gunnar and Lucy. Gunnar took the middle, keeping himself between me and Lucy, no doubt. An undercurrent I was already aware of, no matter that they were all six or seven years older than me, that he should have been looking at me like I was nothing more than a lost child.

It was late afternoon. The sun hanging over the ocean. We rode back toward Beverly Hills, but this time we cut north, heading up Laurel Canyon Boulevard, into the Hollywood Hills. The road twisted and turned as we went higher and higher. There were houses on either side of the road. Big money boxes. Bold statements of modern architecture. Some of them hanging off the edges of the cliffs, daring an earthquake to tip them over into the canyon below.

We passed Mulholland Drive, then a private gated road with a smartly dressed guard sitting in his little white guardhouse. Up another hairpin turn, then another. Julian pulled the car over onto the shoulder. Everyone got out. They seemed to know their parts in the play, exactly what they were supposed to be doing at every moment. Julian took a good look around, making sure we were out of anyone else's direct sight. He went right up to the edge of the gravel shoulder, where there was a dense growth of sage and chaparral and other hostile-looking plant life, all leading down into the canyon. Gunnar joined him on the edge. He gave Julian a quick hug, turned to give the rest of us a wave, and then disappeared into the brush.

Ramona scanned the canyon below us with a pair of binoculars. Julian produced a cell phone. While the two of them kept watching Gunnar's progress down the canyon, Lucy popped open the trunk.

"Here," she said, handing me the jack. "Make yourself useful."

I gestured to the wheels. Which one?

"Doesn't matter. Take your pick."

The right rear tire seemed to be on smooth level ground, so I hooked up the jack back there, put the tire iron in the slot, and started cranking. It was a solid idea, I realized. If somebody drove by, it would look perfectly natural for us to be here. We could even finish up and drive away if we really needed to, and then come back later.

"Our man's upstairs," Ramona said. "I don't see the bodyguard."

She kept watching. Julian stayed ready with the phone. I was ready to look busy with the tire if I heard a car coming up the road. Lucy was pacing now, muttering to herself. She looked more nervous than the rest of us put together.

Finally, the phone made a low buzzing sound and seemed to jump in Julian's hand. He pushed a button and listened.

"We're trying to locate the bodyguard," he said. "Just hang tight."

Ramona kept peering through the binoculars, moving them back and forth slowly.

"There," she finally said. "The guard's upstairs now."

I looked down the canyon and saw a residential road, about a quarter mile below us. On the far side of that road was another large ultramodern house, one of the most impressive of all. Nothing but shining metal and glass. The yard was gravel and Japanese topiary. A long black sedan sat in the horseshoe driveway, partly eclipsing the front door.

As I kept watching, I saw a figure crossing the road, moving quickly but not frantically. Hurrying but not rushing. He went around the car and stopped directly in front of the door.

"You're clear," Julian said into the phone.

Gunnar opened the door, stepped inside, and then closed the door behind him.

That's when I heard a car coming up the road. I tapped on the back of the trunk to alert the others. They hid the binoculars and the phone while I went around to the side of the car, as if inspecting the tire.

A little red Porsche rounded the curve, winding through its gears. I saw sunglasses, blond hair, and then the car was gone. The driver didn't even slow down.

Ramona went back to the binoculars.

"He's on his own now," she said. "Do you see anything?"

"No," Julian said. "I don't see anybody. Anywhere."

"Fuck fuck fuck."

"He's okay," Julian said. "You know he's okay."

"I'm sure that prick has a gun in the house."

"Gunnar's okay."

"I need a drink."

"That won't help."

"It won't help *you*."

"Guys, please," Lucy said to both of them. "Just shut up for a minute, okay?"

"He's okay," Julian said. "Everybody should stop freaking out here."

"I said shut up!"

That got everyone quiet for the next few minutes. I could only wonder how these guys could be the absolute best if they acted this way all the time. Lucy took the binoculars away from Ramona and peered down at the house. Julian kept scanning the landscape, looking at the other houses in the distance, no doubt wondering when someone would finally notice us all standing up here.

Then his phone buzzed again. He looked at it without answering it.

"He's in," he said. "He's okay."

"Let's get the hell out of here," Ramona said.

She pulled Lucy away from the edge and opened the back door for her. I pulled the jack off and put it in the trunk. A few seconds later, we were all in the car and Julian was spraying gravel as he pulled onto the road.

"Take it easy," Ramona said. "Don't get us killed, eh?"

"I hate this part so much," Lucy said. "We should all stay together. *All the time.*"

"This is the only way," Julian said. "He'll be fine."

"What time is it now?" Ramona said, looking at her watch.

"We've got a few hours to kill," Julian said. "Plenty of time to go get dressed."

"What about him?" Ramona said, looking over the seat at me.

"Yeah, we've got time for that, too," he said. "Michael, what do you say we go do a little shopping?"

I still didn't know how this was supposed to work. Gunnar had just sneaked into somebody's house, and the rest of us had apparently just abandoned him there. To go shopping.

Now, if it sounds like these guys were just leading me around by the nose, you've got to understand . . . I mean, yes, the Ghost had drilled the rules into my head. You're the specialist. Make sure you understand exactly what's going on before you commit to anything. If it doesn't feel right, you walk away. At the same time, he also told me that these guys on the other side of the white pager were as good as it gets. Unorthodox, yes, but money in the bank. So what was I supposed to do here? Right or wrong, I decided to let it play out. At least for the time being.

So there we were in Beverly Hills. Julian parked the car on Rodeo Drive, and they steered me into the first overpriced clothing store they could find.

"All right, let's do this right," Julian said. "Just trash him up and we'll get out of here."

I didn't know what he meant by that, but it didn't take long for me to find out. The two women dragged me off to the fashion suits and started holding them up to me like I was a dress-up doll. Lucy picked out a suit that was, I swear to God, the brightest red you could ever find in the universe of clothing.

"Hello?" Ramona said. "Black?"

"Black is too easy," Lucy said. "Use your imagination."

"He'll look like Santa Claus, babe. That's not quite the effect we're going for."

"He won't look like Santa Claus, he'll look like Satan. He'll look absolutely evil."

"We don't have all day," Julian said. "Just go with the black suit, okay? Lucy, go pick out a red shirt if you want."

So that's how I ended up with the European-cut black suit and skintight red shirt. No collar. Two gold chains. Thin leather black belt. Black leather shoes with no socks. There was no time to have the suit tailored, so it hung off of me a little bit. But Julian said that was just fine. He said it added to the effect.

He paid for the clothes, and I'll just say one thing about that. Forget being a professional safecracker. Just open a clothing store in Beverly Hills. The working conditions are a lot better, and you'll make a lot more money.

Then they hustled me over to a hair salon and asked one of the stylists to give me a quick once-over. He looked at me and my do-it-yourself haircut and said I was unsalvageable. Julian laid a wad of twenties on him, and he suddenly got a little more motivated.

"Okay, last thing," Julian said when we were back on the sidewalk. He took my cheap sunglasses off and threw them into a garbage barrel. Then we went into a fashion "eyewear" store, and the women had their second fight of the afternoon, this time over my new sunglasses. At least I had served to distract them for a while from poor Gunnar stuck in that house in the canyon.

Finally, with a new pair of ridiculously priced gold-rimmed sunglasses over my eyes, they all looked at me and had me turn around a couple of times. I was pronounced acceptable. We got in the car and took off back to the house in Santa Monica.

I sat in a chair feeling disoriented and quite freaked out actually while the rest of the gang went off to get dressed. Here's where I wish I could talk, I thought to myself. Yeah, here's where talking would be especially useful. So would getting up and walking out the door, for that matter.

Julian came down the stairs, looking even more dressed to kill than I was. His fashion suit was the color of freshly poured cream. He had a purple silk shirt with an actual collar, and the whole outfit looked like it had been especially created and tucked and tailored just for him. He had a bottle of cologne with him. He put some on his hands and slapped my cheeks.

"You're looking sharp," he said. "You're looking like you belong in this town."

He washed his hands in the kitchen sink. Then he poured a couple of glasses of red wine and handed me one. He didn't sit down. He went to the window, looked outside, went to the kitchen, and looked at the clock. Then he went back to the window.

Another half hour passed. Finally, both of the women came down together, their high heels clicking on the stairs. Ramona was in black, Lucy in a dark shimmering burgundy. Skintight, lots of leg, lots of chest. Hair pinned up. Lipstick and long dark eyelashes. Eye shadow almost glowing. Lucy looked especially transformed with all the makeup. The unevenness of her eyes was even more pronounced now, but somehow it made her bone-chillingly beautiful.

Julian looked at them and smiled. "What do you think?" he said to me. "Do they pass?"

"How long has it been?" Lucy said. "Gunnar must be going crazy by now."

"You know how he is," Julian said. "He's the Zen master."

"Let's just go. I can't stand waiting."

We all piled back into the Saab. It was dark now. A cool Thursday night in January in Los Angeles. We rolled down Santa Monica Boulevard again. The traffic was even heavier now. The weekend had already begun, or so it would seem.

Julian turned north and took us right into the heart of Hollywood. A right on Sunset Boulevard, past nightclub after nightclub, all with long lines out front. Eventually, he pulled into a parking lot, just past Vine Street. He chose a spot right near the street and parked nose facing out.

"Okay," he said. "Game faces on. Michael? Just act bored. That's all you have to do."

We got out of the car. Like all the other clubs on Sunset Boulevard, this one had a long line of people waiting to get in. Everybody dressed to kill. Julian led us right to the front of the line. There was a bouncer standing there, a prototypically cast-iron man bulging out of his shirt. He took one look at Julian, gave him a little nod, opened the ropes, and let him in. He gave Ramona and Lucy the same little nod. I got a quick once-over, but he didn't stop me. I took a look back at the people waiting in line as we walked past them. Nobody seemed especially happy to see us waltz through, but nobody looked ready to start a riot over it, either.

As soon as we got inside, my ears were assaulted by the music. The relentless, pounding beat you could feel right up your legs, into your gut. The lights were flashing from every direction. Spotlights and lasers, all in perfect time with the beat of the music. We were still twenty feet from the dance floor, but Julian had his hands up in the air already. He edged his way through the crowd to the back corner of the room, where a tight spiral staircase led up to the balcony level. There was another bouncer at the top of the stairs. Like the first one, he gave Julian a nod and let us go past.

Most of the tables up here on the balcony were already taken. The rich and famous and beautiful. Or so I gathered. They didn't look any different to me than the people downstairs. Julian went to the corner table, in its own little cage like one of those private boxes in an old theater. He unhooked the rope and let us into the cage. There was just enough room for the four of us.

A hundred people were all dancing right below us, as if for our entertainment. The lights kept painting everything red then yellow then blue then green. I sat there, drinking it all in. Wondering what the hell was going on. Wondering how the hell this had anything to do with Gunnar sneaking inside that house up in the canyons.

"Drinks, ladies? Michael?"

Ramona and Lucy wanted champagne to start off the evening. I shrugged my shoulders. Champagne, whatever. I'm fine.

There was a little button set into the frame of the cage. Julian pressed it, and about five seconds later, a woman dressed in what looked like a black wetsuit unzipped halfway down her chest came calling.

Julian ordered a bottle of Cristal, and she was gone. Two minutes later, she came back with a bottle, an ice bucket, and four champagne flutes. She popped the bottle and poured. Then it was time for the toast. Julian looked into Ramona's eyes and said five words.

"A la Mano de Dios."

We all drank to that. Then Julian settled back into his chair and watched the dancing crowd, moving his shoulders to the beat. Finally, a dark figure appeared and leaned into our cage.

"So the party can begin now!"

He was tall and thin. His suit was dark gray with pinstripes. White shirt with the top three buttons undone. His hair was tied back in a tight ponytail. Somewhere in the ocean, a shark was missing its cold eyes because this man had them.

Julian stood up, shook the man's hand and did the half-body hug. The man kissed Ramona's hand, then went for Lucy's. Then he got to me.

"Do I have the pleasure of finally meeting your friend?"

"Indeed you do. Wesley, this is Mikhail. All the way from Moscow."

"I'm honored," he said. "I hope you had a good trip."

"He doesn't speak any English," Julian said. "He refuses to learn even a single word."

That seemed to impress the man profoundly. "I hope you'll enjoy the hospitality of my club tonight," he said, shaking my hand. "Even though I realize you have no idea what the fuck I'm saying."

He laughed at his own joke. Then he whispered something into Julian's ear. Then he was gone.

"You made an impression," Julian said to me. "He thinks you're beautiful, too."

"Americans are suckers for Russians," Ramona said.

Just roll with it, I thought. For once, I'm glad I can't say the wrong thing.

Julian took a sip of champagne, then looked at his watch.

"Now that we know our man Wesley is on the premises . . ."

"Let's go," Lucy said, standing up and taking my hand. "You and me."

Julian and Ramona stayed in their seats. As I stood up, I spotted our host on the other side of the balcony, putting the power schmooze on another table. I nodded toward him, and Julian gave me a little smile.

"Yes," he said. "That's the man we're taking down tonight."

Thirteen

Michigan
July 1999

Mr. Marsh led me out into his backyard. I had been there once before, of course, but it had been dark then, and I hadn't really been paying much attention to the landscaping. In the bright light of day, I could see that the grass had recently been planted, a thousand green shoots poking their way up through a thin layer of straw. There was about a half acre or so, ending in a line of trees that looked like part of an old apple orchard.

"You guys didn't do my new grass any favors, either," he said, pointing to a wide patch of new straw. "I should have waited and made you fix it."

I looked down and saw four different sets of footprints.

"Anyway, if you really want to take this rap all by yourself, you're going to be mighty lonely back here."

Meaning what, exactly?

He walked out into the yard, stopping about twenty yards from the house. He picked up a shovel he had apparently left there. It was brand-new, with a yellow fiberglass handle and a shiny blade that had yet to touch dirt. A few yards away was a wheelbarrow with the price tag still taped to one of its handles.

"They asked me to have some sort of work for you to do for me," he said. "Four hours a day, six days a week. For the rest of the summer. That's a lot of time."

He handed me the shovel.

"I marked it out," he said. "Make sure you follow the lines exactly."

I had no idea what he was talking about. Until I noticed the length of twine at his feet. It was strung along a series of wooden pegs, one inch above the straw. I followed the line, maybe thirty feet or so until it took a right turn. Then three more right turns to complete a large rectangle.

"Don't worry about depth yet. Just start and we'll see how it looks, eh? When you fill up the wheelbarrow, just take it over to that spot by the trees and dump it."

This was going to be a swimming pool. The man actually expected me to dig him a swimming pool in his backyard.

"There's a plastic jug over there by the faucet," he said. "That's how you get your water. You need to take a piss, you use the woods. I'll let you know when it's four o'clock. Any questions?"

He waited for a few seconds, as if I'd actually say something.

"Let's get one more thing straight here," he said. "You're dealing directly with me and nobody else. You don't step foot in the house unless I tell you to. As far as my daughter goes, well, I'm just hoping that if she sees you working back here, maybe she'll realize you're not so terrifying. You hear what I'm saying? I want her to see that you're just a cheap punk and not a monster so she can sleep at night. Beyond that you have nothing to do with her. If I see you so much as look at her sideways, I will kill you. You got that?"

I held the shovel. I looked at him. I felt the sun beating down on my back.

"My son, on the other hand . . . like I said, he's already up in East Lansing, so you probably won't get to meet him. You better pray you don't, actually, because if he ever comes home and sees you . . . let's just say I won't have to worry about killing you anymore."

He stopped, shook his head, and did a bad job fighting off a smile.

"I'll be out later to check on you," he said. "Remember, one word from me and you get sent to the juvie camp. So you sure as hell better get digging."

I watched him walk away from me. He didn't look back. When he opened the door and disappeared, I just stood there for a while, looking around me at the great rectangle marked in the grass and straw. There wasn't a single cloud to pass above me. No trees to offer their shade. I swallowed hard and dug my shovel into the ground. I lifted a small mound of dirt and carried it over to the wheelbarrow. The dirt hit with a hollow thump.

One down. Seven million to go.

There are prison programs where you leave the grounds for a few hours every day to help out on some kind of project or other. Clearing out debris from a demolition, say, or maybe even helping to build something if you have the skills. It's a chance to get out of the prison, ride a bus down a real street, see real women walking along on the sidewalk, then to actually do something constructive when you get there. Most inmates would gladly stick a knife in someone else's back to get that kind of assignment.

It's not like in the old days, like when they made the prisoners themselves build Sing Sing from the ground up. With regular whippings for anyone who didn't pull their weight. No, they just don't do that kind of thing anymore. No more backbreaking labor. No more rock piles and sledgehammers. No more whippings. They sure as hell don't stick you in the middle of a field by yourself and tell you to start digging a swimming pool. That kind of cruel and unusual punishment would get a modern warden fired by the end of the first day.

But I wasn't in a prison. I was here in the Marshes' backyard and would be here everyday except Sundays. For the rest of the summer. I didn't think I had much choice in the matter. I sure as hell didn't want to find out if that juvie camp was an idle threat. So I put the shovel back in the ground, pushed down with my foot, lifted the dirt, and threw it into the wheelbarrow.

I kept going. I filled the wheelbarrow, rolled it over to the edge of the woods, and dumped it. I rolled it back and picked up the shovel again. While filling up the second load, I started to hit rocks. Some of them were big enough I had to shut everything down and spend the next few minutes working around it, until I finally got enough leverage to pry the damned thing free. My hands were starting to hurt already. My back, too. I was pretty sure I hadn't even been digging for half an hour yet.

The sun was punishing me. I put down the shovel, took the plastic water jug over to the house, and turned on the faucet. The cold water felt good on my hands. I knelt down and splashed my face with it. Then I filled the jug and took a long drink. When I turned off the faucet, I could hear Mr. Marsh from inside the house. He was yelling at someone. I didn't hear anybody respond, so I figured he must be yelling into the phone. I couldn't make out the words. Only the anger.

Probably wouldn't be a great idea to have him come out right now, I thought, see me sitting here by the house. I took the jug back with me and started digging again. I could see that I was barely making a dent in the ground. This would have to be something not to think about. At all. Just turn off your brain, I told myself, and keep digging.

Another half hour passed. Another few loads of dirt, moved from inside the stakes to the growing pile at the edge of the woods. The sweat was starting to sting my eyes. I didn't see Mr. Marsh come out of the house. All of a sudden, he was just standing there behind me.

"You're going to destroy your back," he said to me. "You won't last two days like that."

I stopped and looked at him. He was holding a drink, some kind of summer cocktail with fruit and lots of ice.

"Use your legs," he said. "Keep your back straight and use your god-damned legs. Then you *might* last three days."

I pushed the shovel into the ground, bending with my knees. I hit another big rock.

"You can't do this by yourself. You know that."

I wiped off my face, then started working around the rock. This felt like the biggest one yet.

"You're being a fool," Mr. Marsh said. He took a long sip from his glass and squinted as he looked up at the sky. "This sun will kill you. Are you listening to me?"

I stopped and looked up at him.

"You give up the others, I'm telling you . . . I'll let you sit out here under an umbrella."

I went back to work on the rock.

"Fine, keep digging," he said. "Let me know when you're ready to reconsider."

He walked back into the house, shaking his head. I spent the next twenty minutes hauling out a rock the size of a basketball. Things got a little hazy after that. I remember two birds high above me. I could hear one of the birds screaming at the other. When I looked up, I saw that the screaming bird was chasing a much bigger bird, drawing jagged shapes against the blue sky. The bigger bird could have flown away, or it could have turned on the smaller bird and knocked it out of the game entirely. It didn't seem to want to do either, maybe as a point of pride. The smaller bird kept after it, screaming those same notes over and over again.

You cannot do that, a voice coming from somewhere inside my over-heated head. Never mind the flying. You can't even make a sound like that. The most elemental thing that any bird or lowly animal can do . . . it is beyond your abilities.

I started to hit roots, as thick as my arm. I hit them with the sharp edge of the shovel but could not cut them. I stopped and went to refill the water jug. I put my head under the faucet and shocked myself with the electric coldness of the water. I didn't get up for a while. I sat there until I looked up and saw Mr. Marsh looking at me through the back window. His arms were folded and he had a look on his face that didn't need any interpretation. I got up and went back to work.

Another hour passed. I didn't slow down, but there was a strange yellowish tint to everything I was seeing, and the birds above me seemed to turn into vultures. Watching me. Waiting. I kept digging in that one little corner of the rectangle, getting down as deep as I could in that one spot so it would actually look like I was getting somewhere. I knew on some gut level that if I spread out my efforts too much, I'd just end up scraping the top two inches off of everything. And that would make me lose my mind.

The dizziness came next. Every time I bent my head down, I felt like I was going to pass out. I could feel the sun burning right through my shirt. I kept drinking, going back to work, drinking, going back. I didn't hear her as she came up behind me. I didn't notice her at all until I turned to reach for the water jug and saw her black sneakers. I looked up, at faded blue jeans with holes in the knees, at a blinding white shirt that gathered around her shoulders and made her look like she belonged on a pirate ship. At her face. Amelia's face, for the first time in real life. Not a drawing, not a photograph.

Her eyes were dark brown, her hair was light brown. Kind of a mess, like mine, but maybe only half as curly. More like an unruly mop she'd have to push away from her eyes just to get a good look at you. A permanent set to her mouth like she'd just won an argument with you.

I'm making her sound pretty ordinary here. A normal seventeen-year-old, maybe a little un-put-together yet, going through one of those phases, never smiling, never brushing her hair. If you think you have the general picture, then I don't think I'm doing her justice. Because there was something above and beyond about her, something I could see right away, even as she was standing there at the edge of the hole shading her eyes from the sun.

Of course, I know that seeing her drawings first was a big part of it. I mean, how could it not be? It was just a gut instinct at this point, this feeling that there was definitely something different about her. That maybe she'd seen some of the same things I'd seen.

Crazy, I know. Impossible to know so much about someone from just a few drawings, before you even meet them in person. Now here she was, about to say her first words to me.

"You are so full of shit. Do you know that?"

I kept standing there, looking at her. I can't imagine what a sight I must have been. Hair even messier than hers, dirt and sweat all over my face. Like some medieval street urchin.

"I already heard about you," she said. "I mean before you broke into our house. You're the guy from Milford High School who doesn't talk, right?"

I didn't answer. I mean, not with a nod or a shake of the head. I looked at the way the sun made her skin glow.

"Because . . . why? What's the deal with that? Because something happened to you when you were a little kid?"

I couldn't move.

"I can see right through you. Your silent act there. Because believe me . . . you want to talk about things happening to you when you're a kid? We could exchange a few stories someday."

A sound from somewhere, a glass door sliding shut with a bang.

"Or no, maybe not. You'd have to drop the act then, right?"

Her father rushing across the grass now, slipping on the loose straw and nearly falling on his face.

"Nice job on the break-in, too," she said. "That was real smooth."

"Amelia!" Her father grabbing her by the arm. "Get away from him!"

"I'm just seeing what he looks like," she said. "The big bad criminal."

"Get in the house. Right now."

"All right, all right! Relax!" She shook her arm free and went back toward the house. She turned and looked back at me for one second. I couldn't tell what she was thinking, but I did know one thing. What Mr. Marsh had said about her, about how traumatized she was by just the thought of me breaking into her house? About how terrified she was?

Somehow, I wasn't getting that from her.

"I warned you," he said to me. "Did I not warn you?"

Well, yes, I thought. You did warn me.

"If I ever see you . . ."

Then he ran off the rails. What was he going to say? If I ever see you talking to her? Just standing there like you're made of stone while she insults you?

"Look, this isn't going to work," he said. "Can we just cut through the bullshit right now? You don't want to come here every day and do this, do you?"

I looked past him. Amelia was standing next to the sliding door. She was watching me. I picked up the shovel and pushed it into the dirt.

"Yeah, okay," he said. "If that's the way you want it. Looks like you're making some progress on the shallow end here, eh? Just wait until you get to the deep end."

He turned to walk away from me. Then he stopped.

"You've got one more hour out here," he said. "I expect sixty minutes. Not fifty-nine. That's all I'm gonna say."

I carried the shovelful to the wheelbarrow and threw it in.

"Last chance," he said. "I mean seriously, I know I keep saying it, but this is seriously your last chance. You come in right now, you write down the names, and we're good. You hear me? That's all it takes."

What I did next . . . I don't know where it came from. It's not something I'd normally do, not in a million years. Maybe only after digging a hole for three straight hours on a hot summer day, while some middle-aged rich jackass wearing tight shorts gives me one last chance for the seventh time. I made an *F* sign with my left hand, a *K* with my right, brought them together, and then made like I was throwing the whole thing right at his face. Sure, there might be simpler ways to say it. Hell, you can do it with one finger on one hand. But if five years of sign language taught me anything, it was how to do things like this with a little more style.

Then I turned my back on him and rolled the wheelbarrow over to the woods.

"What was that?" he yelled after me. "What the hell was that supposed to be, you stupid little freak?"

He was gone when I came back. I didn't see Amelia anywhere, either. I kept looking at the house for the next hour, but she didn't appear.

I finished up at four o'clock. Then I left. I tried to keep her face in my mind as I drove home. I went right to my drawing paper and tried to capture it. I had such a talent for drawing from memory, after all. That was my "mutant gift," as Mr. Martie called it, being able to re-create every detail, just starting with the basic shape and letting it all come back to me.

Today I couldn't do it. For the first time ever, I couldn't draw somebody's face. I kept trying and failing and wadding up the paper and trying again. You're too tired, I told myself. You can barely keep your eyes open. So I gave up and went to bed.

Waking up the next morning . . . biggest mistake of my life. My back was so tight, I literally had to roll myself out of bed. My legs were sore. My arms were sore. But nothing, and I mean nothing, has ever hurt as much as my hands hurt that morning.

I couldn't open them, for one thing. I couldn't completely close them, either. Then I took a shower and just about went through the ceiling when the hot water hit my blisters. When I was dressed, I rummaged around in the back room of the liquor store and found an old pair of work gloves. Better late than never, I figured. Uncle Lito took one look at me and just about fainted.

"What the hell did they do to you?" he said. "Your face is as red as a lobster. I'm going to call that stupid probation officer right now. Hell, I'm calling the judge."

I grabbed him by the shoulders, which surprised the living hell out of him. I grabbed him and my shook my head. I didn't want him to call anybody or do anything else that would stop me from going back to the Marshes' house that day. I had to see her again, no matter what.

I ate something just so I'd have a little energy, got in the car, and drove over to the Marshes' house, trying to loosen up my hands as I drove. It was a few minutes after noon when I got there. Mr. Marsh was waiting for me in the driveway.

"You're late," he said. "Come with me."

Yeah, yeah, I thought, back to the pool. Just tell me that your daughter will be home again today.

"I want you to meet somebody."

He led me around to the back of the house. There was a man there, kneeling by the door.

"This is Mr. Randolph," Mr. Marsh said. "He's a locksmith."

The locksmith stood up and adjusted his baseball cap. "Mr. Marsh tells me you opened this lock," he said. "I don't see a scratch on it. So I'm calling bullshit." He had a slight Eastern European accent, so bullshit came out as "bullsheet."

"How about it?" Mr. Marsh said. "You want to show us how you did it?"

I put my hands up in surrender. No, I don't.

"It was open," the locksmith said. "Am I right? This door was open so you walked right in."

I should have let it go. Instead I shook my head and made a gesture like I was picking an imaginary lock in the air.

"Come off it," the locksmith said, sneaking a wink at Mr. Marsh. "There's no way you could pick this lock. It would take me quite a bit of work to do it myself."

"Let him prove it," Mr. Marsh said. "Let him put his money where his mouth is."

The locksmith started laughing. "I'll bet you a hundred dollars cash. Real American money, right here on the spot."

"You're not taking my money today," Mr. Marsh said. Then he turned to me. "But I'll tell you what, Michael. You open that lock, and I'll give you the day off. Okay? You up for that? Open it right now and you can go home."

"Here, you can even use my tools," the locksmith said. He pulled out what looked like a large wallet and handed it to me. "Best in the business."

I unzipped the leather case and opened it. I stood there for a moment looking at the contents. I had never seen such a beautiful collection of tools.

"You know how to use them, don't you? Come on, show us your stuff."

There were at least a dozen lock picks to choose from. Three different diamond picks, two ball picks, one double ball pick, at least four or five hook picks. I didn't know their names yet. I wouldn't learn that until later.

"Okay, make that a thousand dollars," the locksmith said. "I'll give you ten to one odds." He was about to take the case back from me, but I turned away from him and took out one of the hook picks. There were four different tension bars, so I knelt down next to the lock and tried to guess which size would work best. I had never had to make such a choice before. It had always been whatever hunk of scrap metal I had on hand.

I took out one of the tension bars. Not the smallest, not the biggest. I slid it into the bottom of the keyhole. I put one finger on the right side and pushed it ever so slightly. Then I took the hook pick and felt along the line of tumblers. I had already done this lock before, of course, so I knew exactly where to go. It was a very basic setup, six pins, one tight combination in the back but otherwise nothing too tricky. It had taken me all of three minutes with a screwdriver and a bent safety pin. With these perfect tools—hell, it wouldn't take me more than thirty seconds.

"He seems to know what he's doing," Mr. Marsh said. "You don't suppose . . ."

"No freaking way," the locksmith said. He wasn't smiling now. "I promise you."

I popped the back pin, worked my way carefully past the fifth. With the good tension bar, it was so much easier to keep the last pin engaged. I felt that satisfying little click with each pin as I made my way to the front. I could feel that I had it halfway done. With the mushroom pins, I knew I had to go back and do them all one more time. There were just the tiniest slivers of metal standing in my way now. Six little notches on six little pins, and then the whole thing would turn free.

The two men were quiet now. I worked my way through the pins again, back to front. I was about to pop that last pin when something made me stop.

Think about this, I thought to myself. Do you really want to prove to these guys that you can break into this house whenever you feel like it? Into *any* house? Is that the kind of thing you want everybody to know?

"Is that it?" Mr. Marsh said. "Are you giving up already?"

"Playtime's over," the locksmith said. A sneer on his face. "Remember this the next time you feel like shooting off your mouth."

Not the right thing to say to me, I thought. I looked the locksmith in the eye as I tapped up that last pin. I turned the knob, opened the door, and gave him back his tools.

Then I put my gloves on and went into the backyard to start digging.

I could hear Mr. Marsh and the locksmith having it out as I picked up the shovel and got to work. Within a few minutes, the locksmith was gone and it was just Mr. Marsh standing there watching me. He had a drink in his hand now. I filled my first wheelbarrow of the day, then rolled it to the woods to dump it. When I came back, he was gone.

It was a little hotter today. I went to fill up the water jug at the faucet. When the water stopped flowing, I could hear Mr. Marsh yelling into the phone again, just like he had done the day before. It may seem like an obvious point, but it was something I realized that day. Do not trust anyone, ever, if you hear them yelling into a telephone.

I spent the next two hours digging and rolling the wheelbarrow and wondering if I'd be able to make it through the day. I felt weaker than the day before. There was no way around that. I knew it was a simple matter of biology and physics. Eventually, I wouldn't be able to do this anymore. It wasn't even a question of pacing myself. I mean, you can only save so much energy when you're digging a hole. Anything less than the basic minimum effort and you're not even digging anymore.

Everything started to turn yellow again, my eyes too tired or too burned by the sun or God knows what. I kept the water jug full and kept drinking as much as I could.

You will collapse, I told myself. This will happen as surely as the sun rises in the east. You will collapse, and they will come and revive you. After a few days of recovery, you'll go to that juvie farm Mr. Marsh was talking about. They won't work you as hard there. Hell, they wouldn't work you this hard *anywhere*. But it'll be so much worse in so many ways. On top of everything else, you'll never see Amelia again.

"I don't know why you're doing this."

I turned around and saw her standing there. That same place on the edge of what would someday be her swimming pool. Today she was wearing cut-off denim shorts that went down to her knees. The same black tennis shoes. White shins and ankles in the bright sunlight. A black T-shirt with some sort of cartoon machine gun on it. It was way too hot to be wearing anything black today.

I stopped digging and wiped my face.

"You'll never dig this whole thing. It would take you a year. Even if you did, so what? You think we're ever going to use a pool back here?"

Extra motivation for me, I thought. Thank you so much. But God you are so beautiful.

"Adam's away to college already. I'll be gone after one more year. Who the hell's going to use it?"

I stood there while she looked around and shook her head and then finally got to the point.

"So are you going to talk today, or what?"

I pushed the shovel into the dirt so that it could stand on its own.

"I'm calling your bluff. Okay? I know you can talk if you want to. So say something."

I reached around to my back pocket and took out the pad of paper and pencil. I know you probably think this was a normal thing for me, having something to write on at all times. Seriously, though, I hardly ever did it then, and still don't. I just don't like writing impromptu notes to people in lieu of real conversation. *I'm sorry, I cannot speak, so I'll write down everything I need to say to you right here on this handy notepad that I carry with me for just such an occasion! Thank you for your patience as I make you stand there with a slightly bemused look on your face while I carefully write down each word so you can then read it and pretend that we're communicating like two normal human beings.*

To hell with that.

But today was different. I had the pad in my pocket just in case I got into exactly this situation. I opened the pad and started writing.

I really cannot talk. I promise you. Really.

I handed her the piece of paper. She took two seconds to read it, then held her hand out for the pencil. Which didn't make any sense, of course, because there was no reason for the writing to be anything other than a one-way process. I gave it to her anyway.

She held the paper down against her thigh and started writing on it. "Amelia!"

A voice from the house, interrupting her writing as I watched the way her hair hung down as she bent over. Mr. Marsh, no doubt, on his way out to warn me off again.

But no. A younger voice. He was approaching from the house, someone our age, wearing an Oriental jacket, baggy pants. Ridiculously way too hot for this weather. Long hair tied together in the back, not just a ponytail, mind you, but with enough ties to make it look like a braid. Smug know-it-all face. A total good-for-nothing prick, I knew it from the first second I saw him. The next second bringing the sick realization, like a horse kicking me right in the stomach, that this was Amelia's boyfriend.

"What are you doing back here?" he said. "Aren't you supposed to be staying away from the criminal?" No genuine worry in his voice. More a double-edged insult, that I was a criminal but a criminal not worth taking seriously. I was already fighting the urge to hit him in the face with the shovel.

"I was just asking him a question," Amelia said. "I thought you were at the gallery."

"It was just boring today. Is anybody home?"

"I don't know. I think my dad went out."

"Is that right?"

"Don't get any ideas. He could be back any second."

"His car's loud enough. We'll hear him."

"I told you, Zeke . . ."

The conversation stalled for a moment. This intimate back and forth I was forced to listen to, and on top of that now the utter ridiculousness of his name. Zeke!

"Come on," he said. "Leave the miscreant to his digging."

"His name is Michael," she said.

"Whatever."

She crumpled up the piece of paper she had been writing on and threw it toward me. Then she walked off with him. She paused to look back over her shoulder at me, until Zeke put a hand on the small of her back. When they were gone, I picked up the paper. She had crossed out my words. Below them she had written her own.

When's the last time you tried?

That was a hard day. It really was. I mean, aside from my hands hurting and my back hurting and feeling like I was two minutes away from heatstroke. I was digging a rich man's pool, working like a slave behind the kind of house I'd never live in. And Amelia . . . who made me ache. If only there was some way to get through to her. To make her see that I wasn't really a criminal. Or a freak.

There's only one way, I thought. I have to draw something for her. No matter how hard I have to work at it, it's my only chance.

Somehow, that thought gave me the energy to keep digging for that last hour. I rolled the last wheelbarrow over to the woods, rolled it back by the hole, which was actually starting to look like a real hole now after eight total hours on the job. I put the shovel in the wheelbarrow and went around to the front of the house. That's when I got my first look at Zeke's car sitting there in the driveway. It was a cherry red BMW convertible. The top was down, so I could see the black leather seats and the stick shift gleaming in the sun. Then, just a few feet away, the old two-toned Grand Marquis with the rust along the edges.

When I got home, I didn't go into the liquor store. I didn't want Uncle Lito to see me and start threatening to call the judge again. I went right into the house. I took a shower. I ate something. Then I sat down to draw.

I had failed so miserably the night before. Trying to capture Amelia on a piece of paper . . . it seemed impossible.

You were trying too hard, I thought. You were turning her into the Mona Lisa. Just draw her like you'd draw anyone else, like she wasn't someone who made you sick whenever you looked at her.

I was still going at midnight. I was so tired, but I was so close now. Maybe that's what I needed, to be so wiped out I could barely see straight. To have to do it all by gut instinct. Just move the pencil and let it come out.

In the drawing, she was standing on the edge of the hole. She was wearing her cutoff shorts and her black tennis shoes and her black T-shirt with the machine gun on it. Her hair all over the place. One arm across her body, holding her other arm near the elbow. Her body language a mixed signal. Her eyes slightly downward. Looking at me but not really looking.

Yes. This was better. I was getting her now. More importantly, I was getting how I *felt* about her. How I saw her in my mind's eye. This was almost passable.

Now all I had to do was to figure out how to get it to her. Could I roll it up, keep it in my pants somehow? Or maybe if I put it in a big envelope, keep it flat. No matter what, I had to have it right there with me, ready to give to her if I saw my chance.

Yes, that's it. If you're patient, the chance will come. For now, take your wreck of a body to bed and get some sleep so you'll be ready for another day.

When I got up the next morning, I felt just as bad as the day before but no worse. I ate something. Then I drove to the Marshes' house. This whole idea with the drawing, it had seemed like the perfect plan at midnight. Now in the light of day I couldn't help wondering if it was a big mistake. But what the hell, right? What did I have to lose?

I got there on time. The drawing was in a large brown envelope, under my shirt, flat against my back. I figured I could take it out and hide it in the woods on my first trip with the wheelbarrow. Leave it out there so it wouldn't get ruined by my sweat. Then if Amelia stopped by at any point during the afternoon, I could go get it for her. I just hoped to God that she'd actually take it from me. That she'd open the envelope and look at it. I didn't think that was too much to ask.

Mr. Marsh was waiting for me. He had the locksmith with him. Not again, I thought. This I do not need today.

"You remember Randolph," Mr. Marsh said to me.

I nodded. The locksmith had a knowing little smile on his face today, like he had a little present for me and couldn't wait for me to open it.

"Come around back again," Mr. Marsh said. "If you don't mind."

I didn't get the feeling that I had a choice in the matter. So I followed them. The locksmith's toolbox was sitting by the back door. The old lock had been taken apart and lay in pieces on the ground. The shiny new lock was in place now, waiting for me.

"The tools, if you will," Mr. Marsh said.

The locksmith took out the same leather case from the day before and slapped it in my open hand.

"How do you feel about serrated pins, kid?"

Serrated pins? That was a new one on me.

"You're giving it away," Mr. Marsh said. "I thought this was supposed to be your big demonstration."

"I'm not worried," the locksmith said, smiling at me. "If he's never done 'em before, knowing what's in there ain't gonna help him."

I opened the case and took out the hook pick and one of the tension bars. If I bend down to do this, I thought, is he going to see the envelope stuck to my back? Maybe I should just give up right now, concede defeat, and go grab the shovel.

"Go ahead," Mr. Marsh said. "What are you waiting for?"

I had to make a show of it, at least. Take a minute to work the lock, making sure my shirt didn't ride up in back. Then stand up and give the locksmith his tools. That was my on-the-spot plan. So I got down on one knee, set the tension bar, and got to work. It didn't take long to feel out each of the six pins. Hell, I thought, this lock doesn't feel any harder than the last one. In fact, the pins weren't very tight at all. No high-low-high-low to make things tricky. I worked from the back, feeling each pin set. It was too easy. When I got to the front pin, I didn't think the plug would turn yet. If these weren't plain block pins, as surely they weren't, there would be a false set on each and I'd have to go back and do each pin again. I kept the tension just right, went back and felt the back pin go up another fraction of a millimeter. Then the one in front of that, and so on until I was back at the front pin.

Okay, here's where you might want to think about what you're doing, I thought. Don't even set the front pin. Just throw your hands up, shake your head, give the locksmith his tools. Let him think he beat you with this lock. Let Mr. Marsh think he's finally got a door that I can't open. Stop having to go through this every day, especially if you plan on smuggling in any more drawings under your shirt.

"I told you he wouldn't be able to open it," the locksmith said.

"It's a shame," Mr. Marsh said. "I was beginning to think this kid could actually do something impressive."

I looked up at the two of them. At their self-satisfied smiles. Then I went back to what I was doing. I pushed up the front pin. I felt it set. Now the plug turns and I'm done.

Except it didn't.

I took the tools out of the lock, feeling the pins fall back into place while the locksmith laughed over my shoulder. I held up one hand to silence him, put the tools back in the keyhole, and started again. Back to front. Set a pin, then the next. I knew these were false sets. I knew I had to go back and bump each pin one more time. This is how a good lock works. False sets, real sets, open.

I got to the front pin again, felt it go up just enough. It was right there now. Every pin should be in place. The plug should turn.

It didn't. The fucking thing didn't turn.

"Never send a boy to do a man's job," the locksmith said. "Did I or did I not say that to you?"

"You did," Mr. Marsh said. "But come on, it's not like you just beat a world-class jewel thief or something."

"Maybe not, but upholding the integrity of my craft—that's a big deal in my book, any day of the week."

"Whatever you say. Just take your tools so the kid can go dig his hole."

I tried to wave him off so I could give the lock one more go, but he grabbed the tools out of my hand. "Just give it up," he said. "This isn't a toy. You can't open it. It's guaranteed punk-proof."

I stood there looking at the door, at the shiny new lock plate. I didn't want to move.

"Go on, get to work," Mr. Marsh said to me. "Playtime is over."

I kept replaying it in my mind as I finally walked away. Each movement in that lock seemed so clear. There was no way I could have overset any of the pins.

My head was pounding. I couldn't breathe.

For the first time, I had tried to open a lock, and I had failed.

Fourteen
Los Angeles
January 2000

There was another staircase leading down to a back door of the club, apparently for use by VIPs only. Lucy opened the door, and we were back out in the parking lot. The night was cooler now, a light wind coming in off the ocean.

We got in the car. I sat up front next to her. She pulled out onto Vine Street.

"You're doing okay," she said. "Just keep it up. Stay cool."

She drove back down Sunset Boulevard, then took a hard right and headed up into the hills. We retraced our route from earlier that day, up Laurel Canyon Boulevard. We took the same turn and stopped in the exact same spot. Now that it was dark, the whole city was lit up and spread out below us as far as the eye could see.

"Get out," she said to me.

She waited for me to come around the car, to where she was standing.

"Take your clothes off."

Excuse me?

"You don't want to mess up the new outfit, do you?" She popped the trunk and took out a pair of jet black coveralls. Then she waited while I took off the suit jacket, the shirt, the pants.

"Shoes, too. I've got a couple pairs here you can try on."

She took my clothes and put them in the backseat. I was standing there on the side of the road in nothing but my underwear. She looked me up and down before handing me the coveralls and a pair of black running shoes. When I was all dressed up in my new simple black, she took my sunglasses right off my face.

"Gunnar will have the phone," she said. "He'll call me when you guys are finished. If he can't for some reason, take the phone from him and press the number nine. That'll ring me and I'll know to come get you. If I don't hear anybody talking, I'll know it's an emergency, in which case I'll find some way to come directly to the house. No matter what I have to do to get there. Do you understand?"

I nodded.

"What button?"

I put up nine fingers.

"Good boy." She grabbed me and kissed me hard on the mouth.

"I really do hate you," she said, "but Wesley was right. You *are* beautiful."

Then she turned me toward the darkness of the sage bushes and the long slope leading down to the house below.

"He'll be waiting for you at the back door," she said. "Now get your ass down there."

Then she pushed me over the edge.

It didn't take me long to get to the bottom. Funny how gravity can speed things along when you're sliding down a fifty-degree slope. When I got to the bottom, I felt like I'd been whipped over and over with a length of barbed wire.

I caught my breath for a moment, looked both ways down the street, and then crossed over to the house. I went around to the back. There was a pool with a dozen underwater lights around the perimeter. The view over the railings would have been spectacular if I had been in any mood to appreciate it. There was so much more light coming from the house itself. So many windows open and no curtains. It was like looking into a giant aquarium. I went to the back door. Before I could knock, Gunnar opened the door and held it with only twelve inches or so for me to squeeze through.

"Move very slowly," he whispered to me.

I slid in and saw that there was a wire running from the top of the door to the frame. It was a magnetic switch that would have activated the alarm if the contact had been broken. It looked like Gunnar had made a small notch in the wires leading to either side of the switch and then had run a jumper wire between them. With the circuit still complete, the alarm wouldn't go off when he opened the door.

The second thing I noticed was that the house was hotter than hell.

"Listen very carefully," he said. "Do you see that unit on the wall over there?"

I looked over at the far wall and saw the rectangle, about four inches by three inches. It had a small screen set into the top half. On the bottom half there was a small black circle.

"The secondary security in this house is passive infrared. Meaning that it picks up the heat in your body as you move across its field. I've cranked the heat up as far as it can go, which will help neutralize the difference between your body and the air temperature. But you still have to be very careful."

He must have used the alarm delay to sneak out of his hiding place and adjust the thermostat, I thought. Then after that, it had just been a waiting game.

"The safe's in the other room," he said. "Follow me and don't go any faster than I do."

He took a slow step across the floor. I followed behind him. Without the superheated air, we wouldn't have had a chance. There's no way we could have moved slow enough, no matter how hard we tried. Even with the heat advantage, we both kept our eyes on that sensor. All it had to do was turn red one time and we'd have to think about pulling the plug on the whole operation.

"There's another sensor in the next room," he said. "So there's no letup. You have to stay slow."

We kept inching our way out of that room, around the corner where I could see into the main part of the house. I saw a huge fireplace, lots of modern art paintings on the wall that looked exactly like the work my old friend Griffin used to do. The big windows and the glowing swimming pool outside. I could even see the lights from the city, and for one second I couldn't help but wonder which one of those lights was reaching up to us from that nightclub where Julian and Ramona were waiting.

We turned another corner finally. There was a big black desk with two space-age lamps suspended above it. Bookshelves. More paintings. Right there, on the wall, just a few feet from us, another infrared sensor.

And a safe.

It was, as Julian had promised, the exact same model he had shown me in his back room. Leaving nothing to chance, he had said. At the time I had wondered if he was taking his preparation to ridiculous lengths. Now I was happy that I'd gotten the chance to practice.

"Very slow now," he said. We were passing just a few feet from the sensor. I kept waiting for that light to go on. I felt so hot now. How could this thing not sense that we were in the room? Gunnar put one foot in front of him, slowly shifted his weight. Put another foot forward, shifted again. It took us another five minutes just to make our way past it.

When we got to the safe, I sank down onto my knees. That finally gave me a moment to catch my breath and to wipe the sweat from my eyes. Funny how exhausting it is to move so damned slowly.

"It's the same safe," he said. "You should be able to open it."

No kidding, I thought. I put my hand on the dial and started spinning.

"Because if you can't, we're all pretty much fucked here."

Thanks for the vote of confidence. Now just leave me the hell alone.

As I turned back to the safe, I could feel the sweat running down my back. It felt like the good old days in Mr. Marsh's backyard. The dial was slippery in my hand, but I knew I'd be able to open it. From my practice session, I already knew that there were four wheels. I already knew what the contact area would feel like. All I had to do was work through the dial, then once I had found the numbers, to crank through the combinations. We wouldn't have any problems here.

Not yet.

When I had the right combination, I turned the handle and started to swing open the door. Gunnar put his hand out and stopped it. I had forgotten to be careful.

We both looked over at the sensor. The light was still off.

"Here," he said, slowly pulling a black garbage bag from his back pocket. "Do your thing."

When the door was fully open, I could see that my thing would consist of taking many bundles of cash and putting them into the bag.

"That's what three-quarters of a million dollars looks like, in case you're wondering."

Looks just fine to me, I thought. A hundred twenty-dollar bills in each bundle, that meant 375 bundles. I started shoveling them into the bag, a handful at a time.

"Take it easy," he said. I think he was about to bend down and start helping me when he stopped himself short. "Did you hear that?"

I stopped and listened. I shook my head. I didn't hear anything.

"That's what I mean. It's quieter now."

We both stayed where we were for a moment. It came to him first.

"The furnace. It's off now."

He was right. That constant humming in the background. It was silent now.

"Hurry up and fill up that bag," he said, "but do it carefully."

Impossible to do it both ways at once, but I did what I could. I slid the bag up close to the safe and grabbed bundle after bundle, shoving them all inside.

"Maybe it overheated," Gunnar said. "Or hell, maybe it ran out of fuel. Is it my imagination, or does it not even feel as hot in here anymore?"

I was hoping it was his imagination, but I was afraid it wasn't. I had stopped sweating, even though I was working so hard putting the money in the bag. How long would it take for the room temperature to sink back close to normal?

"We're going to have to be even more careful," Gunnar said. "Are you ready?"

I nodded to him. He reached down and picked up the bag. I closed the safe and got to my feet. He started moving and I followed.

One step, shift. One step, shift.

When we were close to the sensor again, I held my breath. The air was definitely cooler now. There was no doubt about that. Gunnar took a step. Then another step.

The light flashed red.

"Stop," he said.

We both froze.

The light went back off. It stayed off. Now it was decision time. Depending on how the alarm system was set, either it made allowances for the occasional trip, or it didn't and the system was calling the central control board that very second. If the alarm was silent, we'd have no idea. Until the vehicles came roaring down the street.

"Even slower." Gunnar leaned forward, watching the sensor. This time he slid his foot across the floor. One inch. Another inch. We were moving impossibly slow now. It would take hours to get back to the door. It would take days.

Patience, I told myself. If you have nothing else in this world, you have patience.

We were right in front of the sensor now. A tilt of the head would set it off. A blink would set it off. You are a statue. The rotation of the earth is the only thing moving you. Your hair is growing faster than you're moving.

Slowly. Slowly.

It felt like forever, but finally we were past the sensor. Not that we were out of the woods yet. There was another twenty-five, thirty feet of floor to cover. Back around the corner, into the kitchen. Watching the far sensor now. Not assuming anything. Not pushing it. If it went off one more time, we'd probably have to make a break for it.

Step by tiny step. Through the kitchen. To the door. The thermostat was there on that wall, so Gunnar reached out and reset it to normal. Just another way to cover our tracks. He paused for a moment, catching his breath. I could see his legs shaking. Then he started moving again, kept going until he got to the back door. He reached for it, pulled it slowly open. When the door was open far enough, he turned his body sideways. Inch by inch, out the door. I could feel the cool air rushing into the room.

"Really slow now," he said. I'd already figured that part out. The good news is that all that cool air would help bring the temperature inside back to normal, so that it wouldn't even feel like somebody had cranked the heat up. The bad news is that we were more vulnerable now than ever.

A minute later, his entire body was out the door. I did my own slow-motion turn and slide. As I finally worked my way out, he reached above me and gently pulled his jumper wire through the doorway. Then he started slowly closing the door. When it was almost there, he gave the wire a quick pull as he closed the door in the same motion. Either the contact on the magnetic switch would be preserved, or else once again we'd have to hope that the system would have a little bit of tolerance built in for occasional random trips.

Either way, it was time for us to get moving.

We went around the side of the house, stopping before we got to the front, looking up and down the street. Everything was still quiet.

We both crossed the street. The cool air felt good in my lungs, but we had no time to savor it yet. We both ducked in under the thick brush and started making our way back up the canyon slope. As we did, I saw him take out his cell phone and hit a speed dial key.

"We're on our way." He hung up and got back to work climbing. It was a hell of a lot harder going up the slope than it had been coming down, but I knew we didn't want to risk having Lucy come down the lower street. Not if we didn't have to.

We grabbed onto branches and vines and rocks, pulling ourselves up, yard by yard, but eventually we both emerged onto the upper road. Lucy was there by the car.

"What took you guys so long?" she said.

Gunnar gave her a quick kiss and told her to get behind the wheel. He went around and got in the passenger's side. I got in back. When we were finally rolling, he picked up the bag and threw it over the seat to me.

"I'm serious," Lucy said. "What the fuck took you so long?"

Gunnar started laughing. If I could have, I would have joined him.

Lucy drove us back down the canyon road, back to Sunset Boulevard, while I took off the coveralls and then twisted myself back into my fancy suit. It was almost midnight now, but the street was still full of traffic. All of the clubgoers were just hitting their stride now, and the lines still snaked down the sidewalk.

We pulled back into the same parking spot. Lucy turned off the car, and only then did she turn around and really get a good look at me.

"You look like shit, you know that?"

She wetted a napkin with her tongue and tried to clean me up.

"Just go inside," Gunnar said. "Go in the bathroom first."

"He looks like he just rolled down a mountain."

"Just go," he said. "I'll take the car back home. You guys'll get a cab, right?"

"No problem, babe." She kissed him again. A long one this time.

"I'm so glad you're safe," she said.

"It was worth it."

"I don't care. You made it out. That's all that matters."

A little more slobbering over each other and then he finally kicked us out of the car.

"Hold on," she said as the car rolled away from us. "If you're gonna look like that, I need to match."

She bent over and ran both hands through her hair. When she stood back up straight, her hair was an unruly mess.

"Let's go, Michael. Excuse me, *Mikhail*. It's time for Phase Two."

Fifteen
Michigan
July 1999

So after failing to open that lock . . . I didn't think the day could get any worse.

Then it did.

When I was back to work in my hole, I took the envelope out from under my shirt and put it on the ground under the wheelbarrow. I started digging, throwing the dirt into the wheelbarrow until it was full. I rolled the dirt over to the woods and dumped it. Then I hid the envelope behind a tree.

I had worked for two hours straight under the brutality of the midday sun when I saw Amelia come out of the house. She didn't come to me. She didn't come anywhere near me. Instead she stayed on the little back patio, turning a crank on a big umbrella over a table until it was open.

Time for a water break, I thought. A perfect excuse to go over near her, to give her that drawing.

Before I could act, she was gone. Back in the house for a few minutes while I kept digging and watching. When she came back out, there were three other people with her. The dreaded Zeke again, plus one more guy with bleached blond hair done up in spikes, and a girl with hair dyed to look like pink cotton candy. The four of them sat down at the table, laughing and drinking from a big pitcher of ice tea or something. Cool in the shade of the umbrella, young and funny and goddamned perfect. They didn't seem to notice me there at all, not more than twenty yards away.

I was thirsty as hell by then, but I didn't dare go near them. I kept digging and trying not to listen to their laughter. When things got quiet, I looked up and saw the blond guy and the cotton candy girl kissing each other. Zeke and Amelia were sitting close now. They weren't exactly kissing at that moment, but it looked like Zeke was staring into Amelia's eyes and stroking her hair.

A few more minutes of talking and arguing and laughing, then more silence. I was afraid to look up again. When I finally did, they were all staring at me. No, worse than that, they were drawing me. The Lakeland High School art mafia apparently, all four of them, each with a pad of paper and a pencil. Watching me intently and trying to capture the sight forever. The young convicted juvenile probationer repaying his debt to society and to the family into whose house he had entered illegally. Miserable. Sweaty. Filthy. Barely more than an animal. A beast of burden.

"Don't stop!" Zeke called to me. "This isn't supposed to be a still life!"

More laughter.

I started to get dizzy again. The sunlight beating down on me so hard, for so long. I don't know how I lived through that day. I really don't.

When it was over, I retrieved my envelope from behind the tree, put it on the top of the pile, and then dumped my last load of dirt on top of it. A fitting burial.

I can't overstate what that day had done to me. I really can't. When I was new to the school and feeling like I had absolutely nothing, that was a bad time. But now it wasn't just a matter of having nothing. It was having nothing and knowing exactly what it was that I didn't have. What I'd *never* have. I had seen it in living color that day. I couldn't stand the thought of seeing it for one more minute.

Somehow, it all seemed to come back to that one stupid lock. Like if I had been able to open it, everything would have turned out differently.

Crazy, I know, but I fell asleep with that thought ringing in my head. The lock with the serrated pins. The lock that beat me.

I woke up. I sat straight up in my bed and looked around the dark room. That's it, I thought. That's why I couldn't open that lock.

I got out of bed and grabbed the first clean clothes I could find. It was just after 2:00 A.M. I rummaged through the things on my desk, found my handmade tools. The pieces of scrap metal bent into the right shapes. I put them in my pocket, grabbed the keys and a flashlight, and sneaked out of the house.

I drove across town on the dark, deserted roads. I had no business being out there, nothing beyond a simple idea so insane I couldn't even begin to stop myself. I drove all the way to the Marshes' house, seeing it now in the darkness as I had seen it the very first time. Only now I was alone, and I had a different kind of mission to accomplish.

I parked a good quarter mile away, left the car on the side of the road, and began walking. A regular, normal pace. When I got close to the house, I slipped into the backyard. I made my way back to the tree line, picking up the shovel on the way. I found the last mound of dirt I had made, then pushed the dirt aside, making my way down to where I had buried the envelope.

Careful, I thought. You don't want to damage it any more than you already have.

When I found the envelope, I picked it up and brushed the dirt off. I stepped behind one of the bigger trees and switched on the flashlight. The envelope looked a little wrinkled, and of course it was dirty as all hell, but it had stayed pretty flat. I opened it and took out the picture and examined it carefully in the thin beam of the flashlight. The corners were a little dinged up. Some of the lines had been rubbed until they were blurry. Overall, though, it didn't look too bad. Someday I'd have to write a letter to the company who made the envelope and thank them.

Now the tricky part. I turned off the flashlight and made my way to the house. I went to the back door, put my head against the window right next to it, and listened. Last thing I needed was Mr. Marsh standing in the kitchen, raiding the refrigerator for a late-night snack.

Nothing. Silence. It was time to do this. I pulled out my tools and got to work on the lock. As I worked over the pins, I started to appreciate how good the locksmith's tools really were. I would have given anything at that point to have them in my hands. But no, I thought. These will have to do. As long as I have the right idea, these will work.

Serrated pins, that's what the man had said. If a mushroom pin had one notch, then a serrated pin must have more than one, right? That's what "serrated" means. So instead of one false set on each pin, there were many. Like what, three? Four? Five?

It was time to find out. I set the back pin, started working my way to the front. All six pins set, go to the back again, set them all again. Here's where you have to be so careful, just enough tension to keep everything in place. One tiny bit too little and you lose it, one tiny bit too much and you can't feel it anymore. I worked through the second sets, got to the exact point I had gotten to before, with the locksmith laughing over my shoulder. This time I knew to keep going.

Back pin again, third set. Work my way to the front. Damn, it was like balancing a house of cards. You have to keep going, but it gets harder and harder with each one, and one false move makes it all fall apart.

I got almost to the end of the third sets, lost the tension, and felt the back pins start to give. So hard to keep the front pin set and go back and fix the back. I let the whole thing go, took a deep breath, shook out my hands, and looked around the empty backyard. I heard a motorcycle revving its motor, maybe a half mile away. I started over.

I got into the fourth sets this time, felt them all start to slip again. These amateur tools, I thought. These worthless hunks of scrap metal.

I stood up and stretched. This is just beautiful, I thought. What the hell are you going to do now?

Try the garage maybe? If you can get through the exterior door, the inside door shouldn't be too hard to crack, if it's even locked at all. But hell, if it's an automatic opener, how do you even get through that? God damn it all. If you hadn't shown off and opened it the first time, I said to myself, then Mr. Marsh wouldn't have switched out this lock. You'd be in the house already.

One last time, I thought. One more shot at this and then I give up. Drive home like an idiot and go back to bed.

I went for that last pin again. Only this time . . . hell, why don't I try setting it all the way? Go through every notch until I get to the last one . . .

No, that won't work. Think about it. As soon as you get to the first set on the next pin, you'll have to let up the tension and you'll lose the back.

Wait. Wait one minute here . . .

I pushed the last pin up, felt it go through all of the sets. Five of them. That last one being the true set. So what if instead of keeping it there . . . I push it past the last set? I overset each one until I get to the front, then I release enough tension . . .

I tried it. It was like picking a lock in reverse. I overset the back pin, then the pin in front of that one, and so on until I had gotten through them all. With all six pins overset, all I had to do was let up just enough . . .

Six little clicks. Six pins falling back to the sheer line. The plug turned and the lock was open.

I stepped into the kitchen. The same kitchen I had been in, how many nights ago was it now? The same feeling came back to me. My heart beating faster. My breathing shallow. Everything in sharp focus. My mind perfectly clear for the first time since . . . well, since the last time I broke into this house. Only this time, I didn't have three accomplices stumbling around, putting fireplace pokers through aquariums. This time it was just me, and I felt in complete control.

It felt good. I admit it.

I stood there in the kitchen for a long time, listening carefully for any movement. I could hear a clock ticking in the next room, and nothing else. I made my way through the house, to the stairs. I paused again, listening. Then I went up the stairs, slowly. There was a single night-light plugged into one of the hallway outlets. I went to Amelia's room, thankful that I knew exactly which door it was. My previous criminal activities coming in handy already. I stopped at her door and listened again. Then I took the drawing out from under my shirt. I was about to slip it under the door. That would have been my last chance to do something halfway smart that night. Instead of doing that, I tried the doorknob. It was locked.

I looked at the knob. There wasn't even a keyhole, just a single round hole in the center. I took my pick out, slid it through the hole, hit the simple release lever, and slowly let it out so it wouldn't make any noise. In my whole life, I'd never crack an easier lock.

I pushed the door open an inch. I stood there listening to the sound of her breathing. She was still asleep. I opened the door a few inches more, enough to peek inside and see her bed. A faint shaft of moonlight coming through the window. She was wearing shorts and a T-shirt, and she was wrapped up in her sheet like she'd been wrestling a boa constrictor.

I took a few steps into her room, put the drawing on her dresser. It looked good there. Good enough to make this whole little adventure seem worthwhile. I paused there for a few moments, watching her sleep, fighting off the urge to touch her skin. I should have felt shame then. Shame and guilt for this violation. I certainly wouldn't have let any other person in the world do this to her. I would have fought to the death anyone else who would dare invade her bedroom and stand over her while she slept.

I backed out of the room, pushing the lock button on her door and then closing it behind me. I moved with quiet speed down the stairs, to the kitchen and out the back door. I locked that door behind me, too. Leaving no other trace except that one single gift. Which I had left unsigned.

I'm crazy, but I'm not stupid.

I was dead tired the next day. When I got to the Marshes' house, I knew things could go one of two ways. One, Amelia gets up, sees the picture, freaks out. She tells her father and all hell breaks loose. I'll have to play dumb, pretend I've never seen the drawing before. Hope they believe me. Hope they believe there's no way I'd actually risk breaking into the house again. Maybe they'd go talk to Zeke the artist boyfriend instead.

Or two, she sees the picture and keeps it to herself. At least for now.

Option two was looking good as I pulled into the driveway at noon. There were no police cars waiting for me. No Mr. Marsh tapping his free hand with a baseball bat.

I went around the house to the backyard and grabbed the shovel from where I'd left it the night before. Before I could even put it in the ground, the back door opened. It wasn't Mr. Marsh coming out to get me. It was Zeke, and he was moving fast. He was wearing another jacket today, this one even more ugly, with a crazy pattern that looked like he'd splattered every color of paint on it. His hair was still braided down the back. He came right up to me and tried to grab me by the shoulders. I pushed him away.

"What the hell did you do to her?" he said. "Huh? What did you do?"

Okay, I thought, now this is interesting.

"I don't know what the hell your problem is, but you'd better stay away from her. Do you hear me?"

Not really. Maybe you'd better say it again.

"You will really regret it, believe me. I promise you. You just stay away from her. Or else . . ."

Or else what?

"I mean, just . . . You'll see."

He turned and walked back to the house. Amelia was there waiting for him. She gave him an exasperated look. Then she looked over his shoulder. At me.

That look.

She didn't give much away. But it was enough.

It was all I needed.

A couple of hours passed. More hard digging for me, of course, but it was the first afternoon in that hole that didn't feel like a death march. It wasn't any cooler that day, but maybe I was already getting a little bit stronger. Maybe Amelia had something to do with it, too.

I kept watching for her to reappear again, but she didn't. No sign of her. No sign of Zeke. Or even Mr. Marsh. None of his daily yelling into the phone. For all I knew, the house was empty now.

About an hour later, I heard a car pull into the driveway. Amelia, I thought. Please be her. I just want to see her again. I went to the faucet for some water, heard Mr. Marsh yelling inside. All was right with the world again. A few minutes later, a man came walking out the back door. He was wearing a white dress shirt with a tie that he had undone so it hung loose around his neck. He was about the same age as Mr. Marsh, but he didn't look like an overaged jock. Instead he had a slick polish on him like he'd be perfectly at home on a used car lot. He came over to where I was working. He stood there and lit a cigarette.

"Are you seriously digging this thing by hand?" he said.

I showed him the shovel.

"Okay, by shovel. You know what I mean. God, I thought I had a shit job."

I kept working.

"He told me to come out here and cool off. What is it, like ninety degrees back here? Stupid jackass."

He blew out a long stream of smoke.

"You been working for him long?"

I shook my head.

"You don't talk much, do you?"

I shook my head again.

"I can respect that. World needs more people who know enough to keep their mouth shut."

Mr. Marsh came out the back door and called to him.

"Case in point," the man said. "I'll catch ya later. Looks like you'll be here a while, eh?"

I didn't look up. I didn't think about seeing him again, and I didn't care either way. Little did I know.

The two men drove away together, leaving me there alone. As it got close to four o'clock, I gave in to temptation and left a few minutes early. I had important things to do, after all. I went right home and got out my drawing paper, sat there for a long time staring at it. You've got her attention now, I told myself. What's the next step? Draw something that will shock her and intrigue her and make her fall madly in love with me. Piece of cake, right?

I started drawing her face again. Trying once again to capture what I saw in her. I realized after a few minutes of work that I was drawing the exact same portrait again. I put it aside and started with a new sheet of paper.

I can draw myself, I thought. A self-portrait that'll help her to see the real me. Not just the dirt-streaked mute digging a hole in her backyard. That's always been hard for me, drawing myself, but I worked on the drawing for a good hour. Then I put that aside, too. I went and got something to eat, came back, and started over.

I knew I was trying too hard. I knew I couldn't win her over with one drawing, no matter how much I wanted to. But I didn't know how else to approach it. I did a quick sketch of myself sitting there at my desk, trying to draw. I drew flames coming out of my body. That's exactly how I felt. Fire! Madness! I drew Amelia floating in the air above me, rays of light shining from her face. Then me again, holding on to my chest. A broken heart above my head. Just stupid nonsense doodling, trying to shake loose an idea.

I thought back to the beginning. The first time Amelia spoke to me. She's standing behind me, slightly above me. I drew the scene, working quickly, just getting the general idea and not obsessing over the details yet. Now, what did she say to me? What were her exact words?

"You are so full of shit, you know that?"

Yes, that was it. I wrote the words over her head, then enclosed them in a balloon. I drew a box around the whole scene. That was my first panel.

You have to understand, comic books were still something from when I was a kid, something to lose myself in during those long days in the back room of the liquor store. I didn't know yet that they had become cooler than cool. I had never even seen a "graphic novel." I remember someone in my art class had done something that looked just like a comic book once, and Mr. Martie had verbally destroyed it for her. "Lowbrow faux-ironic bullshit," I think he called it. So I wasn't naturally inclined to go in the comic book direction with anything. It just sort of happened.

The more I used it, the better it seemed to work. The next panel was me looking up from my digging, turning to see her in the flesh for the first time.

A wider shot for the third panel. I knew instinctively to keep using different viewpoints. Both of us in this one, with her talking again. "I already heard about you. Before you broke into our house. You're the guy who doesn't talk, right?"

Closer shot on me, the streaks of dirt on my face. Just rough it in for now. Don't get hung up on making it perfect. Because here's your chance to answer her. Finally, a chance to say something to her, even if it's only in a thought bubble . . .

Don't be coy, you idiot. Just say it.

"My God, she's even more beautiful in person."

Yes. That's it. Next panel, back to her. Play it back in your head. Every word.

"What's the deal with that? Because something happened to you when you were a little kid?"

Now what? What do I say to that? I drew myself looking away from her, thinking "Yes."

Her again. "It's all an act, isn't it? I can see right through you. Because believe me, you want to talk about things happening to you when you're a kid? We could exchange a few stories someday."

A view of me from behind, her face visible over my shoulder, which I'll have to come back and make just right. Another thought bubble over my head. "If only she knew how much we have in common . . ."

Then a shot of her walking away, me watching her. Then me putting the shovel back into the dirt. The last panel on this page, the last thought bubble. I worked it over in my head for a while. Then I gathered my nerve and wrote down the words.

"If she asked me to, I would dig this hole to the center of the earth."

God, that's ridiculous. So yeah, write that down, too. Recognize how ridiculous that sounds. Another thought bubble, to the right of the first, and slightly lower. "God, that's ridiculous. But I think it's true."

Okay, I thought. Okay. At least you're talking to her now. This might actually do something.

I worked for a couple more hours, filling in all of the details in the drawings. Getting the faces just right. The texture of the dirt. Some background here and there, never so much that it would be distracting. When it was done, I put it in another big envelope. Then I set my alarm for two in the morning.

I tried to sleep. When the alarm rang I was out of my bed in seconds. I put my clothes on, slipped out of the house, and got in the car. The trip I was already making every day, and now apparently even that wasn't enough. There was a police car on Amelia's street as I made the turn. I held my breath, kept driving, and didn't look sideways. The police car passed right by me. I went to the end of the street, turned around, and came back. I parked far

from her house again. Got out and walked in the darkness, once again trying to act like I belonged there.

I ducked behind the house, got the tools out, and opened the lock again.
Tonight it felt as easy and natural as using a key.

When I was in the kitchen, I stood there for a long time listening again.
Feeling my heart beat faster, that same feeling, now so familiar. You could
get addicted to this, I told myself. Just this part right here.

I went up the steps, paused at her door, waited for another minute, listening. This time, when I finally turned the doorknob, it wasn't locked. That
got me a little worried for a moment. I couldn't help wondering if she was
waiting for me on the other side of the door. Ready to turn the lights on,
maybe. Ready to scream her head off.

No. I could see that she was sleeping as I pushed her door open. I stepped
into the room, placed the envelope on her dresser. I froze when I heard a
sound outside the door. I waited. Amelia rolled over, kept sleeping. I listened
to her breathing.

I got that funny feeling again, at the thought of someone breaking into
the house and standing there in her bedroom, watching her sleep. I mean,
it's not like I didn't know it was wrong for me to be there, but somehow it
was like that idea didn't really apply to me, because I knew I was there for
the "right" reasons, and that I'd never do anything to hurt her. I was more
upset that it was so easy to do, and that anyone who really wanted to could
follow in my footsteps tomorrow night and be standing here instead.

Nobody is safe. Ever. Anywhere.

I slipped out the door, down the hallway, down the stairs, through the
back door, and into the night. Back to the car, got in and drove, all the way
home. I tried to sleep for a while. It didn't happen.

The morning came. I was so tired. I didn't even want to look at myself in
the mirror. I took a shower and put clean clothes on, wondering what her
reaction would be to my comic strip. Today it felt like the biggest mistake
ever committed in recorded history.

"If she asked me to, I would dig this hole to the center of the earth." I
actually wrote those exact words down on paper.

When I got to the house, I went right around to the back, picked up the
shovel, and got to work. The hole was getting close to a decent-sized kiddie
pool now. I hadn't even started the deep end yet, but hell, I wasn't thinking
about that today. I looked around for Amelia. She was nowhere to be seen.

I've scared her away. The whole thing was just so wrong and so stupid. I might as well just beat myself to death with this shovel right now.

I had to live with all these crazy thoughts for the next four hours. Another hot day, another half ton of dirt to move into the woods. I still don't know how I got through it. When four o'clock came, I dragged myself to the car. This is it, I was thinking. I won't last one more day here.

When I opened the door to the car, I stood there for a moment, not quite sure what I was looking at. There was an envelope on the driver's seat. It was the envelope I had left in Amelia's bedroom. I picked it up as I sat down behind the wheel. I held it for a moment. My heart was pounding. Then I opened the envelope.

It was my comic strip. Obviously a big "No, thank you" here. Return to sender. Your submission does not fit our needs at this time.

But wait, there was something more. A second page in the envelope. I pulled it out and looked at it. Another comic strip? More panels?

Yes. That's exactly what it was.

Amelia had drawn page two.

Now, I don't have to have it with me, all these years later, to tell you exactly how it went. I can close my eyes and see it again, panel by panel. Every little detail. She was a better artist than I was, that was the first thing I noticed. Maybe not in a technical sense, but in this medium especially, she had a natural ability to reduce everything down to its essentials without losing anything. Just simple, clean lines. Her face. My face. The shovel across my shoulder, one hand resting on the handle.

Her first panel was herself standing on the edge of the hole, saying, "You'd have to drop the act first." Her exact parting words to me that day, which I had left out. Second panel, her walking away. Anger on her face. A dark cartoon squiggle in the air over her head.

Third panel, her inside the house. The dreaded Zeke, sitting in front of the TV with a bottle in his hand. His hair swung around his neck and hanging down to his chest. "What's the matter?" he says. Amelia responding, "Nothing."

Close up on Amelia. Zeke's words coming from off-frame. "I think we should go to that showing tonight. Linda is so cool and I think she's got so much talent and if we get there by," and then the words disappearing behind Amelia's head. She's ignoring him completely, her own thought bubble reading, "Maybe I'm being too hard on him." Him being me.

Next panel, more words coming at her from off-frame. "Are you even listening to me? What the hell's wrong with you today?" Amelia standing up now, looking out the window, thinking, "We're not so different, right? If he can talk to *anybody*, it should be me."

Last panel, me as seen through the window. I'm bent over, picking up a load of dirt with the shovel. Amelia's thoughts at the bottom of the panel. "Why does it bother me so much that he won't?"

End of page. I sat there looking at it for a long time. Finally I looked up and saw Mr. Marsh staring at me from the front porch. I put the car in reverse, backed out of the driveway, and took off.

When I got home, I laid Amelia's page out on my desk, studied it and read it over a dozen more times, still not quite believing it was real. Then I put it aside and got busy with page three.

Okay, what to do here . . . Maybe go to the second day I was there at the house. I wrote "The next day . . ." in the upper left-hand corner. What did she say that day? She told me I was wasting my time digging a pool, that nobody would ever use it. Then she got to the good part. I'll start there.

So first panel, her watching me again. Wearing shorts and a T-shirt that day. "So are you going to talk today, or what?"

Next panel, me looking up at her.

Third panel. What did she say next? "I'm calling your bluff, okay? I know you can talk if you want to. So say something."

Here's where I took out my little pad of paper that day. Wrote down that I really, honestly couldn't say anything. Gave it to her. That was what happened in real life, anyway. Here on this page, though, I could do anything I wanted to, right? I could make my own alternate reality.

So fourth panel. Me talking. Yes, me actually opening my mouth and saying a word out loud. On paper, it was as easy as drawing a dialogue bubble instead of a thought bubble. My first word after nine years of silence . . . She said to say something, so I did. "Something."

Fifth panel. Surprise on her face. "You can talk," she says.

Sixth panel. My answer. A little smile on my dirt-streaked face? No. No smile. Just the truth. "I can talk to you, Amelia. To you and nobody else."

I wanted to keep going. I wanted to fill up ten more pages and give them to her, but that wouldn't be right. It would be like dominating a conversation, something I'd never done, as you can probably guess. No, one page back from me and then it's her turn again.

I went over the panels and filled in the details, trying to be a little more selective this time. Following Amelia's example. The time flew by. Then, as I was about to set my alarm, I stopped and thought about what I was doing. You don't have to break into her house every night, I realized. If you left the envelope in your car, she'd find it.

But then you'd have to wait an extra day. For someone who's waited his whole life for something like this to happen . . .

No. Not if she knew to look for the envelope when you first got there every day at noon. She'd have four hours then to draw her own page and give it back to you. Assuming she's still up for this. So you don't have to take stupid chances anymore.

I knew it was the right way to play it, but at the same time I was disappointed that the idea made so much sense. That feeling I got when I picked that lock and stepped into that dark kitchen . . . I'd have to live without it for a while.

The next day finally came. I got to the Marshes' house a few minutes early. As I got out of the car, I left the envelope on the dashboard, so there'd be no doubt where she could find it. All she'd have to do was look out a front window.

I felt the whole plan unravel when I went around to the back and saw the Lakeland art mafia sitting under the big umbrella again. Zeke was there with Amelia, along with the guy with the bleached-blond spikes and the girl whose hair color today had been switched from cotton candy pink to sour apple green. I did everything I could to ignore them, but I couldn't help hearing the laughter, along with the unmistakable sound of one of them applauding my arrival.

I attacked the dirt for the next half hour or so. Whenever I dared to sneak a glance, Amelia seemed to be doing a professional job of not making any eye contact whatsoever. Finally, on my second trip back with the wheelbarrow, I noticed she was gone.

Another half hour passed. The remaining threesome kept working on whatever it was they were working on. The laughter faded with each passing minute. I caught Zeke staring at me. After another five minutes or so, he got up and went into the house. Ten minutes after that, he came out and said something to Blondie and Miss Green Hair. The two of them gathered up their things and left. Then Zeke came walking out to me.

"I thought I told you to stay away from her."

I kept digging. I didn't even look up.

"I'm talking to you."

I stopped, cupping my hand to my ear like I was deaf. Then I picked up a shovelful of dirt and threw it into the wheelbarrow.

"You goddamned son of a bitch."

He came at me then. I turned and pointed the shovel blade at his neck. That's all I had to do.

"I will get you, you stupid bastard. I promise you."

Then he left.

I went back to work. Every few minutes I looked up at the back windows, hoping to see Amelia. I didn't. When I went to the faucet to fill the water jug, I heard Mr. Marsh yelling into the phone.

Just before four o'clock, I saw the back door open. My heart went into my throat for a second until I realized it was Mr. Marsh. He had a drink in one hand. With his other hand he grabbed one of the patio chairs and carried it out to the hole. He set it down a little too close to the edge, tried to take a seat, and almost dumped himself right into the dirt. He adjusted the chair, sat down again, and this time kept his bearings.

He watched me dig for a while. He took long sips out of his glass until it was almost empty.

"Why are you doing this?" he finally said.

I looked up at him.

"I got all sorts of guys working for me these days. Building things. Trying to make deals happen. You know what I'm saying? All sorts of guys all over the place. And you know what?"

He rattled the ice cubes in his glass and then drained it.

"I'll tell you what. If every one of those guys worked like you do, I'd have absolutely no problems at all. I'd be fucking rich and I'd have no problems."

He took out one of the ice cubes and threw it at me. It went two feet over my head.

"Look at you! You show up here every day. You do your job. Every minute you're supposed to be working, you're working. Every single minute. And the whole time you keep your fucking mouth shut. No complaining. No backtalk. No calling me up and telling me you can't do one simple goddamned thing because this thing happened and that thing happened and this person said goddamned whatever. None of that bullshit at all. Not one little bit. Do you have any idea what I'm saying to you?"

I stayed still. I wasn't sure what the right response would be, or if he'd even notice it.

"Who'da thunk it," he said. "All these guys supposedly working for me and getting paid pretty goddamned well, and the one guy doing the best job is the juvenile delinquent who has to do it for free. Can you imagine?"

No. I cannot imagine.

"You want a drink?" he said. "A real drink? Come on, I'll fix you something."

I put my hands up. No thanks. It's almost four o'clock, and I'm dying to get to my car, to see what might have been left there.

"You sure? I make a mean vodka martini."

I put my hands up again.

He got out of the chair and stepped down into the hole. He came close enough for me to smell the alcohol on his breath.

"I didn't want you to actually dig me a pool. You realize that. I mean, what the hell do I need a pool for?"

Once again, staying absolutely still seemed to be the only way to go.

"You win, okay? No more digging. Put the shovel away. Put the wheelbarrow away. You're done. You win. End of story."

End of story. Yet he was still standing there.

"I'm sorry I did this to you. Will you accept my apology?"

He seemed to really mean it. What else could I do? I nodded my head.

"Can we be friends now?"

Okay . . . not sure *what* to think now.

"Tell me we can be friends."

What the hell. I nodded my head.

"Shake on it?" He switched his glass to his left hand and put out his right. I shook it. It was cold and wet from the drink.

"When you come back tomorrow, we'll think up something else for you to do, okay? Something a lot more fun? More rewarding?"

He's really, really drunk, I thought. Or really, really crazy. By tomorrow, he may have forgotten all about this. Or else it's going to be an interesting day all around.

"It's a little early," he said, "but you go on home. I'll see you tomorrow."

Without another word, he stepped back, grabbed his chair, and dragged it back to the house. I stood there for a while, watching him. Waiting for the big zag after the zig. It never came. So I just threw the shovel in the wheelbarrow and went around the house to my car.

It was empty. No envelope.

I was running the scenarios through my head. Amelia coming to her senses. Or Zeke getting to her somehow. Or hell . . . maybe even Zeke figuring out our little game and taking the envelope out of the car himself.

Before my stomach could turn completely over on that one, I heard something behind me. A door shutting? No, a window. I looked up and saw the brown envelope sailing through the air. The window already shut and the person behind it already gone.

I retrieved the envelope from the front lawn, got in my car, and drove a hundred yards. The craziness with Mr. Marsh already forgotten, because this was something much, much bigger. I pulled over and opened the envelope. First page from me, second from her, third from me again . . .

Page four.

I knew she had had to deal with Zeke for the first hour, so she hadn't had much time to work on it. But here it was. I was expecting that maybe she'd pick up from where I had left off, her standing there at the edge of the hole after I had finally uttered my first words, but the scene was different. The first panel showed the foursome sitting outside under the umbrella. Today? Is that what she was drawing? In the middle distance, there I was, hard at work, while Zeke and the other two artists watched me and laughed. You could only see the back of their heads, Amelia's profile in the foreground. Her thought bubble . . . "You clowns can't even see it. He's got so much more talent than any of you. And he's kind of beautiful, too."

Holy fuck, I thought to myself. Holy motherfucking fuck.

Second panel. Amelia standing up. Zeke looking up at her with dumb surprise. The way she drew him in that panel alone, like he was the most pathetic and ridiculous human being who ever lived. It brought even more pure joy to my heart.

Third panel. Inside the house. Amelia with her back to Zeke, saying, "Get out. I don't ever want to see you again."

Fourth panel. "Later . . ." in the upper left-hand corner. Amelia in her room, sitting on her bed. The thought bubble . . . "He was here. Right here in my bedroom. Two nights in a row."

I swallowed hard, kept reading.

Fifth panel. Silhouette of Amelia on the bed, leaving lots of room underneath for a longer thought . . . "Definitely an uncool thing to do, sneaking into my room in the middle of the night. Absolutely way over the line unfucking-cool, right. So last night, when he didn't come here at all . . ."

Sixth panel. Viewpoint from outside the window. Amelia on the inside looking out, saying it out loud . . . "Now *that* was just fucking cruel."

One page of paper. Wood pulp bleached and then pressed into a thin layer. Marked with the rubbed-off graphite from a single drawing pencil. That's all it was. You understand this.

I held that page of paper in my hands for five minutes maybe, while sitting in my uncle's beat-up old car on the side of a road just outside of Milford, Michigan. On a hot afternoon turning into a hot evening. When I could finally breathe again, I put all of the pages back into the envelope. I reminded myself of the correct procedure for operating an automobile, put it in gear, and pressed the gas pedal. Steered it all the way home.

I went inside and opened the envelope again, took the pages out, and put them on my desk. This lonely cigar-smoke-smelling room at the back of this old house. The miracle that these sheets of paper could even exist within that lonely room's four walls.

I sat down with a clean page in front of me. If I had been capable of laughing out loud, I would have done it. What in goddamned hell could I possibly draw in response to this? Six panels of what exactly?

I tried out a few different ideas. What might happen between us if I broke into her house again. If I slipped into her bedroom in the middle of the night. I wadded up every piece of paper and threw them onto the floor. Every single one.

Eventually, I put my head down on my arms. I had to close my eyes for a minute. Just one minute. As I slipped into a dream, I could hear the water pouring into the room, running down the walls, coming through the window. Pooling on the floor and then rising. Slowly, inch by inch. Until I was submerged in it.

Like every night. Like every dream.

When I looked up again, it was after midnight.

I shook myself awake. You're blowing this, I thought. You're totally letting this whole thing slip away.

I knew I had to draw something. Anything. I had one hour left. Maybe an hour and a half. Then it would be time to go to her house.

What are you really feeling right now? That's what I have to ask myself. Just think about that one simple idea and start drawing.

I took out a clean sheet of paper. In the bottom right corner, I drew myself, here at the desk, my head down, just like I had been a minute ago. A big dream bubble above me, taking up the rest of the page.

Yes. This is it. Not six panels. Just one. A big risk, maybe. Probably totally insane. But here it is. One single page showing her exactly how I see her, late at night, in my underwater dreams.

Sixteen

Los Angeles
January 2000

The back door to the club was locked, so we had to go around to the front. The bouncer did a little double take when he saw the condition of my face, but he clearly remembered us. He opened the velvet rope and let us through.

I found a bathroom and looked at myself in the mirror. I washed the dirt off my face. Then I tried to splash water on my hair and restore some kind of order again. When I had done all I could, I went back outside and found Lucy. As we worked our way across the dance floor, we could see Julian and Ramona sitting at that table high above us. Wesley was sitting there with them. Julian caught sight of us, and his cool might have slipped for half a second, but he recovered just as quickly.

Lucy and I went up the spiral staircase, got past the balcony bouncer, and made our way to the table. Wesley got up like a gentleman and gave Lucy back her chair.

"We were wondering where you ran off to," he said.

"I told you," Julian said. "The man had to go attend to his business. To make sure everything is ready."

"What happened to you?" Wesley said. "You look like you got run over by something."

You don't understand English, I told myself. Don't even look like you're following what he's saying.

"Oh, he did," Lucy said, sliding her fingernails through her messed-up hair. "He got run over real good."

Then to prove her point, she reached over and raked those same fingernails across my cheek. It hurt like hell, but it got Wesley smiling and nodding his head in appreciation.

"Okay, seriously," Julian said. "I think it's time to stop fucking around, don't you?"

It was all part of his act, as I'd realize later. Get right in the guy's face. Act a little too anxious. Push the deal like you can't wait one more minute to make it happen.

"I couldn't agree more," Wesley said. "Let's do some business."

Julian turned to me and said something in Russian. Or if he was making it up, at least it *sounded* like Russian.

I waited a beat. Then I gave him a nod.

"So where do we do this?" Julian said.

"Let me go make a trip to the cash machine," Wesley said. "You guys just hang here for a while, eh?"

"Works for me. Can you send another bottle over?"

Wesley gave him a big smile. "Coming right up, my friend."

He took his leave and walked over to the upstairs bouncer. I kept watching him. As he turned, I could see a sudden flash of condescension on his face. We were all just kids, the look said. It was almost too easy to play us.

That's when the whole setup started to become clear to me. The whole seemingly insane yet totally brilliant idea behind what Julian and his gang were doing. You don't wait for the target to put the money in the safe. You *make* the target put the money in the safe. You get close to him. You get to know him. You find out what he wants. You tell him he can have it. You tell him that you know somebody who knows somebody else who knows exactly how to get it. You tell him you'll arrange the deal so that everybody comes out ahead. You do all of this in such a way as to make him believe beyond a shadow of a doubt that he's smarter than you. That in the end, he's the one who's going to come out ahead.

It doesn't even matter what it is. In this case, it was Ecstasy. Not the cheap, dirty pills you can find in every club. The real thing. One hundred percent. Does that make you a drug dealer all of a sudden? Of course not! It could be rocks from the moon for all you care, because you're not actually going to deliver anything at all.

Of course, your man has every reason to be suspicious, because after all who the fuck are you to appear out of nowhere and to tell him that he can have exactly what he wants? So he knows going in . . . he *knows* that there's a chance you're totally full of shit. He wouldn't be where he is today if he didn't know this. But he plays along, because what the hell, maybe you *can* deliver. He's got nothing to lose, he figures, because he's a smart man and you're a cheap, dumb punk, and he'll make sure he sets it up the right way. So you let it happen. Everything he wants, you give him. You want to see a sample? Here it is. You want us to bring everything to a certain place at a certain time? Whatever you say. We'll be there.

You let him call the shots. You let him gather up his money and hold on to it. Keep it right in his back pocket until you've proven that you can deliver everything you said you could. There's no way he can lose here, because he isn't even *touching* his money until he knows it's a safe play.

Absolutely no way to lose.

Unless . . . Oh, hell, let's just imagine here . . . Let's just say that while he's got all that money sitting in his back pocket, someone else comes along and takes it before the deal can even happen. Yeah, that might be the one slight complication that could get in the way.

This is the way Julian set it up. It's perfect. Your mark's watching you fumble around trying to look cool and to set up the deal. While he's doing that, somebody else sneaks around behind him and picks his pocket. Even if that "pocket" is an eight-hundred-pound iron box protected by two separate alarm systems.

The ladies excused themselves for a moment. Julian came around the table and sat in the chair next to me. He leaned in close and whispered in my ear.

"You're doing great," he said. "You're a natural. You haven't said one wrong word tonight."

He gave me a little punch in the shoulder, grabbed Lucy's champagne flute, and raised it. He waited until I got mine and did the same.

"*A la Mano de Dios.*"

I understood it this time around. To the Hand of God. That's what you call this kind of operation. When young con artists get together with young burglars and set up the perfect crime.

"Here's the important part," he said, leaning in close again. "When he goes home to get the money, and he sees that it's gone . . . his head is going to go through the fucking roof, right? When that happens, it's our job to put *our* heads through the fucking roof even higher than his. We tell him he's a no-good fucking con man, what kind of bullshit move is this, et cetera, et cetera. You get what I'm saying?"

He paused and took another sip of champagne.

"We play it all the way through. Right in his face, all the way out the door."

The ladies came back to the table. Ramona grabbed Julian like she had no plans to let go that night. Lucy bent over and wrapped her arms around my neck. I was overwhelmed by her hair, by her scent, by the feel of her skin against my cheek.

She was just playing her part, I knew. But still.

"Have some more champagne," she said to me. "It'll numb the pain."

I wasn't sure what pain she was talking about. The pain in my body from everything I'd done that night? The pain in my heart? Or something else entirely.

Either way, I drank some more champagne. In this nightclub in this city on this night, with these lights flashing and this music pounding away on the dance floor below me . . . I couldn't help wondering what would happen next. With these strange, beautiful people . . . it seemed like it could be *anything*.

Wesley came back. His face was red and his ponytail was undone. Julian gave me a quick wink as he stood up. Then I watched the two of them go at it. Wesley waving his arms around, Julian sticking his finger right in Wesley's face. The upstairs bouncer had to step between them, and all hell broke loose for the next minute until we were all stumbling down the back steps and out into the night air.

Julian hailed a cab and we all squeezed into the backseat. Ramona gave the driver an address and we were off, rolling down Sunset Boulevard. Between the champagne and the company and the night itself, I was starting to feel disoriented.

Then we were going east on an expressway. The lights whizzing by us.

Then we were crawling slowly down a narrow street where people were dancing. They had to move to let us pass, one by one, inch by inch.

Then we were out of the cab and going into another club. This one was called El Pulpo. It was crowded and it smelled like spicy food and everyone was speaking Spanish.

Then I was dancing. Me. Actually dancing on a dance floor. I stopped dancing and drank a bottle of Mexican beer. Then I was dancing again.

I was dancing and feeling warm and almost good. Almost wonderful. As close to wonderful as it was possible for me to ever get, in my whole life.

All these strangers around me, speaking a language I didn't know. Yet I felt like I belonged there. There was nowhere else to be that night except this sweaty little crowded nightclub in East L.A.

Lucy was in front of me now. Her arms in the air, a distant smile on her face. She was dancing, and it felt good to be close to her. I reached out and touched her. One hand on each hip.

Another man put his hand on her shoulder, turned her toward him, and said something into her ear. She took his hand and with one smooth motion twisted it all the way around until he was down on his knees. She kicked him once in the stomach and let him go. He crawled away, and she turned back to me like nothing had happened.

The music got louder. People were shouting.

More dancing. The way I felt connected to Lucy now. In a way I hadn't felt since Amelia. Not just her but Julian, too. And Ramona. Even to Gunnar, still wiping the sweat from his face now, back at the house. Counting all that money.

More shouting. Louder and louder.

A thought came to me. If I ever talk . . . it'll be on a night like this. I'll just open my mouth and—

Lucy was saying something to me. I leaned in closer to hear it.

"You're one of us now," she said, her lips touching my ear. "You belong to us."

Seventeen
Michigan
July 1999

Even now, when I think back on that day . . . the day Amelia gave me that last page . . . that hope I felt, for the first time in my life. That's the part I want to remember most. That hope that was so real it was like something I could touch. Like it was right *there* in front of me. Those few hours I spent with nothing more than that one piece of paper in my hands. Waiting for the night to come. Being scared and unsure of myself, and having absolutely no idea about what would happen. But having hope that it would be as good as I could possibly imagine.

The sun went down. I waited for midnight to come. Then one o'clock. I made myself wait, told myself that I couldn't afford to go any earlier than normal. Who knew how late anyone stayed up in that house? Two o'clock had been safe before, so that's the time I would go.

I left at one thirty-five. I drove over to the house. I had my tools with me, of course. I kept telling myself, relax, calm down, or you'll never be able to open the back door. But when I finally got there, the door was unlocked. Another new thing, this little message to me. I listened for a few minutes. Then I opened the door and went in.

Through the kitchen, to the stairs. Quietly up each step, into the hallway, to her room. I tried her doorknob. It, too, was unlocked. I turned the knob, but I did not press the door open. I stopped dead.

It was my last moment of doubt. Because this whole idea . . . it was obviously too good to be true. It was all a setup. A hoax. There'd be a movie camera on the other side of this door. The lights would snap on. Maybe all four of the art mafia would be there waiting for me.

Do I open the door or do I turn and run away? This was the moment.

I opened the door.

It was dark in her room. I stepped inside and closed the door behind me. I stood there for a long time, waiting. I had the envelope with me, my new page added to the rest. I put the envelope down on the dresser in its usual spot.

"It's about time." A voice in the darkness.

I didn't move.

"Did you lock the door behind you?"

I reached around and locked it.

"Come closer."

I took a step toward the voice. I couldn't see her yet. My eyes still hadn't adjusted to the dark.

"Over here."

There was a soft click. Then a thin beam of light hit the ceiling. I saw her sitting on the bed, holding the flashlight.

"I was starting to think you wouldn't come tonight. I fell asleep."

I stood there, six feet away from her. I didn't move.

"Are you going to sit down, or what?"

I sat on the edge of the bed. She was wearing shorts and an old T-shirt. Same as ever.

"I won't bite."

I slid down a little closer to her.

"I guess I've been waiting for something like this to happen," she said. "Ever since the first time I saw you. But now that you're here . . ."

She repositioned herself, sitting Indian style now. Her bare knees just a few inches from me.

"I guess this is a little weird, huh?"

I put one hand on my chest, then gestured to the door.

"No. You don't have to leave. I mean, I haven't seen your new page yet."

I stood up, took the envelope from the dresser, then gave it to her. I watched her open it. She held the flashlight with one hand as she paged through the comics with the other. When she got to my new page, she picked it up and looked at it carefully.

"This is . . . me."

She moved the flashlight back and forth across the page. On this drawing that had come from somewhere inside me.

A mermaid, with Amelia's face. Underwater, her hair free and floating with the current. One arm crossed over her chest, for modesty's sake. Her tail curving into a long U shape.

I closed my eyes. Somehow I had done the impossible, with a drawing that was both childish and salacious at the same time. The most ridiculous thing ever put on paper.

"I don't even know what to say."

That you hate it? That I should leave immediately?

"It's beautiful," she said. "It's amazing. How did you know?"

I opened my eyes.

"How did you know I've always had this thing about being a mermaid?"

She looked up at me. The flashlight made a deep shadow across half her face.

"Is this how you really see me? When you're dreaming about me?"

I nodded. Just the slightest movement. I looked at her mouth.

"If you want to kiss me, you better go ahead and—"

I put one hand on the back of her neck, drew her mouth to mine. No other thought in my head except for how much I wanted to do that, without waiting another second. She slid her arms around my waist, pulled me closer. I felt us both slowly tilting toward her bed. Then falling. Her tongue touching mine and then everything melting. A word I'd read in how many books, melting, when two lovers come together, and yet this is exactly what it felt like. Both of us stretched out on her bed now, wrapped together, our hands finding each other's, clasping and almost pushing away, like it's all too much.

"Oh God." Her voice close to my ear. "You have no idea how much I wanted this to happen."

I was seventeen years old, remember. Before this night, I had kissed one girl for about two seconds. It had been over before I even knew what was happening. Now I was *right here*, in Amelia's actual bed. I knew how everything else was *supposed* to work, and God knows I wanted it to, but I had no practical idea of exactly what to do next.

"Are you okay?"

I nodded. She sat up.

"I promise I won't ever ask this again . . . Can you really, really not say a word to me?"

I shook my head.

"Not even a little sound?"

I swallowed hard.

"It's okay," she said. "It's okay. I think that just makes you more amazing."

We were both silent for a while. The flashlight was lying on the bed now, the thin beam bouncing off her wall and casting a pale glow on both of us. Amelia's face half hidden behind her hair. She drew closer to me again. I kissed her, slowly this time. The taste of her. The smell of her. This was really happening. She pulled me down again, and a dozen different thoughts ran through my head at once. What might happen next. What was *going* to happen next unless one of us did something to stop it.

Then we heard the noise. In the hallway, footsteps, then the creak of a door. Amelia put one finger to her lips to shush me, then seemed to realize how little sense that made. "Just wait," she whispered to me. "It's my father."

We listened for the sound of the toilet flushing, then the footsteps again as Mr. Marsh made his way back to his room. I couldn't help wondering what he would have done to me if he had woken up a little earlier and found me sneaking around in his house. I wondered further what kind of prison I'd get sent to, and if they'd be able to accommodate the fact that I'd have been crippled tonight and forever confined to a wheelchair.

We waited a few more minutes, long enough to make sure he had gone back to sleep. By then, the spell seemed half broken. I wondered if that would be it. For tonight, anyway.

Then she stood up. She grabbed the bottom of her shirt and pulled it over her head. Her skin was glowing in the window's faint light. I swallowed, reached forward to touch her. I put both of my hands against her collarbones. She put her hands on mine, slid them down to her breasts. She closed her eyes.

She reached for my shirt. We pulled it off together. Then my pants. Then my underpants. She pulled her shorts down and kicked them away.

She took my hand and led me back to her bed.

"This is crazy," she said. Afterward. "You don't have to creep into my room in the middle of the night anymore. Even if I'm strange enough to actually like it."

She pulled me to my feet. We stood there in the middle of her room with our arms around each other. The room was so dark, with the wooden floor painted so black it seemed like we were floating in outer space.

"My summer just got a hell of a lot more interesting," she finally said. "Will you keep drawing for me?"

I nodded.

"I will, too. I guess it's my turn."

She kissed me again. Then she let me go. She went to the door, opened it a few inches, and looked into the hallway.

"It's clear," she said, "but be careful."

I slipped past her, took a step onto the thick carpeting like I was coming back to earth. When I was halfway down the stairs, I heard a sound behind me. I stopped dead, expecting to hear Mr. Marsh's voice. Hoping he didn't have a gun in the house. When I turned, I saw Amelia looking down at me. She gave me a little smile and raised one eyebrow a quarter of an inch. Then she waved good night and shut her door behind her.

From one summer night . . . to the very next morning. How quickly the whole world can turn on you. How much I'd give to stop everything right there. Those few hours in Amelia's bedroom. Finish my whole story on that note. Close the book. The End.

But no.

That's the one thing prison teaches you. You can close your eyes and dream about the way you wish things could be. Then you wake up and everything comes back at you at once. The isolation and the locked doors and the crushing weight of the stone walls all around you. It all comes back and it feels worse than ever.

So maybe you shouldn't dream at all if you're in a place like this. Not that kind of dream, anyway. Don't dream that kind of dream unless you don't plan on waking up.

I left her house that night. I drove home. I went inside. I sure as hell didn't sleep that night. I kept smelling her scent on me, kept feeling her lips against mine. Alone in the darkness of my room, my heart still beating as fast as a hummingbird's. Until the sun finally came up and I was on my feet again, ready to go back to her house.

It felt funny to drive over there that morning. I couldn't help worrying that the whole thing would fall apart in the light of day. That she'd see me and shake her head, put up her hands as if to say, no, that was just a mistake. Just go to the backyard and keep digging and forget it ever happened.

I didn't see her when I pulled in and got out of the car. I stood there in the driveway for a few moments, waiting for her face to appear in one of the windows. It didn't happen.

There was a strange car there. Somebody new in town. I didn't think anything of it yet. I went around the house, remembering what Mr. Marsh had said to me the day before. About how I was through with the pool-digging, and that he'd be finding something else for me to do. Something more rewarding, he had said. Whatever the hell that meant.

He was just drunk, I thought. By today he'll have forgotten the entire conversation, and I'll be right back to work, filling up that wheelbarrow and dumping the dirt in the woods.

But there in the backyard, waiting for me, was a big surprise.

I saw the white tent first. It was as big as one of those huge white tents you see at outdoor weddings, big enough to cover the area where I had been digging every day. I blinked a couple of times, taking it all in, then finally seeing the two men standing in the shade underneath the tent. It was Mr. Marsh and my probation officer.

When Mr. Marsh spotted me, he stepped out into the sun. "Michael! Come on over!" He had a maniacally big smile on his face.

"Look who's here," he said, gesturing to my PO. "We were just talking about our little project back here."

The PO stepped out and shook my hand. He peered into my face. "Good to see you, Michael. Boy, you look a little red."

"I told the kid, you should always wear sunscreen, eh? Skin cancer? Melanoma? You think he listens to me?"

Mr. Marsh gave me a playful punch on the shoulder.

"I finally got this tent for him," he said. "I've been meaning to get one, anyway."

"Sure's a beaut," my PO said, looking up at it. The fabric was blinding white in the sunlight. "Turns your whole backyard into a real oasis."

"You picked the right word," Mr. Marsh said. "An oasis. As you can see, we're really trying to do something special back here. Michael's been such a huge help."

"It's gonna be impressive, all right. I better not bring my wife over here, or she'll have me digging up our backyard in no time."

The two of them kept smiling at me, their teeth as blinding white as the tent. I looked away from them and finally got around to noticing all of the stuff someone had dragged out here. There were a dozen potted plants, each one bigger and more multi-fronded than the next, all sitting on the ground. A large black tarp was draped down into the hole. My wheelbarrow was filled to the brim with rocks as big as volleyballs.

"Mr. Marsh was trying to describe how this is going to look when it's done," my PO said to me. "I can't wait to see it when you've got the fountain set up. Although how are you going to . . ."

He looked all around his feet at the straw and the stubby new grass. "You'll need an electric line back here, won't you?"

"Oh, yeah, yeah," Mr. Marsh said. "Of course. That's the last step. We'll need an electrician to run the wire from the house."

My PO followed an imaginary line to the house, nodding his head in agreement. "It's a shame you can't do that yourself."

"The union would complain, eh?" Mr. Marsh put his hand on the back of my neck. I could feel the strength in his fingers.

"Well, it's good to see that things are working out so well. I'll be glad to report this as a success story."

"I was just telling Michael yesterday . . . all the people I pay good money to work for me, and not one of them works as hard as he does."

"That's great. That's outstanding."

"Like you say, a success story. That's exactly what this is."

I still didn't know what was going on, but the two men shook hands and smiled some more, and then Mr. Marsh showed my PO to his car. When he was done with that, he came back around to the back of the house. I was standing there next to the pretend oasis, marveling at how much effort had gone into the illusion. I hadn't dared to go under the tent, figuring that even the shade itself would be forbidden to me. That he'd tear the whole thing down now that my PO was safely gone. Pull up the tarp and tell me to get my ass back to work.

Instead, he came back to me and put both hands on my cheeks. Grabbed me right by the face. "I tell you what," he said. "Your stock is up today, young sir."

He gave me one last little slap in the face and then let go of me. "Just hang loose for a while. I'll be needing you inside in about a half an hour."

Hang loose, he says. I didn't know how to do that. I walked around the tent, looking for the shovel. I found it over by the edge of the woods. It felt so strange to be there without that wooden handle held tight in my hands. But what the hell, right? It sure looked like the pool was on hold today. I dropped the shovel and went back to the tent, looking up at the windows.

Please show yourself, I thought. Everything would feel a hell of a lot better if I could just see you smiling at me for one second.

I finally went under the tent and sat down on the edge of the hole with my feet on the plastic tarp. I kept waiting.

Finally, Mr. Marsh came back out through the back door.

"Come on in!"

He held the door open for me. I went inside, feeling the sudden chill of the air-conditioned air.

"Right this way, Michael."

He showed me to his office, the same room where we had had our first extended conversation, about seven thousand shovelfuls of dirt ago. The same stuffed fish was there, the great blue marlin frozen in midair above his desk.

"Have a seat," Mr. Marsh said. "Can I get you something to drink?"

I put my hand up to decline.

He didn't look interested in taking no for an answer. "A Coke, maybe? Dr Pepper? I know we've got something. Let me see."

He went to the wet bar on the far wall and rummaged around in the little refrigerator. "You want ice?"

I didn't think it would matter if I did or not. I didn't even try to stop him.

"Here we go," he said, pouring a can of Coke into a glass filled with ice. The glass looked like crystal. He handed it to me and put the can on the desk in front of me. Then he sat down behind the desk.

"Let me tell you why I brought you in here. My daughter Amelia, she told me something very interesting about you this morning."

Oh shit, I thought. Here we go. I didn't figure on an early death today.

"She says that you're a very good artist, and that you shouldn't be spending all your time digging in our backyard. Those were her exact words."

I started breathing again.

"You surprise me every day, Michael. That's all there is to it. I mean, you've already proven your loyalty to me. After all that hard work . . . after not giving up your friends like that. By the way, I apologized yesterday, right? Did I already apologize?"

I nodded.

"I was so upset about what happened. What you boys did. You and those Milford High School punks."

He cut himself off with a visible effort. Then he put his hands down on the desk.

"But that's no excuse for abusing you like that. I'm just trying to explain where my head was. Okay? You understand? And you forgive me, right?"

I nodded again.

"Thank you, Michael. I appreciate that. Seriously. Why aren't you drinking your Coke?"

I took a sip, feeling the bubbles go up my nose.

"So here's what we're going to do now. First of all, I meant what I said. Your days as pool digger are over. Okay? No more digging. Instead, well, I thought maybe if you're such a great artist and all . . ."

He paused for a moment, leaning back in his chair. The huge fish just above his head.

"Amelia had this little friend . . . Zeke. Ezekiel. Whatever the hell his name was. You probably saw him around here, right? Anyway, I guess he's history now. Can't say it breaks my heart. I mean, his family has a lot of money and all, but he's just a little too weird for me. Anyway, now that he's gone . . . well, I know Amelia always likes to have somebody else around to do her art stuff with. So I was thinking . . . do you see where I'm going with this?"

No, I thought. I absolutely do not see where you're going with this. Because there's absolutely no way that you'd seriously be offering me this chance.

"Amelia has had a really tough time of it. I mean, since it's just been the three of us here. Hell, the two of us now, with Adam gone. She spends way too much time alone. I just don't know how to reach out to her sometimes, you know?"

No way. There's no way you're going to ask me this.

"So what I'm saying is, if you could come here and instead of digging . . . If you could spend time with her, while she's drawing, or whatever you guys want to do. It would make me feel a lot better, to know she had somebody to be with. To talk to. I bet you're a great listener, am I right?"

Yes. Yes I am.

"Now, if you're worried about the probation officer . . ."

No. I'm not worried about the probation officer.

"I'll just tell him you're doing some other jobs for me. Down at the health club. I'll make sure that's covered, is what I'm saying. I'll make sure you're covered here. Totally covered."

The catch is coming. There has to be a catch here.

"I'm having a little barbecue tonight. You think you could stay for it?

There's somebody I'd like you to meet. His name is Mr. Slade. He's my partner, actually, at the health club. Along with some other stuff. We've got a lot going on these days. I think he'd really enjoy meeting you. Whaddya say?"

That's the catch? I have to meet your partner?

"And maybe . . . I don't know. Maybe if we have a problem that you could help us solve sometime? You think maybe that would be a possibility? You helping us out, I mean?"

Okay. Here it is.

"I'm just saying. You have a lot of skills. In fact, I bet Mr. Slade would be very interested to see them. You think you could show him? Maybe even tonight, after the barbecue?"

That's when I heard the footsteps. I looked up and there she was, standing in the doorway. She had jeans and a simple white shirt on, untucked. Beads around her neck. Her hair tied up in a ponytail.

"Tell you what, you just think about it," Mr. Marsh said to me. "You think about it, and we'll talk later."

"What's he supposed to be thinking about?" Amelia said.

"Just an adjustment to our work agreement," Mr. Marsh said. "I think everybody will be a lot happier. You included."

She didn't look convinced. I'd find out soon just how well she knew him. For as much as she loved him, the only parent she had left, she knew he was full of shit at least half the time.

"You guys run along," Mr. Marsh said. "Go do some art stuff or something."

"He doesn't have to dig today?"

He smiled at his daughter. Then he gave me a little wink.

"No. Not today."

I don't know if I realized it yet, but he had me. Before I could even get out of the chair. I had no idea what he'd ask me to do. Or who he'd ask me to do it for. All of that would come later.

But for now . . . yes. He'd played the Amelia card, and he'd played it perfectly.

He had me.

Eighteen
Los Angeles and Monterey
Early 2000

I was still in L.A. when I turned eighteen that month. February of 2000. Lucy had asked me for my birthday. Just out of curiosity, I thought. I had no idea they were planning anything. But on that day, Julian and the gang put a blindfold on me and took me out to the street. They took the blindfold off and there it was. A Harley-Davidson Sportster with a big red bow on the seat. The most beautiful motorcycle I had ever seen, even better than that old Yahama my uncle had given me.

I had already moved into the little apartment that was attached to the garage. It didn't take long to bring in all of my stuff, which at that point could still fit into the two luggage bags from my old bike. Julian apologized to me about how small the space was, but damn . . . after setting out on my own, figuring I'd be living in motel rooms or God knows where else . . . this was as close to a real home as anything I could have hoped for.

I still had a lot of questions about these four people. The White Crew. First of all, you can only spend so much time stealing money from rich people. What else did they do all day?

As it turned out, Julian had grown up in a family of wine snobs, so he took that background and he turned it into a business. He had a storefront in Marina del Rey, not far from the docks. There was a climate-controlled wine cellar beneath the store with well over a million dollars' worth of bottles. The very finest, most expensive wine in the world. The kind of stuff that only a very rich person would even think of buying. That's how he made many of his first contacts in this community of obscene wealth, mostly from the people who'd dock their yachts in the harbor. At the same time, it gave him a way to launder some of the money he made from the robberies.

There was a kind of symmetry to my life now, if you think about it. A man who sold cheap liquor took me in when I needed him most. Now, it was a man who sold overpriced wine.

Ramona spent most of her time at the store, too, along with members of her extended family, especially her three sisters. Like her, they were ridiculously attractive Hispanic women who could charm you right out of your undershorts. The few times I was around the store, I'd hear them talking Spanish to each other at a million miles an hour, and it would often disintegrate into shouting matches. By the end of the day, they'd make up. It was a tight family. They loved each other like crazy and would kill for each other, I could tell. I was envious of that.

As for Gunnar, he was a tattoo artist. He had a little shop right there in Santa Monica. When he wasn't there, I often saw him working out in the backyard. Even now that he was hooked up with Julian and had some money in his pocket, he still liked to use junkyard equipment like cinder blocks and tire chains.

He didn't talk to me much. Then again, the more I hung around the more I noticed that he didn't really talk to *anybody*. I mean, he lived in the same house with these people. He had dinner with them almost every night. When it came time to put a big job together, he would literally entrust these people with his very life. But he was different from them. That much was clear. There always seemed to be a subtle undercurrent in the room, with Julian especially, and now me. Like there's no way on this earth he'd be spending so much time with us, if it weren't for our one common interest.

Lucy? She was the one member of the gang who hadn't found her daytime calling yet. She'd worked a number of jobs since getting out of rehab, but nothing had seemed to stick. Her latest kick had apparently been painting. Some of her work was hanging around the house, and Julian had arranged for some pieces to be shown at one of the local art galleries. Most of her work was these almost psychedelic paintings of birds or dogs or even jungle animals that I'm sure she'd never seen in person. It was good, I thought, but she didn't make many sales.

Because she was the one with the most free time, I'd often end up hanging around while she was painting or cooking or whatever else. One day, she caught me drawing a picture of her on my pad of paper. Nothing much, just a quick pencil sketch, but she took the paper from me and looked at it for a long time.

"One more reason to hate you," she said as she flipped it back at me.

They still had the safe in the back room. For the rest of that month, she kept trying to open it. I'd watch her, and I'd do whatever I could to show her exactly what I was feeling when I got to the shorter contact areas, but I knew there was no way to *make* her feel it. It would either come to her or it wouldn't.

No matter how hard she tried, she couldn't feel it.

Julian made me throw away my fake New York driver's license. He told me he'd find me a *real* fake identity. So I was no longer William Michael Smith.

A friend of a friend of his had a young neighbor who hadn't gotten his California driver's license yet. In fact, he would have had to lose about two hundred pounds before he could even think about trying to fit behind the wheel of a car. So for a certain amount of cash delivered to his door every month, he agreed to "loan" me his identity. I could open up a bank account in his name if I wanted to. I could even use his Social Security number if I wanted to go out and get a real job.

That's how my new fake name became Robin James Agnew.

I still had the pagers with me, of course. One day, the green pager went off. This was the one that had been silent for years, according to what the Ghost had told me. He didn't even know if anyone still had the number.

Well, apparently someone did.

I called the number on the screen. The man who answered asked me if I was the Ghost. When I didn't answer, he asked again, swore a few times, then hung up.

So much for the green pager, I thought. I kept it anyway. I made sure the batteries were fresh, just like in all the others. They sat in the shoebox under my bed, and I checked them every day.

On the first day of February, the yellow pager went off again.

I thought about ignoring it. I finally went to a pay phone down by the marina and dialed the number. It rang twice, and then I heard the voice.

"Is this Michael?"

He knows my name, I thought. Yet he doesn't seem to know I can't answer him.

"This is Harrington Banks," he said. "Harry. Do you remember me? I met you at that junk store in Detroit."

Yes. I remember you. You came in and asked a few questions. I saw you the next day, in your car. You were just sitting there. Watching.

"Is there someplace I can meet you, Mike? I think we really need to talk."

He got his hands on the yellow number. I wonder if he can tell I'm calling him back from L.A.? Hell, maybe he's tracing the number right now. Right down to this exact pay phone next to the docks.

"I think you might have gotten yourself in way too deep," he said. "Are you listening to me? I think you'd better let me try to help you."

I hung up the phone and left. I rode my motorcycle back to the house. When I went back inside, I could hear the yellow pager beeping again. It was the same number.

I was two seconds away from smashing the stupid thing. No matter what would happen to me if the man in Detroit found out about it. Instead, I just took out the batteries and left it lying there dead in the box.

Gunnar was getting restless. He didn't wear it well.

"Julian only knows one way to do this," he said to me. We were sitting at the dining room table. Julian and Ramona and Lucy were in the kitchen. "It takes him like six months to set up a score. *Six months.* Everything's gotta be just right, you know? We gotta know every single last detail about the guy. If he gets up in the middle of the night to take a piss, we gotta know about it."

He drained the last bit of red wine from his glass.

"Meanwhile, Julian gets to play around in his wine store and him and Ramona get to go out with all these big shots. Wine and dine them. Me and Lucy, we just sit around waiting. Until it's finally time to *do something.* Then I get the grunt work, of course. I'm the guy who sits in the fucking closet for six hours. You saw that. And Lucy, either she doesn't get to do anything because Julian can't trust her, or else she ends up being the bait for some horny old guy."

He picked up the bottle and started to fill up his glass again. He got a couple of tablespoons' worth, then nothing but a dribble. He put the bottle back down on the table with a loud thump.

"Life's too short for this, know what I mean? We could be out there *hitting people.* As long as you move fast, you can take a little chance now and then. You don't have to wait so goddamned long. Be such a fucking yellow-ass pussy all the time."

I don't know why he was confiding in me like that. I was the new member of the gang, after all. But hell, I guess I shouldn't have been surprised. You can tell me just about anything and be pretty sure I'm not going to repeat it.

But no matter how anxious Gunnar got, Julian never wavered from his approach. He made his contacts. He developed them. Slowly. Carefully. He got to know everything he could about his marks. Until he would finally see the right opportunity. If it came at all.

Only one time had he ever miscalculated. He had picked the wrong mark, at the wrong time, and it *should* have gotten him killed.

Instead, he got the Ghost. Then me.

"Your man in Detroit," Julian said to me. "This is how I first met him."

It was a few nights later. After another big dinner, just me and Julian and Ramona sitting there with two empty wine bottles on the table. Gunnar and Lucy out riding around somewhere. Julian was telling me this story now, finally, like it was the most important thing he'd ever tell me. It probably was.

"I knew he was a heavy hitter the moment he walked into the store. You've seen him. You know what I'm talking about. I mean, he's not the biggest man in the world, but it's like, he takes up more *space* than anybody else. You know what I mean?"

I nodded. Yes. I know.

"This was a couple of Septembers ago. What he does, apparently, is he leases a big yacht, gets some other really serious guys together, and they start up in Oregon, play some golf up there, work their way down the coast, stop at marinas every couple of days, come ashore for a while, play some more golf, maybe run over to Vegas when they're here in L.A. Sounds like a pretty fun trip, right? A nice little pleasure cruise?"

I thought back to the two times I'd met the man. It was hard to imagine him golfing or sitting on the deck of a boat. Or doing anything remotely human.

"It's all just a warm-up. They push off from here and head down to Mexico, and on their way they start playing poker. No limit hold-'em. Seven, eight guys. Half-million-dollar buy-in. No credit. Strictly cash. So they've got like four million dollars sitting on that boat, Mike. Can you imagine what I was thinking when he told me that? I mean, here he is, standing right in my store, sharing this with me like it was no big deal. This man I'd never even seen before. Anyway, he said he came in to buy some more wine for the boat, but I'm thinking, the universe woke up this morning and decided you've got way too much money, sir. That's the only reason why you're here."

Ramona was sitting next to him. She smiled and shook her head.

"I wasn't quite sure how to make the play," Julian said. "It was such a short window of time, you know? He was heading back to the boat. They'd be leaving the next day. All that money on its way to Mexico. I was thinking, hell, I don't know . . . what could I do? He seemed so open and candid about everything. At least if I could spend a little more time with him, maybe I'd see an angle. So I told him I'd get together the best wine I had, some really nice bottles, bring them all out to the boat personally. And he was like, that would be very kind of you. Come on out, I'll show you around the boat. The whole thing, you know? Really friendly about it. Which should have been a red flag right there. But I was stupid! Four million dollars. It makes you lose your balance.

"So I go out to the marina. He's got the boat there. Biggest boat in the place, by far. Just dwarfs everything else. It wasn't his, remember. He just leases it for the month. Complete with crew, I'm sure. Anyway, Ramona and I are both there, we've got a few cases of wine with us. Ramona's put together some nice flower arrangements. Some cigars. The whole thing, right? We're walking all this stuff up the gangway, Ramona's wearing her bikini top, flirting with Mr. Bigshot there. Everybody else is still on shore, so the rest of the boat is pretty much empty. I figure I can take a little walk around the cabins, right? Take some flowers with me? Open up a few doors, see what's inside. If he sees me, I can just play it off, say I was putting some flowers in the cabins, being a nice guy. Going the extra mile for him. I mean, it's not like I expected the money to just be sitting out there in a pile or anything, but if I could figure out where it was . . . at least we might have a shot, right? If it was all in a safe, maybe Lucy could open it, I was thinking. She'd been working real hard on it back then, and I was just hoping, if the safe wasn't a great one . . ."

He stopped to think about it for a moment. Ramona's smile had disappeared.

"It was really dumb, I know. To just improvise like that. I totally lost my head. Of course, the whole thing turned out to be a setup, anyway. I'm poking around in the cabins, and I actually find the safe. It's right there in one of the cabins. Not a great-looking safe, either. I was pretty sure Lucy could open it. So I'm excited now. When all of a sudden I hear this voice from behind me. I turn around, and there's this other guy there with a gun pointed at me. Some guy I didn't see before. Real strange-looking. You ever meet him? He's got this lazy kind of face, like he's half-asleep all the time?"

I nodded. Oh yes. We've met.

"I started giving him my excuse. 'I was just putting some flowers down here, friend.' But he's not buying it. Hell, it sounded lame to *me*. So he gets me up on deck and there's Ramona with Mr. Bigshot, and all of a sudden nobody's friendly anymore. He sits me down and he asks me to give him one good reason why he shouldn't just take me with them out into the ocean and dump our bodies there. I'm trying to think of something to say, when Ramona pipes up. 'Because sharks don't like Mexican,' she says. Which gets the guy thinking. He says, 'But your boyfriend here isn't Mexican.' And she says, 'Who's talking about *him*?' Which got this guy laughing, at least. But then he got real quiet, and he said, 'Somebody told me you guys were good. So I had to see for myself. Is this the kind of scam you usually run? Wait until a rich man shows up on a boat? Go snooping around the cabins?' And I'm like, 'No, sir. Not at all, sir. And how did you even hear about us in the first place?' Because at that time there was no way he could have known about us. I mean, *no way*. But he gets real close to me and he says, 'I know everything. That's all you have to remember.' And I'm thinking, okay, this is it. We're dead. The lazy-looking guy is getting ready to put a bullet in our heads.

"Then he let us go. Under two conditions, he said. Number one, well, thanks for all the wine and cigars and flowers. That was very thoughtful of you to deliver all of this stuff to the boat. And number two, here's a phone number. 'If you guys live long enough to learn how to do this right,' he says, 'then you'll probably need a good boxman.' We just have to remember to always pay him ten percent off the top. Which is how we got to meet the Ghost."

"Lucy told you about going to visit him," Ramona said. "About her trying to learn from him?"

I nodded.

"Things have a way of working out," Julian said. "We got you instead."

Yeah, things worked out, I thought. And here I am. Working with a guy who tried to set up the wrong target. The absolutely worst target in the world.

No wonder he's so careful now.

———

About a month later, the next score finally came together. It was time to get back to work.

The mark was a smooth, suit-with-no-socks kind of guy who lived up in Monterey, apparently in some ridiculous house perched right on the ocean. He'd been coming down to L.A. every week on some sort of Hollywood-related business. He liked expensive wine, and he *really* liked women who were beautiful in unique, quirky ways. Which is where Lucy came in. She was playing the bait, just like Gunnar had told me.

So on a clear day in April, Julian got his car out of the garage and we drove all the way up the coast to Monterey. Six hours up the Pacific Coast Highway. We stayed overnight in a little hotel, and then the next day it was time to take down Mr. Moon Face. That was our pet name for him.

Julian, Ramona, and Lucy went to his house for dinner that evening. Mr. Moon Face fancied himself quite the gourmet, so he made some kind of poached sea bass or some damned thing and they drained a couple bottles of wine Julian had brought up with him. While the man was distracted, Julian took out a little razor blade and sliced a thin line through the electric foil that ran around the perimeter of one of the man's seaside windows. All of the windows were foiled like this, of course, but now when the man activated his security system, the one window would show a disconnection in the closed circuit. When he looked at the window and found nothing wrong, he'd have to call the security company to get it fixed. Of course, if he was on his way out for a night on the town and a possible shot at sleeping with the young Lucy, the little chink in his security armor would get put aside until the next day.

When they finally left the house, it was time for Gunnar and me to do our thing. The house was close to the road and to some other ridiculous houses hanging on the cliff, so we only had one good way in. We took the car Gunnar had rented in town and parked down by the shore, at one of the observation points. We climbed down the rocks and made our way across the beachfront, finally climbing our way back up to the house. It was a longer climb than either of us had anticipated, and the weather was turning bad fast. The wind picked up. The waves below us were getting higher. It was dark and hard to see exactly where we were going.

The Pacific Ocean, right below me as I struggled my way up those wet rocks. One false step, I thought. That's all it would take. Not the way I wanted to die today. Then in that very next moment I lost my footing and I felt myself starting to fall. I could already feel the cold water against my skin. The waves turning me over and dragging me to the bottom. How quiet it must be down there, compared to this violent roar on the surface.

Then Gunnar reached out a hand and grabbed me by the belt. He saved my mortal life right there. When I was back on the rocks, I shook it off and we kept climbing, until we finally got to the house.

Gunnar located the window with the deactivated foil, put a wad of modeling clay on the glass, and then started cutting a hole, just large enough for us to climb through. We obviously weren't going for a clean in-and-out this time. There's no way you can cover your tracks when you cut a big hole in a window, after all. Julian was confident we wouldn't need it this time. Not with Mr. Moon Face. So we made the forced entry, and within two minutes we were standing inside the house. There was no infrared motion detector to worry about this time, so we were clear. Julian, Ramona, and Lucy would be sure to keep Mr. Moon Face out for another couple of hours, at the very least.

We walked in through the kitchen, past the remains of their fancy dinner. A half-dozen wine bottles sat empty on the table. We found the man's office, where the safe stood tall and proud in the corner. No hidden wall safes for this guy.

I eliminated the tryouts first, then got to work.

Find the contact area, park the wheels, spin and count. Three wheels, check.

Back to 0. Find the area again, feel for the short contact.

3. 6. 9. 12. 15.

I started getting nervous around 30. Were all three numbers high on the dial? Most people don't do it this way.

45, 48, 51.

Damn. Damn.

72, 75, 78.

I was starting to sweat.

93, 96, 99.

Nothing.

I stopped and shook out my hands.

"What's the problem?" Gunnar said.

I shook my head. No problem, man. Everything's cool.

I could hear the waves crashing on the rocks outside. I could smell the salt in the air. I started again.

This time, when I got to 15, I thought I was getting close to something, but the difference felt so faint to me. It was like tuning in a radio station from a thousand miles away.

I shook out my hands again. I tried to clear my mind. I didn't even bother asking myself what the problem was, because at that point I knew.

I hadn't been practicing enough. Simple as that. I hadn't been spinning the dial enough on the safe in Julian's house. I hadn't been spinning on my portable lock. I just hadn't been doing it. I had just assumed I could pick it back up again, any time I wanted.

So I had to spend the next full hour finding my touch again, while Gunnar paced back and forth and tried very hard not to strangle me. I finally narrowed the numbers down, and even then I wasn't totally sure about them. My face was dripping with sweat now.

I'll never take this for granted again, I promised myself. Just get this thing open and I promise I'll practice every single day.

I spun through the possible combinations. Every single damned one of them. None of them opened the safe. So I had to go back and redo my contacts, go through them again and find the number I had gotten wrong. When I finally did that . . . when I *hoped* I had done that . . . I had to go back and do the combinations again. We were going on two hours inside the house now.

I cranked through each possible combination. The waves were getting louder. From somewhere in the room I could hear a clock ticking.

Then . . . finally. Finally! I hit the right combination and turned the handle. Gunnar pushed by me and started shoving money into his bag. I got up and stretched out my back, walked around a little bit and saw the headlights through one of the front windows.

Son of a bitch.

I ran back and helped him finish putting the money in the bag. Then I slammed the door shut, and we went back to the hole in the window, keeping our heads down. We jumped through it like circus performers, rolling in the sand and gravel outside and scrambling down onto the rocks.

When we were down on the beach, we ran back toward the rental car, the waves even higher now, our legs getting soaked. We climbed back up to the car. We stood there catching our breath for a minute. Then Gunnar grabbed me by my shirt. He got his face up close to mine, and I was waiting for him to yell at me for taking so fucking long to open the fucking safe. But he didn't.

"Lucy's mine. Do you hear me? She's the only person I've ever loved. Like in my whole life. You understand me?"

I looked at him. Was he really telling me this now?

"Do you understand me or not?"

I nodded my head. Yes, I understand.

He let go of me. He threw the money in the backseat and got behind the wheel. I got in beside him and made two promises to myself.

Stay away from Lucy.

And practice.

Nineteen

Michigan
July 1999

I knew it was too good to be true. I knew the catch was coming. For the moment, I didn't care. I was outside, not digging but sitting in a chair, next to Amelia. With the official approval of her father.

Somehow it felt different now. You're another person when it's late at night. Here it was . . . just us, our real daytime selves. Two seventeen-and-a-half-year-olds who went to different high schools and otherwise lived in different worlds. Only one of whom could speak.

"You feel weird?" she said.

I nodded.

"Would you rather be digging?"

I didn't think I had to answer that one.

"So . . . how are we gonna do this? I mean, how are we going to communicate?"

I was about to make the writing gesture, so maybe she could go find me a pad of paper, when she came right out of her chair and grabbed me. She kissed me for a long time, long enough for me to forget about pads of paper and everything else in the whole world.

"You must know sign language," she said, sitting back down. "Teach me some stuff. Hello is . . ."

I waved my hand. It made me think of Griffin, asking me the same thing once upon a time.

"Yeah, okay. Duh. How 'bout, 'You look good.'"

I pointed to her. You. Then I drew a circle around my face. Look. Then a simple thumbs-up. Good.

"What if I wanted to tell you to kiss me again?"

With each hand, I put my fingers and thumb together, like a gourmet ready to say "Magnifique!" I brought one hand to my lips, then put both hands together.

"That's 'kiss'? Are you kidding me? That's the lamest thing I've ever seen!"

I shrugged it off. I wasn't around when they made that up.

"We need our own secret sign language for 'Kiss me,'" she said. "How about this?"

She grabbed me again and took me inside the house. Up to her bedroom. I looked around for her father on the way, figuring this might be one sure way to die. Maybe not the worst, but still. He had apparently run off somewhere, so for the moment we seemed to have the house to ourselves.

We did some things next that we'd need a whole different set of sign language for. When we were done, we lay in her bed, staring at the ceiling. She kept running her fingers through my hair.

"It's nice to be around somebody who doesn't talk all the time."

If that's really true, I thought, then you came to the right place.

"Are you going to draw something for me today?"

To be honest, I didn't feel like drawing just then. Or doing anything at all except exactly what I was doing. But we had to get up and get dressed eventually. She found a couple of big sketchbooks and a few pencils, and for the next hour or so we sat on her bed drawing. We were drawing each other in the act of drawing each other. Her with one strand of hair falling over her face, me with a serious expression on my face, bordering on sadness. On melancholy. I was surprised to see that in her drawing of me. It was my first truly happy day in a thousand days. How must I have looked before then?

A couple more hours went by. It was four o'clock already. Amazing how much faster the time went by when I wasn't killing myself outside and counting the minutes until I could go home. We heard her father's car pulling into the driveway, so we went downstairs, back out to the chairs outside.

Cut to a barbecue in the backyard, a few hours later, this day getting more unlikely with every passing minute. I was sitting on top of a picnic table, next to Amelia. I was holding a beer in my hand, three and a half years away from being able to drink it legally, but what the hell on a hot summer night. The beer had been given to me by Mr. Marsh himself, after I'd just spent two solid hours in the close company of his daughter in her bedroom. The only dark cloud being Amelia's brother, Adam, who was home for the evening from East Lansing. He was wearing a ripped tank top, his arms bulging like they'd been stuffed with coconuts. His hair had been cut high and tight, with a faux Mohawk running down the middle. As soon as he saw me there in his backyard, he looked very much like he wanted to kill me.

"You're the little bitch who broke into our house?" he said.

That's when Mr. Marsh came to my rescue. He told him I was a stand-up guy and how he should leave me alone and forgive me and not kill me, et cetera. Ever since then, though, Adam hadn't stopped glaring at me from the other side of the yard. He had five former Lakeland football players standing around next to him, with more on the way, apparently. Mr. Marsh was grilling hot dogs and hamburgers at a frantic pace to keep up with their appetites.

Amelia took my right hand in her left, lacing our fingers together. Nobody else seemed to even notice this. She seemed barely aware of it herself, as she stared out at the night sky.

"Nights like this," she finally said, in a voice low enough so only I could hear. "You'd think we're a nice, normal, happy family."

She turned to look at me.

"Don't believe it. Not for a second."

I wasn't sure what she was getting at. I'd never thought of them as nice, normal, or happy. I wouldn't even know what that looks like in the first place.

"If I asked you to, would you take me away from here? As far as we could get?"

I squeezed her hand.

"You're a criminal, after all. You can kidnap me, right?"

I took another sip of beer, feeling that same little lightheaded feeling I had the night we broke into this very house. It was another night that felt like it was opening up right in front of me. Like anything could happen again, good or bad.

The night got darker. The moon was shining. The smoke from the grill hung in the air. Mr. Marsh played the Beach Boys on his boom box. His favorite group, apparently. At least on a warm summer night. His partner Mr. Slade showed up just in time to get the last hamburger. I realized as soon as I saw him that I had seen him before. Then I remembered. He was the man who had come out to watch me dig for a few minutes, before going inside to meet with Mr. Marsh. Today he was once again dressed in a suit, with the tie knotted tight against his neck. His hair looked slightly wet, like he had just come from the gym.

When Amelia went inside for a moment, Mr. Marsh cornered me and officially introduced the man.

"Michael, meet Jerry Slade. My partner."

"I believe we've met," he said, shaking my hand. "Good to see you again."

"I don't think Jerry believes you can do what you can do," Mr. Marsh said. "You still think you could show him?"

Amelia came back outside and saved me.

Mr. Marsh grabbed me and whispered in my ear. "We'll show him later." Then he slapped me on the back and went back to his grill.

A couple of hours later, Adam and his friends rolled off to hit another party. It was just the four of us now.

"Gotta get this boy home to bed," Mr. Marsh said, wrapping an arm around my shoulder. "We might just have him out digging again tomorrow."

"I thought he was done with that," Amelia said.

"I'm just kidding, honey. I'll let you two kids say good night. Actually, can you stop in to my office on your way out, Michael? I wanted to ask you one more thing, you know, about our new work arrangement."

He turned off the music. Then he and Jerry went inside. It was quiet and dark now in the backyard. The big white tent seemed to glow in the moonlight.

"What is he having you do now?" Amelia said, wrapping her arms around my waist. "And why is Mr. Slade here? That guy gives me the creeps."

I shook my head. Hell if I know what's going on.

"Just be careful, okay? Those two guys get together, God knows what they'll come up with."

I wasn't sure how to take that, but I figured I'd find out soon enough.

She kissed me good night. I didn't want her to leave. I wanted to stay right there in the backyard with her for the rest of the night. But I knew the men were waiting for me.

She went up to her room. I went to the office. They were both standing underneath the giant fish. As soon as I came in, Mr. Marsh took out a leather case and gave it to me.

"Do you remember these?"

I opened it and saw the same lock-picking tools I had used in our little exhibitions with the locksmith.

"Can you show Mr. Slade what you can do with them now?"

I looked back and forth between them. They were dead serious. This wasn't just a bar bet.

"Now, I know we've got those fancy unpickable locks on the doors now, but there's gotta be something around here . . ."

As he rummaged around in his desk, I stood there sorting through the picks and tension bars. Such a perfect set of tools. I couldn't help it. I had to try them again. So I gave them a little wave and had them follow me out the back door. When all three of us were outside, I locked the door and closed it.

"What are you doing?" Mr. Marsh said. "You can't open this lock, remember?"

I bent down, took out the tension bar and a diamond pick, and got to work. Using the same idea for these serrated pins . . . oversetting all of them, and then letting them fall back down just enough, one by one . . . with the good tools, it was a snap.

Two minutes later, I turned the handle and pushed the door open.

"Holy Christ," Mr. Marsh said. "How the fuck did you do that?"

"I'm impressed," Mr. Slade said. "I mean, I know what you told me, but seeing it in person? God damn."

"What else can you open?" Mr. Marsh said. "Can you open *any* kind of lock?"

He pushed in past me, into the kitchen. He started rummaging through a junk drawer. Then he pulled out an old padlock.

"I don't even know the combination to this thing anymore. Can you open it?"

I took it from him. A cheap padlock off of one of his kids' gym lockers, probably. Thrown into the junk drawer forever.

"This I gotta see," Mr. Slade said.

He didn't realize that this would be easier. A *lot* easier. But what the hell. I spun through the sticking points, found the obvious last number. Cleared it and started through the super sets, using the good old number families. I got lucky, because the first number was a three. So it didn't take me more than a minute to snap it open.

They both stood there with their jaws open, like I had just levitated or something. I mean, it really was no big deal to me.

"Did I tell you or what?" Mr. Marsh said. "Is he or is he not amazing?"

"He is amazing."

I gestured for something to write on, so I could give them the combination and they'd have this padlock back in service. They obviously had much bigger things in mind.

"What do you think?" Mr. Marsh said. "Can he use him?"

I didn't know who they were talking about. I wasn't sure I liked the sound of it, but Jerry Slade was already smiling and nodding his head.

"Damned straight. How could he *not* use him?"

"This could be it," Mr. Marsh said. "This could be our ticket out of hell."

It was just after midnight when I got back to Milford, but the liquor store was still open. Uncle Lito was behind the register, the phone to his ear. He slammed it down when I stuck my head in the door.

"Where in blazes have you been all night?"

I made a digging motion.

"Since noon? You worked for what, twelve hours?"

I gave him the thumbs-up and backed out the doorway. I heard him calling to me, but I kept walking. Back to the house. To my room. I sat down at my desk. I didn't feel like sleeping. I didn't feel like drawing. I just sat there and wondered what I'd gotten myself into.

I took out the leather case from my back pocket. I opened it and sorted through the tools. At least I've got these now, I thought. I'll take care of these like fine jewels.

I didn't know any better. I didn't know that once you've proven yourself useful to the wrong people, you'll never be free again.

The next day, my uncle was still pissed at me for leaving him hanging all night. Sitting at the kitchen table, eating his cereal. "That guy you work for," he said, "you know he's crazy. He could have killed you and buried you in his backyard for all I knew."

I made a fist and rubbed it in a circle against my heart. He'd never been great with the sign language, but he knew that one. *I'm sorry.*

"You're growing up. I know that. You're at that age, you think you know everything."

I nodded at him, wondering who he was even talking about. Certainly not me.

"I was seventeen myself once. I know that's hard to imagine. Of course, I hadn't dealt with half of what you've had to deal with."

I couldn't help wondering where he was going with this.

"You know, when I was seventeen, there was only one thing I wanted to do."

Oh, please. Don't go there.

"Okay, two things, but there's one in particular I'm talking about here. Can you guess?"

I shook my head.

"Come on out to the store with me. I was going to give this to you yesterday."

I followed him out of the house and around to the liquor store. He put a key in the back door and disappeared inside. When he came back out, he was pushing a motorcycle.

"It's a Yahama 850 Special," he said. "It's used, but it's in great shape."

I stood there looking at it. The seat was black with a bronze trim. The chrome exhausts shone in the bright sunlight. If he had rolled out a spaceship, I wouldn't have been any less surprised.

"One of my regulars couldn't cover his tab. He offered me this bike if I would call it all square."

That must have been one hell of a tab, I thought.

"Come on, saddle up. Hold on, I got you a helmet here."

I took the handlebars from him while he went back inside. He came back out with a helmet and a black leather jacket.

"You need this, too," he said. "I hope it's the right size."

I would have been speechless even if I could speak. I put the jacket on. Then he helped me put on the helmet. I sat on the bike and felt the whole thing bounce up and down under my weight.

"New shocks, he told me. New brakes. Tires are okay, not great. We'll get you some new ones soon."

I still couldn't believe it was happening. I was actually supposed to ride this thing?

"Take it nice and easy at first, eh? Go ahead, give it a try."

After he showed me how to start it, I tried putting it in gear and giving it a little gas. It just about took off from right underneath me. I tried again and made sure I was ready for it. After a couple of circles in the parking lot, I was on my way down the street. I took it slow at first, afraid I'd end up on the hood of somebody's car. Then I started to get the hang of it. It was much easier to stay balanced than I would have imagined. And I had to say, the whole experience felt pretty damned good.

I took the bike back, but my uncle was already stationed behind his cash register, ringing up his first customer of the day. He gave me a wave, told me to go back out and get to know the bike. He gave me a few bucks to fill up the tank. Then I was off.

I spent the rest of the morning riding. You don't realize just how much pickup one of those babies has. From an absolute dead stop, if you really crank it, it feels like you're on a rocket. I headed west on the back roads, out into what was then still farmland. I found a new hatred for dirt roads that have been freshly oiled, nearly killing myself the first time I hit one. After that I stuck to pavement and didn't have any other close calls. It was just me and the sound of the machine between my legs and the wind whipping against my helmet. I wanted to share this feeling with Amelia. To take her by the hand and sit her down on the back of the bike. I could already feel her hands wrapped around my waist.

I made one more stop to buy a pair of sunglasses. And another helmet for Amelia. Now I had everything I needed in life. I got back on that bike and headed straight for her house.

So I rode out to that big white castle of a house gleaming in the sun, feeling like I owned the whole world. Feeling like this could be the day that I start talking. I mean, why not? Maybe this is what it would take.

Today, though, I was going to get something a little bit different.

I saw Mr. Marsh's car in the driveway, but when I knocked on the door, nobody answered. I knocked again. Nothing.

I wandered around the house to the backyard and looked under the tent. The plants Mr. Marsh had dragged back there were all starting to wilt, so I went looking for a watering can and spent the next few minutes walking back and forth between the tent and the faucet.

Then I knocked on the back door. When nobody answered, I pushed the door open and went inside. I walked through and peeked into Mr. Marsh's office. Nobody there. I looked up the stairs and saw that Amelia's door was closed. I went up and knocked.

"Who is it?" she said from inside.

I knocked again. What else could I do?

"Come on in."

When I opened the door, I saw her sitting at her desk. Her back was to me. She didn't say a word. I hesitated, finally came into the room and went over to where she was working. I wanted to touch her shoulders, but I didn't.

She was drawing something. Buildings, an alleyway. Lots of shadows. There was a long figure in the foreground, but it was hard for me to see exactly what she was doing with it. I stood there for a long time, watching her work.

"If I don't talk," she said, "it's going to be pretty quiet in here, huh?"

She turned around, finally, and looked me in the eyes for the first time that day.

"My mother killed herself. Did you know that?"

I nodded. I remembered Mr. Marsh telling me that, on that very first day, before I had even seen Amelia.

"Today's the anniversary. Five years ago."

She still had the pencil in her hand. She twirled it in her fingers like a miniature baton.

"Five years ago exactly, at one o'clock in the afternoon. Give or take a few minutes. I was in school when it happened."

She got up and went over to her dresser. She went through a stack of papers and drawings and pulled out a portfolio. I wasn't about to tell her so, but this was the same portfolio I had looked through the night we had all broken into this house. It was the first time I had seen her drawings, the first time I had seen her face. I remembered there were some other drawings in there, too. Of an older woman. These were the same drawings I was about to see again.

"This was her," Amelia said, putting each drawing, one by one, onto the bed. Her mother sitting in a chair. Then outside, on a bench. "I was twelve years old then. She was in this institution they sent her to for a while. I got to go visit her."

I could see it now, in the drawings. The manicured lawn, the path running a straight line, in front of the bench. Everything in its place. These were some pretty damned excellent drawings if they were really done by a twelve-year-old.

"I was so happy, because I knew she'd be coming home soon. Three months later . . ."

She closed her eyes.

"Three months later, she sealed up the garage and started the car. By the time I got home from school, she was dead. I wasn't the one who found her. I mean, my brother found her. He came home first and she was. I mean, she was there in the car. In the garage. This was at our old house. Before we moved here. Anyway, there was no note. No nothing. Just . . . checkout time."

She started putting the drawings back into the folder. She didn't look at me.

"It wasn't the first time she tried something like that. Did you know that women are twice as likely as men to try to commit suicide? But most of the time they don't actually do it. Men are four times more likely to actually kill themselves."

She was talking a little too fast now. Like she didn't want there to be any silence again.

"I looked that up last night, because I wanted to try to understand what happened to you. I mean, I know the general story. I know they called you the Miracle Boy."

I saw one single tear on her face.

"It's been five years for me," she said. "For you, it's like what, nine years? In all that time, you never tried to . . ."

She wiped the tear from her cheek, finally turned and faced me.

"I mean, is this it? Are you seriously never going to talk to me? Ever?"

I closed my eyes. Right there, at that moment, in Amelia's bedroom . . . I closed my eyes and took a deep breath, and I told myself that this was what I had been waiting for. I had never had such a good reason to try before. All I had to do was just open up and let go of the silence. Just like those doctors had said, years ago. It was as true on this day as it had been then. There was no physical reason why I couldn't speak. So all I had to do was . . .

The seconds passed. A minute.

"Some men came and took my father away," she finally said. "About an hour ago. I don't know where they were going. I don't even know if they're going to bring him back. Seriously . . . I mean, I thought it might be him when I heard you in the driveway."

I reached out to touch her. She turned away from me.

"I am so freaked out right now, Michael. I don't know what I'm going to do. Do you have any idea how much trouble my father is in these days? What if they—"

She looked up.

"God, is that him now?"

She went to the window and looked down at the driveway. When I stepped behind her, I saw the long black car, then the three men all getting out at the same time. One from the driver's door. Two men from the backseat. Then finally, a few seconds later, another man. Mr. Marsh. He blinked in the bright sunlight and straightened his shirt. His face was bright red.

"Oh, fuck." She turned and ran out of the room.

I followed her. Down the steps. Through the front door. She passed right by her father and went for the driver of the car. She took a wild swing at him.

"I'm calling the police, you fucking goons!"

Mr. Marsh tried to grab her from behind while the driver fended off her blows with a big stupid grin on his face. He was wearing a fishing hat of all things, and Amelia finally managed to knock it off his head. The grin disappeared, and he raised his open right hand as if to give her a good slap. That's when I caught up and threw myself right into the middle of it.

One of the other men grabbed me by the collar. He was shorter than the other two men. He was ugly and his eyes looked half shut, and as he pulled my shirt tight around my neck, he put his face right up into mine.

"Do you have a death wish, son?" he said. "Or are you just incredibly stupid?"

"Let him go," Mr. Marsh said.

"I asked you a question," he said to me.

The third man was still on the other side of the car. He was tall, and he had a mustache that was too big for his face.

"Let go of the kid," he said, "so we can get the hell out of here."

The man with the sleepy eyes tightened his grip one more notch, enough to choke me. Then he pushed me away.

The driver picked up his fishing hat, tipped it to us, and got in behind the wheel. The other two men got in back, and as the doors closed we could hear them already arguing. The car shot backward onto the street, then roared off. As it did, I got one more glance at the man in the backseat. Those sleepy eyes on the other side of that window, staring back at me.

Not for the last time.

The three of us kept standing there in the driveway. Amelia was crying now. Not wailing away, just softly crying in almost total silence. She wiped her face off. She went to her father and stood before him. He reached out to her, just as I had tried to do. She knocked his hand away.

"You promised me," she said. "You promised me you wouldn't get into this kind of shit again."

Before he could even try to answer, she turned and went back into the house, slamming the door behind her.

Mr. Marsh let out a long breath. He paced back and forth on the driveway a few times. Slowly, like a much older man.

"Look," he finally said to me. "I know we started to talk about this the other day, but I need you to help me. Help *us*. Me and Amelia. Will you help us out? Please?"

I rubbed my neck, where the fabric had left a raw crease in my skin.

"I owe these people a lot of money, okay? I just . . . If you can just help me out here this one time . . ."

He reached into his pocket and took out a small slip of paper.

"I need you to go see somebody. Today. Nothing bad will happen, I promise. Just go see this man, okay? He'll be expecting you. This is his address. It's in Detroit."

I took the paper. I looked at the address.

"You'll know him when you see him," he said. "They call him the Ghost."

He wasn't more than forty miles away, this man who would change my life. I didn't want to get on the expressway with my motorcycle yet, so I worked my way down the secondary streets to Grand River, then took that straight into the heart of the city. From block to block, I could see every social class. The landscaping thinning out, the buildings going from glass and steel to gray cinder blocks and iron bars.

There were lots of stoplights. Lots of opportunities for me to change my mind. The lights kept turning green and I kept going forward. When I hit Detroit, I started to look at the street numbers. A couple more blocks and I knew I was close. I waited for a break in traffic, then swung the bike around to the other side of the street. The whole block reeked of desperation and wasted second chances. It was the west side of Detroit, just inside the border.

I counted down the addresses. There was a dry cleaners, then a hair salon, then a store that appeared to sell both discount clothing and music and small appliances out of an impossibly small space. Then an empty storefront. It was hard to tell exactly where my target was, because not all the buildings had numbers above the door. I finally narrowed it down to a business called West Side Recovery. It was twice as wide as most of the other businesses, with windows that could have used a good cleaning a decade ago. There was a CLOSED sign hanging inside the glass door.

I rechecked the address. I was sure this was it. I knocked on the door.

Nobody answered. I knocked one more time, was about to turn and leave when the door finally opened. The man who stuck his head out was about sixty years old, maybe sixty-five. He was wearing a sweater vest, and he had reading glasses hanging from his neck. He had thin, white hair and a complexion so pale it looked like five minutes of direct sunlight would kill him. He blinked a few times as he gave me the once-over.

"Am I supposed to be expecting you?"

I handed him the piece of paper Mr. Marsh had given me, with his address on it. He slipped his reading glasses on and gave it a look.

"Is that your bike I heard?"

I turned back to where it was parked, halfway down the block.

"So apparently you wish to have it stolen today? Is that your plan?"

I shook my head.

"Bring it over here, genius. You can pull it inside here."

I went back and got the bike and pushed it down the sidewalk to where he stood, holding the door open. It was so dark inside the store, it was like rolling the motorcycle into a cave.

He closed the door behind us and kicked something aside. It took my eyes a few seconds to adjust, but when they did I saw a huge collection of scrap metal, old furniture, cribs and high chairs, a couple of refrigerators standing side by side. Basically it looked like a good portion of the city dump had been transferred here.

"This way," he said. I kickstanded the bike and followed him back through the store. He traced his way down a mazelike path through the junk to another door, through which I could see the flickering blue light of a television set. There was a faint haze of dust in the air that I could almost taste.

"I'm closed on Mondays," he said. "Reason the lights are off. I'd offer you a beer, but I'm fresh out." There was a better selection of junk in this second room. Besides the television, there were probably a few hundred items stacked on floor-to-ceiling shelves. A washboard, an iron, some old green bottles. Stuff like that. A few shelves on one wall were bulging with books. This whole place had so much more junk than the junk store back in Milford. I wondered why all the better items seemed to be hidden away here in the back room. But more than that, I wondered why I was sent here.

"They said you don't talk much." He was standing next to a desk that didn't have one free square inch on it. There were a dozen lamps on it, along with cigar boxes and trophies and a three-foot-high Statue of Liberty. The man slid the statue in just far enough to give himself a surface to lean on.

"They call me the Ghost," he said.

Yes, I thought. That makes sense. Just look at you.

"That's the only thing you can ever call me. Are we understood? To you, I'm the Ghost. Or Mr. G. Nothing else."

The dust and mildew were starting to get to me. That plus the fact I still had no idea what the hell was going on here, or what was expected of me.

"You really don't talk. They weren't kidding."

I was thinking maybe it was time to ask the Ghost for some paper so I could write out a few questions, but he was ready to move on.

"This way. I've got something you might like to see."

He pushed open another door. I followed him down a short hallway, squeezing my way past several bicycles until we came to yet another door.

When he opened it, we were outside. Or rather half outside. There was a makeshift awning above us, long strips of green plastic with gaps here and there that let the sun in. It ran all the way to the back fence, which was over-run with thick sumac and poison ivy.

"Here we go." He pushed through a collection of old lawn mowers, past a rusted-out barbecue grill. He picked up an iron gate, something that looked like it came from a haunted mansion somewhere, and moved it aside. He was surprisingly strong for a pale old man who looked like a retired English professor.

He stepped aside and ushered me into this small clearing within the greater chaos. There, arranged in a perfect circle, were eight safes of various heights, their combination dials facing the center. It was like a Stonehenge of safes.

"Not bad, eh?" He walked the circle, touching each safe one by one. "Every major brand. American, Diebold, Chicago, Mosler, Schwab, Victor. This one here's forty years old. That one over there is new, hardly ever been used. What do you think?"

I did a slow 360, looking at all of the safes.

"Take your pick," he said.

What, he wanted me to pick out a safe? So I could take it home, strapped on my back while I rode my motorcycle?

He put his reading glasses on again. He tilted his head so he could peer over the lenses at me. "Come on, let's see you do your thing."

My thing, he says. He wants me to do my thing. This man actually wanted me to open one of these safes.

"Today would be good." He stood there in the green-tinted shade, finally taking his glasses off and letting them dangle from his neck again. I stood there. I didn't move.

"Are you going to open one of these safes," he said, speaking very slowly, as if to a simpleton, "or aren't you?"

I went to the safe closest to me, one of the tall boys. It was as big as a Coke machine. The combination dial was a finely engineered machine of polished metal, like something you'd see on a bank vault. I grabbed the handle next to the dial and gave it an experimental pull. Yet more finely engineered metal said fuck you and did not move the slightest fraction of an inch.

"All right, now you're joking around, right? Now you're being a comedian?"

I looked at him. What on earth could I possibly do here? How could I communicate that this was all a big mistake? How could I make this man believe that I was sent here because of two absolute morons and that I was simply wasting his time?

A few more seconds of us both standing there, and at least the bottom line became clear to him. "You can't open any of these, can you?"

I shook my head.

"Then what the fuck are you doing here?"

Hands up. I don't know.

"I cannot even believe this. You have got to be fucking kidding me. They're gonna send this kid over. He's a natural, they say. An absolute natural. He's the Golden Boy."

He turned away from me, walked away a few paces, and then came back at me.

"You're the Golden Boy, all right. You fucking—"

He stopped and seemed to be working very hard to contain himself.

"Okay. Count to ten here, huh? The Golden Boy ain't so golden. It's not the end of the world."

He closed his eyes for a moment, put two fingers from each hand on his temples, and started rubbing in little circles. He took a few deep breaths and then opened his eyes.

"You're still standing here," he said. "Why is that? Are you seriously trying to make me have an aneurism?"

I took a step toward the door, not sure I could even find my way back through the maze.

"There you go! Now you've got it. You can't open a safe, but you know when to leave. Give you credit for that."

He pushed by me and led me through the lawn mowers and barbecue grills. When he opened the back door, we were plunged into darkness again, and I almost killed myself on the gauntlet of bicycles in the hallway.

"Graceful, too! What a bonus. I'm so glad you came to visit today."

He hurried me through the television room and through the main room to the front door.

"Get your bike, Golden Boy."

He held the door open for me while I fumbled with my motorcycle and then finally wheeled it outside.

"That's right," he said when I was finally on the sidewalk. "Get the fuck out of here and don't come back."

He closed the door behind him and that was it. A rousing success! It was hard to see with all the confetti and streamers flying around.

What the hell, I thought. If that was a job interview, I was kinda glad I hadn't passed. I rolled the bike to the street and started it. Then I was flying up Grand River, honestly believing that I'd never return.

I drove right back to the Marshes' house. I went in through the front door, went up the stairs. I knocked on her door. She was either out somewhere, or else she just didn't want to deal with anybody right now. Even me.

I turned to go back down the stairs and saw her standing at the bottom.

"What are you doing?" she said. "Why did you come back?"

I went down the stairs.

"Where did you go, anyway?"

A pen, I thought. Paper. Why the hell don't I carry them around with me?

"Michael, what are you doing for my father?"

I made a writing motion. Let me tell you.

"I probably don't even want to know, right?"

I tried to grab her by the shoulders. No, not grab her. Just put one hand on each shoulder so she'd stand there and stop talking for one minute while I found something to write on. She pushed my hands away.

"I should have seen right through this," she said. "I mean, I know he'll do anything to get what he wants. But look at you. One day he's trying to kill you. You have to break into the house at night just to see me. The next day, all of a sudden you're his right-hand man. Invited to the family barbecue . . . You're the Golden Boy."

Again with the Golden Boy. Where did this come from all of a sudden?

"I was the prize, wasn't I? Whatever you've done for him, I'm your reward."

Now's the time, I thought. Time to speak. Make a sound. Anything. Do it right now. Just do it.

"Don't you get it? He's going to drag us down with him. Both of us."

Open your mouth. Right now. Let it come out.

"I can't be here anymore. Not one more minute."

You stupid fucking mutant freak. *Say something!*

She tried to push past me. I grabbed her arm. For real this time.

"Let go. Please."

I took her hand, lacing my fingers into hers. I pulled her through the door and out into the driveway.

"What are you doing?"

I took the helmet off the seat of my motorcycle and tried to put it on her head.

"What is this? Where did this motorcycle come from?"

I held the helmet out to her, waiting for her to put it on.

"I'm not wearing that."

I threw it into the grass and got on the bike. I started it. I moved up to the front of the seat and waited for her. I didn't even look back. I just waited.

Finally, I felt her climbing onto the back of the bike. I felt her hands slipping around my waist. Yes, I thought. If this is the only good thing I'll get to feel all day . . . I'll take it. This moment right here.

"Take me away," I heard her say behind me. "I don't care where we go. Just take me away."

I knew I couldn't do it yet. Not for real. Not forever. But for one day . . . a few stolen hours . . . yes. We could get as far away from here as this bike would take us.

I put it in gear and we took off down the street.

Twenty
Los Angeles, Arizona
July, August, September 2000

As the summer came to Southern California, everyone was back in their holding patterns. Julian and Ramona were selling fine wine and looking for the next mark. Gunnar was doing his tattoos and grumbling about how slow and careful Julian and Ramona were being. Lucy had given up her painting by then. She tried to learn to guitar for a while. Then after maybe one week of that, she started spending a lot more time with Gunnar down at his tattoo parlor. She had finally decided to learn the craft herself. So I was on my own a lot more during the day. I'd either spin my locks or draw. Or I'd get on my bike and go out riding around in the city.

Then I got another call on the green pager. The last time around, they had asked for the Ghost, remember, and had freaked out when I didn't say anything. So I wasn't expecting much this time. But when I called the number, the man on the other end gave me an address in Scottsdale, Arizona. It was less than four hundred miles away, a straight shot down I-10, so I got on my bike and hit the road. Five and a half hours later, I was sitting outside a gas station on Indian School Road, drinking as much water as I could physically get down my throat. I finally got off the bike and sat down with my back against the hard brick wall. When I woke up, the sun was in my eyes.

I waited around for another hour or two. Until the temperature had once again climbed over 110. Then I got on the bike and headed back to Los Angeles.

Six more hard hours on the road, and when I got back I could feel the tension in the air. Julian and Gunnar had been fighting again.

"Oh, and this guy," Gunnar said when I walked in the door. "This guy gets to go out and do freelance jobs any time he wants! He gets a call, and boom, he's out of here! Opening up a safe for somebody else, making money.

While I have to sit here playing with myself, waiting for you to put something together."

It was a bad day to hit me with that line. I didn't care if he could kill me with his bare hands, I went right up to him, took out my wallet from my back pocket, and took out whatever money I had. A few twenties. A hundred bucks, maybe. I slapped the money against his chest and walked out.

The next day, I went out to the backyard and picked up one of Gunnar's low-tech barbells. It was a metal pipe with sandbags tied to each end. I tried curling it a few times. Then I saw Gunnar come charging out of the house. I put the barbell down, figuring I'd just earned myself a hard lesson in keeping my hands off other people's property. Instead he picked up the bar and gave it back to me.

"Didn't anybody ever teach you to do this the right way?"

He showed me the correct form for a biceps curl. Feet hip-width apart, chest out, abs tight, back straight, elbows tucked into my sides. Keep the elbows still, pause and contract at the top. Inhale on the way down.

"It's about damned time you worked out," he said to me. "I need you to keep up with me when we're out on a job."

Then he made me reverse with the triceps. Everything in balance, he told me. From that day on he became my personal trainer. He started killing me in the backyard every other morning. I mean absolutely killing me. I think it's safe to say he enjoyed it.

Until that one morning . . .

I was doing bench presses with his iron pipe, cinder blocks chained to each end. The pipe a little too thick to grip properly and the cinder blocks threatening to swing over and bash me in the head. Why he never got real weights, I'd never know. God knows he had the money now.

In any case, he was spotting me and I was working hard. I was getting toward the end of my set. We had our shirts off in the morning sun. The bench was nothing but a wooden plank set on more cinder blocks. He hardly ever talked to me when we were working out, but today was the exception.

"I suppose Julian told you the story about the man from Detroit."

I was breathing hard, holding the pipe just above my chest and getting ready to lift it again.

"He told you how he met him? How they went out on his boat? Checked out the safe and everything? What did you think of that?"

I squinted as I looked up at him. What the hell was he talking about?

"Think about it. This guy comes through with four million dollars cash in his safe. Julian goes on board and gets busted trying to case out the boat, right? Guy puts a gun to his head, makes him piss in his pants? Takes all his wine and cigars? Does that seem a little funny to you?"

I couldn't get up. Not with the weight on my chest. I was trapped there until he finished his pitch. Every last word of it.

"You know what we could do, Mike? When that boat comes back through this year . . . you and I could sneak on board and take all of that fucking money. What do you think?"

I started shaking my head. No. You're crazy. No.

"I know this guy owns you, Mike. I know that. I know he's supposed to be real scary, too. I'm just saying . . . if somebody would finally grow a set of balls around here, we could take this guy down."

I kept shaking my head.

"I'm not afraid of him," Gunnar said. He finally pulled the bar off my chest. "I'm not afraid of anybody."

I sat up and started to put my shirt on.

"What if I told you I've developed another contact on the boat? Somebody who could help us."

I stopped.

"Somebody who works for one of the other players. I know Julian thinks he's the only one who can put these things together. Like the rest of us aren't smart enough. But this guy, I'm telling you . . . he's in the same position we are, you know? Always having to answer to somebody. He gets tired of it. Just like you do, I'm sure. So when we got talking, it was like, hey, maybe we can work something out. Something that'll be great for all of us."

I stood up and walked away.

"Just think about it," he said. "We've got some time. Just think about it."

There was nothing to think about. It was insanity. It was suicide. But Gunnar wouldn't let it go. He kept hitting me with it, whenever we were alone.

"He treats you like a dog," he said to me once. Talking about the man from Detroit, of course. Like he could see the image I'd always had in my mind. Me being the dog with no place to sleep, who nevertheless had to come running whenever the master called.

"Maybe for once in your life you should think about biting the hand that feeds you."

Around the end of that month, the green pager went off again. I walked down to that same pay phone and called the number. Even though I was expecting the same clowns who had made me ride all the way out to fucking Scottsdale, Arizona, for nothing.

But no, it wasn't them this time.

"Michael, it's Banks. Are you there?"

What the hell?

"I know you can't speak. I apologize, I didn't know that last time. I didn't know anything about you. Now I do, and you've got to listen to me."

I was standing on Santa Monica Boulevard. Traffic crawling by me on a hot summer night.

"The men who called you on this number before . . . They're out of the game now. For good. The same thing's gonna happen to everybody, sooner or later. Are you hearing me? If you trust me, I can get you through this. I'll do everything I can to help you. I know you must feel like you don't have a choice anymore. But you do."

The half-dirty air coming in off the ocean. The sound of the cars. My own heart beating hard in my chest.

"Your uncle is worried about you, Mike. Your uncle Lito. I talked to him. He wants you to come home."

I pressed my forehead against the glass.

"I'm in California now, Mike. I know you're here, too. Let me give you an address."

I hung up the phone and walked back to the house.

The summer went by. September came, but the heat didn't break. There was one day . . . one slow, hot afternoon. Gunnar was at the tattoo parlor. Lucy was in my apartment, watching me draw. She seemed a little rattled, which probably meant she had gotten into another fight with Gunnar. She liked to hang out with me whenever she was upset, because she knew I wouldn't start peppering her with questions. Or with advice on how to improve her life. She kept watching me for a while. Then she asked me if I had any drawings I could show her.

I didn't want to show her the pages I was still doing for Amelia every day, but I had plenty of other stuff, including some more drawings of herself and the rest of the gang. She sorted through them one by one, looking at each one carefully.

"How do you do this?" she said. "You just get us all so perfectly here. I mean, look at this."

She pulled out a drawing I had done of Gunnar, right after he had been working out in the backyard. Every muscle and tendon standing out in the sunlight. The scar above his lip. The spiderweb tattoo on his neck. It was one of my better spontaneous drawings, I admit.

"This is the best drawing of him I've ever seen," she said. "I mean, it's better than a photograph. It's like it's just . . . it's *him*. How did you do that?"

I had no answer for her. She kept looking at the drawing. When she finally put it down, she went through a few more, finally picking out a drawing of Amelia. I hadn't even realized it was in there.

I had an urge to take it from her. To tear it right out of her hands. Then in that very next moment I realized how useless it would be. It was just scratches on a piece of paper, after all. A faint representation of someone I'd never see again. Someone I'd lost forever.

She looked at the drawing for a long time.

"This is her," she said. "The girl you love."

I nodded.

"It hurts, doesn't it? Wanting something so much."

She looked at me. Her hair a complete wreck, as always. The one eyelid slightly heavier than the other.

"You know that painting of the lion I did? The one Julian hung up?"

I remembered. It was probably her best, because it wasn't a cutesy fuzzy lion like some people would do, or a proud and noble lion, either. It looked ragged and half starved. A lion that would rip your face off in a second.

"When I got off the drugs . . . I mean, I kicked it, but I knew it wasn't gone for good. Julian always makes it sound like I got clean in one day and me and Gunnar just joined up with him and Ramona and everything's been a big party ever since, but he doesn't realize how hard it is. He doesn't know what it feels like, when it's still out there, all the time, just waiting for me to come back to it."

She put the drawing down.

"Did you ever see two lions having sex?"

I shook my head. Slowly.

"It's violent. It's dangerous. It must feel good, but at the same time you might get yourself clawed to death."

I was watching her lips as she talked.

"Imagine if a lion loved you too much. If it *wanted* to have you too much. That's what I'm saying. That's what it would feel like."

She reached out to me. She put her hand on my throat.

"What's inside you, anyway? Why won't it let you talk to me?"

I swallowed hard, feeling her cool fingers against my neck. I closed my eyes.

"Let me see you try talking."

I can't do this, I thought. I tried so hard for Amelia. I couldn't do it. Not even for her.

I pushed her hand away and stood up. A second later she was behind me, so close I could feel her breath on my neck.

"What's her name?" she whispered. "Tell me the girl's name."

When I turned she kissed me. She was so unlike Amelia in every way, a different creature entirely. So much more like me really, all broken and fucked up but she was right here and her arms were around me and I could feel her heart beating in her chest. When she took her clothes off . . . her body looked even more naked than Amelia's had. More pale and vulnerable. I saw the tattoos that Gunnar had given her. A Chinese symbol on her left shoulder blade, a black rose on her right ankle, and finally Gunnar's name itself, not in big bold letters but in letters so small I could barely see them, in the small of her back. He had literally marked her with his name to claim her forever, yet here she was with me in my little borrowed apartment in the backyard on a late afternoon and I had no idea what I was doing. It felt good and yet not good and it was all over too quickly. Then as we lay there afterward I heard the faint beeping from under my bed.

"What's that noise?" she said.

I got up and pulled out the shoebox. Another call from my good friend at the FBI? Just what I needed.

No. This one was for real.

"Who is it?" she said, looking into the box. "Who's paging you?"

I picked up the red pager.

It's the master calling, I said to her in my mind. If you'll excuse me, I have to run barking all the way home.

Twenty-one
Michigan
July 1999

The next day, when I rode out to the Marshes' house, I saw the car parked in the driveway. The same long black car from the day before. The car was empty, but as I got off the motorcycle, I could hear the car's engine still ticking in the heat. They hadn't been here long.

I went to the front door and knocked. A voice from inside told me to come in. As soon as I pushed open the door, I saw the three men in the living room. The same three men. All of them now making themselves at home. The man with the tan fishing hat was standing on one side of the aquarium. The tall man with the mustache that didn't quite go with his face, he was on the other side.

The third man, the one with the slow, hooded eyes that made him look half asleep, he was just sitting there on the couch.

"You're late," he said to me. "They're waiting for you. In the office."

The other two men looked up at me. I stood there wondering what the hell was going on. And where Amelia might be.

"Today would be nice," Sleepy Eyes said.

I took a few steps forward, pausing at the bottom of the steps. I could see that Amelia's door was closed.

"Hey!" Sleepy Eyes said. "Are you deaf or what? Get your ass in there right now."

Fishing Hat and Tall Mustache both seemed to think that was funny. Sleepy Eyes pointed one finger at them and was about to say something, but I didn't hear it. I opened the door to the office and stepped inside.

Mr. Marsh was in his usual chair, and in the guest chair sat a man I'd never seen before. He had a gray suit on. A white shirt. A red tie. He had dark hair and dark eyebrows. There was something a little rough and sand-papery about his skin. He was smoking a long cigarette.

"You're here," Mr. Marsh said. "Come on in! Have a seat!"

He jumped up to pull over the other guest chair.

"I'd like you to meet somebody," he said. "This is, um . . ."

Everything stopped in its tracks right at that second. The man with the cigarette looked up at Mr. Marsh. Mr. Marsh ran his tongue along his lower lip.

"This is another business associate of mine," he said. "Please sit down. We've got something we want to, um, talk to you about."

I sat down. Mr. Marsh sat back down in his own chair, wiping sweat from his face.

"So you're the young Michael," the man with the cigarette said. "I've heard a lot about you."

"All good," Mr. Marsh said. "All good things."

The man with the cigarette looked over at Mr. Marsh and raised one of his eyebrows. Maybe a quarter inch. Mr. Marsh put up both hands and then kept his mouth shut for the next three minutes.

"I understand that you went to see Mr. G yesterday, and that the results, at least from this preliminary meeting, were not so good."

I sat there, looking at him.

"Would you agree with that assessment?"

I nodded my head.

He leaned forward in his chair, pinching the cigarette between two fingers and being careful not to spill ashes on his pants. I could smell the cigarette and maybe the cologne he was wearing. It was an expensive and exotic smell that I'd never forget.

"You don't speak," he said.

I shook my head.

"You don't speak *ever.*"

I shook my head again.

He leaned back in his chair. "Okay then. That is something I can appreciate. In fact, that's a gift that I wish you could pass on to others."

He didn't look over at Mr. Marsh. He didn't have to.

"Norman here tells me that you broke into this house. Is that true?"

I nodded.

"He tells me that you refused to give up any of your accomplices."

I nodded again.

"You're two for two here, Michael. You sound like the kind of man I could trust."

I looked over at Mr. Marsh. He was smiling and nodding his head. He had his hands clasped together tight.

"But then we get to the business with the locks," the man said. "Because here I was led to believe that you can open up *anything*. Hence my disappointment when I heard back from Mr. G."

I didn't know how to react to that. I sat there wondering if Amelia was up there in her room, if she was scared out of her mind or pissed off or what.

"Now, I know that Mr. G can be a little abrupt sometimes. So I'm wondering if maybe the two of you just got off on the wrong foot. Is that possible?"

I didn't move.

"Michael? Is that possible?"

I shrugged. The man kept watching me.

"Here's the thing. Mr. Marsh and his partner, Mr. Slade, both have certain obligations right now, and I'm afraid that neither one of them have been meeting those obligations. In Mr. Slade's case, well, he seems to have disappeared completely, so I'm not sure how we're going to deal with him when he does eventually show his face again."

He finally looked over at Mr. Marsh. Mr. Marsh was staring at his own hands now. The giant fish loomed over everything.

"Give Mr. Marsh credit for one thing," the man said. "At least he's facing up to the situation. He wants to make good on those obligations, which I appreciate. So I'm willing to work with him. The problem is, he's sort of overextended himself right now. With the one health club and the plans for another, and these plans for a new housing development . . . well, I'm afraid he's already leveraged all of those assets about as far as he can go. Do you understand what I'm saying? The poor man doesn't have anything else of *value* that he can use in place of actual cash. But what he does have . . ."

He leaned forward in his chair again.

"Is you."

I looked over at Mr. Marsh again. He wouldn't meet my eye.

"Don't get me wrong. I know you're not his property, but as I understand it, you were sentenced by the court to perform certain services for him, for the rest of the summer. Whatever he sees fit for you to do. Within reason, of course. Which means that while he doesn't own *you*, he does, in fact, own a certain amount of your time. A set number of hours, every day. Every week. And that, Michael, is the closest thing to a real commodity that he's got right now. So in the grand scheme of things, what else can he offer me to help make things right?"

I watched the smoke from his cigarette curl toward the ceiling.

"So both of us would like you to think about giving it another shot with Mr. G. I've already spoken to him. I've explained that you sound like a young man with a lot of promise—which now that I've met you I can see is most definitely true—and that you deserve another chance."

"It would really help us out," Mr. Marsh said, finally finding the courage to speak again.

"It would," the man said. "It would help me out, because I'm very interested to see just how good you really are. And it would certainly help out Mr. Marsh. And his family, don't forget. The son, he's already off to college? Getting an early start on his football career?"

"Yes," Mr. Marsh said.

"Excellent. And your daughter?"

Mr. Marsh closed his eyes.

"Is there a problem?"

"No, not at all. She'll be a senior in high school."

"Very good. What was her name again?"

"Amelia."

"Amelia. That's a beautiful name. Don't you agree, Michael?"

He saw me holding on tight to the sides of my chair. He didn't say a word about it, but I could tell he was registering my reaction.

"I think we're all on the same page now," he said. "Michael, if you'll excuse us. We have a few more things to talk about. I know Mr. G is waiting, so you might want to go ahead and make your way down there. I'm sure the two of you will have a much more productive time of it today, huh?"

He sat there and waited for me. I stood up.

"It was a pleasure, Michael," he said to me. "I'm sure I'll be seeing you again."

I opened the door and left. I walked past the three men, who were all sitting together in the living room now. They had apparently found their way into the refrigerator, because they were all holding beer bottles.

"How'd it go, lover boy?"

I didn't know who said it and I didn't care. I went right up the stairs and knocked on Amelia's door. She wasn't there.

"She's gone," Sleepy Eyes said. He was standing at the bottom of the stairs, looking up at me. "Daddy sent her away."

I went back down the stairs and tried to go around him. He grabbed my arm.

"You were already on my list, remember? When I say something to you in the future, you'd better not walk away from me."

He stared me down for a few seconds, his fingers digging into my arm.

"Go on, get going. You've got business to take care of."

I went outside. I stood there for a while with the hot sun in my face, thinking about what to do next. I played the whole scene back in my head, right up to the part where the man with the cigarette said Amelia's name. Just the sound of her name on that man's thin lips . . .

I got on my bike and headed for Detroit.

I've had more than one moment like this in my life. These moments when I could have taken myself right out of the game. Cut my losses. Taken the whole thing to my probation officer, maybe. I can't help wondering how differently my life might have turned out if I had played it that way. Even once.

That's not how I played it. Not that day. I rode down that same road to that same place. All the way back to West Side Recovery on Grand River Avenue. The clouds gathered in the rising heat, and then the rain came down hard for a few minutes. Then it stopped and the steam rose from the hot pavement.

I rolled my bike right up to the door this time. I knocked on the door and waited. The Ghost, or Mr. G or whatever the hell I was supposed to call him, opened the door and peeked out at me. He was wearing the same worn-out sweater vest. The same glasses hung from the chain around his neck. He didn't say anything to me, just shook his head and let out this theatrical sigh like I was a huge inconvenience to him. Then he held the door open for me so I could roll in my motorcycle again.

"You're back," he said. "I'm so delighted."

I parked the bike and stood there waiting for whatever was going to happen next.

"They tell me you're probably the best I'm going to get. God help us all."

He turned and headed toward the back of the store, tracing his way in the near darkness, around the piles of junk. I followed him. To the back room, the television on again, through the narrow hallway crowded with bicycles. Out the back door to the green-lit shade of the yard. The air even heavier today, with the wet heat and the smell from the rain on the sumac and the poison ivy. The Ghost looked a little older to me today. Somehow older and even more pale to the point of being translucent. His hair was like thin straw, with a dozen age spots showing through and scattered across the top of his head. Yet he was so light of foot, like an old athlete or even a dancer. He walked quickly and never looked back to see if I was behind him. He went right to the safes and stopped in the dead center. He put his glasses on, and only then did he finally look at me.

"I'm losing my eyesight," he said. "That's the first problem."

He held up his right hand, palm facing the ground.

"My hands are starting to shake, too. Which is not good."

From where I was standing, I didn't see any shaking. His hand looked rock steady.

"My daughter's husband ran out on her, too. Left her with a couple of kids. She's in Florida, you understand, and even though I hate every fucking square inch of that whole state . . ."

He went behind one of the safes and produced a rolling office chair. There was plywood here on the ground, in the circle created by the safes. He spun the chair a half revolution and sat down on it backward.

"What I'm saying here is . . . I mean, that's it. That's all you need to know about me. Anything else is none of your fucking business. You understand?"

I nodded once.

"Do you want to try again with the safes today, or do you really not know anything at all about opening them?"

There were eight safes, perfectly arranged. One on each point of an imaginary compass, or maybe even on the real compass for all I knew. With another safe positioned exactly halfway between each point. In a building with so much junk in it, here was the one and only place where everything else was pushed aside. A perfect circle carved out of the chaos.

"What exactly *can* you do?" the Ghost said. "Should we start with that?"

I held imaginary lock picks in my hands and worked them together. That seemed to impress him about as much as me making balloon animals, but nevertheless he took me over to a workbench set up against the outside wall of the building. We had to work our way through a miniature city of paint cans, but when we got there I saw that he had some kind of lock-picking laboratory set up. There was a clear Lucite cylinder attached to the workbench with screws, and set into the cylinder was a key lock. He pulled the lock right out and slid off the top of the plug, exposing the pins. He put on his glasses and examined them, then pulled out one pin. There was a little chest of drawers sitting nearby. He opened up one of the drawers and replaced the pin with another, being careful to load the spring on top of it. He worked his way down the line, setting up his own custom configuration of pins. Hard or easy, or whatever. I had no idea. When he was done, he slid the top of the plug back on and replaced the plug in the clear cylinder. He started rummaging around on the workbench, looking for a set of picks, I was guessing. I took the leather case out of my back pocket and showed it to him.

"You always carry those around?"

I nodded.

"If the police ever stopped you, you wouldn't want them to have any doubts, huh? Make their life real easy?"

He didn't wait for me to field that one. Instead, he just gestured to the lock and took a step backward.

"Whenever you're ready, hotshot."

I took out a tension bar and diamond pick and got to work. It felt good to finally do something I knew how to do. I set the tension and felt for the first pin. As I did, I could sense him standing right behind me, looking over my shoulder. I could practically feel his breath.

"I'm not bothering you, am I?"

I kept going. Second pin, third pin, fourth pin, fifth pin, sixth pin. The lock sprung open, without me even having to go over them again. Apparently, these were straight block pins.

"Okay, then. You can do an easy one. Hooray for you. Let's make them a little harder."

I stepped aside as he slid the top off the plug and swapped out all of the pins. I could see the little notches on the new pins he was putting in. He struggled with the springs this time, bending down to his work until his face was just a few inches away.

"If I could just see one goddamned thing . . ." he said under his breath. When he was done, he took his glasses off, rubbed his eyes, and then stepped back. I took his place in front of the lock and went to work.

This time, he held up his left arm and looked at his watch. "Ten seconds," he said, "and counting. You'd better hurry."

I set the tension and felt for the pins.

"Twenty seconds."

Ignore him, I told myself. Shut him right out of your head.

"Thirty. We're getting impatient here."

Set the pin, feel it catch. Just enough. Move on.

"Forty seconds! You need to hurry!"

All the way down the line. Keep that tension just right. Not too much. Don't let him throw you. Don't tense up. Just like that . . .

"Fifty seconds! Are you kidding me?"

Work my way down again, feel for that pin, feel for that little give, ever so slight.

"One minute! This whole building will be crawling with cops soon!"

I felt a line of sweat dripping down my back. An angry insect was buzzing away, somewhere in the weeds behind us.

"They're beating down the door! You idiot!"

Another pin. Hold the tension. Not too hard.

"*Bam!* Hear that? *Bam!*"

I closed my eyes. I held myself completely still. I let up on the tension bar, one millionth of a millionth of an inch.

"We're totally fucked now! They're all over the place!"

Three more pins. Two more.

"It's too late! Run, you fool! Run!"

One more. I felt it give. The whole thing turning. I pulled the tools out, and it took everything I had not to smack the Ghost right in his pale stupid fucking face.

"That took a while," he said, eyeing me coolly like he hadn't spent the last minute and a half screaming at me. "I've never seen somebody hold a pick quite the way you do, either. I don't know who the hell taught you to do it like that."

He was back to rummaging around on the workbench. He started a small avalanche of washers and nuts and bolts.

"Of course, lock pickers are a dime a dozen these days. You can find them anywhere."

When he finally found what he was looking for, he picked it up and tossed it to me. It was a combination padlock, but not a cheap one.

"Simple three-cam lock, right? What do you do with it?"

I pulled the shackle out and started turning the dial, feeling for the sticking points. The usual routine, finding the last number and then using the number families to narrow down the possible combinations.

The Ghost watched me as I did this. Last number 25, so start with 1, super-set the second numbers and start cranking them out.

"What the hell are you doing?"

I looked up at him. What do you think I'm doing?

"You're not seriously going to cheat the numbers, are you? You think you can get away with that on a *good* lock? They don't use those patterns like they do on cheap pieces of shit, for one thing. For another thing . . . I mean, God damn, how much of an amateur are you, anyway? Don't you have any sense of touch at all?"

He didn't wait for me to respond to that. Not that I had any answer. He grabbed the lock from my hand and started to spin the dial.

"You have to feel it, okay? There's no other way to do this. I mean, shit, if you can't do that on a fucking padlock . . ."

He took one quick glance at the dial. Then he put the lock near his left ear for a moment and kept turning. He closed his eyes.

"Either you can feel it or you can't. Okay? It's that simple."

He opened his eyes and started spinning the dial in the opposite direction.

"I can do this in my sleep, hotshot. I mean, literally. I can do this while I'm driving a car. While I'm talking on the phone. While I'm having sex."

He turned the dial a little more, stopped, changed direction one more time.

"Do you understand what I'm saying? I can do this while I'm not even *thinking* about it one little bit."

He pulled the shackle out and tossed the now open lock back to me.

"Sit down here and work on it. When you can open it like a real boxman, let me know. In the meantime, I'm going to lunch."

Boxman. That was the first time I heard the term. It rang in my ears as he left me there alone in that green-shaded back lot, in the middle of those great iron safes.

A real boxman.

The sun was going down when I finally left that place. I had the lock in my pocket. My first piece of homework was to keep spinning the dials until I could feel the cams lining up the right way. Until I could open the damned thing purely by touch, without cheating.

I should have gone straight home to practice, but instead I rode back to the Marshes' house. Every window was dark when I pulled into the driveway, but I could hear music coming from somewhere inside. I opened the front door and peeked inside. The stereo was blasting "Wouldn't It Be Nice" by the Beach Boys. Mr. Marsh's favorite band, I remembered. It was loud enough for a party, but the lights were all off, and I didn't see anybody.

I went into the living room. The big aquarium cast an eerie glow. Then I saw a thin line of light under the door to Mr. Marsh's office. I went upstairs first. I opened Amelia's door and flipped on the light. She still wasn't there.

I turned her light off and left. I went downstairs. There were a few seconds of silence as the song ended. Then another Beach Boys song came on. "You Still Believe in Me." I went to the office door and pushed it open. The music got louder.

The first thing I noticed was that the giant stuffed fish was gone. The second thing I noticed was that it wasn't so much gone as just taken down from the wall and rammed through the window. The back half was still inside, the front half outside.

The third thing I noticed was the desk chair, facing away from me. I saw an arm hanging down one side. I stood there for a few seconds, waiting for some sign of life.

Then the chair turned. Mr. Marsh was slumped down with a drink in his other hand. He looked up at me without the slightest hint of surprise.

"Good to see you," he said. "Make yourself a drink."

I saw a legal pad on his desk. I grabbed it, along with a pen, and started writing. *Where is Amelia?*

When I gave it to him, he held the pad out in front of him and then started tromboning it back and forth to make it come into focus.

"She's gone."

I took the pad back one more time. *Where did she go?*

That one seemed to deflate him. He closed his eyes for a while. So long I thought he might have drifted off on me. Then he cleared his throat.

"I sent her away. Somewhere safe. I think she wanted to call you, but . . . well, it's kind of hard to do that, you know?"

He drained the rest of his drink and then put his glass down on the desk. He did it carefully, like it was something that took every ounce of his strength and skill. I couldn't help but remember the very first time I saw him sitting in that chair. The overtanned man in his tank top and shorts, with the perfect teeth, the flashy wristwatch, the fifty-dollar haircut. Lots of attitude and big words then, but today he was so scared he could barely keep his hands from shaking.

"If I talk to her, I'll send her your, you know . . . I mean, I'll put in a good word for you. I'll tell her you're helping me. And that she'll be able to come home soon."

I walked over to the great tail fin of the fish. The way it was stuck there in the shattered window, it looked like it was trying to escape this place. A completely understandable feeling.

"Besides, you need to focus right now," Mr. Marsh said. "I need your absolute best effort here. Are you with me?"

I didn't even look at him. I turned away and walked to the door.

"They will kill me."

I stopped.

"I need you to believe that, Michael. They will kill me for sure. Or if they think I'm more useful to them alive . . . they may hurt Adam. End his football career."

His voice was flat, devoid of all emotion.

"Or Amelia . . ."

No. Don't even say it.

"I don't even want to think about what they might do to her."

This is not happening, I thought. This is worse than a bad dream.

"It's a terrible thing to put on you," he said, "but I don't have a choice."

He didn't say anything else to me.

He didn't have to.

Twenty-two

Ohio
September 2000

The Ghost had made it clear to me. I knew the rule. When the red pager goes off, you call the number as quickly as a human being can pick up a phone and call a number.

"That was fast," the voice said. A rough voice that I knew I'd heard before. "Good boy. Now write this down because I'm only gonna say it once. We need you to get yourself to Cleveland. We'll be down there on Friday morning, bright and early, like around eight o'clock. So you've got what, two and a half days from now to get there. Here's the address . . ."

I wrote down the number and the street name.

"It's a bar. Restaurant, whatever. Just go on inside and hang out until we get there. Oh, and one more little detail. Things are kinda hot right now, so do *not* fly there. You got that? Do not get on a fucking airplane. Are we crystal clear?"

He actually seemed to be waiting for me to say something.

"Can you press a goddamned button or something to let me know you're there? Once for yes, twice for no, how's that?"

I pressed one of the buttons. One time.

"There you go. We figured out how to communicate. So I'll see you in Ohio. Getting there won't be any more fun for me than you, believe me. So don't bitch at me about it."

He hung up. I looked at the address on the pad. I tore it off, put it in my pocket, and started writing on the next page.

I need to go. Back in a few days.

I put the pad on the table. As soon as somebody came back here looking for me, I knew they'd find it.

I did a quick packing job. Then I hit the road.

———

Ohio was over two thousand miles away. A hell of a trip, but I didn't figure I had much choice. I hit Las Vegas by the time the sun was going down. I was just past St. George, Utah, when I stopped for the night. I checked into a little motel, paid cash for a room, and fell asleep on the bed with my clothes still on.

The sun was hot on my face when I finally woke up. Galaxies of dust floating in that one ray of light that shone through the gap in the curtains. I got up, grabbed some breakfast, and hit the road again.

I made it through Utah that day, then through Colorado. I could feel my hands going numb. The road was dead straight by the time I hit Nebraska. I kept the bike between the lines and just rode and rode. This is a test, I thought. It's impossible to do this, but they want me to do it anyway.

I stopped at another motel outside of Grand Island. It was hard to walk when I got off the bike that night. I paid for the room, took a shower, and tried to sleep. I was exhausted, but I couldn't close my eyes. I sat up, turned on the light, and started drawing. I had all of my stuff with me, of course. I couldn't imagine going anywhere without it. So I drew myself sitting there in the bed, in that little motel room so close to the road I could feel the walls shake every time a truck went by. Another chapter in my ongoing story for Amelia. Michael on his way to Ohio to do God knows what.

In the morning, as I was packing up again, I heard the blue pager go off. The guys from New York? Did they somehow know I was already halfway there? Thinking maybe I could swing by and do a second job on the same trip?

I picked up the phone right there in the motel room and dialed the number. It didn't even finish the first ring before the man on the other end picked up and started talking.

"Michael, you have to listen to me."

It was Banks. First yellow, then green. Now he had the blue pager number.

"Time is running out, my friend. You need to face reality. We're almost past the point where I'm going to be able to help you."

I looked out the window. I had a sudden feeling that I was being watched, at that very moment, right here in the middle of Nebraska. That the door would come busting down and a dozen men would jump into the room and yell at me to lie down on the floor with my hands behind my head.

"This might be your last chance. Are you listening to me?"

But no, he wouldn't call me first. If he knew where I was, he'd just come get me. He wouldn't bother with the phone call.

"Michael. Don't hang up. Okay? Just stay with me here. I want to help you."

They can trace this. I'm sitting here in a motel room and they can trace this call.

I hung up the phone and got out of there.

I hit some heavy traffic around Chicago. Then I lost another hour in the time zone change. It was after midnight when I finally got to Cleveland. I stayed at my third motel in a row, this one by the airport. I stared at the ceiling for a long time, wondering what the next day would bring.

When the morning came, I got myself together and rode over to the address I'd been given. It wasn't eight o'clock yet, but I could see the long black sedan in the parking lot. The same car I'd seen before, back in Michigan.

I parked the bike next to it and was about to go inside. That's when Sleepy Eyes came out the door.

"Welcome to the mistake by the fucking lake," he said. "What took you so long?"

I pointed at my watch.

"Yeah, yeah. Save it. Let's go."

He went back inside and got the other two men.

"The kid is here," the first man said, looking me up and down. "In the flesh." He wasn't actually wearing a fishing hat today, but he'd always be Fishing Hat to me.

"How was the trip?" the second man said. Tall Mustache. It had been a year since I had last seen these guys. They didn't look any different at all. Which wasn't necessarily a good thing.

Sleepy Eyes opened up one of the back doors for me. As he did that, the other two men got in front. Sleepy Eyes shook his head and muttered darkly to himself. I could see that the wonderful team chemistry in this crew hadn't changed, either.

The morning sun was in our eyes as we drove down the expressway. So we were going east. Through Cuyahoga Heights, Garfield Heights, Maple Heights. A lot of Heights out here in the suburbs of Cleveland. It was a warm pale blue morning in the Midwest, like the days I knew when I lived in Michigan. I didn't want to be here. Not like this.

"So let me ask you something," Sleepy Eyes said, tapping my arm.

I turned to look at him.

"Do you know how far we had to drive down here, from Detroit?"

"Oh God," Tall Mustache said. "Here we go."

"I know you just rode across the whole fucking country, but hell, you were on a bike. That's different."

"Just knock it off," Tall Mustache said.

"So here's my question," Sleepy Eyes said, ignoring the other man. "How come it's always me who has to sit in the fucking backseat? Can you answer that for me, please?"

"You can't drive," Tall Mustache said, "because you lost your license, remember? And it wouldn't make any fucking sense for you to sit here in the front, because you're like a foot shorter than me."

"A foot is twelve inches. I am not twelve inches shorter than you."

"My legs are a lot longer than yours, is what I'm saying. That's why you're in the back."

"Will you two knock it off!" Fishing Hat said. "Do you *always* have to do this?"

"On the way back," Sleepy Eyes said, "it's me and the kid in front. Whaddya say? Then when we drop him off, it'll just be me by myself."

"I'd say you'd have to kill both of us first," Tall Mustache said.

"One more word," Fishing Hat said, "I'll turn this car right around and take you kids straight back home."

That got Tall Mustache laughing.

"Yeah, that's funny," Sleepy Eyes said. "I'm dying of laughter back here."

Nobody said anything for a while. I thought about the three hours it would take to get to Detroit from here. I hadn't been back to Michigan yet. I couldn't help but wonder what Amelia was doing at that very moment.

"I always get the shit end of the stick," Sleepy Eyes said to me. "Any time there's an unpleasant job to do? Somebody's garbage taken out? Something hot and boring and dangerous? Who do you think does it?"

"Blah blah blah," Tall Mustache said.

"Somebody's gotta be cramped up in a fucking backseat or stuffed into a little cabin on a stupid boat for two weeks at a time?"

"Oh yeah, that's a tough job," Tall Mustache said. "Sailing on a fucking *yacht* for two weeks. I'm really crying for you up here."

"You think I get any fun out of that? Eight big-shot assholes playing poker, and all I get to do is stand around like a fucking piece of furniture?"

Here it is, I thought. The big boat trip.

"Two weeks on the Pacific Ocean," Tall Mustache said. "All the food you want. Wine, women . . . you name it."

"What women are you talking about? It's just a bunch of men. Every one of those guys has their own bodyguard, you know that? So that's what, me and seven fucking coked-up moonbats? You think we each get our own cabin? Huh? You think we're living in luxury?"

"Oh, excuse me. You've got to share a cabin on the yacht."

"We're all in the same cabin, you fuckhead. Seven fucking moonbats on steroids trying to act tougher than anybody else, all of us sleeping in one fucking little room. Like we're on a fucking World War II submarine or something. Does that sound fun to you?"

"What's a moonbat, anyway? Huh? You keep saying 'moonbat,' and I don't know what that word means."

"A moonbat is a guy who's packed into a little sardine can for two weeks in the middle of the fucking ocean who will *kill* you for looking at him sideways. Okay? That's what a moonbat is. That's what I get to live through every single fucking September."

"Will you two fucking shut up for one second!" Fishing Hat nearly drove us off the road. When he was back between the lines, an uneasy silence reigned.

I thought about what Gunnar had told me. Was it possible that he really had another contact on this boat? One of these "moonbats"? Was he actually thinking that we could hit that boat and get away with it?

Julian was right. It would be suicide.

A half hour later, we hit a town called Chagrin Falls. It kind of reminded me of Milford. There was a river that ran through the middle of town. There were lots of little shops and restaurants. We rolled right through and out to the other side of town, where the trees and houses started to thin out and you could see for miles across the flat horizon.

We turned onto a long gravel driveway. I saw a farmhouse ahead of us. There was a barn and a couple of other outbuildings. We passed by an ancient plow. As we got closer, I could see that someone had spent a lot of time and money restoring the whole place. That plow was a rustic decoration and nothing else.

We came to a stop beside the house. All three men got out. I joined them. Sleepy Eyes went to the back door of the house and knocked. I noticed then that he was wearing black gloves. The other two men, as well. I stood there wondering what the hell was going on. If we were supposed to be hitting this house, well . . . you usually don't go up to the door and knock.

A man opened the door. He was sixty years old, maybe. Distinguished-looking. Gray hair at the temples. Expensive golf sweater.

"What are you guys doing here?" he said.

That's all he could get out before Sleepy Eyes punched him right in the stomach. The man went down hard, so Sleepy Eyes had to step over him to get into the house. He grabbed the man by the shirt collar and started dragging him inside.

"Don't bother helping out here," he said to his two partners.

They each took one leg and helped guide the man through the mudroom and into the kitchen. I could see a full breakfast for one laid out on the table.

"Close the door already," Sleepy Eyes said to me.

I stood there, unable to move.

"I said close the door!"

I closed it.

"What do you guys want?" the man said. He was lying on the floor, still holding his gut. "I told Mr. Fr—"

Sleepy Eyes kicked him in the ribs.

"Don't you dare say his name out loud, you stupid fuck. I don't want to hear his name cross your lips. Do you understand me?"

The man was gasping for breath now. I was waiting for that feeling to kick in, that feeling of complete calm I'd get whenever I had broken into a strange house, but it wasn't happening. I guess I shouldn't have been surprised. This was nothing like any other break-in I'd ever been a part of.

"Where's the money?" Sleepy Eyes said. "Huh?"

The man couldn't speak. Sleepy Eyes got down on his knees and grabbed the man's hair.

"Where is it?"

"He can't breathe," Fishing Hat said.

"Shut up," Sleepy Eyes said, without looking up. "Go look for the safe."

Fishing Hat and Tall Mustache exchanged yet another look. Probably look number 1,001 from just that day alone. Then they split up to search the house.

"Mr. Assemblyman, meet the Kid. Do you know why he's here?"

The man kept gasping for air.

"He's here just in case you won't tell us the combination to your safe. Or in case we kill you first. Either way."

Turn off the switch. Feel that sense of detachment, like it isn't really happening. Like I'm not here in this man's kitchen watching the last hours of this man's life.

He was starting to breathe again. He shook his head and spat blood on the kitchen floor. Fishing Hat stuck his head into the room and announced that the safe had been found. In the basement.

"To the basement," Sleepy Eyes said.

He pulled the man to his feet, took him over to the stairs, and then pushed him down. The man let out a yell, and then the next thing we heard was his body hitting every single step, all the way down.

"Was that necessary?" Fishing Hat said.

"I told you to shut up," Sleepy Eyes said. "Now get down there and see if he's still alive."

It was a nightmare. Just put it that way. If you happen to live in Ohio, you might even remember what I'm talking about. What happened in that basement in September of 2000, I was there to see the whole scene from beginning to end.

The man was out cold when we got to him. The basement was unfinished. The original brick foundation from years before, whenever the house had been built. They propped him up against those rough bricks and started slapping his face to bring him back to life. There was a freestanding safe along the opposite wall.

"Let's have a little race," Sleepy Eyes said to me. "You start opening that safe, and we'll see if we can get the combination out of him first."

I stood right where I was. I measured the distance to the stairs. If I wait for them to be distracted, how big a head start can I get?

Sleepy Eyes came over to me and looked into my eyes.

"Do you have a problem with all of this?"

"He's not coming around," Fishing Hat said. "Nice going."

"We don't need him to come around," Sleepy Eyes said. He was still staring into my eyes. "That's why we brought the Kid."

"If you had just given him a chance, he would have told us the combination."

"What fun would that be?"

"You're fucking crazy," Fishing Hat said. "You know that? You're a total fucking psycho."

"You're not the first to notice that, believe me."

"Hold up," Tall Mustache said. "I think he's coming to."

He lightly slapped the man's face again. The man opened his eyes and tried to focus. He ran his tongue over his broken teeth.

"What's the combination?" Tall Mustache said. "Come on, save us all some trouble here."

"Go fuck yourself," the man said.

"The man's got balls," Sleepy Eyes said. "You gotta give him that."

He went over and kicked the man in exactly that area.

"For fuck's sake," Fishing Hat said, "will you back off for two seconds, please? What the hell is wrong with you today?"

When the man was done moaning and gasping and spitting up more blood, he finally gave up the numbers. Fishing Hat had to lean down to hear him.

"Twenty-four. Forty-nine. Ninety-three."

"You're the expert," he said to me. "Get dialing."

I hesitated for a moment. Then I went to the safe and started spinning those numbers. Four turns to the right, three to the left, two to the right, one to the left. Until it stopped. Turn the handle. Open the door.

There was money inside. Stack upon stack of it.

"Who's got a bag?" Fishing Hat said.

Nobody had one, so he went up the stairs. A couple minutes later, he came down with a trash bag and started stuffing the money inside it.

The man's head was slumped down to his chest now. There was blood and spit and tears and teeth and God knows what else all over his shirt.

Sleepy Eyes went over to him. He pulled out a gun from his jacket.

"When you're paid to perform a service," he said to the man, "you should go ahead and perform that service. It's just common sense, right? You understand what I'm saying?"

The man looked up. The blood was pouring from his mouth now.

Fishing Hat and Tall Mustache both stepped away. They put their hands over their ears.

Sleepy Eyes didn't shoot. He came back over to me and looked me in the eye again. Then he offered the gun to me, handle first.

"You got off easy on the safe," he said. "So why don't you go ahead and finish up here?"

I looked down at the gun. I didn't take it. I wasn't going to touch it. No matter what else happened to me that day, I was not going to touch that gun.

Sleepy Eyes kept waiting me out. His two partners finally dropped their hands from their ears.

That's when he finally turned and shot the assemblyman in the head.

Sleepy Eyes turned back to me with a smile on his face. "That's all you have to do," he said. "Is that so hard?"

Then he raised the gun again and shot his partners.

Fishing Hat first. In the neck. Tall Mustache in the chest. Both men went down with surprised looks on their faces. They both lived for most of the next minute before finally dying, their blood spreading out slowly on the basement floor.

"My two friends here . . ." Sleepy Eyes said, putting his gun away. "They've both been having little secret meetings with an FBI agent."

He came over to me and looked me in the eye.

"If someone like that ever contacts you? Someone who smells like a Fed? Wants to have lunch or just get together for tea or something? I would recommend that you decline the invitation."

He looked over the whole scene one more time. Then he gestured to the stairs.

"After you."

I stepped over a spreading pool of blood and went up the stairs. We both went outside. Sleepy Eyes got behind the wheel and threw the garbage bag full of money into the backseat. The keys were dangling from the ignition. If I had made a break for it, I thought, I might have had a chance to get away. It was too late now.

I got in next to him.

"See what I mean?" he said, stretching out his legs. "This is what I'm talking about. Is this a hell of a lot more comfortable, or what?"

He drove me back to the restaurant. Thirty minutes in the car, sitting next to him. He started whistling a tune, like he was on his way back from a good day's work painting a house. When we were at the terminal, he slipped the car into park and put a hand on the back of my neck.

"I know this might have seemed like a wasted trip to you," he said. "Riding all the way out here like that. But you've been out there in L.A. for what, almost a year now? Living with that crazy bunch of kids? It's good to keep in touch, you know?"

He reached back for the bag of money and pulled out a single stack.

"It's good to remember who we both work for."

I took the money. I did. I took it. Then I opened the door and got out. When I looked back, he had rolled down the window.

"Have a good trip back home," he said, "and keep that pager right next to your pillow. I'll be talking to you again soon."

After he drove off, I sat there on my bike for a long time. I hadn't even left the parking lot yet. I kept thinking about the blood. The way it ran like a dozen little rivers across the floor.

I will never be free of this, I thought. There is no way out.

And now I have to turn around and drive for three days straight, all the way across the country. To a houseful of thieves. To the only place where I will ever be welcome.

All those miles. And I am so tired.

Unless . . .

No. I can't.

Yes. I have to. It may be my last chance. I may never be this close again.

I started the bike and pulled out onto the road. But instead of going west, I went north.

Two hours later, I was in Michigan.

Twenty-three
Michigan
July, August 1999

I didn't know where Amelia had gone. Where she was hiding until her father let her come back home again. And of course because I am not a normal person, she couldn't just call me on the telephone. She couldn't call me and talk to me and tell me she was okay and that we'd be back together soon. Not like any other two young lovers who might find themselves separated.

No. If I couldn't see her in the flesh, she might as well have been taken to another planet.

No messages. No words. Just gone. And as impossible as this may seem, I knew that there was only one way for me to bring her back.

I had to learn how to open a safe.

I worked on the lock most of the night. I kept turning the dials, trying to feel whatever the hell it was I was supposed to be feeling. Then I rummaged around for my old combination locks, found the old lock I had cut open and sat there studying the damned thing for the next hour.

It was really so simple. You line up all three notches, the shackle opens. There's no way I shouldn't be able to do this.

I went back to the lock the Ghost had given me. I was so tired now, after everything that had happened that day. I kept seeing that giant fish half out the window.

Just feel it. Turn the dial and feel it.

I fell asleep. I woke up, with no idea what time it was. The lock was still in my hand. I spun the dial again and this time I *thought* I was feeling what I was supposed to be feeling. I pulled the shackle and the lock opened.

I could barely see straight. Maybe that was the key. Maybe every other signal in my head had to be so weak and fuzzy before the "lock" signal could break through and be heard. Whatever it was, I kept working at it until I felt like I could zero in that signal. Until I finally had to close my eyes again.

So big freaking deal. That nagging voice in the back of my head, sounding exactly like the voice of the Ghost. You can open a cheap little combination lock now. That voice stayed in my head until the next morning, when I headed back down to Detroit. The air was heavy with the threat of rain. Finally, the clouds opened up and I was soaked through in a matter of seconds. I got to West Side Recovery and rolled my bike to the door. I knocked and waited another full minute in the rain before the Ghost appeared and let me in.

"How did you do with the lock?" he said. "Try not to drip on everything."

I took the lock from my pocket and held it up for him.

"It doesn't look open to me."

He stood and watched me work on it while the rain pounded away outside. Right, left, right. Boom. I pulled the shackle open and handed the whole thing to him.

"Don't start acting like a smart-ass," he said, snapping the lock shut. "I'll throw you back out in the rain."

He turned toward the back office. I followed him. About halfway, he picked up another combination lock off an old table and threw it directly over his head. I wasn't expecting it, and as usual the light level was about one-quarter what it should have been. I was lucky to snag the lock out of the air just before it hit me in the face.

I was still working on it when we had passed through the office, down the narrow hallway, and out into the backyard. The rain rattled off the green plastic, so loud we might as well have been standing inside a giant snare drum.

"Okay, then," he said. Then he stopped when he saw I didn't have this second lock open yet. Even while walking in near darkness, trying not to trip over a thousand pieces of junk, I was supposed to have it open already? He folded his arms and watched me, maybe two minutes going by, but each of those minutes feeling like an hour. When I finally got it open, he grabbed the lock from me with such utter contempt I was sure I was headed for the front door again. Instead he just threw it on the workbench and told me to wait where I stood.

He pushed open a sliding door. A dozen rakes and hoes and other assorted garden tools came tumbling out at him. He swore and karate-chopped his way through them until he was standing inside a storage room. There was a single naked lightbulb in the center of the ceiling. When he pulled on the string, nothing happened.

More swearing. More junk being kicked aside or tripped over. Then the Ghost backing out of the room, pulling out something on a dolly and struggling with the weight of something covered in a dusty white sheet.

He rolled it back away from the door, telling me to get the hell out of the way before he gave himself a hernia. He stopped and let the thing settle on the floor. Then he tried to catch his breath.

I knew what it was, of course. Four feet high, maybe three feet wide, two and a half feet deep. The exact shape of a medium-sized safe. But why was this particular safe kept in the storage room, hidden under a sheet?

"This is the first thing you have to see," he said, wiping his forehead with a handkerchief. "Get ready, because this is about as obscene as it gets."

He pulled the sheet off, raising a cloud of dust. It was a safe, all right, but it had been torn apart in every way you could conceivably tear apart a safe. On one side, the outer shell had been stripped away, the middle layer of concrete apparently hammered at until the inner layer was finally exposed and somehow pried open.

I walked around the back of the safe and saw that a square-foot rectangle had been cut straight through. Then as I got to the next side I saw yet another rectangle, this one with blackened edges. Finally coming around to the front, I saw that a half-dozen holes had been drilled. On the top of the safe, there were three more holes.

"I'm going to go through this once," the Ghost said. "So pay attention."

He closed his eyes for a moment and took a deep breath.

"As you can see, this particular safe has been violated. The man who did this was experimenting with several methods of forced entry. On this side, you'll see brute strength at work. Actually prying open the damned thing like it's a big tin can. Then gouging out the concrete. It must have taken days to do that."

He moved around to the back.

"Here, a high-speed disk cutter. Again, a lot of time, a lot of noise. Then over here . . ."

He went around to the rectangle with the black edges, started to put his hand down, and then pulled back like the thing was still molten hot.

"You can use an oxyacetylene torch to cut right through the metal like this. Of course, that means lugging a big tank of fuel and another tank of oxygen. A thermic lance will get even hotter. Like six thousand degrees. You realize how hot that is? If there was something inside that safe, what do you think the chances are it wouldn't be ashes by the time you got through? Hell, you can burn the whole building down."

He stood there shaking his head for a moment, then walked around to the front of the safe.

"Our man drilled through here. Which at least uses a *little* bit of intelligence. A little finesse. I mean, you have to know exactly where to drill to bypass the whole locking mechanism. It's different on every safe. Some have special protective plates now that make it a lot harder, so sometimes you have to come at it from a different angle."

Finally, he let himself touch the safe, putting a finger in one of the holes drilled on the top. Then he knelt down by the dial.

"On some safes you can punch the dial." He pulled the dial right off and handed it to me. As I held it I noticed the chips along the edge, where it had apparently been pried away.

"Older safes, you can still use explosives," he said, running his hand along the edge of the door. "Gelignite is a plastic explosive, similar to nitro. Just a little bit in the right place. A jam shot, they call it, and you're in business, assuming you don't blow your hands off."

He pulled the door open and showed me the inside. It was strange to see the green-filtered daylight coming through the various holes, big and small.

"Like I said, newer safes make it a lot harder to do any of this stuff. Besides those plates, there are lock-out mechanisms that get triggered when you try to go through the outer walls. Some have a steel cable running all along the perimeter. You break the wall, you break the cable, and it jams up everything. I mean, it makes the whole thing useless, even for the owner."

He closed the door, took the dial from me, and tried to replace it. When he moved his hand away, it fell to the ground. He didn't bother to pick it up.

"Point is . . . no matter how well made a safe is, you can get it open if you try hard enough. You take it away to a warehouse somewhere, you put enough time into it. Enough sweat, enough heat, enough noise . . ."

He pushed himself up, back to his feet, wincing as he straightened his back.

"They all open eventually. If you don't care how much brutality you have to inflict on it. If you don't care what the safe looks like when you're done."

He grabbed the sheet, one corner in each hand. He billowed it open and let it settle on the safe. Hiding it once again, the way you'd draw a sheet over a dead body.

"I told you this would be ugly," he said. "I hope you agree. If you don't feel the same way that I do about this, you should leave right now."

I wasn't totally sure what he meant, but I wasn't about to leave.

"These are the methods of crude men. They can't face the challenge that a safe presents to them. They can't face the safe on its own terms. So they do what? Same thing men have been doing for thousands of years, right? They resort to violence."

He grabbed the dolly and tucked it under the safe.

"No patience. No skill. No intelligence. Just brute strength. They have to *break* something. It's the only way they know."

He pushed down on the dolly, tried to tilt the safe back. Then he stopped.

"Here, you do it. Wheel this thing back into the storage room. I can't stand it being out here another minute."

He stepped aside so I could take my turn with the dolly. I grabbed it by the handles, tried to tilt the thing back. It was way too heavy.

"Imagine trying to wheel this thing out of a building," he said, "so you can take it back home with you and break it open. Can you even conceive of doing such a thing?"

I pulled back harder, felt the damned thing move a little bit. On my third try, I finally got it tilting and then had to fight the momentum. One more inch and it would have flipped right over.

"Easy, Hercules. Why don't you go put this thing away before you kill somebody."

I got it rolling in the right general direction. My forearms were burning by the time I got it halfway there. The very same forearms I thought were so strong now, after all that digging in the Marshes' backyard. I clipped the side of the storeroom door, which rocked the whole wall. With one last-gasp effort, I muscled it into the back corner and let the safe drop into position, the handles ripping right out of my hands. I stood there in the near darkness, catching my breath, listening to the blood pounding in my ears.

When I finally stepped back out, the Ghost was sitting in the rolling office chair, directly in the middle of the Garden of Safes.

"Come and look at these magnificent creatures," he said. "Absolutely fucking magnificent. What do they make you think of?"

I stood just outside the circle, in the gap between two of the safes. I listened hard to what he was saying.

"You touch a safe the way you touch a woman," he said. "Never forget that. Do you hear me?"

I nodded.

"The greatest puzzle in the world, young man, the greatest challenge a man can face, is solving the riddle of a woman's heart."

He rolled his chair, slowly, to one of the safes.

"This," he said, putting his left hand against the safe's door, "is a woman. Come closer."

I took one step into the circle.

"This," he said, putting his right hand on the dial, "is a woman's heart."

Okay, I thought. I'll go with this.

"You want to open this, what do you do? Hit her over the head with your club, drag her back to your cave? You think that'll work?"

I didn't even bother to shake my head.

"Of course not. You want her to open, you start by understanding her. You understand what's going on inside her. Come here and see."

I went closer. I got down on one knee.

"This safe's name is Erato," he said. "She's very special. Very open. Because unlike most safes, you can really see what's going on inside her."

He gently removed the felt-lined panel from the inside of the open door. Then he removed the little metal plate from behind the locking mechanism. As he turned the dial, I could see that there was a drive cam turning in perfect sync, behind a set of three wheels. He showed me how the notches in each wheel could be made to line up perfectly, using the right combination, of course, so that the fence above the wheels would fall down into this newly formed channel, which in turn would lower the lever and release the bolt. Letting the handle turn free.

"So simple," he said. His voice was low now. I could hear the distant sound of traffic on the street. I could hear insects buzzing in the tangled weeds beyond the fence. With the right combination dialed, he turned the handle, and all ten bars were retracted into the door itself, three on each side, two on top, and two on the bottom, each bar two inches thick and made of solid steel.

"That's how you open a safe," he said. "Every other safe in the world is just some variation on this same idea."

I stayed down on one knee. This whole business with the safe being a woman, having a name. That might have sent some people running from the room. But not me.

"It's easy when you know the combination," he said, closing his right hand like he was holding something. "But what if you don't?"

He opened his hand, like a magician showing his audience that it was empty.

"That, my young fucking hotshot, is where the *art* comes in. Are you ready for this?"

I nodded my head. One time, very slowly.

He looked at me for a long time without saying anything.

"You have to be sure about this," he finally said. "So do I."

I didn't move. I waited for him to decide whatever it was he had to decide.

"Okay, then. Pay attention. This is how a real artist opens a safe."

Now, there's a certain code I'm probably going against here. The Ghost passed this information down to me, and made it clear that I should keep it to myself. That I should keep it between fellow artists. Maybe one day, if I found the right person, I'd be able to pass it on, but only to that one person. Somebody I'd choose very carefully. Somebody who could handle such a burden. Look what it had done to me, after all. What price this unforgivable skill.

Really, though . . . it's not like I can just tell you how to do this. I mean, I think I've already given you the basic idea. You've seen me do it, right? Eliminate the presets first, on the off-chance that the owner was too lazy to change it.

After that, it gets tricky. As you turn the dial, you have to picture that notch on the drive cam. You have to feel where the lever is touching one side of the notch, then, with a little more turn, where it's hitting the other side. That's your "contact area."

Unless you already know how many wheels are in the lock, you spin the dial a few times and park all of the wheels, somewhere far from the contact area. Dial back and count how many times the drive pins pick up another wheel. That's how many wheels you have. That's how many numbers are in the combination.

That much I could probably show you how to do in a few minutes. What happens next is the part that I can describe to you, but I'll never be able to actually show you how to do it. You either can or you can't. For most people, on most safes, you just can't.

This is the part where you park all the wheels at 0 this time, then you go back to the contact area. You "measure" how big that area is. It's going to be a little bit different every time you go there. And if any one of the wheels happens to have a notch around that number, the range will be slightly shorter. According to the Ghost, most safecrackers actually write down the number ranges on a little graph, but if you have a good enough memory, you can remember the ranges. Go back and park at 3, measure again. Then at 6, and so on. It takes a while. Most dials go to 100.

When you've worked your way through, those numbers with the shorter contact areas are approximately the numbers in your ultimate combination. You have to go back and narrow those down. If it's a 33, you measure at 32 and 34, et cetera. Until you've got your final numbers.

The last part is a little bit more grunt work, because while you know your numbers now, you don't know the order. If you've got three numbers, you've got 6 possible combinations to try. If you've got four numbers, you've got 24 combinations to try. Five numbers, 120. Six numbers, 720. Which is a hell of a lot of combinations, but not so bad if you're fast on the dial. And remember that you only go as far as you have to, until you find the right combination. If you're lucky, it'll come early.

As mad as the Ghost had gotten when he saw me try to grind through the numbers on a little combination lock, the ironic thing is that on a big safe, once you've gotten those numbers, you have no choice but to work your way through them one combination at a time.

That's the basic idea. Problem is, the better the safe, the quieter the dial is going to be. Feeling your way through those contact points . . . that takes a special kind of touch, the kind of touch that the Ghost was talking about, caressing the safe like it's a woman, feeling the slightest tiny movement deep inside her. This was the kind of touch I just didn't have yet. No matter how much I hushed those singing voices in my head, no matter how close I got to the safe itself, with my cheek resting against the cool metal, my right hand on the dial . . . I turned it and felt only the general idea of that lever hitting the contact points. He ran through the whole procedure seven or eight times for me, let me try it on my own. He even gave me the numbers so I'd know exactly where to find them. I went to the 17. I felt the first touch. The emptiness in between. The second touch. Yes, I've got it. It's right there. Go to 25 now. It should feel different now. Feel the first point, the second. Is it different? Can you feel it?

No. I couldn't feel it. Not that first day.

He gave me more homework, a safe lock to take home. An actual dial and wheel set. It was no bigger than my fist, and it didn't weigh more than two or three pounds. I could take it anywhere and practice the general method anytime I wanted. It wasn't the same as doing it on a real safe, but it was something to get started with.

That's what I did. All that day. All that night. Every waking moment. As long as Amelia was still away, what the hell else was I going to do, anyway?

I still wasn't feeling it. Not even close.

When I went back the next day, there was an actual customer in the store. I'd come to learn that the Ghost had intentionally made the place as uninviting as possible. He kept it dark, he kept most of the worst junk up front, and when somebody actually came inside, he was as charming to them as he was to me most of the time. If they actually wanted to buy something, he'd make up a ridiculous price and not budge from it by one penny. Obviously, selling junk to people off the street was not the real reason for this particular junk store's existence. That was as much as I knew then.

So when this day's customer was shooed away, the Ghost took me back to the safes and ran through the procedure again. Not that he had to. I certainly knew how it was supposed to work by then. I just couldn't do it yet.

"Did you practice on the lock I gave you?"

I nodded.

"Did you open that yet?"

I shook my head.

"Sit. Practice."

I did. For the next four hours, I did nothing but turn the dials. I moved from safe to safe, hoping to find one that would feel a little easier. I dialed and listened and tried to feel those contact points. By four o'clock I was sweating and my head hurt. The Ghost came in and didn't even have to ask me how I'd done. He sent me home and told me to practice with the lock set some more. And to come back the next day a little earlier.

I came back the next day. More of the same. Spinning. Working myself beyond exhaustion, so I could bring Amelia back home.

Then the next day. More spinning. Going home with the practice lock and spinning some more.

The next day, I had to take a break and keep an appointment with my probation officer. He looked a little tired and overworked, and I had no idea what he might say when he sat me down in his office.

"I talked to Mr. Marsh this morning," he said.

This could be interesting, I thought.

"He says you're still doing a fine job. Around the house. At the health club now? He's got you working at the health club? He's really got you doing everything, eh?"

I nodded. Yeah, everything.

"How's that pond coming, anyway?"

I gave him a little shrug. Not bad.

"I'm anxious to see it when it's done."

Yeah, me, too.

"You know, we should talk about what happens when you're done with your hours over there. You'll still have about ten months left on your probation, which means I'll be talking to the faculty at your high school. You know that perfect attendance is part of your compliance, right?"

I nodded. Yeah, sure.

"All righty then. I guess we're good for today, eh?"

Couldn't be better, I thought. I shook his hand and left the probation office. Got on my bike and drove down to Detroit for another day of safe-cracking school.

I kept working at it. I spent so many hours in the back of that store, it started to feel like home to me. One day, the Ghost left me alone for a few hours. He said he had to go run some errands, and that if anybody came into the store, I should just stay in the back until they gave up and left.

A couple of hours passed, just me and the safes. Until I looked up and saw a man standing there, watching me. He was tall. He had dark hair that looked slicked back against his head, like he had spent a fair amount of time that morning getting it just right. He was wearing a blue suit, with a white shirt and a wide red tie.

"Sorry, didn't mean to scare you," he said. Even though I was sure I had shown no sign of being scared.

"I'm looking for the owner. Is he around?"

I shook my head.

"What'cha got here, anyway? A bunch of safes?"

I took my hand off the dial. I sat up straight in my chair.

"These are some beauties."

He ran his hand down one of the smooth metal sides.

"You sell these? You should have them out front."

I looked around. I wasn't exactly sure what to do. Something about this man, the way he had walked all the way back here. Through the darkness, down the hallway . . . it wasn't the kind of thing most people would do.

"My name's Harrington Banks," he said. "Most people call me Harry."

He stuck out his right hand. I hesitated for one beat and then shook it.

"You don't mind me being back here, do you? I figured it was part of the store."

I kept looking up at him. He was already tall enough without me being way down here in my rolling chair.

"You're not in charge here, right?"

I shook my head.

"Of course not. You're way too young."

He slapped his hand on top of the safe I was sitting next to.

"Well," he said. "Maybe I should let you get back to, uh . . ."

There was a whole world in the space between the words, as he looked from one safe to the next.

"Back to work here, huh?"

He backed away one step.

"I'll stop by again. Maybe I'll catch the owner next time. Your name was . . ."

I didn't move.

He raised his right hand, as if to grab my name from the air. "I'll get that next time, too. Right? Until then . . ."

He stood there nodding to himself for a while. Then finally turned to leave.

"See you later. Have a good day."

Then he left. I would have let the Ghost know about the visit, but I swear, I completely forgot about it because of the other strange thing that happened that same afternoon. The Ghost was still gone, and I was back in my chair, feeling especially frustrated because I still wasn't getting anywhere. That's when I heard the beeping noise.

I sat up and looked around. It was just loud enough to hear, a constant string of beeps. I tried to ignore it and go back to the safe, but the sound kept distracting me. I got up and looked around the backyard, heard it getting a little louder when I went down the hallway, louder yet when I got into the back room. There were only about seven thousand items in the room, so I had to narrow it down gradually, until I came to a shoebox on the desk. When I opened it, the beeping doubled in volume.

Now, you have to remember, this was 1999. Not every single damned person in the world had a cell phone yet. Some people still had pagers. I don't think I'd ever actually held one, until I picked up that pager from the shoebox. It was still beeping away like crazy. There was a little screen on top, with ten bright little red numbers. A phone number, I assumed.

Before I could even think about what to do with it, the pager stopped beeping. I put it back in the box with the others. There were five in total. All of them black, but each with a piece of tape on it, in different colors. Red, white, yellow, blue, green.

The Ghost finally came back about an hour later. I picked up the box and showed him the pager that had gone off. It was the one with the red tape on it. He grabbed it from me and read the number. I didn't think it would have been possible for him to get any paler than he already was, but it happened. He ran over to the phone and called the number, waving me away when he saw me watching him. I went back to the safes.

When he came back out a few minutes later, the Ghost looked like he had seen a ghost. "I've got company coming over," he said. "So you'd better get the hell out of here."

I got on the bike and started for home. It felt strange to be out of there in the middle of the day. I drove by Amelia's house. Just because. The grass looked so long now you could have made hay out of it. Which I'm sure the Lake Sherwood neighbors were real thrilled about.

There was another car in the driveway today. A red BMW. It looked vaguely familiar to me. I could see somebody sitting in the driver's seat. I sat there and watched for a while, waiting for something to happen. Finally, the driver got out of the car. It was Zeke. Good old Zeke.

He was holding something as he walked to the door. A red rose? Yes. A single red rose. He went to the door and left it on the mat. He reached into his back pocket and took out a piece of paper and put it down next to the rose. A heartfelt letter, no doubt. Maybe an overwrought love poem.

He didn't knock on the door. Meaning he must have known that Amelia was gone. Hell, maybe he made this same trip every day now. Maybe this was a ritual for him.

As he came back to the car, he saw me sitting on my motorcycle. I flipped my visor down and took off. I didn't bother to see if he was following me.

Then when I was close to home—when I was about to make that last turn onto Main Street—that's when I saw the flash of red in my rearview mirrors. I turned around and saw the BMW convertible, closing fast.

It was him.

I made the turn and took off down Main Street. If you know anything about motorcycles, you know that even a midsized bike will out-accelerate anything on four wheels. I left him far behind me, pulled off and waited a while, then looped back into town.

After so many empty days . . . with no sight of Amelia. No luck with the safes. So much time frustrated and alone, with nothing to show for it except this. I avoided getting run over by Amelia's ex-boyfriend. That's it.

I didn't think he'd be waiting for me. I mean, really. But as I took the turn off Commerce Road, there was his car, parked at the gas station. He came out in a blur and surprised me. I gunned it down Main Street again, but it's not like it was an open road or anything. One little bobble and I would have ended up on somebody's hood or plastered all over the sidewalk.

He was right behind me as both vehicles came to the railroad bridge. I slowed down just enough to avoid the embankment. Zeke slowed down just enough to avoid death, but not enough to avoid the sickening sound of the entire left side of his car being scraped away on the concrete. Sparks flew and the car came wobbling out of the turn, air hissing out of his left front tire.

I paused for one brief moment, watching the car finally stop a few yards away from the liquor store. I pulled the bike into the parking lot and sat there, waiting for whatever was going to happen next.

The driver's side door opened. Zeke came out, looking unsteady on his feet. There was a thin line of blood running down the left side of his face. When he saw me sitting there on the bike, he found his legs and he came at me like a bullet. I hopped off the bike, threw off my helmet, and met him somewhere in the middle, ducking under his wild swing and then waiting for him to try a few more. He finally clipped me over the eye, but that was good, it was beautiful, because I *wanted* him to hit me. After everything that had happened, I wanted to bleed a little bit and to mix my blood with his.

He swung again, but I was already inside his reach. I nailed him in the chin with an uppercut and then in the stomach and then the best one of all—on the side of his stupid fucking wealthy ponytailed head.

I stood there waiting for him to get up. He didn't. I turned around and went into the liquor store. Uncle Lito was standing by the front door, looking out through the glass. His face was bright red.

"Who the hell was that?" he said. "And since when did you start hitting people?"

I went into the back room. The same back room where I had spent so many hours as a kid. Where I had first taken apart a lock and figured out how it worked. I sat in my old chair and took out the safe lock the Ghost had given me. My heart was racing. I could hear a siren in the distance.

Chaos. Noise. The voices screaming in my head.

I turned the dial to the right. I felt what was going on inside. I heard it. In some far corner of my mind I could *see* it. I turned the dial back to the left. Then to the right.

The sirens were getting louder.

I need this. I need this.

The heartache, the misery, the loneliness, the pain, the eight-year-old boy still living inside me, the only one who can do this.

I could feel it. I could feel the slightest touch of metal on metal in that lock now.

So what? Fuck this, I thought. This doesn't matter. I need the real thing.

I need the real thing because I know what's waiting for me there.

So I went right back outside and got on the bike. A police car was on the scene now. Another police car was pulling up to join the first. I pulled out onto the street and gunned it. Going too fast, weaving in and out of traffic, somehow managing to keep it together and not crack myself up on the way down Grand River. These same miles I'd been riding every single day. I knew it would be different this time.

I knew it.

I got to the store. I parked on the street. Let someone steal the motorcycle, I thought. I don't care. The Ghost appeared at the door, on his way out it looked like. Done for the day, but then he saw me. This man who had never once seemed to take the slightest interest in how I was doing, he stopped me and asked me what the hell was wrong with me. Why I looked like I was out of my fucking head. I pushed past him and went through the store, throwing things out of my way in the darkness.

I went to the safes. I sat in the chair and pulled it up to the safe named

Erato. The Ghost's favorite. I leaned my head against the cold face and felt my heart pounding in my chest.

Quiet now. Everybody quiet. I have to listen.

Quiet quiet quiet.

That's when I heard it. The sound, like someone breathing. Steady but shallow.

Spin a few times. Park at 0. Go to the contact area.

The sound was coming from inside the safe.

Park at 3. Go to the contact area.

There was somebody inside the safe. Suffocating.

Park at 6. Go to the contact area.

If I didn't open it in time . . .

Park at 9. Go to the contact area.

Then he would die.

Park at 12.

He would run out of air.

Go to the . . .

He would die inside the safe and stay there forever.

. . . contact area. It feels different now. It feels shorter.

I parked at 15. The contact area back to normal.

18. Normal.

21. Normal.

24. Boom. There it is again.

I got 6. I got 24.

You have to hurry. You have to get him out of there right now.

27. 30. I kept going. Parking at each three spot. Testing. Feeling. I worked my way through, got my three rough numbers. I went back and narrowed down each one until I had 5, 25, 71.

I cleared the dial and started cranking. The Ghost appeared behind me.

"Easy," he said. "You don't have to go so fast. Just get it right."

I kept working through the combinations, faster and faster.

"Relax, will you? You can work on the speed later."

I'm ignoring you, I thought. You are not even here. It's just me and this big metal box.

The air is gone. He can't survive this.

The sweat was running down my back now. I dialed left three times to 71, right two times to 25, then left until the dial was finally sitting at 5. As soon as I grabbed the handle, I could already feel it.

It might be too late. He might already be dead in there.

Nine years, one month, twenty-eight days. That's how much time had passed since that day.

Nine years, one month, twenty-eight days. I pulled the handle and the door swung open.

The next day, Amelia came home.

Twenty-four
Michigan
September 2000

It felt strange to be back in the state of Michigan. I never thought I'd be able to come back here, and with every passing mile I kept wondering if I had made a huge mistake. Still, I kept going. This sudden unexpected chance to see Amelia one more time, even for just a moment . . . it was more than I could resist.

I rode through Milford first. It didn't look much different. Until I got to the bend in the road and I got my first big surprise. The Flame was gone. In its place was a generic-looking family restaurant now, the kind of place you'd go after church on Sunday. More importantly, the liquor store was gone, too. Replaced by a wine store, of all things. Not quite as upscale as Julian's, but still. On another day, it would have made me laugh.

I didn't know if Uncle Lito would still be in the same house. I mean, if the liquor store was gone . . . he could be anywhere now.

I made the turn into the little alley that ran along the wall of the building, back to the house. I didn't see the old two-toned Grand Marquis there. I parked the bike and walked up to the front of the house. I peeked through the window. I saw the same table there, the same wooden chairs. The same threadbare couch.

I took out the tools and did a quick job on the front door. One of the first locks I had practiced on, way back when. Today it didn't take me more than a minute.

When I was inside, I was greeted by that same familiar smell of cigar smoke and loneliness. I walked in through the house, through the front room and kitchen, back to my old bedroom. There were piles of laundry on the bed. Otherwise it was exactly the same. It felt so strange to be back here.

After all of the things I had been through . . . the calendar said only a year had passed, but to me it was a lifetime.

I came back out to the front room. I paged through all of the newspapers on the table. The racing forms. I had remembered my uncle saying on more than one occasion, when he was done with the liquor store he'd spend every day at the racetrack. That's probably where he was today.

But I could see it wasn't as simple as that. It wasn't just a man retiring to do what he always wanted to do. There were plenty of bills on the table. Collection notices and threatening letters. There were three new bottles of prescription medicine, too. Medicine I knew he wasn't taking when I was still living here.

Then something else caught my eye. I went over to the kitchen counter. There, next to the pile of dirty dishes, was a cell phone.

That was a surprise in itself, but then it also made me wonder why he didn't have it with him. I mean, why get a cell phone if you're just going to leave it at home?

I turned it on and saw that it was fully charged. I checked the call history. It was empty. Not one single call coming in or going out.

I checked the address book. There was one entry.

BANKS.

I turned the phone off and put it in my pocket. One of two things happened here, I thought. Banks gave this phone to my uncle so he could call him if I ever came home. So he could have me taken into custody for my own good. I could see him selling my uncle on that one.

Or else he gave it to my uncle so that my uncle could give it to me. So I could call Banks myself. Either way, it made me feel suddenly very vulnerable. I went to the front window and looked outside. Banks could be out there right now, I thought. Watching me.

I went out to my bike, scanning in every direction. Looking for someone walking by on the street. Or a man sitting behind the wheel of a car, maybe reading a newspaper. The way he had done it before, back when he was watching West Side Recovery.

I dug out the bundle of money Sleepy Eyes had given me that very morning. I went back inside and put it on the kitchen counter, where the cell phone had been. Remembering that old coffee can that had sat next to that register in the liquor store for all those years. HELP OUT THE MIRACLE BOY. With the yellowed newspaper clipping next to it.

Here you go, Uncle Lito. Just don't lose it at the track.

_____

As I got to the stoplight at the end of town, a police cruiser pulled up next to me. I could feel myself being examined. I didn't look back at them. When the light turned green I took off, waiting for the siren to come on, already planning where I'd go if I needed to make a break for it. But it didn't happen.

I rode east. Those same four miles I knew so well. The most important four miles of my life. There were more new houses being built, in a spot that had once been an empty field. Each one bigger than the next, stacked almost on top of each other, using up every inch of land. It was still the same road, though, and I knew exactly where I was going. I could have done it blindfolded.

When I got to her subdivision, I saw a dozen cars parked in the driveway and spilling out onto the street. A party of some sort was going on. Maybe for Amelia? Was I going to walk right into the middle of it? Talk about a surprise party.

I parked my bike on the street, took off my helmet, and went to the front door. I rang the doorbell twice, but nobody came to the door. So I went around back.

There was a pool there now. An honest-to-God in-ground swimming pool in the very spot where I had started digging. There was a white fence around the whole thing. Tables and chairs everywhere. Green tablecloths and flowers. Forty or fifty people all stood around with plastic glasses of white wine. I didn't recognize anyone.

They started to notice me, one by one. I just stood there. Finally, the back door opened and Mr. Marsh came out, a bottle of wine in each hand. He looked good, I'll say that much. He was obviously back to his suntanned, king-of-the-world self. He stopped when he realized that everyone was staring at something. He followed the invisible arrow until he finally spotted me. He processed this information for the next two seconds, doing a heroic job of not dropping his wine bottles.

"Michael," he said. "What are you doing here?"

He handed off the wine bottles and came over to me, turning me by the shoulder and half pushing me back around to the front of the house.

"It's good to see you," he said, "but I thought . . . I mean . . . how are you?"

Such sincerity, I thought. It brings a tear to my eye.

"We're having a little party here, as you can see. I finally opened up that second health club. Now I'm working on the third."

We finally stopped walking when we were in the driveway. Away from the party. Away from anyone who could hear us.

"Listen," he said, "I know I owe you a lot. I mean, I don't know if saying thank you is enough. But thank you. Okay? You gave me the chance to get out from under those guys. I got totally paid up and everything's good now. They're not going to bother me anymore. Or anybody in my family."

That might be true, I thought, but for reasons you'd never guess.

"You remember Jerry Slade, right? My old partner? He kinda disappeared off the face of the earth. I never did see him again. Just goes to show you. You gotta stick around and face the music, you know what I mean? Just stay positive until things start to go your way."

You are so full of shit, I thought. If you weren't Amelia's father . . .

"But I don't know if you're supposed to be here, you know? I mean, I don't know if that's a good thing, is all I'm saying. But it is great to see you. Don't get me wrong. I'll tell Amelia, I promise."

I pointed up to her window.

"Yes, she's doing just fine. I'll be sure to tell her you were here."

I waited him out. I wasn't about to leave.

"She's studying art, just like she always wanted to. Isn't that great?"

I kept waiting.

"She's in London, if you can believe it. She absolutely loves it there."

London . . .

"I'll tell her you were here. She calls me every week."

She's in London.

"Look, I really should get back to the party. If you ever need anything . . . I mean *anything*. You let me know, okay? You take care of yourself."

He put a hand on my shoulder. Then he went back to his party.

I wasn't sure what to do then. I stood there in the driveway for a while, looking up at her window. Wondering if her bedroom still looked the same. The garage doors were open, with several large tubs filled with ice. This is where he kept the wine, along with the bottles of water and soda pop and whatever else. I grabbed a bottle of Vernors. I figured he owed me that much. One bottle of cold ginger ale in exchange for saving his life, his home, his business, his family. His old Mercedes was parked there on the other side of the garage. He'd be trading it in for something new, no doubt, as soon as the new health club took off. I was about to turn and leave. Then I noticed the stickers on his back window.

Michigan State University.

And above that . . . the University of Michigan.

I knew his son Adam the football star was at MSU. And if I remembered right, from all that bragging he had done when I first met him, that was Mr. Marsh's alma mater, too. So why the hell would he have a University of Michigan sticker on his car?

Only one reason, genius. Although you had to hand it to him. Art school in London. He came up with that one pretty quick.

I couldn't even blame him.

After all those hard miles to get here, it was only forty more to get to Ann Arbor. A beautiful September afternoon as I headed down to where I thought the center of campus had to be. There were students walking all over the place. Backpacks over their shoulders. Maize and blue T-shirts. Young smiling faces.

I rode down State Street, looking at the buildings. The biggest of all had eight huge columns in front, and right next to that was the art museum. I figured I had to be getting closer, but I didn't see the art school anywhere. I finally parked and walked around until I found a campus map. It looked like the art school was up on North Campus, a whole separate area of town. I got back on the bike and headed up that way, passing the huge hospital. It looked vaguely familiar now. I must have come down this very road when I was nine years old, to see some supposed expert about getting me to speak again.

There were blue buses running back and forth on the main road. This was how the students must have traveled between the two campuses. I kept going until finally I saw the art building. It was all metal and glass, and in the late afternoon light it was already starting to glow from the inside.

I parked the bike again and walked through the building. The people there, the art students . . . they didn't seem to be moving as quickly as the students on the main campus. They were dressed a little better. Hell, they were just flat out a little more attractive and more put together. They wouldn't make any money when they graduated, but at least they'd have more fun.

This is where I should be, I thought. If everything hadn't gotten turned inside out. One more year of a regular life, and this would have been me.

I hadn't planned on everything being quite so big, so I wasn't sure what to do next. Write her name on a piece of paper? Start showing it around?

No, not yet. I decided to go back outside first, to get on my bike and to keep looking. I went up the hill and found a big dormitory. It seemed to be the only dorm on North Campus, the only dorm anywhere near the art school, so I figured there was a good chance she lived there.

Inside, there were two women at the front desk. They both looked like students themselves. Like maybe this whole town was run by people in their twenties. I went up to them and made a writing motion. They looked at each other, until finally one of them produced a pen and a piece of paper. I wrote down *Amelia Marsh* with a question mark after it.

The first woman took the paper from me and read it. "Okay, umm . . ." She looked over at the other woman. "I'm not supposed to do this, but why don't you go on up and leave a note on her door yourself? Who knows, you might see her."

She gave me directions to the sixth floor. I walked down the long hallway, passing students on their way to dinner, I assumed. I went up the elevator to the sixth floor. Down the hallway to the room number they had given me. I heard music coming from every open doorway I passed. Finally I got to her door and knocked. Nobody answered.

I sat down right there in the hallway, my back against the hard wall. There was music coming at me from two directions, and I was tired and hungry, and not sure now if this had been a good idea in the first place. Maybe this was the sort of thing you just don't do to a person. You don't just show up after a year and expect her not to slap you right across the face. I put my arms across my knees, put my head down on my arms.

The time passed.

"Michael?"

It was Amelia. She looked beautiful. Incredible. Amazing. Of course. She had long black shorts on. A black sleeveless shirt. Black work boots. Her hair was tied up to one side of her head, but otherwise as unruly as ever.

I got to my feet. I stood there in front of her. In the hallway of her dormitory, having not seen her in a full year. Having run away from her without a word.

"I've got one question for you," she finally said.

I prepared myself.

"What the hell did you do to your hair?"

I sat on her bed. She sat at her desk. I watched her reading my pages. I watched her catching up on the last year of my life. Starting with the day I left her. Riding east. My first job. Ending up in New York City. The horror in that house in Connecticut. Then the long trip west to California, and everything that had happened there.

I hadn't had the chance to cover the last few days, of course. What had happened with Lucy. Then this trip out to Cleveland to witness three murders, before deciding on the spur of the moment to come up here and find her.

Even so, it was enough.

The tears were running down Amelia's face as she followed my story. Page by page. This is why I'm here, I thought. This is the whole reason right here. If one person in the world can understand what I've been going through. One person who really knows me. That's all I could ask for.

When she was done, she put the pages together carefully and put them back into the envelope.

"You're telling me," she said, wiping her face, "that *my father* got you into all of this?"

I gave her half a nod. It wasn't quite so simple, but basically yes.

"You became . . . a *safecracker*. That's why you had to leave."

Yes.

"Are you going to stop now?"

I didn't have an answer.

"Why did you agree to do it in the first place?"

I did it for you, I thought. But I don't want to tell you that.

"You know," she said, leaning closer to me, "the way you drew some of these pictures . . . it's like you really get into this stuff."

I looked away from her. Out the window at the fading light. What a long day this had already been.

"Michael. Look at me."

I turned back to her. She gave me a pad of paper and a pen.

"Why did you keep doing this?"

I wrote on the pad. *I didn't have any choice.*

She looked from the pad back to my face.

"But . . . you did. You always did."

No. I underlined the word.

"There's more to this . . ."

I swallowed hard. I closed my eyes.

"This is about what happened to you, isn't it . . . when you were a kid."

I wasn't surprised at this leap. She was the one person in the world who could have made it.

"I told you everything," she said. "About my mother killing herself. About what I was going through last summer. Everything."

I shook my head. This part . . . This is not why I came here.

"You said we had all this stuff in common, remember? If that's true, how would I even know that? You still haven't told me anything."

I pointed to the papers in her hands. It's all right there.

She wasn't buying it.

"What happened to you?" she said. "Are you ever going to tell anybody?"

I didn't move.

She took a few deep breaths. She took my hand for a moment, then she let go.

"I don't know why I feel this way about you. Okay? I try not to, because it's just . . . it's just crazy. But I swear to God, I will kick you out of my room and you will never see me again, ever, unless you tell me what the *fuck* happened to you to make you this way. Right now."

There were cars passing by under her window. People walking in the evening. Normal people. A thousand of them all around her, playing music, talking, laughing. While I sat there on her bed, with a pad of paper in my lap. I started writing again.

I want to tell you.

"Then go ahead."

I don't know how.

"Start with where it happened. Draw me the house."

I looked at her.

"I'm serious. You were eight years old, right? Isn't that when it happened? Where did you live?"

I thought about it for a while. Then I put the pad down. I stood up. I went to the door and opened it.

She bit her lip as she watched me.

"Okay, fine," she said. "Good-bye."

I stayed there at the door.

"What? What is it?"

I picked up the pad.

Let's go, I wrote.

"Where are we going?"

I'm going to show you where it happened.

It was getting dark now. It was crazy to be doing this. I had no business taking her where I was about to take her, but I had been on the run so long . . . I was so tired, and I had already lived through enough in the past few days to last me for the rest of my life. So maybe the fact that I had no idea what I was doing was a good thing just then. Maybe that was exactly what we both needed.

She got on the back of my bike. Just like old times. It felt just as good as ever to have her hands around my waist. We rode out of Ann Arbor, heading due east. I knew where I was going. I had always known. Even though I hadn't gone anywhere near it in ten years.

I got off the highway, right before it took us into the heart of the city. I wandered in a slow zigzag toward the water. I knew we couldn't get lost now. All we had to do was keep going until we hit the Detroit River.

It was coming up on midnight when we hit Jefferson Avenue. We turned north. We passed the enormous steel plant on the river. The taste of the smoke and the grit in the air already, punishing us as we got closer and closer. Amelia wrapped her arms tighter around my body.

I kept going. I knew we were close. Then I saw the bridge.

The bridge over the River Rouge.

I looked at the street signs. Just before we got to the bridge, I took that last left turn. The last turn before the river. We were on Victoria Street now. I rolled to a stop.

"Is this it?" she said. The wind was still buzzing in my ears. "Is this really where you lived?"

Now understand, this has nothing to do with the city of River Rouge. Or the people who live there or the businesses or the streets or the river itself. It is a place like any other place, where you grow up and you go to school and you make your stand against the world. If you go to this particular street, though, you'll be just as amazed as Amelia was when we got off the bike and looked around and breathed that air.

There are six houses on the southern side of Victoria Street. On the northern side is the plant where they make wallboard, a city unto itself of brick and steel, of pipes and smokestacks and water towers and huge mounds of gypsum.

"Is the air always like this?"

Amelia covered her mouth with her hand. Besides the gypsum, there was the salt from the salt plant just up the river, the coke and the slag from the two iron plants. Not to mention whatever came out of the wastewater plant. Or from the storm drains, whenever it rained.

"Which house did you live in?"

I walked down to the street and stopped in front of the house. She followed me. It was a simple one-story house. Inside, a small living room, a small kitchen. Three bedrooms. One bathroom. An unfinished basement. At least that's what I remembered. I lived here from the time I was born until that day in June of 1990. Kindergarten, first grade, second grade. Playing outside in the tiny backyard on those days when the air wasn't too bad. Inside on all the other days.

As I looked at the house, I knew it was empty. I knew it had been empty for ten years. Nobody would buy this house. Nobody would live inside these walls. Never mind the air or the industrial blight across the street. You wouldn't go into this house for one second if you knew what had happened here.

And everybody knew. Everybody.

The whole street looked abandoned. I opened up one of my luggage bags and grabbed a flashlight. Then I took Amelia by the hand and led her up the two front steps to the door. I tried the knob. It didn't turn. I got out my tools and started in on the lock.

"What are you doing?"

It didn't take long. Less than a minute. I turned the knob and pushed the door in. I took her hand again and led her inside.

The first thing that hit me was how cold it was. Even after a warm September day, the unnatural chill in this place . . . the lights from the plant came streaming in through every window, so it wasn't that dark, but still I felt myself wanting to reach for a light switch. To fill the place with a warmer light than this pale glow that made everything look like it was underwater.

Amelia didn't say anything. She followed me as I walked through the living room, our footsteps creaking on the wooden floors. There was no carpet. I remembered that. Other things coming back to me, like where the television was. Where the couch was that my mother would sit on while I was on the floor, watching cartoons.

We went into the kitchen. The tile had curled up in places. The old appliances were still in place.

"Why is this house still here?" she said. "Why haven't they torn it down?"

Yes, I thought. Tear it down. Burn the lumber and everything else that will burn. Take the ashes and bury them in the ground.

I led her back out, through the living room to the hallway, where it got much darker. She gripped my hand tighter, and I took her past the bathroom, past the master bedroom, past my own bedroom from way back when. To the extra room at the very back of the house.

This door was closed. I pushed it open.

It was empty. There was still a roller blind on the window. I went to open it and the whole thing fell off the window with a crash.

"Okay, I'm getting a little nervous in here." Her voice was small in the middle of this emptiness.

I looked along the floor for the faint indentations in the wood. Four of them. They were centered against the back wall.

I took out my pad of paper and my pen. I started to write, holding the pad up to the dim moonlight that came in through the window. Then I put the pad back in my pocket. There was no way I could do this and make her understand what it felt like. This whole trip was a horrible mistake.

"So show me," she said. "I want to see what happened."

I shook my head.

"There's a reason we're here. Show me."

I took out the pad again. I started to draw a picture. But I didn't have room on the pad. How could I do this on a stupid little pad of paper? I ended up throwing it against the wall.

That's when I got the idea.

It was plaster, with a simple coat of off-white paint. It had always been that way. No bright colors for this house. No wallpaper.

I turned on the flashlight. I went to the wall, and I started drawing with my pen. Amelia came over to me and watched over my shoulder. I drew a picture of a little boy reading a comic book in a living room. I drew a woman smoking a cigarette and watching television. My mother. On the couch next to her . . . this was the tricky part. A man with a drink in his hand. But not the father. How do you make that clear? This man is not the father.

"Michael, do you have stuff out on your bike? Pens? Pencils?"

I nodded.

"I'll be right back."

What? You're going to leave me here?

"It'll only take a second. You keep doing what you're doing."

She left the room. I heard her footsteps, and I felt the air shift as she opened the front door. It was just me and the ghosts for a long minute or two. I fought off the feeling that I was trapped here forever now. That the door was locked and she'd never come back.

Then the door opened again, and she reappeared in the room. She was carrying my wooden art box. Everything I'd need to do this for real.

Especially if she helped me.

When I finished the first panel, she came behind me and started filling in some of the details. The second panel went a lot faster. I just sketched in the general idea, and then she finished it while I went on to the third.

That's how we did it. That's how I finally told her this story. On this one September night, in this half-dark empty room, me and Amelia together again, filling up the walls.

June 17, 1990. Father's Day. This is the day that happened then and is still happening. This is the day that lives outside of time.

I am sitting on the floor of the living room, reading a comic book. My mother is on the couch, smoking a cigarette. The man I call Mr. X is sitting on the couch next to her. He is not my father, but even though it is Father's Day, there he is on the couch with my mother.

His last name really does start with the letter *X*, but it's a name I can never quite remember. Xeno? Xenus? Something like that. Anyway, that's why he is Mr. X.

He's been coming around a lot lately. I don't mind too much because for the most part he treats me okay. He brings me lots of comic books, for one thing. The very comic book I am reading on this day had come from him. From the little suitcase that he brings with him sometimes. He buys the comic books and he gives them to me and then sometimes he goes into the bedroom with my mother while I am reading them.

I am eight years old, but I am not a dummy. I know the comic books are a way to keep me occupied. I play along because, hey, what can I do to stop them? They're going to do what they're going to do, and at least this way I'm getting comic books!

I remember I used to see my father on weekends sometimes. Back when I was five or six years old. We'd go to Tiger games and movies, and I believe one time we went on a big steamboat on the Detroit River even though it rained all day. Then he disappeared for what seemed like forever to me. Even when he was away, my mother would still get phone calls from him. She'd send me out of the room while she talked to him. Then she'd go outside and sit on the steps and smoke a cigarette.

She works at one of the plants down the river. Mr. X is actually her boss, I believe. The first time he came over, they went out and I got stuck with a babysitter all night, but then after that he started coming to the house and staying longer and longer. That's when he started bringing the comic books.

So Father's Day. Here we are, all sitting there in the room, when we all hear a noise at the front door. My mother gets up and looks out the little window, but she doesn't see anybody. Before she comes back to the couch, she hooks that little chain on the door. That little chain with the knob that fits into that little slidey hole thing. No matter how old I am, I realize that a little chain like that is not going to stop somebody if that somebody really wants to get into the house. Not that anyone would want to. But if.

There is a back door in the kitchen, leading out into the tiny yard with the wooden fence around it. So there are two doors plus seven windows, which I know because I have counted them, plus the one tiny door on the side of the house from a long time ago when the milkman used to come. That was before I was born, but we did use that door the one time we got locked out of the house. I was just small enough back then to fit through it.

But that back door. That's the door my father came in. Who I haven't seen in two years. All of a sudden, it isn't just my mother and Mr. X on the couch watching television while I sit on the floor reading my comic book. It's my mother and Mr. X on the couch watching television while I sit on the floor reading my comic book and my father standing there in the doorway like it's the most perfectly natural thing in the world, leaning against one wall with his feet crossed and saying, "So what are we all watching, huh?"

Mr. X gets up first and my father hits him across the face with something. It's a rolling pin, which he's picked up from the kitchen. Mr. X bends over with his hands on his head, and my father kicks him right in the face with his boot. My mother is screaming now and trying to get off the couch and getting tangled up with the legs of the coffee table while I keep sitting there the whole time watching everything happen. My father hits Mr. X in the head again, and then he goes after my mother, who is trying to get the front door open now except she can't because of that stupid little chain.

Then he spins her around a few times like they're dancing, and my father asks her if she missed him. She's trying to hit him and she's screaming and finally she claws him right in the face. He pushes her down right next to me. Mr. X is trying to get up now, so my father picks up the rolling pin and hits him in the head again. And again and again and again and again. The sound of that wooden rolling pin hitting his head makes me think of one thing, which is the sound of a bat hitting a baseball.

My mother is screaming at him to stop, so he throws the rolling pin at the television. It hits the screen and knocks out one half of it while the other half goes black. Then while my mother is trying to crawl away, my father gets down on his knees and he comes over to me finally.

My mother is begging him to leave me alone, but all my father does is he takes my comic book from me and he looks at it.

"I'm not going to hurt our son," he says. "How could you even think that?"

Then he hits her across the face with the back of his hand.

"Go in the bedroom," he says to me, his voice dropping into a gentle tone. "Go ahead. It'll be all right. I promise."

I don't want to move for one simple reason, and that is because I have pissed all over myself and I don't want him to see the puddle on the floor.

"Go ahead," he says. "Go. Right now."

So I finally get up, puddle or no puddle. I go to the bedroom, and when I look back my father is taking his shirt off and my mother is crying and trying to get away. I go into my room and I try to open up my window, one of the seven windows in the house, but it has this lock on the top that is jammed tight and I can't move it one little bit. My pants are all wet and I want to change but I can't remember which drawer my pants are in and it doesn't even occur to me that I could just start opening them until I find the right one. I can't think straight at all. Not with those sounds coming from the living room.

There is a pile of comic books in my room and a desk with a pad on it where I had been trying to draw pictures of superheroes and a single bookshelf with my books on it, plus a trophy on top of that from T-ball, which I pick up now, thinking this might be something I could use because it would really hurt if it hit you on the head.

I open up the door to my bedroom, cracking it open the way I do at night when I'm supposed to be in bed but I want to see what's on television. But of course now the television is half gone and all I can see is what my father is doing to my mother in the living room. I could draw an exact picture but it still wouldn't make any sense, the way she's bent over the coffee table with her hair hanging to the floor and the way my father is behind her with his pants off, moving his hips against the back of her again and again.

He doesn't see me coming out of the room with my T-ball trophy in my right hand, getting closer and closer until I can see what he has done to Mr. X's body. How he's taken Mr. X's pants off just like he's taken his own pants off except there's blood all over Mr. X's legs because he has cut off or pulled off or whatever else he has done to Mr. X's private areas, as my mother calls it when I'm in the bathtub.

I run back down the hallway except this time I go into the spare bedroom where we keep my old bed I've grown out of, plus the old gun safe that used to be my father's but was too heavy to get out of the house.

I am not allowed to open that safe or even touch it under any circumstances, my mother has said more than once. There's something about the bolts in the door that are extra dangerous. Because they have springs in them that automatically lock when you close the door. But today seems like good circumstances to me all of a sudden after what I've just seen, and I don't want my father to do to me what he's done to Mr. X, so I pull the safe door open and I get inside. It's empty now, of course, because my father doesn't live here and he doesn't have any guns or anything else to put in it, so I have just enough room if I sit cross-legged. Then I pull the door closed.

That's when I realize that there is no handle on the inside. I can't get back out even if I want to. Not without somebody on the outside spinning the right combination. I start to wonder if I really will suffocate or how I'll even know if I am. I remember all those times when I'd be under my blanket and the air would get heavy until I stuck my nose out and the air would be so cool and delicious. It starts to feel like that, the heavy part I mean, but then I notice that there's a thin line of light on the side of the door where the hinges are and if I put my nose up to it I can almost smell the fresh air.

So I stay in there with my legs crossed and my nose up against the side of the door. I can't hear what's going on outside the safe very well, but I know one thing for sure. As much as I've ever known anything in my whole life. I have to be quiet.

Waiting.

Waiting.

Waiting.

Until I finally hear the footsteps. Into the room. Then out. Then into the room again. My father's voice.

"Michael?"

Then farther away. Then closer.

Then right next to the safe.

"Michael? Are you in there?"

I must be quiet.

"Michael? Seriously, did you go inside there? You know you shouldn't be in there."

Quiet, quiet. Not a sound.

I feel the safe being tipped over a few inches.

"Michael! Come on! You didn't really go in there, did you? You're gonna die in there! There's no air!"

I feel the warmth spreading in my pants again.

"Michael, open the door, okay? You've got to open it."

I can hear the dial being spun now.

"I don't remember the combination! You have to open it!"

More spinning. Such a simple idea. If those three numbers come into his head, he will spin those numbers and the door will open.

"What was it? Fuck! It was two years ago! How am I supposed to remember?"

A hand slamming down on the top of the safe. I stop myself from crying out. Nothing. Not a sound.

"Listen to me. You have to open this thing right now. Just reach up and turn that handle. You have to do this, right now!"

Be quiet. Be quiet.

"Come on, Michael. Turn that handle."

There is no handle.

"I promise you, it won't hurt. Okay, buddy? I swear to God. It won't hurt. Just come out and we'll do this together, okay? You and me."

Be quiet.

"Come on, Mike. I can't do this by myself. You have to come with me, okay?"

There is no handle. Be quiet. There is no handle.

"It'll be so quick. You won't even feel it. I swear to you. I cross my heart and hope to die. I want us both to be together when we do this. Okay?"

I keep my nose against the edge of the door, but I'm getting dizzy.

I hear my father crying. Then I hear him go away. At last. At last he's gone.

The relief and the panic all at once. He's gone but now I'm going to be in here forever.

Then the footsteps again. A crinkling noise, all around me. The light getting dim.

"We'll go out together," he says. "I'm right here with you. I wish I could see you one more time. It's okay. Don't be afraid. We'll go out together."

The air getting thinner and thinner. My mind starting to shut down. A pinhole of light, at the bottom of the safe. Whatever he has wrapped around it, he isn't covering the whole thing. He's trying to cut off my air but . . .

Everything's black for a while. I think. I'm out and then I come back. I can hear his breathing.

"Are you still there, Michael? Are you still with me?"

That's when I feel the whole world tilting. I hear the steady squeak of the wheels underneath me. The rumbling across that wooden floor. Down the steps. Whump whump whump. A fresh blast of air through that crack along the safe's door. Waking me up. We are outside now. We are on the sidewalk. Hitting every crack. Bump bump bump. Onto the smooth road. A car passing by us, honking its horn. Then the motion of the safe almost stopping. I can hear my father laboring outside now, fighting for every inch. We must be on rough ground. The dirt and weeds and gravel beside the road. Where are we going? We can't be going toward the river. We can't be.

A few more feet. Then we stop.

"You and me, Michael. You hear me in there? You and me. Forever."

Then the fall. The impact, slamming me against one side of the safe. The sudden darkness.

Then the water, seeping in through the crack. It's cold. It fills up the safe, one inch at a time. It's squeezing out the rest of my air.

The seconds ticking away. I feel the water covering my face.

I can't breathe. I am cold and I am dying.

I can't breathe.

I close my eyes and wait.

I finished the last panel. Amelia was right behind me, darkening the lines and making everything stand out as if we had burned it into the wall. For the second time that night, the tears were running down her face.

We stood back and looked over what we had done. The panels started in the room where the safe had been. They wrapped around three walls and out into the hallway. They continued into the living room and finished on the wall opposite the front door, right where the couch had been. The last panel was the biggest of all. A complete underwater panorama, with the trash collected there on the bottom of the river. An old tire. A cinder block. A bottle. A piece of lumber with the nails still in it. The stringy weeds pushing up through the debris and swaying with the current.

In the middle of everything, tilted slightly with one corner submerged in the sand, the great iron box. Sunken. Abandoned. Never to be brought back to the surface again.

That was it. That was the very last panel.

"Why does it stop here?" she said. "They got you out. They saved you."

I understood what she meant. In the reality she was thinking about . . . yes, they got me out. It was a cheap safe, after all. That's why the door didn't quite seal shut, and why I was able to keep breathing, at least until I was in the water. That's why the men who pulled the safe from the river were able to open it. With a big crowbar? With the Jaws of Life? I didn't know. I wasn't awake to see that part. It didn't really matter. In my own mind, the safe was and always would be at the bottom of the river. With me locked inside forever. That was the only real part for me. As real as anything had ever been real.

"You're not in that box anymore," she said, wiping her cheeks. "You're free now. You can leave the box here."

I looked at her.

"Now that you've done this. Can't you leave it all right here in this house?"

If only it were that easy.

She kissed me, in that room where the worst parts of that day had begun. She kissed me and she held me tight. We both sat down on the floor and stayed there for a long time. Just the two of us in that house.

When I opened my eyes again . . . it was so late. Past the middle of the night. We had been here in this house so long. We collected our things. We went outside and got on my bike. Then I took her back to Ann Arbor.

As we left, I knew that if anyone else ever dared to come inside this house, they would see this story. They would know exactly what had happened here.

When we were stopped in front of her dormitory, she got off the bike and stood there next to me for a long time, not saying anything. She reached into her shirt and pulled out a necklace. It was strung through the ring I had given her, a year ago.

"I still have this," she said. "I wear this every day."

I wanted to say something so badly. I wanted to open my mouth and talk to her.

"When you left . . . I tried not to care about you anymore. I really did."

She kissed me.

"I know we can't be together right now. So just . . ."

She stopped. She looked up at the stars.

"I can't do it. I can't just let you ride away again."

I reached back into my bag for a pad of paper. I took out a pen and wrote two sentences for her. The two most important sentences I'd ever written for anyone.

I will find a way to come back. I promise.

She took the paper from me. She read it. Then she folded it up and put it in her pocket. Whether she believed it or not . . . well, I wouldn't have blamed her if she didn't. But I did. I knew I'd find a way back. Or die trying.

"You know where to find me now."

She turned to go inside. As I rode away, I hoped to God that it would always be true.

It was another long trip, all the way back to Los Angeles.

I started out slow, but halfway there, the decision came to me. As crazy as it sounded . . . as desperate and hopeless . . . I knew it might be my last chance to be free.

I'm going to do this, I told myself. No matter what, I'm going to try.

For the last thousand miles, I was flying.

Twenty-five
Michigan
August, September 1999

I passed the fresh scrape in the bridge embankment, edged with cherry red paint, as I rode out to her house that morning. She was there when I arrived. A duffel bag over her shoulder. Moving back into her own house after her little "vacation" with relatives up north. When she saw me, she dropped the duffel bag, came over to me as I was getting off my bike, and held me tight for a few long minutes straight. She kissed me and told me how much she had missed me and otherwise made me feel absolutely numb with such sudden happiness.

It was my first lesson in how everything in your life can change if you just do one small, specific thing perfectly well.

I helped her bring her stuff inside. Another small measure of pure joy for me when I saw all of Zeke's love notes in her garbage pail, along with the dried-out roses. She wanted me to take her out on the bike, right then and there, but it was getting close to noon. My first taste of the conflict I'd have to live with every day for the rest of August. Mr. Marsh covered for me today, at least, telling Amelia that I had to go to work at his health club, and that he was sure I'd be able to see her again later. When she was distracted by something, he gave me a little wink and a thumbs-up.

In the end, that's how it had to work. I still had my court-ordered obligations to Mr. Marsh, after all. Beyond that, I still knew that working with the Ghost was the one thing that was keeping everybody safe and happy. Even though Amelia didn't know it yet, I was busy keeping the wolves from her door.

I wasn't naive about what I was doing. I really wasn't. I mean, when I let myself think about it, I knew I wasn't learning all this stuff so I could open up my own little locksmith shop on Main Street. I knew these men would want me to actually open a safe for real at some point. I mean, open a safe that belonged to someone else. I figured I could live with that. Open one safe, let them do what they had to do. Then walk away.

I thought it could be that simple. I really did.

By the end of that week, I could do all eight safes in one sitting. Rolling that chair from one to the next. It took all afternoon, and by the time I opened the last safe my back would be wet and my head would be pounding, but I could do it. The next day, the Ghost would have all of the combinations reset and I'd do the whole thing again.

By the end of the next week, I could do them all without killing myself, in about half the time. I still had the portable lock set at home, too. I'd go see Amelia in the evenings, of course, but then I'd spin every night when I got home, just to keep my touch.

One day, another of the pagers went off. I could tell it was a different pager, just from the sound. The Ghost left the room to make a phone call, but this time when he came back he wasn't shaking like a little kid called down to the principal's office.

"Buncha fucking amateurs," he said. Saying it to himself and not really to me. "Aren't there any real pros around anymore? Guys who know what the fuck they're doing?"

I listened to him say stuff like that, but I still didn't really know what he was talking about. Who these people were on the other end of these pagers. I just kept doing my thing. Getting better and faster. I'd go down to Detroit every day, spend my time with the Ghost, then go have dinner with Amelia. Sit in her room, draw, go out on the bike. Come back. End up in her bed sometimes. More and more often, actually, as it occurred to me that nobody was stopping us. Her father would leave the house for hours at a time. Even when he was there, he'd make a big point of staying in his office, like there was no way he'd ever come upstairs and bother us. It's kind of sick looking back at it now, just how much liberty he must have felt he owed me. Even in his own house.

Then, finally . . . the day came. It was the middle of August. I went down to West Side Recovery, and from the moment I walked in the place, I could tell that something was up. The Ghost sat me down and rolled up his chair in front of me. Then he started talking.

"First rule," he said. "You work with people you trust. Nobody else. Ever. You got me?"

I sat there looking at him. Why was I getting this today?

"I need you to let me know that you're hearing what I'm saying," he said. "I don't think that's fucking too much to ask, is it? So give me some kind of indication here. Are you with me on the trust issue or not?"

I nodded.

"Okay. Thank you."

He took a moment to settle himself down. Then he continued.

"I know you don't know shit about anybody yet. So you're gonna have to use your gut. You get a call, you hook up with somebody, you ask yourself one simple question. You ask yourself, do I trust this person with my life? *With my life?* Because that's really what you're doing. You look them in the eye and you ask yourself that, and your gut will tell you. If there's anything wrong . . . I mean *anything*, you walk away. You turn right around, and you walk. You got me?"

I nodded.

"Being a little nervous is okay. But if they look too nervous? Jumping all over the place? You turn and walk. They're loaded? They're high on fucking speed or something? You turn and walk."

He fiddled with the chain that held his glasses as he thought about it. This man who dressed like a homeless ex-librarian, telling me these things.

"Too many people. You turn and walk. What's too many, you ask? Depends on the situation. Simple in and out, deal with an alarm maybe, somebody looking out, somebody driving. You got what, four people? Five, maybe? So what happens if you show up and you see ten fucking guys standing around? It's like bring-a-friend-to-work-day or something? You turn and walk. Because that's the last thing you need, right? A few more idiots to get in the way? Or run their mouths about it afterwards? Let alone the fact that your share gets smaller with each extra guy on board. Who needs it, right? You turn and walk."

I kept sitting there in front of him, with my hands locked on my knees. I felt a little numb.

"You know what else? Here's another thing. You don't carry a gun. You do not so much as *touch* a gun unless it's an emergency. You got that?"

I nodded. That one I could agree to without a problem.

"It's not your job to carry a gun. It's not your job to do *anything* except open a box. That's the only reason you're in the fucking room, and that's the only thing you do. You're like the doctor in a maternity ward, right? They've got nurses to do all the other shit, run around like crazy while the baby's getting ready to come out. Then when it's time, and only when it's time . . . call the doctor! He comes in, boom. Baby's out, everybody's happy. Doctor goes back to the wherever, the doctors' lounge. He acts like he's too good for everyone else, and his time is way more valuable than anybody else's time. Because, yes, you're damned right! It's the truth! He knows it and everybody else knows it. He's the doctor and everybody else ain't worth shit."

I was too hot under the big green plastic shade. It was one of those late August days that didn't get the memo about summer being almost over.

"Bottom line, kid. Bottom line. You are an artist. So you get to act like a fucking prima donna. They expect you to. If you didn't, they'd think something was wrong. Hell, they'd pull the plug on the whole thing. We were expecting an artist, and instead we got this schmuck. So what the fuck, eh? Let's all go home."

He inched his chair a little closer to me.

"There aren't many of us left," he said. "That's the simple truth of the matter. Without you, they gotta go in, they gotta carry that safe out, they gotta do God knows what. You've *seen* what they have to do, ripping that box apart. Without you, it turns into a fucking demolition project. So you get to call your shots. You hear me? Never be afraid to do that."

He looked especially tired today. Especially pale and old and used up. I couldn't help but wonder if this had done that to him, this work he was telling me about.

"Let me show you what I've got here," he said, picking up the shoebox from the floor and putting it in his lap. "This is very important, so listen carefully."

He opened the shoebox and picked up one of the pagers.

"You know what these are, right? Pagers, beepers, whatever you want to call them. Somebody wants to reach you, they just dial a certain number and the pager will go off. Their number will get stored right here in this little readout. You see this screen? There's a memory, so you can go back and find the number if you don't happen to see it."

He pushed a little button and showed me.

"It'll usually be a secure number they leave, in case you're wondering. A pay phone, maybe. Or some kind of temporary situation. As long as it's clean. Anyway, you get a number on one of these, you call it."

I waited for him to see through to the obvious problem. He gave me one of his rare little half-smiles and shook his head.

"Yeah, I got it, hotshot. I know you don't call people all that often. Don't worry. The people who need to know about you will know that you're just calling to listen. If they don't, then hell, that's just one more way to know who not to work with. You don't even have to leave the house."

He put the pager down, picked up another.

"As you can see, I've got these all marked with different colors. Make sure you keep them straight. The green one here . . . hell, I don't think this one's gone off in two years. I don't even know why I have it anymore."

He put it back in the box and picked up another.

"The blue one . . . they don't call that often. Once a year, maybe? Twice a year? From the East Coast, mostly. They're pros, so you can feel good about it if these guys call. Okay? You got that part?"

That one went back in the box. Another came out.

"Okay, yellow. You'll get beeped on this one. Problem is, you'll never know exactly who you're dealing with. Or where the call is coming from. Hell, it could be from fucking Mexico or something. That's why I've got it yellow, you see. Yellow, as in yellow pages, meaning that just about anybody can get this number and call you. Also, yellow as in proceed with caution. You got it?"

Back in the box, one more out. He shook this a few times.

"The white pager," he said. "Never a problem here. These guys are money. Okay? They're fucking money in the bank. They stay out west mostly, and I gotta admit, they're a little unorthodox. Whatever they set up, it's usually some kind of slow play. They set up a situation and they know they won't see you for a few days, but they know you're the guy they need and they'll be willing to wait for you. If it rings, you go, because like I said, these guys are as good as it gets."

He put that one back, picked up the last one. He held it carefully, as if even the pager itself would be more dangerous than the others. He moved his chair another inch toward mine.

"Okay, here it is," he said. "The red one. I'll put this in simple terms so there's no chance of misunderstanding. If this pager goes off, you fucking call the number as soon as you can. You listen to what the man says. If he wants to meet somewhere, you go and you meet him. Are you hearing me?"

I nodded.

"The man on the other side of the red pager is the man who allows you to do what you do. Everything else that happens, happens because he lets it happen. In fact, if any one of these other people ever uses your services, this man gets a cut right off the top. You got that? He's the boss, and if you ever get on the wrong side of that, you might as well just go kill yourself and save everybody else the trouble. Because this man will fuck you and everyone else around you in ways that you have never even imagined. Are we totally clear on this point?"

I nodded again. I had a fairly good idea I knew who this man was. The man I had met in Mr. Marsh's office. The man in the suit, with the strange cologne and the foreign cigarettes.

"The red pager goes off," he said. "What do you do?"

I made a telephone with my thumb and little finger, and held it to my ear.

"How soon do you do it?"

I pointed to the floor. Now.

"I know that seems to contradict everything else I was telling you about being a prima donna and walking away from things. But trust me. When he needs you, you better come through."

He put the red pager back in the box and closed the lid.

"Don't worry," he said. "He won't call that often. It's not like he needs a lot of help in life."

He held out the box to me. He waited for me to take it.

"You're ready. Take them."

No, I thought. I am most definitely not ready.

"You realize, this isn't something for you to choose at this point," he said. "You already chose. Not to get too heavy or anything, but that next call on the red pager will be for you, whether you like it or not."

I took the box. The Ghost got up from his chair.

"Make sure you keep spinning, every single day. You know if you stop, you'll lose your touch."

He reached into his pocket and took out a ring of keys. He tossed them to me.

"That big one's the front door. The silver one's the office. Some of those others are for the cabinets in there, I think. That last one's for the back gate. Probably doesn't even open anymore."

I looked up at him. What the hell did I need these for?

"I don't suppose you feel like running this place. So you'd better keep it locked up. Make up a sign, say we're closed for renovations or something. You can still come in and practice."

I pointed at him. Where are you going?

"I told you," he said. "My daughter needs me. In Florida. Dream come true, right? She lives in one of those 'manufactured homes,' which is just a fancy way of saying a double-wide trailer. A swamp out back with alligators that come out and eat all the little dogs."

I gestured to everything around us.

"Yeah, how could I ever leave this? Don't worry, I'm not that sentimental about most of it. None of it's mine, anyway."

I put my hands out.

"Who owns it, you're asking? Who do you think?"

He pointed to the red pager.

"Now if you'll excuse me, I want to say good-bye to the ladies."

I knew who he meant, of course. I left him there in the back lot of West Side Recovery, so he could spend his last few minutes in the Garden of Safes. I rolled my bike out onto the sidewalk, the shoebox tucked under my arm. There was an overflowing garbage can just a few yards away, in front of the dry cleaners. I could just leave this box right on top, I thought. Ride away and never come back.

Instead, I opened up the little storage compartment behind the seat and put the box in. It just barely fit.

As I was standing there on the sidewalk, I saw the car parked across the street. I got one look at the driver's face, before he picked up a newspaper and hid behind it. It was the man who had come to visit the store that one day, the man who had walked all the way back to the safes. The name came back to me. Harrington Banks. Who his friends call Harry.

Gotta be a cop, I thought. I mean, who else would be doing this? I could go knock on his window, get a pad of paper and write down everything I know, before it goes any further.

I put my helmet on and took off for Amelia's house.

Amelia's father was gone. She was upstairs in her room. As soon as I saw her, I knew something was up.

"How was work today?" she said.

I gave her a shrug. It was okay.

"It's funny, I went by the health club and you weren't there."

Uh-oh.

"Nobody had ever even heard of you there."

I sat down on the bed. She turned around in the chair to face me.

"What are you doing for my father every day?"

This is not good, I thought. What the hell am I supposed to tell her?

"Tell me the truth."

She picked up a pad of paper and a pen. She brought them over to me and then sat on the bed next to me. She waited for me to start writing.

I'm sorry I lied to you, I wrote.

Then I crossed that out and wrote something different.

I'm sorry I let your father lie to you.

"Just tell me," she said. "I want to know what he's making you do."

He's not making me do anything.

"Michael . . . Tell me what you're doing."

I thought about it for a few seconds. Finally, I wrote the only words I could think to write.

I can't tell you.

"Why not?"

I'm trying to protect you.

"Bullshit. Is it illegal?"

I had to think about that one.

Not so far.

"Not so far? What does that mean?"

I'll tell you someday. As soon as I can. I promise.

"Whatever you're doing, it's the reason those men aren't coming to see my father anymore. Is that true?"

I nodded.

"It's the reason he let me come back home."

I nodded again.

She took the pad from me.

"How do I even figure this out? I am so mad at him for what he's gotten all of us into. I am so mad at *you* for going along with whatever stupid idea he came up with."

She got up and put the pad on her desk. Then she stood there, looking down at me.

"And I am so mad at myself for wanting to be with you every single second. No matter what."

She put her right hand against my left cheek.

"What the hell am I supposed to do?"

One idea came to me. I pulled her down onto the bed with me and showed her.

My trips down to West Side Recovery . . . they remained the one secret I kept from her. Even though it felt strange to be there without the Ghost. Just me and the safes. Me and the ladies. Almost like I was cheating on Amelia with these eight mistresses.

I didn't see Banks again. Either he was no longer watching the store, or else he was getting better at hiding it. I'd look around for him, and then I'd open the door with the key the Ghost had given me, stumble over the junk in the darkness, and spend a couple of hours spinning in the back. All the while I'd keep imagining that I was hearing footsteps.

The last few days of summer went by. Then it was time to go back to school. I was a senior at Milford High now, remember, and Amelia was a senior at Lakeland. Along with good old Zeke. So that first day back at school was tough. Griffin was long gone to Wisconsin, and even my old art teacher was nowhere to be seen. He was out with some sort of chronic fatigue syndrome and wouldn't be back on the job until God knows when. So we had a long-term substitute art teacher, some sixty-year-old ex-hippie with gray hair down his back. Who was way more into three-dimensional art than "flatlander art," as he called it.

So it was already looking like a long year.

When I got back home that afternoon, I took my helmet off and put it on the seat. The engine and the wind were both still roaring in my ears. So I almost walked away from the bike without hearing the beeping noise.

I opened the back compartment, took the box out, and lifted the lid. I sorted through them until I found the pager that was going off. It was the red one.

Go to the park, I thought. Go down to the river and throw the whole box in. Watch it float away. That's the first thing that came into my mind.

I went inside and dialed the number. Someone picked up on the other end. A voice I'd heard before. He didn't say hello or who is this or how may I help you. Instead, he simply gave me an address on Beaubien Steet, in downtown Detroit, and a time, eleven o'clock sharp. Tonight. Knock on the back door, he said. Then he hung up.

I was with Amelia that evening. We had dinner to mark our first days back at school. For better or worse. She told me she hated being back at Lakeland.

Especially now, knowing that I was across town at Milford. I kept checking my watch, because I knew I had somewhere to be at eleven. When I left her house a little after ten . . . well, she knew something was going on. I could never hide that from her. Not then, not ever. But she let me go.

I road down Grand River, passing the darkened windows of West Side Recovery. All the way down into the heart of Detroit. I swung around the bottom of the big circle where all of the streets come together in Grand Circus Park like the spokes of a wheel. I hit Beaubien Street around ten fifty.

The address turned out to be a steak house in Greektown. This was the first year for the big casinos in Detroit, and the place looked like it was doing a good business. I rolled into the lot and parked the bike. I went around to the back door, past the garbage cans and the empty produce crates. It was a heavy metal door, just like at the liquor store. I knocked on it.

A few seconds passed before the door opened. The bright light from the kitchen spilled out into the night, casting two shadows. Mine and the man who stood there looking at me. He was a big man, and he was wearing a big white apron with the belt tied tight around his waist.

"Come on in." He led me through the kitchen, where another man in an identical apron was hard at work at the grill. The first man opened the door to the pantry and stood aside for me to enter. I saw three men standing inside the room, which was otherwise filled floor to ceiling with canned tomatoes and olives and peppers, jugs of vinegar and cooking oil, and every other nonperishable thing you'd ever need to run a restaurant. When I stepped into the room, I recognized the three men immediately, and my first impulse was to turn and run out the back door.

"You're early," Fishing Hat said. He was cutting slices from a big stick of pepperoni and passing them to the other two men.

"I didn't realize you were the second coming of the Ghost," Tall Mustache said.

That left Sleepy Eyes to be heard from. He came over to me, moving slowly. "Why do we keep running into you, kid?"

"Relax," Fishing Hat said. "This is him. This is the Ghost Junior."

Sleepy Eyes kept staring me down for another long moment, until he finally backed away.

"You want some?" Fishing Hat extended the big stick of pepperoni to me.

I put my hands up. No thanks.

He looked over at Tall Mustache, and the two exchanged smiles with each other.

"We heard you don't talk much," Fishing Hat said. "He wasn't kidding."

"We heard you don't talk *at all*," Tall Mustache said. "Like ever! Is that really true?"

I nodded once, then looked back out into the kitchen. I could feel Sleepy Eyes drilling a hole in my back.

For the next few minutes, nobody bothered to make small talk. They just stood there and ate their pepperoni and looked at me.

"What do you say?" Fishing Hat finally said, looking at his watch. "Is it time to go to work?"

"Blow that whistle," Tall Mustache said.

"Consider it blown."

They led me back out through the kitchen, back into the parking lot. We all piled into the same black car that had rolled into Mr. Marsh's driveway that day. Fishing Hat at the wheel, Tall Mustache riding shotgun. That left me and Sleepy Eyes in the back.

"Okay, let's have some fun," Fishing Hat said. He put the car in gear and pulled out onto the street. He went down to Jefferson Avenue, took a left, and started heading east along the Detroit River. He kept it slow, and he stopped at every yellow light.

Sleepy Eyes was still looking at me. "How old are you?" he finally said.

I flashed him ten fingers, then seven more, but he didn't look at my hands.

"You're the boxman now? Is that what you're telling me?"

I'm not telling you anything, sir. You can go back to being quiet and that'll be just fine with me.

"He must have extra-good hearing," Tall Mustache said. He turned around to look at me. "Is that true? Do you have extra-good hearing? I mean, on account of not being able to talk?"

"What the hell are you talking about?" Sleepy Eyes said.

"When you lose one of your senses, the other senses get better. Haven't you heard of that?"

"Talking is not a sense, you idiot."

"Yes it is. You know, seeing, hearing, touching, speaking . . . What's the other one? Smelling, right? Is that five?"

"You have no idea what you're talking about."

"Will you guys shut the hell up!" Fishing Hat kept both hands on the wheel, his eyes locked on the road.

"I don't work with kids, is all I'm saying. I got enough problems."

"If he can do it, he can do it," Tall Mustache said. "That's all that matters."

"I said enough," Fishing Hat said. "Can we have a few minutes of peace here so we can prepare ourselves?"

Everybody was quiet for a while. Sleepy Eyes finally stopped staring at me. I put my head back against the seat and closed my eyes.

We kept going east on Jefferson. We passed the Waterworks Park. We took a left on Cadillac and started heading north. Then Fishing Hat slowed the car. Everyone seemed to be focused on a little check-cashing joint on the left side of the road. It was closed, but the neon letters still advertised its services. CHECKS CASHED! MONEY ORDERS! GET YOUR INCOME TAX REBATE NOW!

It was just past eleven thirty. The street was fairly quiet but not deserted. It made sense to me, to be doing this now. Any later and sure, it might be even more quiet, but then you'd really get noticed by the one guy who happened to be awake, or the cop driving by on the night shift. Fishing Hat hung a left down the street, looped around a residential block and came back out toward Cadillac, then hung a right into the parking lot behind the store.

There was a fence back there, maybe six feet high. A security light above the back door, but it was a simple round bulb, so the light wasn't directed anywhere specifically. A few of the houses had line of sight, but nobody was outside. We all sat in the car and waited for a few minutes. One man came by, walking his dog. Cars kept driving by on Cadillac, one every few seconds, but none came down the side street.

It was quiet in the car, the only sound the breathing of four men. Another minute passed. Then Fishing Hat raised one hand. "Okay," he whispered. "The alarm system should be off."

"Should be?" Sleepy Eyes didn't sound too happy.

"Yes. That's what my man tells me."

I didn't know anything about alarm systems yet. Hell, I didn't know anything period, beyond how to open a lock or a safe.

Sleepy Eyes opened his door. I assumed I should do the same. The other two men sat tight.

That made sense when we got to the back door. There was no reason for all four of us standing around while I worked on the lock. I took out my picks and set the tension bar. A place like this would have a great lock on it, I thought. Nothing easy about it. With all the time I'd spent working on the safes, I hadn't been doing this for a while. The tension bar felt strange and foreign in my hand. God damn it all, what if I couldn't get this open?

I could feel Sleepy Eyes getting restless already. He was standing too close to me. I stopped and gave him a quick look. He took a step backward.

"Make this quick, will ya?"

I cast him out of my mind and focused on the lock. You've done this so many times. It's so easy. Set the tension, start working your way through the pins. One at a time. Yes, that's it. Yes.

A car turned down the side street. It passed by us, maybe twenty-five feet away. It didn't stop. It didn't slow down.

I kept the tension exactly where it was. I told myself to relax. I kept going.

The seconds ticked by. One pin. Two. Three. Four. Five. Nothing yet. I'm sure these are mushroom pins, at the very least.

Sleepy Eyes breathing hard now. Shut him out. Just shut him right out. Nothing exists in the whole world but these little pieces of metal.

Nothing else. Not even Amelia.

I paused for a moment.

"What's the matter?"

I went back to it. Second set. One. Two. Three. Four . . .

I touched the last pin, felt the whole thing give. The knob turned, and I pushed open the door.

Sleepy Eyes went in first, taking a flashlight out of his back pocket. I followed, and heard someone else come in behind me. It was Tall Mustache, who would apparently serve as the second lookout. Fishing Hat stayed in the car. That's how they were going to play this.

The safe was right there in the back room, not ten feet from the door. It was a six-foot behemoth, a Victor brand with a beautiful black finish. I couldn't even imagine how much this thing would have weighed. No wonder the man who owned this place made no effort to hide the thing. Hell, he could have put it on the sidewalk and it would have been just as secure.

I went to the dial. First things first, make sure it's actually locked up. It was. I tried out the couple of Victor presets I knew, but neither of them hit.

Okay, then. I grabbed a chair from a nearby desk, made myself comfortable, and started doing my thing.

"How long is this going to take?" Sleepy Eyes said.

"Just leave him alone," Tall Mustache said.

Sleepy Eyes stepped through to the front room. I could see him hunched down behind the counter. Once again, I forced the clown out of my head and concentrated on my work.

Find the contact area. Spin a few times. Park the wheels. Go back the other way. Pick up one . . . two . . . three . . . four. And that's it. Four wheels, like I was afraid of. An extra-tough safe for my first time out, but we'll give it a shot. Spin a few more times. Park at 0. Go back to the contact area. Feel for it. Feel that exact size. Let the safe tell you what's going on inside it.

Yes, like that. Park at 3, back to the contact area.

I kept the side of my face against the metal. Time slowed down. Everything else disappeared. I kept working. I found the areas shortening up around 15, 39, 54, 72. I went back, worked those down to 16, 39, 55, 71.

I shook out my hands. Tall Mustache had the door open just wide enough for him to see out with one eye. Sleepy Eyes was sitting on the floor now, watching me.

One last step here. Four numbers means twenty-four possible combinations. I started spinning them all out, starting with 16, 39, 55, 71. Then switching the last two numbers. Then switching the second and the third, and so on.

I did twelve combinations. I did thirteen. On my fourteenth try, the handle moved.

That brought Sleepy Eyes off the floor. He came over and hovered behind me as I turned the handle all the way and opened the safe door.

It was empty.

"Are you fucking kidding me?" Sleepy Eyes turned around and went back out toward the front counter.

"What is it?" Tall Mustache said. He was still standing at the back door. He had no idea how unhappy he was about to become.

Me? I had a strange mix of feelings, standing there looking into that empty space. There's nothing quite as *empty* as an empty safe, for one thing. It's always given me an oddly elated hollow feeling in my chest, swinging that door open and seeing absolutely nothing. Like the emptiness of outer space.

So that feeling mixed with the triumph of knowing that yes, I really could open up a safe in this kind of environment, using only my ears and my fingers and my mind. I could really do this.

Mixed with oh shit, this safe is fucking empty and these three guys are about to go insane. It may not be my fault exactly, but I'll still have to deal with it.

That's as far as I got. Two or three seconds of that before it all fell apart. The next sound we all heard was the distinctive sound of four tires leaving four black marks on the pavement just outside the door. Followed by Tall Mustache swinging open the back door and running out into the night like he had been shot out of a cannon. The last part of that chain reaction was Sleepy Eyes climbing over the front counter, slamming his whole body into the front door, fumbling with the latch and getting it open remarkably quickly, and then falling out onto the sidewalk.

That left me, an empty safe, and a long shadow in the back doorway.

I made a break for the other door, thinking it would be a real good idea to follow in Sleepy Eyes's footsteps.

"Stop right there or I'll shoot you right in the fucking back."

I stopped.

"Turn around."

I turned. The man was in his sixties maybe. With a rough face. The kind of man who clearly hadn't taken a lot of shit from anybody in the past and wasn't about to start now. He was wearing a black leather jacket that might have been a little too young for him, but that wasn't the biggest problem. The biggest problem was the very real gun in his right hand.

It was a semiautomatic. It looked like the gun my uncle had under his cash register. It was pointed right at my chest.

"Your friends are all gone."

His voice was perfectly calm. He took a step closer to me, right into a thin beam of light that came into the room, filtered through the front window. I saw his face more clearly. He had a big nose. He had red cheeks. He was badly in need of a shave.

"I think you need new friends," he said, taking another step closer. "Don't you agree?"

No arguments there.

"You're just a kid, eh? So how about this, I'll make you a deal. You tell me who those other guys were and I won't put a bullet in your head."

I didn't move. He came closer.

"Come on, kid. Don't be dumb. You think any of those guys wouldn't have given you up in two seconds? Just tell me who they are."

That's going to be a problem, I thought. I don't think I'm going to be able to help you here.

The man shook his head and smiled. It looked like he was going to step away, but in the next instant he was right on top of me. He grabbed me by the front of the shirt with one hand. With the other he pressed the gun right into my neck. I smelled the cigar smoke on him. It took me right back to my bedroom in Uncle Lito's house. A million miles away.

"It's a little rude not to answer my question, don't you think? Are you going to tell me or what?"

This is it, I thought. This is it right here.

"Who are they?"

The gun barrel pressed harder into my neck. He had it angled upward. The bullet would go right up through my brain.

"Okay," he said. "Okay. Maybe you don't know their names. Is that it? Huh?"

He's going to kill me.

"Just tell me where you know them from. Can you do that? Who set you up with these guys?"

My last minute on earth. It's right here.

"Say *something*, kid. Tell me something right now or I swear to God, I will pull this trigger."

Worse things could happen.

"Three seconds. Talk or die."

Worse things than having to live like this.

"Three."

Maybe it's the only way out.

"Two."

Even if it means never seeing Amelia again.

"One."

I wished I could have said good-bye to her, at least.

"Zero."

A few seconds passed, the gun still pressed into my neck. I kept breathing. From outside, I could hear a car pulling into the lot. The headlights came through the open door and swung across the room.

The man lowered the gun. He wrapped one arm around my head and pulled it against his shoulder. For one second I thought he was going to break my neck.

But no. He was hugging me.

"Okay, kid," he said. "Okay."

Fishing Hat came in through the back door. Followed by Tall Mustache. Followed by Sleepy Eyes.

Followed by the Ghost.

"I told you guys," the Ghost said. As pale as ever, and he seemed agitated and totally out of place here. "Did you think I was making a fucking joke? The kid doesn't talk. And he wouldn't rat you out, even if he could."

"You were right," the man with the gun said. He must have been the owner of this place. Doing somebody a favor by letting these guys use it for a theater, and getting into the act himself.

"I told you he'd be able to open the safe, too. Did I not?"

"Correct again."

Looking back on it, the whole thing did seem a little too choreographed. But at least I had passed the test, right? Local kid makes good, proves himself to criminals.

They took me back to the restaurant in Greektown. The Ghost didn't come inside with us. He stood in the parking lot and said good-bye to me again. For real this time.

"It's official," he said to me. "You own the franchise."

He got in his car and drove off. The other men took me inside and got me a drink from a bottle I recognized from my uncle's shelves. I choked down a swallowful.

"Sorry if we were riding you a little hard," Fishing Hat said, grabbing me by the back of the neck. "We had to see how you handled it, you know? Make sure you could handle your business. See how big a pair you had if it all went to shit on you."

Big enough, apparently. For what that was worth. The closing act was when I got taken over to a private table, separated from the rest of the restaurant by a folding partition. There were three couples sitting at the table, but there was no mistaking who was in charge of the evening. It was the man I'd met exactly one time before. The dark eyes, the thick eyebrows, the long cigarette hanging from his lips. That same aroma in the air, the smoke mixing with his cologne and whatever else, the combination vaguely foreign and powerful and different from anything I'd ever smelled before.

That smell, by itself, would have told me everything I needed to know. Like the Ghost said, this was the man you do not fuck with.

"It's good to see you again," he said to me. "I knew I had a good feeling about you."

I didn't move.

"A man who doesn't talk. What a beautiful thing, eh?"

Everyone else at the table nodded at this. Two other men in suits. Three women in diamonds and dressed out to here.

"If you see Mr. Marsh, tell him I'm sorry to hear that his partner Mr. Slade is still missing. He should be more careful who he does business with."

That brought some laughter from around the table. Then I was dismissed. Sleepy Eyes ushered me away and pressed a wad of bills into my right hand. When I got outside, I opened my fist and saw five crumpled hundred-dollar bills.

I still had the pagers in the motorcycle's back compartment. I was wondering what would happen if I were to take them back into the restaurant. If I were to place them on that table and then walk away. I was trying to picture exactly what might happen, when I heard Sleepy Eyes calling to me.

"Over here," he said. He gestured me over to the long black car, the same car I'd seen parked in Mr. Marsh's driveway.

"The boss wanted me to show you something," he said. "He thought it might be . . . what's the word? Beneficial?"

Sleepy Eyes took a quick look around, then opened the trunk. As the light popped on, I saw the lifeless face of Jerry Slade, Mr. Marsh's partner. The trunk lid got slammed back down before I could register anything else. How he might have died, or if the rest of his body was even intact.

"I don't make a point of parking in the middle of a city with something like that in the trunk," Sleepy Eyes said, "but we finally caught up to him today, and well . . . it seemed like good timing. Do your little test tonight and make a lasting impression, all at the same time."

I kept standing there. My mind couldn't make my muscles do anything yet.

"Welcome to real life, kid."

He smacked me once on the cheek and went inside, leaving me there alone in the dark.

I went to school for two more days. That was it for my entire senior year of high school. On Thursday night, the blue pager went off. I called the number. The man on the other end had a thick New York accent. He gave me an address in Pennsylvania. Just outside of Philadelphia. He told me I'd be expected in two days' time. I sat there for a long time, looking at the address.

I'm going to need a note, I thought to myself. I'm going to need a note, excusing me from school tomorrow so I can go to Pennsylvania and help some men rob a safe.

The next morning, I bought a pair of luggage bags. They hung over the backseat of my motorcycle, one on each side. I came back and put as many clothes as I could fit inside them. Toothbrush, toothpaste, the usual things you need every day. I packed my safe lock. I packed the pages that Amelia had drawn for me that summer. I packed the pagers.

I had about a hundred dollars of my own saved up, plus the five hundred the men had given me after the fake robbery. Minus the thirty bucks for the motorcycle luggage. So about $570 in total.

I went to the liquor store, going in through the back door in case Uncle Lito was taking one of his morning naps. When I went through to the front, there he was slumped over the counter, his head resting on his forearms. If someone walked through the front door, he'd snap awake in a half second and try to act like he hadn't been sleeping.

I slipped around him and stood in front of the cash register. I pushed the magic button on the register and the drawer popped open. I did a quick count. There wasn't much, and what there was, I put right back. I couldn't take it. When I closed the drawer, Uncle Lito came to.

"What? What's going on?"

I put my hand on his back. Not my usual thing to do.

"Michael! Are you okay?"

I gave him the thumbs-up. Never better.

"What are you doing? Shouldn't you be at school?"

He looked old today. My father's brother, this man who felt responsible for what had happened to me, who had taken me in despite having no aptitude whatsoever for taking care of another human being.

But he tried. Right? He tried.

And he gave me one damned fine motorcycle.

I hugged him for the first and last time. Then I went out the door.

Here is the part that kills me. I had one more stop to make. The antique store down the street. I went inside and waved to the old man, the very same old man who had sold me my first locks, way back when.

I wasn't buying a lock today. I went to the glass counter and pointed to a ring. I didn't know if the diamond was real. All I knew was that I had seen it before, and that I had liked it. And that I had enough money to buy it. It was only a hundred dollars.

When I had the ring in its little box, tucked inside my jacket, I rode over to Amelia's house. The place was empty. Mr. Marsh was off at the health club or wherever else he went during the day, now that I'd earned his life back for him.

Amelia was at school, of course. Like any normal seventeen-year-old.

The front door was locked. I went around to the back. That was locked, too. One more time, for old times' sake, I took out the tools and opened that door. It made me remember that first time, when I had broken into the house with the football players. Then the time after that, when I had broken in just to leave a picture in Amelia's room.

I didn't regret any of it. I still don't, to this day.

When I was inside, I went upstairs and sat on her bed for a while. Amelia's bed, officially the greatest square footage on the planet Earth. I sat there remembering everything, and then for the last time that day, I tried to talk myself out of it.

You can go get her right now, I thought. Go get her out of school, give her the ring in person. Take her with you. You love her, you can't live without her, you'll find a way to make it work. Why else would you feel this way? Why do you even have a heart inside you if it tells you that this is the person you want to be with for the rest of your life and you can't make that happen?

And so on. Until the truth finally came back to me. As clear as sunlight. As clear as that look on her face when those men came to the house, with her father in the backseat.

I can't take you with me, I thought. I can't let this touch you. Any of it. I can't even tell you where I'm going.

I stood up. I took the ring box out of my jacket. I put it on her pillow.

I did all of this for you, Amelia. And now I have to do one more thing.

Twenty-six

Los Angeles
September 2000

Gunnar was in. Of course. It was his crazy idea to begin with.

Julian and Ramona were out. No surprise there, either.

"I told you before, it's suicide," Julian said. "You know it is."

"It's foolproof," Gunnar said. "We hit, we run. We have our tracks covered. Four million dollars."

"You don't think they're gonna know in two seconds who took the money? You might as well draw a big fucking neon arrow from that boat to this house."

"No," Gunnar said. "You don't get it. I told you, I've got another contact on the boat."

"Who's this contact you keep talking about? Give me a name."

"You don't know him. His name won't mean anything to you."

"How did you meet him?"

"I was doing a tattoo on this one guy who knew this other guy who was gonna be going on this big boat, he said. Being a bodyguard. So I followed up on it. You know, the same thing that you do all the time."

"You're insane," Julian said. "You've totally lost your mind."

"You just don't want to face the fact that I was the one who set this up. For once, it's *me* who puts together the perfect score, and you can't take it."

Lucy watched them going back and forth. She was as silent as I was. Eventually, she went upstairs and didn't come back down until the evening. By then, it had come down to one simple declaration. Anybody else in the house was welcome to join us, but if we had to, Gunnar and I would do it alone. I knew it was a bluff and Julian and Ramona probably knew it, too. But in the end . . . they were in.

It was just too much money to turn down.

And if you thought about it long enough, you had to admit . . . if we did this just right, we might actually get away with it.

So the next few days were all about preparation. Putting the goods together, first of all. The wine, the cigars. Everything. Julian had done this once before, of course. He had delivered it all as part of his repayment to the man from Detroit, in exchange for being allowed to walk off that boat without a bullet in his head. Now he just had to come through again, with a little help from the rest of us.

It wasn't expected, mind you. No official promise had been made. Still, it was a reasonable cover story. It was a way to walk right onto that boat like it was the most natural thing in the world. It was also a card to play if everything fell apart and we were asked what the hell we were doing there.

We cased out the marina itself. Even though Julian already knew the place, he wanted nothing left to chance. He wanted to know the exact slip where the boat would be moored. The exact schedule. Who would disembark and when, where they'd go, how long they'd be there. So we could put together our plan, choreograph every last movement, down to the second.

We went over it again and again. Until everybody knew exactly what they had to do.

Now all we had to do was wait for the boat to arrive.

Lucy was acting strange. After what had happened between us . . . that one single afternoon . . . she was distant to me. She wouldn't come over in the afternoons to hang out anymore. At dinner, she barely looked at me. I started to worry about her. Is she really ready for this? Will she be able to carry off her part of the operation?

The night before the big day, Julian was walking back and forth from one end of the house to the other, muttering to himself. Ramona didn't want to be alone, but she didn't want to talk, either. She spent the last hours putting together the gift baskets, with all of the expensive goodies spread out on the table. The wine, the single malt whisky, the Cuban cigars, the Dunhill cigarettes. She wouldn't let anyone help her. God help you if you came within three feet of that table.

Gunnar was doing a light workout in the yard. Alone in the darkness. Lucy sat in a chair with earphones on, listening to music.

Me? I spent the time drawing, of course. I was trying to capture everything about that one last empty evening. The way we all looked as we were getting ready. For better or worse, nothing would ever be the same again.

Midnight came. We tried to sleep.

Then the next morning . . . Gunnar got the call from his contact. The ship had changed its plans. It wasn't docking at Marina del Rey, after all. It was heading directly to Mexico.

"Four million dollars," Gunnar said. "Four million dollars on that fucking boat and it's not coming to shore? Can you fucking believe this?"

"Maybe they got tipped off," Julian said. "They know something is up."

"Don't be an idiot. These guys are smart, but they're not *psychic.*"

"Maybe the card game's getting serious," Julian said. "Maybe they just want to skip all that other shit. Coming ashore and golfing, or going to Vegas . . ."

"We should just get our own boat," Gunnar said. "Something *fast.* Ride out there and take them down, right on the ocean."

"Yeah, that would work. That's a great idea."

"I'm serious, Julian. I'm not fucking around."

"You go ahead, give that a try. They'll cut you in half and feed you to the sharks."

"I'm glad we're not doing this," Lucy said. She had taken her earphones off. It was the first time she had spoken in two days. "I had a bad feeling about it."

Gunnar stared her down for a long moment. Then he picked up one of Ramona's carefully wrapped gift baskets and threw it across the room. It exploded against the wall, filling the room with cigars and crinkly green tissue paper and the warm scent of whisky.

After that, everyone drifted off in their own direction. Nobody ate dinner together.

Just before he went to bed, Gunnar got the second call. The boat would be stopping in San Diego in the morning, his contact said. At one of the marinas in Coronado, at the north end of San Diego Bay. If we were there bright and early, we just might catch it.

Julian drove. Ramona sat beside him in the front seat. Gunnar and I were in the back. Lucy was between us. The sun was just starting to come up.

"This will work," Gunnar said. "They'll never see it coming. It's just like you always say. Hit 'em where they ain't looking, right? Eight heavy hitters with a half million each? What will they be worrying about? Pirates at sea? The *banditos* in Mexico? What's the one time they'll have their guard down? On a spur-of-the-moment stop! Their last stop in America!"

"We've never even been down here," Julian said. "We have no idea what we're getting into."

"For once in your life," Gunnar said, "you have to improvise a little. You move fast, you're in, you're out. Then you're gone. We can do this."

"What do you think?" Julian said to Ramona.

"Now you're asking my opinion? While we're already on our way down there?"

"Yeah. Now I'm asking."

"My opinion is we go make our deliveries. If it doesn't feel right, we can bail out. Nothing lost."

"Four million dollars," Gunnar said. "That sounds like a hell of a loss to me."

"How about your life?" Ramona said. "How's that for a loss?"

"It won't happen."

"You've never met this guy," she said, turning to face him. "You've never looked him in the eye like I have."

"Everybody stop talking," Lucy said. "Just stop right now."

They did. They all stopped talking and joined me in the tense silence. Julian kept driving. For all of his doubts, he was the one taking us there at a mile a minute.

The sun broke over the San Marcos Mountains just as we got close to the northern end of San Diego Bay. From one moment to the next, the ocean was suddenly glittering in the sunlight. We took the bridge to North Island. As we pulled up near the marina, we could see the yachts all lined up in a row. We parked at the service entrance. Julian popped the trunk, and we started carrying our load down onto the dock. The crates of wine. The gift baskets.

We were all in our game day outfits, of course. Julian, Gunnar, and I in identical black pants and white golf shirts. Looking as nondescript and interchangeable as possible. Like every other faceless man who spends his working day waiting on people.

Ramona and Lucy, on the other hand, stripped down to their short shorts and bikini tops. For maximum distraction.

We walked out onto the long dock, each of us with our arms full. As we walked by each ship, we saw crew members hosing off the decks. We saw rich people with tanned ankles and docksiders, sitting high above us, enjoying their breakfasts while the seagulls screamed for handouts. We kept walking.

"I don't see it," Julian said. "Where's the fucking boat?"

Down toward the end, there was a long gangway leading up to the biggest boat of all. It had to be two hundred feet long. It was parked facing out, with a gangway leading up to the stern's second deck. There were two men standing there at the foot of the gangway. Both large, both dressed in black. Both doing a professional job of looking unfriendly.

"This isn't it," Julian said. "This isn't the boat."

"It has to be," Gunnar said. "Let's check it out."

Gunnar went up to the two men, slipping into his role. A not so bright delivery man, just trying to get rid of his packages.

"Hey, guys, what's up? Is this the boat we're looking for, I wonder?"

One of the men raised an eyebrow.

"We might be looking for another vessel," Julian said, stepping into his role. "These guys were on the *Skylla*."

"That was last year," one of the men said. "This is the new boat. Excuse me, the new 'vessel.' "

The two men exchanged a look. Then they started noticing Ramona and Lucy, and everything tipped in our favor.

"We've got all this stuff to set up on the boat," Gunnar said. "If you don't mind . . ."

"Yeah yeah," the man said. "Go ahead. Take your time."

Gunnar went up the gangway. Julian and I followed while Ramona and Lucy lagged behind for a little extra face time. There were a few feet of clearance between the dock and the back of the boat, so I couldn't help noticing when we were directly above the water. The gangway trembled beneath my feet with every step. When we were finally on deck, we put our crates down on the bartop.

"I don't know this boat," Julian said. "This might be a problem."

"So what the fuck," Gunnar said. "It's gotta be the same setup, right? We just find the safe."

Ramona and Lucy arrived on the deck.

"One hell of a boat," Ramona said.

"It's even bigger than last year's," Julian said. "Just remember to split up when we start going back."

Julian and Ramona stayed at the bar, taking their time unpacking the wine and keeping a lookout at the same time. Lucy, Gunnar, and I went down the hall to the staterooms. Lucy pushed open the first door and set down her gift basket. The room was small but comfortable. One bed. A television. Everything done in fine wood and polished brass.

Gunnar opened the next door, gave a quick look up and down the hallway, and pointed me to the last few doors. He took the gift basket from me and left me there in the hallway.

I poked my head into each room. I saw more beds, more fine wood, more luxury.

No safes.

"We can't stay on too long," Gunnar said when we were both back in the hallway. "It'll look suspicious."

We went back out to the bar and down the gangway, Gunnar giving Julian a quick shake of the head as we walked by. Julian waited a few minutes, then followed us. When we were back at the car, we all loaded up with wine crates and gift baskets again.

"You guys go first," Julian said. "We've got to keep it spread out."

Gunnar and I walked back down the dock. Ramona and Lucy were chatting up the guards now, asking them where the boat was going, who was on board, how often they worked out to get such nice bodies. The two men were eating it up.

I noticed the water again as I passed over it, found myself taking a step too close to the edge and feeling the weight in my arms pulling me over. I regained my balance and kept going, suddenly rattled in a way that never happened when I was on the job.

This time we went downstairs to the lower level. The first room we looked in was by far the largest we had seen so far. A pool table was pushed all the way over to the side of the room, and a half-dozen army cots were carefully arranged to maximize every square inch. This must have been the room Sleepy Eyes had told me about, where all of the bodyguards bunked together and drove each other insane.

He slept right here in this room, I thought. I couldn't help feeling a shudder run down my back.

Gunnar looked into the next room, but I was already focused on the door at the end of the hallway. I could see that it had a better lock than all of the other doors. When I went down and turned the knob, it didn't move. So

I got down on one knee and took out my lock picks. Tension bar in. Quick rake and boom, it was open. Our first lucky break of the day.

I stepped inside and saw enough scuba gear to outfit the Navy SEALs. On another wall there were a dozen high-end deep sea fishing poles. Then against the far wall, a safe. Our second lucky break of the day.

I shook out my hands and stepped up to the safe.

There was no dial. Only a touchpad.

It was an electronic safe.

Now, there are ways to break into an electronic safe. Apparently, somebody figured out how to program a computer to send out a special wireless signal to the locking mechanism in an electronic safe, working at lightning speed through each possible combination until the right one is hit.

Of course, I didn't happen to have a computer with me at the time, programmed to send out a special wireless signal or otherwise. In other words, I was totally fucked.

I stood there letting the reality soak in for a while. Then I left the room and closed the door behind me. Gunnar was just coming down the hallway with another gift basket. His eyes got wide when he saw me.

"What's the problem?"

I motioned him over to the door, opened it for him, and pointed to the safe.

"What? What is it?"

I made a stabbing motion with my finger, like I was keying in a combination on the touchpad. He looked back and forth a few times. Me. The safe. Me. The safe. Then he got it.

"Oh, fuck. Are you kidding me? You can't open that thing?"

I shook my head.

"There's got to be a way."

I shook my head again. He looked like he was about to do his patented gift basket throw again. Then he got his composure back in the next second. He opened up the nearest stateroom door, slammed the basket down on the little table next to the bed, then went up the stairs to the second deck.

Gunnar, Julian, Ramona, and Lucy were all standing at the bar when I finally went up there. I could tell that Gunnar had already told them the news.

"This is all a joke," Julian said. "You guys are playing a joke on me. There's not really an electronic touchpad down there."

"Yeah," Gunnar said. "It's a joke, all right."

"The other boat had a regular safe. I swear."

"Well, good. Let's go find that boat and rob it. Whaddya say?"

"What do we do now?" Ramona said.

Julian took the last bottle out of his crate and set it down on the bartop. "We finish our deliveries like good little boys and girls. Then we leave."

"Four million dollars," Ramona said. "In a safe. On an empty boat. And we can't touch it."

"We could hijack the whole boat," Gunnar said. "Just take it."

Julian just looked at him.

"It's all right," Gunnar said, slapping my shoulder a little too hard. "I should have known it was too good to be true."

"Give him a break," Ramona said. "It's not his fault."

"Yeah. I know. They didn't cover this in safecracking school."

He walked away from us. He left the ship, went down the gangway, paused for a half second at some smart remark from one of the two guards, then kept walking down the dock.

The rest of us followed. When we were all at the car, we got the rest of the stuff and carried it back on board. I wouldn't have been surprised if Gunnar just sat there in the car and let us finish the job without him, but he grabbed a big crate of wine and carried it back to the boat. When we were all on board again, we split up to distribute the rest of the baskets. Nobody said a word.

I took my basket down to the lower level. As I walked into one of the rooms, I couldn't help noticing the faint aroma. The exotic cigarettes, mixed with the cologne. This was *his* room. The man who owned me and apparently would keep on owning me. Forever.

It felt strange to be standing there, right next to the bed where he would be sleeping every night. A half million dollars of his money just next door in that safe.

I put the basket down on the table. The only thing I would accomplish that day, a thoughtful delivery of various amenities to make his trip a little more enjoyable. Some fine Cuban cigars. A bottle of Lagavulin, aged sixteen years. A German Birko straight razor, complete with shaving brush and shaving cream. A can of L'Amande talcum powder, from Italy. May you enjoy it all, sir. Glad to be of service.

I left the room, went halfway down the hall.

Then I stopped.

I went back to the room and looked at the gift basket. I loosened the cellophane wrap and took out the can of talcum powder.

Then I went back out. To that last room. I opened the door.

"Michael!" It was Lucy's hushed voice, from somewhere behind me. "Where are you going?"

I went to the safe. I poured out some talcum powder into my hand. Then I held the powder up about two inches away from the touchpad. And blew.

"What are you doing?" She was standing right behind me now.

I looked around the room and found a flashlight in one of the drawers. I brought it back and shined it on the touchpad. I played around with the angle, moving my head, moving the flashlight, until I finally achieved the effect I was trying for.

"Are you telling me . . ."

I nodded without looking at her.

"I'll go tell those guys to stall a little bit. Good luck!"

She left the room. It was just me now. Me, the touchpad, the flashlight, some powder, and four visible fingerprints on four of the numbers.

I knew how to do this last part. It was just like when I would narrow down the numbers on a dial, and then go back and try out each possible combination. With four numbers, that meant twenty-four possibilities, assuming each number was only used once. I started going through them, hitting the ENTER button and then watching the little indicator light. Around the fifth try, I started to wonder if there would be some kind of lock-out mechanism if you tried too many incorrect combinations.

I held my breath and tried the sixth possibility.

Or you know what? Maybe too many incorrect tries sets off an ear-splitting alarm. That would be fun.

I tried the seventh combination.

Right about now, I thought. If this next one is wrong, something bad is going to happen. The alarm will go off, and those huge men will come storming onto the boat with guns.

I tried the eighth combination. The little light went from red to green. I turned the handle and opened the safe.

Now, I know what a stack of hundred-dollar bills looks like. A hundred bills in one stack equals ten thousand dollars. A hundred stacks equals one million. Off the top of my head, I was guessing we could fit a hundred stacks into one empty wine bottle crate. So I left the safe open and hurried back up to the second deck. And walked right into a party.

The two guards had come up the gangway and were standing at the bar now. Each with a bottle of Mexican beer. The women were still smiling and laughing, still playing their parts, but as I caught Ramona's eyes I saw the flash of helpless desperation. Julian and Gunnar were still rearranging everything on the bar, moving all the wine bottles around and otherwise trying to look like they still had a good reason to be there.

I knew we needed several empty wine crates downstairs, as quickly as possible, but there was no way we could take them down there and fill them with money. Not while these guards were here.

"You guys about done?" one of the men said.

"Oh, just about," Julian said. "Making sure everything's perfect."

"Maybe you need to show us around the boat," Ramona said. "As long as we're here . . ."

"That could be arranged," the man said. "For a reasonable fee."

She gave that one a little laugh. I could see the muscles in Gunnar's forearms straining as he slammed a wine bottle down on the bar.

"Show us what's up here," Ramona said, pointing to the upper deck. "Like, is there a place where you can get a good tan?"

"We can show you the sundeck, sure. Maybe the staterooms, too?"

Ramona was practically pushing the man up the stairs. Lucy followed with the other, giving Gunnar a quick look as she did.

"Come on, let's go," Julian said, when they were gone. He grabbed two of the empty wine crates and headed down the stairs.

Gunnar didn't move.

"We're wasting time," Julian said. "You gotta focus here."

"I will fucking kill that guy if he touches her," Gunnar said, grabbing two more wine crates.

When we were all back in the safe room, Julian and Gunnar started packing the bundles into the crates. While they did that, I took the talcum powder back to the room where I had found it. I slipped it in the gift basket and then went back to the safe room to help with the money.

"There's too much here," Julian said. "We're not even halfway through it."

"This isn't four million dollars," Gunnar said. "Is that possible?"

"What did they do, double the buy-in this year? I think there's fucking *eight million dollars* in this safe."

"There's no way they're just playing poker. Something else is going on here."

"Does it matter? Just keep moving!"

A few minutes later, we had all six of our wine crates packed tight. There was still about two million dollars left in the safe.

"Come on," Gunnar said, "let's get these to the car, so we can come back for the rest."

"This is enough," Julian said. "It's six million dollars."

"We gotta come back anyway, right? You're gonna leave two million dollars here?"

So each one of us took two crates apiece, one under each arm. Probably fifty, sixty pounds of total weight, so it was hard to move fast, especially as we got down to the end of the gangway and had to keep going down the whole length of the dock. When we finally made it to the car, Julian was breathing hard.

"This is what you get for not working out with us," Gunnar said. He opened up his two crates and dumped the money into the trunk. "Mike and I will go get the girls and the rest of the money. Start the car and have it ready to go."

Julian looked at him for a moment, not accustomed to being the one receiving the orders. Then he gave us a nod and took out his keys.

"Did you see how he just let Ramona go off with that guy?" Gunnar said as we were running back to the boat. "It didn't seem to bother him one bit."

All part of the job, I thought. What the hell else was he supposed to do? But no matter. We had two more cratefuls of money to pack up, and then we could all get the hell out of there.

Up the gangway, moving so fast now it lunged up and down like a trampoline. Back down to the lower deck. Shoving the rest of the money into the last two crates. Then, just as we're finishing up, we heard the noises from upstairs.

"What the hell is that?" Gunnar said.

I closed up the safe while he went to the door and peeked down the hallway.

"Come on, I think we better get out of here."

We were halfway down the hall, each of us carrying a crate, when we heard the men on the second deck. We ducked into the nearest stateroom.

"Now what?" Gunnar said. "We're totally fucked now."

I put my hand on his arm. I didn't think we had a huge problem.

"No, you're right," he said. "We just made one more trip. Now we're all done. So what if we're carrying these? Just pretend they're empty."

I nodded.

"Okay, let's go."

We walked up the stairs. Just two deliverymen finishing up their work. That's when we saw the limos.

They were pulling up to the gangway, as the two guards ran down to greet them, followed by Ramona and Lucy. Lucy took a quick look back and spotted us, her eyes growing wide, but she couldn't help us now. I saw one limo door opening. I saw Sleepy Eyes getting out. Followed by the man from Detroit. A red-faced man who must have been the harbormaster ran up to them and started yelling. Not happy about the limos driving on his dock, no doubt. Ramona and Lucy used the distraction to slip away without being seen—but we were still trapped.

"We can't go down there," Gunnar said. "They've never seen me, but you . . ."

He didn't have to finish the thought. Even though they knew I was in California . . . seeing me here on the boat . . . right now . . . it would break the spell and ruin everything. We might as well just slit our own throats right here on the spot.

"We gotta find another way off this boat."

He went over to the stairs, took one more quick look down the gangway, and then scrambled up to the top level.

"Come on, what are you waiting for?"

I followed him up the stairs, even if it seemed hopeless to me. The boat was pointing nose out, after all. There was no other way off.

"This way. We have no choice."

I followed him down the side rail, to the sundeck at the front of the boat. Gunnar went to the very tip of the nose and looked down. We were maybe twenty, twenty-five feet above the water, but it might as well have been the edge of the world.

"Hold on to your money," he said. Then he jumped.

I heard the splash below. I looked over the edge and saw his head surfacing. He started treading water, working hard to keep his hold on the crate.

"Get the fuck down here!" he said to me. "Hurry up!"

I didn't move. I kept looking down at the water.

"Mike! Just jump already! It's not that high!"

The height's not the problem, I thought. I have no problem with heights.

"God damn you! Jump!"

I could hear the men coming up the gangway. Another few seconds and I'd be caught dead.

"Don't think about it! Just jump!"

One more look behind me. Then a step up onto the gunwale. Then I did it. I jumped.

I hit feet first and went straight down, all the way to the bottom. When I opened my eyes I saw rocks and green shadows all around me and nothing else. Everything else in the world was obliterated now. It was just me and the water, all around me and over me. The thing I had feared for so long, reclaiming me at last. Like the water itself had waited with such great patience for all of this time and now this time it would never let me go.

I looked up at the surface. So high above me it was like outer space. My lungs were burning. A few more seconds and I'd have to give up. I'd have to draw in one final mouthful of water and swallow it and then lie down right here on these green-lined rocks.

Then I saw a fish.

It was a tiny thing, no bigger than my finger. It swam toward me and stopped like it was looking me up and down and trying to figure out what the hell I was doing there. It was so close to me I could have reached out and taken it in my hand.

Instead I pushed myself off the bottom, letting go of the crate. The fish darted away as I rose toward the surface. When I broke free I was choking and gulping down the cold air like I couldn't breathe enough of it.

"Michael, quiet."

I looked over and saw Gunnar a few yards away. He was against the hull of the ship, watching me.

"Get over here. Hurry."

I dipped back under the water, trying to propel myself. I came up one more time, went down again. Then I felt a hand grabbing my shirtsleeve as he pulled me up next to him.

"What the hell's the matter with you? Just stay right here, until we can make a break for it."

I tried to keep kicking my legs to keep my head above the water. I grabbed at the boat's hull, but it was as smooth as an ice floe.

"As soon as they're ready to push off, we have to go over there." He pointed to the much smaller boat parked parallel to us, a good thirty yards away. "We should stay underwater, and not come up until we're on the other side. Can you do that?"

I shook my head.

"Yes, you can. You have to."

We waited for a long time. It was hard to even tell anymore. What a minute felt like, or an hour. Then we heard the engine starting, and it was time to move. Gunnar pushed off from the boat, and as I watched him swim it occurred to me that he was still holding on to his crate of money. He used it as dead weight to help keep himself underwater, as he kicked and swam with his free arm and made his way over toward the other boat.

I took one last deep breath and followed him. I couldn't go as deep, but I imitated his motions and somehow I willed myself through the water. I taught myself to swim, right there on the spot, because it was either that or die. Either that or never see Amelia again, after everything I had done that day to help make it possible again.

That day in her backyard, the very first time I saw her. Standing there on the edge of that hole, looking down at me. That's what I thought about. The sunlight on her face.

Gunnar was waiting for me on the other side of the boat. "I wasn't sure if you were gonna make it," he said.

We stayed there in the water until the big boat finally motored its way out of the marina. Then it was finally time to get out. But Gunnar had one more thing to do first.

"Where did you drop the money?" he said. "That was a fucking million dollars."

I shook my head. No idea.

He shook his head and handed me his crate.

"I gotta do everything around here," he said. Then he dove back down under the water.

I had a big beach towel wrapped around my shoulders. I stared out the window as we drove back north along the coastline. Nobody said anything. Nobody was celebrating. Because even though we had all gotten out of there alive, our plan was still only half done.

Two hours later, we were back at the house. Ramona and Lucy brought out their hair dryers and started in on the wet bills. Julian was back to his pacing. Gunnar sat on the couch, staring at his phone.

"I hate this," Julian finally said. "This is the part we have no control over."

But it's the part I really care about, I thought to myself. It's the only part that matters to me. I don't care about the money.

"My man is on it," Gunnar said.

"These guys know each other. They're not going to believe that one of them would rip off the others."

"They *hate* each other, okay? They take this trip every year just so they can show each other up. You think they trust each other?"

"I don't know. It's just—"

"Why the hell do you think they bring their bodyguards with them? Eight mobsters, eight bodyguards, all armed to the teeth. Does that sound like a pleasure cruise to you? One little spark, my guy says. One little spark and *boom*."

"And he knows exactly what to do?"

"Piece of cake," Gunnar said. "Talk to all the other bodyguards, like hey, something's funny here. I saw these guys carrying all of these boxes, throwing them overboard. There was this other boat I could see coming up in the distance. You don't suppose they found out the combination to the safe, do you? He'll sell the whole thing, don't worry. Just like I told you. He'll come by in a few weeks, by the way. He'll be happy to find out his share got doubled."

"I still don't think we should be sitting here. We should be moving, just to make sure."

"It's as good as done," Gunnar said. "Just relax."

So we kept waiting. When the money was dry, we put it all in the safe. That very same safe in the secret room, which Julian had bought for me to practice on before that first job in the Hollywood Hills. It was just big enough to hold eight million dollars in hundred-dollar bills.

Then more waiting.

Then more waiting.

Then just after ten o'clock that night, Gunnar's cell phone rang. He hit the button and listened. He didn't say a word.

When he finally hung up, he just looked at us, one by one.

"It wasn't pretty," he said, "but it worked. The two men we wanted fed to the sharks got fed to the sharks."

Nobody said anything. We all knew exactly what we were doing, every step of the way. But now it was real. Two men were dead. Two men who wouldn't be missed, of course. Two men that the world would keep revolving quite nicely without. Nevertheless they were both dead because we made it happen.

Julian and Ramona hugged each other. Gunnar kept looking at his phone. Lucy came over to me and put a hand to my cheek. I turned away from her and walked out of the room.

I went back to my little apartment next to the garage. This one little room, my home for the past year. I couldn't help thinking back on all of the things that had happened here. All those times I had checked those pagers . . . Kept the batteries charged . . . my ritual, every single day. See if a call has come in. See if you're needed somewhere. Call back immediately. Especially if it's that red pager.

No more.

I was no longer owned by the man from Detroit. I would never again have to answer one of these pagers. My days as a safecracker for hire were over.

I was free.

The next day, I wrote a letter to Amelia. I actually had an address for her now, after all. Care of that dormitory in Ann Arbor. I didn't fill up the letter with drawings this time. I didn't try to capture everything that had happened the day before, with the boat and the money and me in the water. There'd be time for that later. For now, all I wanted her to know was that I was on my way back home.

I figured we could work out the details when I got there. I mean, she was in art school, and I'd never take her away from that. Hell, maybe I could buy myself another new identity and start life over. Maybe even register for classes there. Buy a house not far from the school and have her live there with me. Anything was possible, right? I had money now, and there was no reason I couldn't go back and make it all happen.

I went out to mail the letter. When I had done that, I kept riding around on the motorcycle, amazed at how different it felt already. Not having to think about the pagers or the next big job. Or anything at all.

Eventually, I rode down to the Santa Monica Pier and walked right out to the very edge. I leaned over the railing and looked down at the ocean.

You can't have me, either, I thought. Not even you.

It was late afternoon when I rode back to the house. Already wondering how long it would take me to pack and say good-bye to them. Wondering what it would feel like to leave, knowing I'd probably never see them again.

Until I went inside.

I knew right away that something had happened. There were newspapers and magazines on the floor, like somebody had knocked them off the table. From somewhere upstairs, I could hear water running.

The sound got louder as I went up the steps.

I looked in Gunnar and Lucy's bedroom first. There was nobody there. Nothing looked out of place.

I went into Julian and Ramona's bedroom. The mattress was slightly askew, like someone had pushed their way past the bed and not bothered to fix it. The sound of the water was louder now. It was coming from their bathroom. I didn't want to open that door. But then I did. I had to.

I stood there and let the whole scene wash over me. Julian. Ramona. Every little detail. The water running in the tub, mixing with their blood. I took it all in and then I closed the bathroom door.

I bent over, feeling the blood rush to my head. I thought I would pass out right there. Then the feeling passed.

How did this happen? Who did this?

And who got it first?

They brought them upstairs. They bent them over the edge of the bathtub. One by one. They blew the top of Ramona's head off. Then Julian's.

Or did they do Julian first?

That's all I could think of. For some reason, it mattered to me.

I wanted to know who went first.

Then the very next thought . . . Where are Gunnar and Lucy? Are they dead, too?

I went back across the hall to their room and pushed open their bathroom door, getting myself ready for another horrible sight. But no, it was empty.

I went downstairs and back out the front door. I looked up and down the street. Then I went back around to my apartment. It was empty, too.

You knew this had to happen, I told myself. In the back of your mind, you knew. Sure, you killed the man from Detroit and Sleepy Eyes. You killed them just as surely as if you had thrown them in the water yourself. But it's not that easy. It's *never* that easy. How could you ever think it would be?

Somebody else figured out where the money went. That somebody else is hunting you down now. You don't even know who he is. He, they, whoever. You have no idea in the world. All you know is that you're dead. You're as dead as Julian and Ramona. As dead as Gunnar and Lucy will be, wherever they are right now.

You can't even call them. You can't warn them. You can't do anything.

There is one thing, I thought. There is one thing you can do.

I took out the box of pagers, pushing them aside until I found the cell phone I had brought back with me from Michigan. The cell phone I had taken from my uncle's kitchen counter. It was the first time I had even turned it on since coming back here. As I did, I saw that there were a dozen voice mail messages. Which didn't surprise me. If Banks found out I had been back in Michigan, and had taken this phone, he'd keep calling until he finally got through to me.

I didn't need to hear any of his messages right now. I knew what the general idea would be. Turn yourself in before it's too late, I'm only trying to help you, same old story. I never believed it. But now, well . . . everything had just changed. The way Julian and Ramona had been killed—that would be me someday. If not today, someday soon.

And if I really went back to Michigan, then it might be both of us. That same scene. Amelia and I together.

I looked up the one single number stored on the cell phone and hit the TALK button. It rang twice. Then Banks answered.

"Michael, is this you?"

I kept the phone to my ear as I went back, stepping over Gunnar's barbells on the way.

"I'm glad you called. Here's what I want you to do. Are you near a police station?"

I went inside the house and sat down at the table.

"Hello, Michael? Are you there? Just stay on the phone, okay?"

That's when I saw that the bookcase door was slightly open. The door to the secret back room. I ended the call and put the phone down on the table. I closed my eyes for a moment, took a deep breath, then got up and went over to the bookcase.

As I pulled it open, I saw Gunnar kneeling by the safe. Another man was standing over him.

It was Sleepy Eyes.

When he saw me, he drew out his gun and aimed it at my chest. Not that he had to worry. I was too surprised in that moment to do anything. He came over to me and pulled me into the room.

"It's about time," he said to me. "Your friend here's having a little problem with the safe."

"Michael and Lucy are always changing this combination," Gunnar said. Which was true. She'd reset it and I would open it. Keeping up with my touch. "So he's the one who can open it."

He was acting way too calm, I thought. He's not being forced to do this.

"Just open the safe." Gunnar's voice was totally flat, devoid of any feeling. "Don't make this any harder."

"You didn't even know," Sleepy Eyes said, that sick little smile on his face. That smile I hated so much. "A Judas in your midst and you had no fucking idea."

That's when it all started to make sense to me. Gunnar did have a contact on the boat. Sleepy Eyes. Everything else was an illusion. They set this whole thing up together.

Why didn't I see it coming? They were so much alike, now that I thought of it. They even sounded alike, the way they complained about always having to do the grunt work. Resenting everyone else around them. Gunnar just did a little better job of hiding it.

"I'm not going to say I'm sorry," Gunnar said to me. "Not to you, anyway. I believe I did tell you to stay away from Lucy, right? Did I not say that?"

"Where is she, anyway?" Sleepy Eyes said. "That's the little redhead, right?"

"Look, you got everything you wanted," Gunnar said. "You've got four million dollars coming. You even got rid of your boss."

So they did pull off that part of the plan. The man from Detroit is dead. For Sleepy Eyes, this whole day is a dream come true.

"I asked you a question," Sleepy Eyes said. "Where's the redhead?"

"She's gone. Don't worry about her."

She can't be involved in this, I thought. Gunnar, I can almost believe. But Lucy? No way. He must have just kept her in the dark, and then sent her away when it was done. She's probably waiting for him right now. Somewhere out there. With no idea of what happened here.

Sleepy Eyes kept staring him down. Then he turned his attention back to me.

"How about you?" he said. "You got any surprises for me?"

I wish I did. A gun in my pocket, say.

"So just open the safe, okay?"

Gunnar stood up so I could take his place. I didn't move.

"I'll ask you one more time," Sleepy Eyes said. "Please open the fucking safe."

Nothing, I thought. You get nothing.

Sleepy Eyes raised his gun to me. For the first time, I really looked at it. The barrel was so much longer with the suppressor screwed onto the end. It was the first time I had ever seen one.

"Pretty please."

Then he turned and shot Gunnar between the eyes.

It was a hollow sound, not at all like a real gunshot. It took me a moment to realize that it had even happened. Gunnar kept standing there for a long moment, a look of surprise on his face. Part of his forehead suddenly gone and a splatter of red on the wall behind him. Then he went down.

"Open the safe," Sleepy Eyes said. "Right now."

I kept standing there in front of him. Going all the way back in my mind, to that robber in the liquor store, remembering the way he held that gun. More scared of it than we were.

How different it was now. All these years later, another man and another gun, but this man wasn't scared at all. He would shoot me as calmly as a man turning on a television.

"I'm going to put a bullet in your left leg," he said. "Then your right leg. I'll keep going until you have the safe open. Do you understand?"

I still didn't move.

"I've done it before. My record is twelve shots. With a reload. It was a man who wouldn't type in a password on a computer, but same idea. Would you like me to try for thirteen today?"

He pointed the barrel at my left leg. That got me moving finally. I went down on one knee and started spinning the dial.

"I always kinda liked you," he said. "I hope you know that."

Four spins to the left. Three to the right. As soon as I turn this handle, I thought, he's going to kill me. I think that's pretty much guaranteed.

Two spins to the left.

I was one more spin away from dying. Hell, if he knew about safes, he could have killed me right then and just made the final spin himself until it stopped.

I spun a few more times to the left. Time to start over.

"Stop with the stalling, okay? Just open it."

I cleared the numbers, spun again, four to the left, three to the right, two to the left. I looked up at him.

He gave me that little smile.

I spun the dial to the right. Now all I had to do was turn the handle.

The voice came from the open bookcase door. "Drop the gun."

Sleepy Eyes looked up.

"Drop it. Right now."

Harrington Banks stepped slowly into the room, his gun still aimed squarely at Sleepy Eyes's chest. I could see three more men behind him, with enough firepower to cut him in half.

Sleepy Eyes gave me one last little smile before he dropped his gun.

It was the cell phone that had brought them there. I know this now, about how when a cell phone is left on you can track the signal to its approximate location. It brought them to the right block, at least. All they had to do was work their way through the houses until they got to this one. If it had been one more house, I probably would have been dead already.

A few minutes later, Sleepy Eyes was taken away in handcuffs. Banks took me out to the table and sat me down. He asked me if I wanted something to drink. I shook my head.

I wouldn't get to see Amelia again. That was the only thing I was thinking about. I wouldn't get to keep my promise.

"You're a hard man to catch up to," Banks said to me, "but I'm glad you called."

When we all stood up, one of his partners started to cuff me.

"Don't even bother," Banks said. "No need to embarrass ourselves."

Twenty-seven
Still Locked Up Tight
but Another Day Closer

So I come back to where I began. I've been right here in this cage for almost ten years now. Ten years. Do you remember what I said about how this all works, back when I was arrested that first time? You get on the wrong side of the law, it turns into three or four people all getting together to decide what to do with you. Nothing more.

In my case, I had a few things going for me. I was the Miracle Boy, first of all. The product of a broken home. Traumatized. Psychologically damaged. Beyond that, well, I was doing things that weren't completely voluntary, if you looked at it the right way. I mean, if you squinted real hard and held your head a little sideways . . . I was a teenager practically brainwashed into being a safecracker, right? I did not fully understand the full ramifications of what I was doing.

You get the picture. That's how my lawyer played it. That same lawyer who got me the probation after that first break-in.

But my strongest card of all was what I could tell them about the jobs I did and who I did them for. Or even the jobs where I was just along for the ride. Especially that assemblyman in Ohio. They were particularly interested in that one. The orders came from Sleepy Eyes's boss, of course, the same man who was my boss. The same man who owned us all, and who was now very much dead. But Sleepy Eyes himself? He was a much bigger fish than I was. He was as big as that fish hanging on Mr. Marsh's wall.

Funny how it works out, huh? Because of Gunnar's double-cross, Sleepy Eyes ended up living. And in the end he was worth a lot more to me alive than dead.

Add it all up and I was sentenced to a term of imprisonment of at least ten years and no more than twenty-five. I was eighteen years old when I was arrested. Nineteen by the time I was finally sentenced. I ended up right here, and you should have seen these people for that whole first month, treating me like I was the amazing Houdini, able to escape from any prison in the world. Like I'd actually be able to break my way through my cell door, then the block door, then the wing door, and probably seven other doors before I got to the outside world. It was almost laughable.

But like I said, ten to twenty-five. Leaning toward ten, I'd like to think. And ten's just about up. So now I'm in the zone, right? Any day now, I could get the news.

Any day now.

I've had a lot of time to think, of course. What else am I going to do? I play everything back and I see the places where I could have gone down another road. How that would have made everything turn out differently.

In the end, I regret most of it. But I don't regret anything that happened with Amelia. I'd do it all again if it meant being with her.

I got my first letter from her about four years in. Yes. I say letter, but it wasn't a letter at all. It was a page of comic book panels. Just like old times.

The first panel was Amelia wearing a wedding dress. I practically died right there, seeing her in that dress. Knowing that she was moving on with her life. Getting married to somebody else. I couldn't stand it. I mean, why would she even send this to me?

That's the kind of thing that was going on in my head, before I even got to the second panel. She's looking at herself in the mirror, everybody fussing around her dress and not noticing how unhappy she is. There's a thought bubble over her head. "Why can't I forget him?"

She's leaving the room in the next panel. Everyone running around behind her, yelling at her, asking her what the hell she's doing.

She's in her car. She's driving somewhere.

She stops the car on Victoria Street. Yes, right by the old house. Where we spent that night drawing on the walls. This time, instead of going to the house she goes right down to the river. She's slipping her big wedding dress over her head now. Leaving it there on the riverbank. Taking off the rest of her clothes. Yes. She draws the scene from behind, as she stands naked on the edge of the river.

Then she does it. She dives right in.

She's in the River Rouge now. The dirty water so thick she can barely see through it. She's swimming down, all the way to the bottom. As she does this, her legs disappear. Or rather, they come together and form a single tail.

That's right. That's what she drew.

She's a much stronger swimmer now, with the tail. She can go anywhere in the river she wants. She can stay down there forever. But she's looking for something specific. She's looking for the safe.

Finally, she finds it. She starts spinning the dials. Another thought bubble over her head. "Good thing he gave me the combination."

Crazy, I know. But I know exactly what she meant by that. I gave her the combination. Her and only her.

She dials the last number. She turns the handle and opens the door.

And there I am.

I'm an adult. Midtwenties, looking a little tired, but very much still alive. There are bars across the safe door. I am sitting in my miniature prison cell, inside the safe.

"What took you so long?" I say. Saying the words to her, out loud. Even though we're underwater.

That was it. The last panel.

That's how it began between us. Again.

We've kept this up for the past five and a half years. This is how we stay in touch with each other. It's like we both live in this imaginary world where we can be together, every single day. It's still not easy to be in here, believe me. But with Amelia waiting for me, I think I'll make it.

I still haven't said a real word yet. I'm sure as hell not going to try as long as I'm in this place. But when I get out . . .

The first time I see her again . . .

I don't even know what the first word will be. But it'll be there, waiting to come out.

After all these years, I'll say something.

I know I will.

Turn the page for a sneak peek at
Steve Hamilton's new novel

MISERY BAY

Available June 2011

CHAPTER ONE

It is the third night of January, two hours past midnight, and everyone is in bed except this man. He is young and there's no earthly reason for him to be here on this shoreline piled with snow with a freezing wind coming in off of Lake Superior, the air so cold here in this lonely place, cold enough to burn a man's skin until he becomes numb and can no longer feel anything at all.

But he is here in this abandoned dead end near the water's edge, twenty-six miles from his home near the college. Twenty-six miles from his warm bed. He is outside his car, with the driver's side door still open and the only light the glow of the dashboard. The headlights are off. The engine is still running.

He is facing the lake, the endless expanse of water. It is not frozen because a small river feeds into the lake here and the motion is enough to keep the ice from forming. A miracle in itself, because otherwise this place feels like the coldest place in the whole world.

The rope is tight around his neck. He swings only slightly in the wind from the lake. The snow will come soon and it will cover the ground along with the car and the crown of his lifeless head.

He will hang here from the branch of this tree for almost thirty-six hours, until his car runs out of gas and the battery dies and his face turns blue from the cold. A man on a snowmobile will finally see him through the trees. He'll make a call on his cell phone and an hour later two deputies will arrive on the scene and the young man will be lowered to the ground.

On that night, I know nothing of this young man or this young man's death. Or what may have led him to tie that noose and to slip it around his neck. I am not there to see it, God knows, and I won't even hear of it until three months later. I live on the shores of the same lake but it would take me five hours to find this place they call Misery Bay. Five hours of driving down empty roads with a good map to find a part of the lake I'd never even heard of.

That's how big this lake is.

"It's not the biggest lake in the world. You guys do know that, right?"

The man was wearing a pink snowmobile suit. He didn't sound like he was from downstate Michigan. Probably Chicago, or one of the rich suburbs just outside of Chicago. The snowmobile suit probably set him back at least five hundred dollars, one of those space-age polymer waterproof-but-breathable suits you find in a catalog, and I'm sure the color was listed as "coral" or "shrimp" or "sea foam" or some such thing. But to me it was as pink as a girl's nursery.

"I mean, I don't want to be a jerk about it and all, but that's all I hear up here. How goddamned big Lake Superior is and how it's the biggest, deepest lake in the world. You guys know it's not, right? That's all I'm saying."

Jackie stopped wiping the glass he was holding. Jackie Connery, the owner of the place, looking and sounding for all time like he just stepped red-faced off a fishing boat from the Outer Hebrides, even if he'd been living here in the Upper Peninsula for over forty years now. Jackie Connery, the man who still drove across the bridge once a week to buy me the real thing, Molson Canadian, brewed in Canada. Not the crap they bottle here in the States and criminally try to pass off as the same thing.

Jackie Connery, the man who wasn't born here, who didn't grow up here. The man who still couldn't cope with the long winters, even after forty years. The one man you did not want to poke with a sharp stick in January or February or March. Or any kind of stick, sharp or dull. Not until the sun came out and he could at least imitate a normal human being again.

"What's that you're saying now?" He was looking at the man in the pink snowmobile suit with a Popeye squint in his right eye. The poor man had no idea what that look meant.

"I'm just saying, you know, to set the record straight. Lake Superior is not the biggest lake in the world. Or the deepest."

Jackie put the glass down and stepped forward. "So which particular lake, pray tell, are you going to suggest is bigger?"

The man leaned back on his stool, maybe two inches.

"Well, technically, that would be the Caspian Sea."

"I thought we were talking about *lakes*."

"Technically speaking. That's what I'm saying. The Caspian Sea is technically a lake and not a sea."

"And it's bigger than Lake Superior."

"Yes," the man said. "Definitely."

"The water in the Caspian Sea," Jackie said, "is it saltwater or fresh?"

The man swallowed. "It's saltwater."

"Okay, then. If it's *technically* a lake, then it's the biggest, deepest *saltwater* lake in the world. Apples and oranges, am I right? Can we agree on that much?"

Jackie turned, and the man should have let it go. But he didn't.

"Well, actually, no."

Jackie stopped.

"Lake Baikal," the man said. "In Russia. That's fresh water. And it's *way* deeper than Lake Superior."

"In Russia, you said? Is that where it is?"

"Lake Baikal, yes. I don't know if it has a bigger surface area, but I know it's got a lot more water in it. Like twice as much as Lake Superior. So really, in that respect, it's twice as big."

Jackie nodded his head, like this was actually an interesting fact he had just learned instead of the most ridiculous statement ever uttered by a human being. It would have been like somebody telling him that Mexico is actually more Scottish than Scotland.

I was sitting by the fireplace, of course. On a cold morning on the last day of March, after cutting some wood and touching up the road with my plow, where else would I be? But either way I was close enough to hear the whole exchange, and right about then I was hoping we'd all find a way to end it peacefully.

The man in the pink snowmobile suit started fishing for his wallet. Jackie raised a hand to stop him.

"Don't even bother, sir. Your money's no good here."

The man looked over at me this time, as if I could actually help him.

"A man as smart as you," Jackie said, "it'll be my honor to buy you a drink."

"Well, okay, but come on, don't you—"

"Are you riding today?"

"Uh, yeah," the man said, looking down at his suit. Like what the hell else would he be doing?

"Silly me. Of course you are. So why don't you head back on out there while we still have some snow left."

"It is pretty light this year. Must be global warming or something."

"Global warming, now. So you mean like our winter might last ten months instead of eleven? Is that the idea? You're like a walking library of knowledge, I swear."

"Listen, is there a problem here? Because I don't—"

"No, no," Jackie said. "No problem. You go on out and enjoy your ride. In fact, you know what? I hear they've got a lot more snow in Russia this year. Up by that real big lake. What was it called again?"

The man didn't answer.

"Lake Baikal," I said.

"I wasn't talking to you, Alex."

"Just trying to help."

"I'm leaving," the man said, already halfway to the door. "And I won't be back."

"When you get to that lake, do me a favor, huh? I'm still not convinced it's deeper, so can you drive your snowmobile and let it sink to the bottom with you still on it? You think you could do that? I'd really appreciate it."

The man slammed the door behind him. Another drinking man turned away for life, not that he'd have any other place to go in Paradise, Michigan. Jackie picked up his towel and threw it at me. I ignored him and turned back to the fire.

They have long, long winters up here. Did I mention that yet? By

the time the end of March drags around, everyone's just a few degrees past crazy. Not just Jackie.

The sun was trying to come out as I was driving back up my road.
It was an old unpaved logging road, with banks of snow lingering on
either side. When the snow started to melt, the road would turn to
mud and I'd have a whole new set of problems to deal with. By the
time it dried out, it would be time for black fly season.

I passed Vinnie's cabin first. Vinnie "Red Sky" LeBlanc, my only
neighbor and maybe my only true friend. Meaning the one person
who truly understood me, who never wanted anything from me, and
who never tried to change me.

I passed by the first cabin, the one my father and I had built a million years ago—before I went off to play baseball and then become a
cop—then the next four cabins, each bigger than the one before it,
until I got to the end of the road. There stood the biggest cabin of all,
looking almost as good as the original. I'd been rebuilding it for the
past year, starting with just the fireplace and chimney my father had
built stone by stone. Now it was almost done. Now it was almost as
good as it was before somebody burned it down.

I parked the truck and went inside. Vinnie was already there, on
his hands and knees in the corner of the kitchen, once again working
harder and longer than I ever did myself, making me feel like my debt
to him was more than I could ever repay.

"What are you ruining now?" I said to him.

"I'm fixing the trim you put down on this floor." He was in jeans
and a white T-shirt, his denim jacket hanging on the back of one of
the kitchen chairs. He had a long strip of quarter round molding in
his hand, the very same strip I had just tacked down the day before.

"You're ripping it up? How is that fixing it?"

"You used the wrong size trim. You need to start over."

"It's not the wrong size. Damn it, Vinnie, is it any wonder it's taking
me forever to finish this place? You wanna rip the ceiling off, too?"

"You got a good half-inch gap here," he said, pointing to the gap
between the floor and the lowest log on the wall.

"That's a quarter inch."

"Here it might be, but over on the other side of the room it gets wider. You have to measure the gap at its longest before you go out and buy your trim."

"Vinnie, what the hell's wrong with you?"

"I told you, you bought the wrong size. And as long as you're buying new molding, get something with a little more style, too. Quarter round is boring."

"Nobody's going to notice it. It's on the floor, for God's sake."

He turned away from me, shaking his head. He grabbed another length of molding and ripped it up like he was pulling weeds.

"Something's eating at you," I said. "I can tell."

"I'm fine. I just wish you'd do things right for a change."

First Jackie and now Vinnie. Such a parade of cheerful people in my life. I was truly a lucky man.

"It's actually trying to get nice outside," I said. "We might even have some sunlight soon. Will that make you feel better?"

He didn't look up. "You know one thing that bothers me?"

"What?"

"How long have you been living in this cabin?"

"Ever since I've been working on it. It just makes things easier."

"I think you're done now, Alex. You've got the floor down. You've got the woodstove working. As soon as I redo your trim, this place will be ready to rent out again."

"It's been a bad winter for the snowmobile people. You know that."

"You could have this place rented right now. It's your biggest cabin. You're just wasting money."

"Since when are you my accountant?"

He stopped what he was doing and sat still on the floor. He finally turned to look at me. "You need to move back into your cabin. You can't keep avoiding it."

"I will." It was my turn to look away. "As soon as I'm done here."

Vinnie didn't say anything else. I got down on my knees and helped him tear up the remaining strips of floor molding. An hour later I was on my way to Sault Ste. Marie to buy the new strips, five-eighths instead of half-inch, cloverleaf instead of quarter round. As I passed that first cabin, I made a point of not even looking at it.

That was how the day went. That last day in March. It started with breakfast at the Glasgow Inn and ended with dinner in the same place. It was like most every other day in Paradise. Vinnie had helped me finish the baseboard trim, then he'd gone over to the rez to sit with his mother for a while. She'd not been feeling like herself lately. Maybe just one more person who was tired of winter. I was hoping that was it, that she'd feel better once the sun came back. That we'd all feel better.

Vinnie gave me a nod as he came through the door. Back from the rez, then a shift at the casino dealing blackjack, stopping in now because that's what you do around here. Every night. Jackie was watching hockey on the television mounted above the bar. Vinnie went over and stood behind him, just like I had told him to do.

"Hey, Jackie," he said, "I heard something interesting today."

"What's that, Vin?"

"Did you know Lake Superior isn't really the biggest lake in the world? Or the deepest?"

Jackie turned and glared at me.

"I'll throw you right out on your ass," he said. "I swear to God I will."

Finally, something to smile about, on a cold, cold night. I looked back into the fire and watched the flames dance. My last hour of peace until everything would change.

We're not supposed to believe in evil anymore, right? It's all about abnormal behavior now. Maladjustment, overcompensation, or my favorite, the antisocial personality disorder. Fancy words I was just starting to hear in that last year on the force, before I looked into the eyes of a madman as he pulled that trigger without even blinking.

In a way, I've never gotten past it. I'm still lying on that floor, watching the light in Franklin's eyes slowly going out. My partner, the man I was supposed to protect at all costs. Later, in the hospital, they pulled two slugs from my body and left the one that was too close to my heart to touch. It's been with me ever since, a constant reminder of the evil I saw that night, all those years ago on a warm summer evening in Detroit. You'd never convince me otherwise. No, I'd seen evil as deep as it could ever get.

But like Jackie and his beloved lake, you'd never know there was something deeper out there until somebody came to you and told you about it. A deeper lake. A lake you've never seen before. Even then, you might not believe it. Not unless he took you there and showed it to you.

It was about to happen. Minutes away, then seconds. Then the door opened and the cold air blew in and the last person I expected to see that night stepped inside, carrying a big problem and looking for my help.

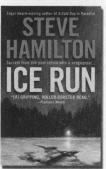

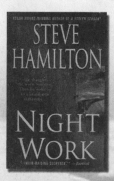